A London childhood [...] the mixed pleasure of having four elder bro[...] the country, I declined to stay there more than a month or two as an evacuee, and returned in good time for the Blitz. Later schooldays were spent watching doodlebugs flying overhead or ducking those that failed to fly overhead.

Working life was, first, a long connection with the *Reader's Digest*. I worked for its chairman, travelled to other *Digest* companies in Europe and America, and learned from my boss anything I know about the writing of English.

Marriage eventually meant separation from London. My husband and I moved out of the shelter of a huge concern, to try running our own small one. We missed the boom, caught the backwash, and finally failed . . . back to being employed again. This time, to broaden our experience if not our minds, we entered the groves of Academe.

Then I entered a magazine story competition and, astonishingly, won it. Now, many stories later (published by *Woman's Weekly*, *Woman & Home*, Mills & Boon, Piatkus, and Corgi) I am an addict, and reach for my pen as an alcoholic reaches for a glass.

My husband's and my retirement from Oxford University brought us to the green hills of Somerset, and the pleasurable oddities of village life. We like to roam about Europe, or contentedly apply ourselves to the other good things of life – friends, food, wine, music, and our garden.

*To the memory of a
whole and seldom man*

THE SNOWS
OF SPRINGTIME

Sally Stewart

CORGI BOOKS

THE SNOWS OF SPRINGTIME
A CORGI BOOK : 0 552 14163 1

First publication in Great Britain

PRINTING HISTORY
Corgi edition published 1994

Set in 10/11 pt Linotype Sabon by
Phoenix Typesetting, Ilkley, West Yorkshire.

Corgi Books are published by Transworld Publishers Ltd,
61–63 Uxbridge Road, Ealing, London W5 5SA,
in Australia by Transworld Publishers (Australia) Pty Ltd,
15–25 Helles Avenue, Moorebank, NSW 2170,
and New Zealand by Transworld Publishers (NZ) Ltd,
3 William Pickering Drive, Albany, Auckland.

Reproduced, printed and bound in Great Britain by
Cox & Wyman Ltd, Reading, Berks.

1898

'For I am one who has had much,
But not the heart's desire.'
                              Ruth Pitter

I

Lavinia Mary Louise St Clyst was ready for her wedding at last. Her cousin's superior French maid, lent for a final inspection, tweaked without enthusiasm at the orange blossom in the bride's fair braids, then departed again, leaving her to stare at the strange, pale-faced reflection of herself in the cheval mirror.

'I'm afraid Arlette washes her hands of me,' she murmured to the small girl standing by her side. 'Just as well, perhaps; she was making me very nervous.'

'Well, 'cording to my way o' thinking, you look real lovely, miss. No need to take notice of 'er; she's full of daft *foreign* notions.'

Lavinia's strained face broke into a smile at the indescribable scorn poured into that word 'foreign'. 'Quite right, Jessie; still, being French, the poor thing can't help herself – we must remember that!'

She glanced round the little room she was leaving for almost the last time. Airless in summer, bitterly cold in winter without the fire her cousins had always been so reluctant to have lit, it had nevertheless been her only refuge for the past eighteen months. A mere year and a half out of her twenty-four, but it seemed more like a lifetime since the death of her father and the sale of their home to pay his debts. She'd tried to feel grateful to her relatives in London, but there'd been time enough to discover that charity given without true kindness was ashes in the mouth of those who had to eat it.

Thanks to the man she was about to marry, she need eat it no longer. Compared with that blessing, nothing

7

else mattered – not this elaborate, uncomfortable dress that didn't suit her at all, not the absurd wreath of orange blossom in her hair that would probably fall off, not even the much worse fear hidden deep inside her that she was marrying a man she scarcely knew. He'd been brought to the house by her cousin's husband – a handsome, courteous man who seemed not to have noticed her own lack of looks, and who had liked talking to her about his home in Cornwall. He'd seemed no more comfortable in London than she was herself and that had endeared him to her.

'Better go down, miss,' Jessie's gruff little voice advised. 'His lordship'll be getting in a fuss.' She swept open the door, and sank into an impromptu curtsey. Lavinia bowed in return, and went down the staircase to meet her uncle – already waiting in the hall, of course, and certainly in a fuss, with the front door held open.

From then on the events of the day seemed to become increasingly unreal: the drive to Hanover Square, the congregation of people she scarcely knew gathered in St George's Church to witness a sacrament that meant nothing to them. She felt very cold, stumbled on the hem of her dress, and heard with sheer disbelief the opening bars of music announcing their arrival. Surely even Cousin Julia couldn't have picked something quite so unsuitable without deliberate intent?

Ill-timed, dangerous amusement grew inside her as they raced up the aisle in time to 'The Trumpet Voluntary'. The amusement needed to be shared, but her uncle was looking red-faced and fierce, and Julian Bossiney, when she reached his side, stared only at the priest who waited to marry them. She stared too, unwilling to believe that any respected member of the cloth could so nearly resemble a parrot as this one did. Her aching desire to laugh – or was it really panic? – seemed to be growing beyond control. This wedding ceremony wasn't real; she was trapped within a grotesque nightmare, beseeching rescue with cries that no-one else could hear.

'Dearly beloved, we are gathered here together in the sight of God . . .' The *voice* of the parrot only made matters worse; she must do her best not to listen to it or disgraceful hysteria would finally overwhelm her.

'. . . Wilt thou take this man to be thy lawful wedded husband . . . ?' At last the twittering sound ceased and silence fell. It was a blessed relief, but now the silence itself felt ominous. What were they all waiting for?

She glanced at the man beside her, noting a gesture already becoming familiar as his hand nervously brushed up the ends of his moustache. Then she saw the agonized gaze of the curate. It was fixed on *her* and his lips were desperately mouthing the words 'I will'.

She must have repeated them aloud because the service went on. Shocked by the nearness of disaster, she listened intently now, responded, moved when required, and found at the end of it that she was no longer Lavinia St Clyst but the wife and possession of Julian Bossiney. *That* felt as unreal as everything else, but she smiled at the people who stared at her and told herself that she would somehow get used to an idea that for the moment seemed very strange.

An hour later she stood in her cousin's drawing room in Green Street and decided that she could finally stop smiling. Their guests were all received, her husband was enjoying a conversation with a turbanned dowager, and she could pretend that she was alone, not in this hot, crowded, alien room at all.

'Lavinia, my dear – may I call you that when we haven't even been formally presented?' The voice was pleasant, with a hint of humour in it.

She opened her eyes to find a late newcomer in front of her – a stranger, except that in this very first moment of meeting he seemed not strange at all. His smile, and the kindness in his face, were familiar to her – known in dreams long since, and lost also long ago.

'I expect you've guessed – I'm Julian's brother,

9

Jonathan,' he explained when she stared blankly at him.

'He said you couldn't . . . no, said you *wouldn't* come, I think. You were too – too busy somewhere on the Continent.'

' "Frittering away my time" is how I expect he phrased it! In fact, I was finishing a course at Heidelberg . . . but suddenly decided that if I stirred myself I could just get back in time to see you married. The intention was good, I promise you, but Channel fog is no respecter of wedding arrangements. Forgive me for missing the ceremony.'

'I'm glad you did,' she said suprisingly. 'I found that getting married was a . . . a strangely unnerving business. Julian was better at it than I.'

If he thought it a curious admission for a bride to make, Jonathan didn't say so. He smiled instead, and she thought it almost certain that he knew and understood the afternoon's near-fiasco, and didn't despise her for it.

'What now?' he asked. 'Home to Cornwall, or a wedding journey first?'

'Paris and Rome, then Cornwall – all equally strange to me,' Lavinia said. 'My home until eighteen months ago was in Devon, but I loved it so much that I'm afraid I never troubled to cross the River Tamar.'

Her voice trembled despite all her effort to keep it even. Jonathan watched her sad, intelligent face, and wondered greatly about his brother's marriage.

'So . . . you came after all,' Julian's voice said behind him. 'I'm glad to see you, Jonathan, but you might have got here in time if you were coming at all. Lavinia, my dear, has your brother-in-law presented himself?'

'Yes . . . yes, we're already acquainted.'

'Then in that case you'd better come and apologize to your host, Jonathan – Lavinia's uncle, the Earl St Clyst.'

The title was rolled out with so much satisfaction that one thing about the marriage at least was immediately clear. At last Julian was where he had always wanted to be – linked by the closeness of family ties to the real, the *old*, aristocracy; the earldom of St Clyst went back to Norman times. The Bossineys had been baronets for just on fifty years, and before that mere merchant adventurers in the filibustering seaport of Fowey. He allowed himself to be shepherded across the room, thinking that he could also guess what had brought Lavinia St Clyst to the unnerving business of marrying his brother. He remembered the expression on her face when he had first caught sight of her – stoic pride concealing her fear that some irretrievable and terrible error had been made.

The wedding journey began not altogether badly. The first gale of the autumn had blown away the Channel fog and the crossing was rough and squally. Julian was a good enough sailor not to mind but Lavinia suffered and was allowed to arrive in Paris still a virgin. She was grateful for the gale, although aware that her husband might have chosen to wait for the Hotel Crillon in any case. The conditions there were more worthy of his wedding night, and she had already learned that appearances were important to him.

She supposed afterwards that it was an introduction to the rites and mysteries of married life less brutal than many women endured in the closing years of Victoria's reign. Julian was considerate, and although there was no joy in it, she hadn't expected any . . . knew she didn't deserve any. A virtuous woman in Victoria's reign was not supposed to *enjoy* having her husband's body thrust into her own; she had only to accept it as the price of being taken care of. Lavinia accepted also that there might have been more pleasure in giving herself to a man she loved. It wasn't Julian's fault but hers, that she had married him to escape the penance of being her cousin's unpaid drudge.

One fear gradually dwindled. Julian showed no sign of being dissatisfied with a wife whose thin body was anything but voluptuous and whose nature was reserved. He seemed to enjoy his rights in their shared bed, slept soundly afterwards, and treated her publicly with perfect courtesy. She noticed with wry amusement what an excellent impression he made – the other hotel guests, male and female, clearly admired an above-averagely handsome man who behaved towards a below-averagely attractive wife more attentively than she deserved!

The days gradually became wearisome, nevertheless, to both of them. To Julian one picture gallery or church was exactly like another, and he seemed scandalized rather than amused by her habit of watching for the oddities she relished in other people. A week after their arrival in Rome, just as she was wondering whether it would be tactless to suggest returning to England earlier than planned, Julian himself made it easy for her.

'I received a letter from Jonathan this morning,' he said over the breakfast table. 'Father is not at all well . . . quite poorly, in fact.'

'Are you concerned about him – I mean, enough to want to cut short our stay here?' Lavinia asked, trying not to sound too eager.

Julian played with his moustache. 'He's no great age, of course – in fact, only fifty-three – but he didn't feel strong enough to attend our wedding, you remember. I should hate to be away from Prospect if . . . if anything were to happen.'

'In that case of course you would rather return at once,' she murmured.

'Yes, I think so, too.' His expression of filial concern faded into complacency. 'After all, there's very little more to stay *for*, is there? I believe we've covered the grandeur that was Rome pretty thoroughly. And very dubious some of it is, in my opinion.'

Lavinia didn't argue with him; nor did she even point out as he stared wistfully at his rolls and apricot jam that perhaps he'd also exhausted the pleasure of continental breakfasts! It was the kind of teasing he didn't enjoy, and she said merely that Sir Edward's health was now the only thing they must consider.

'Yes and, as a doctor of sorts, we must assume that Jonathan is some judge of *that*, at least.'

She stared at him in astonishment. His only reference to his brother had left her with the impression that Jonathan Bossiney was a useless dilettante, idling away his life in foreign travel. 'A *doctor*? Where does he do his doctoring?'

'He hasn't done it anywhere, so far,' Julian said rather testily. 'If he's now back in England for good I suppose he'll set up his plate in Wimpole Street and become fashionable.'

She remembered with strange vividness the sense of recognition felt in the few moments she had spent with her brother-in-law; if intelligence and kindness and charm were appreciated in a London doctor, no doubt he would become very fashionable indeed.

Three days after that breakfast conversation the wedding journey was over. The train from Paddington steamed into Lostwithiel station on a damp November afternoon, and Lavinia nerved herself for the real beginning to her new life – a town, a house, and a father-in-law living in it, all strange to her; there was also the knowledge that in crossing the River Tamar into Cornwall she had entered unfamiliar territory. She was only certain that it was a place apart from the rest of the kingdom, steeped in its own ancient mysteries and legends, still scattered with the evidence of people who had lived there immeasurably long ago. Tired and apprehensive, she scarcely listened to Julian's excited chatter during the carriage ride, as he kindly pointed out things she couldn't see and reeled off the names of neighbours she didn't know.

'Prospect isn't right in the *centre* of Fowey, like Place House,' he explained, 'but it's an important part of the town all the same. No point in keeping a carriage of our own, my dear – everywhere's too narrow and steep for that. We hire a conveyance when we need to go outside Fowey.'

She saw what he meant when the horses were pulled up in front of a wrought-iron gate leading not to the drive she would have expected, but to a wet pathway winding down through bare lifeless gardens. At the end of it, grey and solid and ugly as Cornish granite and slate could make it was the home she had come to; beyond and below it was nothing but more greyness, tenuous but just as depressing – grey mist, grey water, and, scarcely real at all, the faint dark hint that there might be land on the far side of the estuary. The house was built on rock, its retaining walls their only defence against the river and open sea. It was a world away from the green, sunlit meadows of Devon, and an old manor-house that had seemed to hold out its arms in welcome to a guest.

She never forgot that first glimpse of Prospect, and feared that she would always hate it. But a fine morning was enough to show her that she might be wrong – for one thing, there *was* colour in this strange place she'd come to, born of the ever-changing light. Even the sullen grey granite walls of the house glinted with a thousand points of light when the sun picked out their particles of quartz. The weather change cheered her gentle father-in-law too. Sir Edward Bossiney had accepted her into his household pleasantly enough but without enthusiasm. With the river visible again, he forgot to sit hunched over the fire in the drawing room and was stationed by the huge bay window instead. Binoculars in hand, he was suddenly full of excitement and happy to share it with his new daughter-in-law.

'Lavinia, my dear, look, down there . . . Do you see the *Ocean Beauty*, leaving on the ebb tide? Oh, lovely she goes. She's bound for the Far East, you know . . . The fastest clipper we own.'

Lovely she *was*, with her white canvas spread to the wind. Lavinia caught her companion's enthusiasm and felt for the first time pride in being part of the family she had married into.

'You must teach me how to recognize *all* our ships,' she said, smiling at him. 'I want to know where they go, what they bring home – everything about them.'

Edward's happiness dimmed suddenly. 'Julian will say you shouldn't trouble yourself with such matters,' he murmured, in a prediction which turned out to be accurate. '*He* isn't interested in ships, and Jonathan unfortunately grew up wanting to be a doctor. I have two sons, but they both leave Chivers to run things for us.' He sounded sad that it should be so, and she found herself wanting to comfort him.

'You and I will be interested,' she promised. '*Someone* must be.'

They were smiling at each other like people who shared a precious secret when Jonathan Bossiney walked into the room. His first impression was that a lonely old man had forgotten to feel melancholy; his next that Julian's wife might be happy in her marriage after all.

'I knew you were back,' he said shyly. 'I'd have called sooner but I thought you might need time to settle in. It looks as if you have.'

'Yes, now that I can see the sun does shine in Cornwall. There's been some doubt about it until this morning!'

The smile she remembered lit his face, wiping away the faint resemblance to Julian. He was less handsome than his brother but unfairly more attractive. 'Think of the tedium, Lavinia, of a sky unchanging blue and sunlight always golden,' he suggested persuasively. 'For *us*, every day is a game of chance, with the odds *slightly* shaded, I'll allow, in favour of a heavy downpour!'

She laughed because he did, or perhaps because the day was bright and she was suddenly happy to be there, after all, the mistress of Prospect.

'Have you come to stay? I'm sure Julian will hope so.'

Jonathan looked surprised, then light dawned. 'Father can't have told you yet – my own home is only a five-minute walk away. Can you think of a more enchantingly

15

suitable address for a doctor, by the way, than Salubrious House?'

She could only think for the moment that her husband had been wrong. 'Wimpole Street, London,' she said faintly. '*That* was what Julian expected.'

'Certainly not – I always meant to practise here, but I had to wait for old Dr Collins to decide that it was time for Fowey's slopes and stairs to wear out a younger pair of legs. At last he's retired and *my* plate is on the door.'

She looked down at the sunlit water of the estuary. A ferry was making its way across the water to Polruan, where a huddle of grey and white cottages climbed the far green hillside. It was *all* beautiful; she felt deeply happy and deeply sad at the same time. Jonathan Bossiney would be a true friend; she had no doubt of it. But even now it was necessary to tell herself what she must always remember – that she owed her deliverance to Julian, not Jonathan.

By the time the bloody opening of the Boer War came to mar the end of Victoria's long reign, Lavinia had grown to love her Cornish home perched on the edge of the sea. She knew the changing colours of the water that ebbed and flowed in their cove below the sea-wall, and lay in bed on stormy nights listening to the waves that seemed bent on sweeping Prospect away. The Bossiney ships were as familiar to her as they were to Edward, and the little grey sea town of Fowey was where she belonged.

She didn't learn to love her husband any more than when she'd married him but there was nothing to dislike in such an equable and courteous man. Their marriage would have seemed unexciting but still something to be grateful for if Jonathan Bossiney hadn't been there to make plain to her what she was missing. In time, it became cruelly hard to give the impression of a contented woman; only pride came to her rescue, and the relief of giving Julian a son. She'd done what he expected of her, and their passionless love-making had at least managed to produce

an heir. She loved Tristram from the moment of first looking at him, but when her daughter, Jenifer, was born two
years later there was only relief from the pain of a perilous
confinement. Jonathan, not Julian, should have given her
the seed for this beautiful scrap of humanity; there would
have been no difficulty then about loving a daughter.

There were no more children after that, because she
was left to sleep undisturbed in the huge bedroom whose
windows faced both the estuary and the open sea. Julian
had the son and daughter he required; now he could give
up the more undignified intimacies of marriage. Understanding him now, Lavinia realized that total love and
longing for another human being was not in his nature. It
would have seemed demeaning to a man who was proud
to be Julian Bossiney of Prospect. He valued his wife,
but mostly for her connections, and for their annual
invitation to stay at St Clyst Castle. Their neighbours
– the Treffrys at Place, the Rashleighs at Menabilly, the
Agar-Robartes at Lanhydrock – were kept informed at
every opportunity about his uncle by marriage, the Earl.

Julian was a careful landlord of his property in the
town, but it didn't occur to him to take a personal interest in the people who lived in his cottages. It was
Jonathan who knew them all by name, tended their ills,
delivered their children, and comforted them when they
were dying. Lavinia excused *him* from concerning himself with the business affairs of the Bossineys; all his
waking moments were given to his patients. But growing
anxiety forced her one day to follow Julian into the
library and to tackle him on a subject he would have
preferred to avoid. He looked pained when she closed the
door behind her; it was supposed to be understood that
he was safe from interruption here.

'I met Chivers down on the quay yesterday,' she began
abruptly. 'He was looking so worried that I asked him the
reason.'

'I expect a tenant was overdue with his rent. That is all
Chivers needs to make him look worried.'

Lavinia walked to the window and stared out at the river below them. 'I can see four . . . no, five steam boats, Julian, and *one* schooner. Isn't it time Bossiney's began switching from sail? Everyone else is doing so.'

He brushed up the corners of his moustache in the gesture that meant he was ill at ease, but determined not to expose the weakness of his case by arguing about it.

'My dear, I don't employ an agent and then do his work myself. It's Chivers' job to run our ships. I suggest that you leave it to him, as I do.'

'I realize that you don't like things to change, and that your father would hate a change even more than you do; but we are getting left behind by our competitors. By the time Tristram comes to inherit Bossiney's there may well be no shipping line left.'

Julian's handsome face was beginning to look flushed, and she recognized its expression of mulish obstinacy.

'You see a string of filthy, obscenely noisy coasters steam past and leap to the conclusion that they spell the end of sail. You're wrong, my dear Lavinia, but even if you were right neither my father nor I would involve ourselves in anything so ill-becoming a gentleman.'

It was on the tip of her tongue to shout that Queen Victoria had done the family a disservice by making gentlemen of them at all in that case; but such a reference to their comparatively recent change of status would offend him deeply. She took a deep breath and tried to speak calmly.

'Even gentlemen must continue to live, and their children after them.'

'I think I am aware of that,' he said stiffly, 'but it doesn't mean that I feel obliged to haggle for merchandise with other shipowners along the quays. I repeat that it's Chivers' job to see to our affairs; I have other things to do.'

Keeping up appearances was one of them, she realized, and probably the one that concerned him most – although there were his butterfly and rare stamp collections to be attended to, and the civic duties that he also prized.

He smiled suddenly to show that he was ready to forgive her if she would leave him in peace. 'Let me remind you of something that *does* concern you, my dear. When the Treffrys arrive for dinner they will expect their hostess to be waiting to receive them, not grubbing on her knees in some muddy corner of the garden!'

He tried to sound amused, but she knew that the incident he was reminding her of had mortified him. It was useless to insist that the Vyvyans, being passionate gardeners themselves, had perfectly understood. Their own grounds at Trelowarren were a byword in the county and they could see what Julian ignored – that out of Prospect's bare, unloved hillside gardens she had begun to create something beautiful. In the four years she had lived there, the transformation had become one of her main joys and comforts in life; she poured into it the passion that she couldn't offer her husband, and wasn't allowed to offer Jonathan.

She didn't make the mistake of talking business again with Julian, and was careful never to draw her father-in-law's attention to the fact that less and less often there were ships to dip the Bossiney flag in salute as they sailed past Prospect.

Edward Bossiney was content nowadays to live in the past, and seemed reluctant to remember that Victoria's place had finally been taken by her elderly son. His stream of reminiscence flowed gently over present anxieties, and Lavinia thought it was only when Tristram used the arm of his grandfather's chair to triumphantly haul himself upright and grin that Edward's contentment was pierced by the slightest fear about the future.

They saw very little of Jonathan, apart from his brief visits to check on his father's health. Lavinia avoided him when she could, because the guard she had to keep on herself in front of him was dangerously exhausting. He loved his work, lived comfortably in Salubrious House watched over by a devoted housekeeper, and married none of the young women or widows of the town who set traps for him.

Julian often chided him for not taking a wife and one evening, when she'd been obliged to join them, invited Lavinia to support him.

'He needs a lady in his life, don't you agree, my dear? Otherwise he'll begin to let himself go.' *Had* begun to, his tone implied, while he smiled in the knowledge that care and discipline were keeping his own figure elegantly trim.

'Mrs Trago's pasties,' Jonathan mumbled in self-defence. 'Every known variety, and all of them delicious but fattening. Still, it doesn't matter because *she* wouldn't like me to take a wife.'

He glanced at Lavinia's thin face, bent over the piece of tapestry she was working on. Evening sunlight caught strands of gold in her smooth hair, shone on temple and cheek-bone, and laid a bright finger of gold down her throat – his brother's wife, forbidden to him by Holy Writ and the most fundamental taboos of their society. He was merely permitted to glance at her occasionally.

Lavinia looked up from her work and found him still watching her. Their eyes, clear hazel and blue, met in a locked glance that suddenly blotted out everyone else in the room. The rest of the world, time itself, ceased to exist for as long as they stared at each other. Then the clock on the mantelpiece struck the hour with its usual noisy grinding of gears, and the spell was broken.

'No, I shan't marry,' Jonathan said again deliberately, and then chose at random another subject for them to talk about – the commotion the suffragettes were making would do.

Lavinia returned blindly to her stitching and only discovered the following day that two lines of the pattern which should have been worked in pale pink were coloured Prussian blue. She left them there until the design was finished, for the remembered heart-stopping joy of a moment when she'd read in Jonathan's eyes that she was loved as she loved him.

Edward Bossiney released his gentle hold on life in the same year that the king died. Lavinia missed his companionship, but was thankful that he didn't live to see the changes that were overtaking the river. More and more steam-driven vessels were belching out their plumes of coal smoke, and now the noise of engines was drowning the traditional estuary sounds of flapping canvas and rigging.

Julian was genuinely saddened by his father's death, but there was comfort in inheriting the title – especially when their neighbour along the Esplanade had just been knighted for his services to literature. Julian congratulated Sir Arthur Quiller-Couch, of course, but couldn't help feeling comfortably sure that the honour for *such* a reason didn't quite make him the match of Sir Julian Bossiney, *Bart*.

As the second decade of the twentieth century began there were more worrying things to think about as well. The Balkans were in more ferment than usual, and even if few Englishmen could remember exactly where they were, much less unravel the mad complexities of their history, they seemed to threaten the stability of Europe. Still, Julian clung to the thought of kinship.

'Kaiser Wilhelm is a cousin of the new king,' he insisted when Jonathan looked unimpressed. 'He's bound to see the madness of allowing his Austrian friends and a lot of Balkan extremists to plunge Europe into war. Good God, man, he's Victoria's grandson – how could he ever contemplate fighting England?'

'His General Staff contemplate little else. They learned from the lesson of the Franco-Prussian war that might is right,' Jonathan said sombrely. 'My dear Julian, the Austrians want to humiliate the Serbs, and the German generals want a war – almost any pretext will do.'

Lavinia feared that her brother-in-law was right, but there were changes nearer home for her to think about. It was time for Tristram to begin his first term at Marlborough, and she hated saying goodbye to him. Julian was almost too preoccupied to notice, because years of effort had finally borne fruit. After being humiliatingly linked with St Austell for far too long, Fowey was to have its identity as a separate borough restored again. The Autumn of 1913 seemed more memorable for *that* triumph than for the settlement of the second Balkan War.

But the pretext for a European war that Jonathan had predicted was found soon enough. The following summer, only days after the assassination of Archduke Franz Ferdinand in Sarajevo, the sequence of international threat, counter-threat, demand, and final ultimatum was complete. By 4 August 1914, Russia, France, and Great Britain were at war with Germany and Austria, and the world they had known seemed to be dying for ever.

2

Julian, at forty-four, was too old for active service but he threw himself into every local war-time activity with an effectiveness that took Lavinia by surprise. He recruited for the Devon and Cornwall Light Infantry, billeted troops sent to Fowey, and organized anything that needed organizing. *She* was only left with the impossible task of offering sympathy to women whose lives were being shattered by the mounting slaughter on the Western Front. With a generosity that she found heart-breaking, they never pointed out that her husband was too old, and her son too young, to be made to fight.

She returned from such a visit one morning to find Jonathan waiting for her. Since that moment of shared glances they had managed not to be alone together, nor to refer to it.

His face looked grave now, and her missed heartbeat righted itself. It wasn't to talk about *them* that he was there.

'Will you say goodbye to Julian and the children for me? If I wait I shall miss the London connection.'

She stared at him, suddenly white-faced, still overwrought by the morning's effort of finding something to say to a woman whose son would never come back from Flanders. 'You aren't just going to London, though,' she whispered. 'You've joined up.'

'Not to fight. I'm a surgeon of sorts as well as a physician – there must be a field hospital where my help would be useful.'

'What . . . how . . . how do we manage here without you?'

'Dr Collins can still do a little, but his younger brother is coming out of retirement to help as well.'

She didn't hear about the Collinses. Field hospitals were where they said they were – in the field; they got shelled and bombed out of existence. Her hands were trembling, but at last she managed to draw out from under the collar of her blouse a fine gold chain and crucifix.

'Wear this, please, Jonathan.' A travesty of a smile touched her pale mouth as she handed it to him. 'I've felt a most terrible fraud, trying to comfort the poor women who live with fear by day and night. I shan't be able to tell them so, but at least I shall now *know* what they suffer.' It was more than she had ever imagined that she would say to him, but what was not said now might never be said, and he must go at least knowing that she loved him.

He loosened his tie with clumsy, trembling fingers and settled the chain, still warm from her body, against his own skin. It seemed the most precious, intimate gift that she could have made him. His eyes examined her face, imprinting it on his memory. Then he suddenly held out his arms and she was gathered into them – home where she belonged. His mouth brushed hers, lingered because her lips trembled under his, and then released her.

'I shall pray for you, every day,' she whispered.

'Mama . . .' It was her daughter's voice, calling from the doorway, sounding fretful as usual.

'Goodbye, my love,' Jonathan murmured softly, and walked out of the room, unaware that he'd forgotten to greet the niece who was staring at him.

He didn't come back to Fowey until three more terrible years were over . . . years of mindless slaughter, of grief, and ever-present fear for adult men and women. But for a schoolboy like Tristram there was excitement, too. Home for the summer holiday, he looked for his friend, Charlie Penwarne, as usual. They were exactly the same age and, on the water at least, had established a friendship that took no account of the difference between Tristram

Bossiney and the son of one of his father's tenants. At sixteen, Charlie was already at work on a fishing boat, but Tristram knew that the fishermen didn't put out to sea on Sundays.

'Why can't you come sailing tomorrow – you always do when I'm home,' Tristram said crossly when his offer of enjoyment had been refused.

'Got something else to do, that's why.' Charlie's brown face split into a grin. 'Walter Jago's short of a deck hand, and there's supplies needed in France. We slip on tomorrow's tide . . . from Albert Quay.'

Tristram shrugged and walked away, but he was careful to go home via the Harbour Master's Office where the tide-tables told him what he needed to know. He was on the quay at 4.30 the next morning, determined that if Charlie Penwarne was old enough to help take supplies to France, so was he. He told the first lie of his life to Walter Jago, and got back to Prospect two days later, too tired to listen to a lecture from his father on the first requirement of a gentleman – consideration for others at all times, but especially to his parents. Lavinia merely wept to see him safely back. He was still the child she loved most, and try as she would to recognize no difference in the affection she felt for him and for her daughter, some lack of understanding persisted between herself and Jenifer. It didn't lessen as Jenifer grew out of childhood into adolescence, and Lavinia supposed that the blame must be hers, because Julian seemed to have no difficulty in dealing with his beautiful but wayward daughter.

The Armistice was signed on 11 November 1918, and Jonathan returned to Salubrious House almost immediately afterwards. He didn't return the crucifix, or refer to it again, and Lavinia never expected that he would. The war was over, their lives and their relationship had returned to normal again.

When he came to Prospect now it was usually in the company of other guests, and the conversations she shared with him were such as anyone might overhear. But one morning, when she was working in the garden as usual, he appeared unexpectedly and came to sit beside her on the stone bench where she was resting for a moment. They shared the immense view of the sea and sky in silence until she finally spoke after a glance at his tired face.

'Is something wrong,' she asked after a moment, 'or do I only imagine that you're feeling sad?'

'Not wrong, exactly, but my old friend Isaac Penwarne died yesterday. It's been expected for a long time, but I shall miss him.'

'A *natural* ending to his life at least; not like the dreadful memories that still haunt your mind.' She turned to look at him. 'They do, don't they? *We*, on the other hand, seem to have gone back to our stately pre-war rituals with shocking ease. Julian is busy with neighbours and stamps and rare butterflies again, and I have nothing more important to consider than whether I should plant a new viburnum barkwoodii just *there*, this autumn.' Her voice trembled slightly, and when Jonathan suddenly reached out his hand to cover hers she had to close her eyes against the threat of tears that might never cease if she once allowed them to fall.

It seemed a long time before he broke the silence between them.

'I saw the children as I came in. It's hard to believe that Tristram's been up at Oxford for a year. He and Jenifer seem to have grown up while I wasn't looking. I only realized for the first time this morning that she is a young woman, not a child any longer, and that she's grown beautiful, besides.'

'She takes after Julian, fortunately; he would have hated a plain daughter! She is also very bored – fears at seventeen that life will pass her by in this sleepy Cornish backwater.'

'Is that how Tristram regards Fowey – as somewhere to escape from?'

Lavinia nodded slowly. 'He'd never hurt my feelings by saying so, but I think he's aware of something missing in our home here that he knows exists elsewhere.' Her clear hazel eyes, the only beautiful feature she possessed, held Jonathan's glance steadily. 'It's my fault, of course . . . not *lack* of love for them, but love choked, like a stream that hasn't been allowed to find its true path to the river. It just . . . peters out, lost in dry ground, without doing any good.' She felt no shame at finally acknowledging the truth, only an aching regret for a situation that couldn't be changed but which they had *all* suffered from.

Jonathan discovered that he still held her hand. It was brown and scratched – the hand of a woman who actually toiled in her garden. 'Not *your* fault at all,' he said at last. 'If I'd arrived in time all those years ago I might have found the courage to stop your marriage to Julian.'

'For what just cause or impediment?' Lavinia whispered.

'For the good reason you already know . . . That you were meant for me, of course.' His face was full of aching tenderness when he smiled at her. 'We've been amazingly good, dear heart, and I don't suppose we shall ever refer to it again, but it had to be said once between us. It hasn't been all waste – you have the children, and Julian who needs you more than you realize, and this miraculous garden you've made. I have less to show, but I think I'm useful to the good citizens of Fowey. Can we make do with that, and the most precious of friendships, do you think?'

His wry, sweet humour, that she'd recognized from their first meeting, made her smile back.

'We have to,' she said slowly. 'There was never any alternative. But it was easier once I knew it wasn't just *me* loving you; after that I could bear it. And there's been time to realize that we have had more richness than many people know.'

He lifted her hand to his mouth and carefully folded her fingers over the kiss he'd left in its palm; then they sat there for a while longer without speaking.

*　　　*　　　*

At nineteen, Tristram was judged old enough to represent his father at Isaac Penwarne's funeral. The congregation, being chapel, not church, and knowing the Wesleyan hymns, could sing very lustily . . .

> "Through the night of doubt and sorrow
> Onward goes the pilgrim band,
> Singing songs of expectation,
> Marching to the promised land . . ."

Tristram did his best, but the hymn tune was as unfamiliar as everything else about the service he was engaged in. The Methodist chapel's plain glass windows let in more sunlight than he was accustomed to in the dim mysteries of the parish church, and the brightness reminded him that the day outside was maddeningly fine and clear – a rare thing for this Cornish summer of 1919. No good holding it against poor old Isaac Penwarne that he was standing here instead of skimming out across St Austell Bay. But added to the discomfort of his funeral clothes on a hot summer afternoon was the growing certainty that his father should have been present himself. The Penwarnes had welcomed him courteously enough, but he felt awkwardly alone and inadequate in the front pew he had been shown to. Father should have forgotten his damned butterflies for once and remembered instead that Isaac's daughter-in-law had been Hannah Eliot before she married into the Penwarne family. Her father, Captain Eliot, might be past the age of taking a schooner to sea, but he had been one of Bossiney's most famous shipmasters, and he still rattled off whatever was in his mind as if an ocean gale might carry the words away.

'Sir Julian not here, I see,' he shouted when they were finally outside in the chapel yard, 'haven't met him down along the quay, either – he's poorly mebbe?'

'Fairly spry, Captain, but . . . but otherwise engaged today, I'm afraid.' Tristram offered an excuse that seemed lame even to him, but he found himself unable to lie to this bright-eyed old man who stood watching him.

'Time was when *you* liked to hang around the boat-slips, askin' questions and gettin' in the way!' Tom Eliot's reminiscent grin faded into a look of sad regret. 'Not much goin' on there these days, though, 'cept a few repairs.'

Tristram nodded, and saw with relief that the dismal business of interment was coming to an end. Soon, now, he'd be able to escape, and there might just be enough of the afternoon left to make an outing worthwhile.

Then another voice spoke behind him. 'You'll come back to the house and take a cup of tea?' Hannah Penwarne offered the invitation not too pressingly, leaving him a slight chance to refuse without giving offence, but with her father's eye on him Tristram knew that there could be no sail that day after all.

He fell into step behind the people beginning to straggle out of the chapel yard and found himself walking beside a girl he scarcely knew. She was bound to be Charlie Penwarne's sister, but she'd grown tall and slender while he'd been away in Oxford. Vaguely, he remembered her as a pretty, gentle child, but now her face was hidden by the obscuring straw boater on her head. It would have been hideous at any time, but for today's occasion she, or Hannah perhaps, had thought it necessary to add an extra bow of funereal black ribbon to express the weight of grief.

He lifted his own hat and murmured politely . . . 'Miss Penwarne? Good afternoon – my name's Tristram Bossiney.'

She half-turned towards him, unaware of the tears trickling down her face . . . Unaware of the effect she suddenly made on a young man who imagined he'd outgrown local beauties. He could now see that tendrils of dark hair framed perfection, and her eyes were of a blueness that had nothing to do with the bright, steely gaze of her maternal grandfather, Captain Tom. Tristram thought confusedly of hydrangeas wet with dew . . . no, not nearly darkly beautiful enough; more like the gentians that his mother persuaded old Simeon to grow in the gardens at Prospect. He hesitated for a second or two, then pulled out a neatly-folded handkerchief from the top pocket of his jacket.

'You've been weeping,' he said awkwardly.

'I know . . . and I know who *you* are; I've watched you on the river often enough with Charlie.'

She scrubbed at her cheeks, hesitated in her turn over what to do next with the crumpled square of linen, and smiled gratefully when he solved the problem for her by taking it out of her hand.

'I expect you were very fond of your grandfather,' Tristram suggested.

'Yes, but twadn't what made me cry.' She blushed for a turn of phrase that her mother would have disapproved of, but they were the words that her grandfather always used. 'I didn't like leaving him *there*. Fowey was too soft for a man from St Just, he always said . . . He wanted to go back home. Gales always blew in from the sea there, and the waves always beat against the land. Seemingly it was never quiet, but that was how he liked it.'

'Couldn't it have been managed to take him there?' Tristram asked shyly. 'I mean, if St Just was what he wanted?'

She shook her head and, as if to add an emphasis of its own, the monstrous black bow on her hat waved too. 'Mother said best leave Grandfather *here*, where she could keep an eye on him.'

Tristram didn't dare smile. Hannah's views on death were probably as matter-of-fact as her approach to life. She would have no truck with visions of the shade of old Isaac leaping out of the grave to dance with fellow spirits when the moon was full; but no Cornishman, even if he *was* waiting to cross the Tamar again and plunge back into the sophistication of student life at Oxford, could bring himself to smile at superstitions. Isaac Penwarne certainly wouldn't have done so; last of many generations of tinminers from the bleak, westernmost region of Penwith, he'd have believed for sure in the underground spirits who had to be taken seriously, and be left the share of pasty crumbs from the day's lunch crowst that would keep them happy.

'I'm sorry my father isn't here,' Tristram said next, holding his companion's arm to pilot her tenderly across the street. She scarcely heard what he said. Her own father, William Penwarne, was a kind and gentle man, her brother Charlie a good friend, and brother John no worse than any other, but none of them had thought to make her feel like a fragile, precious lady before. For a moment she hated the ugly black dress that Annie Tregear had run up for the funeral, then blushed again with shame. It was downright wicked to be thinking about such things when Grandfather Isaac had just been left to lie alone with the cold earth piled on top of him. The dreadfulness of it made her shiver and, when Tristram turned to look at her, her eyes had darkened with the horror of the picture in her mind. It didn't seem strange to him then – only afterwards when he remembered it – that he should have known so clearly what troubled her.

'Your grandfather won't be frightened of the dark,' he promised gently.

Her huge eyes searched his face for the truth of what he said. 'You mean . . . because of being used to being below ground? Well, p'raps he would've said t'was only where he did belong to be.' This time even if she'd been aware of using the Cornish phrase, she would have had no fear that her companion might despise her for it. She could see only kindness in his face. Tristram stared at her, and watched terror fade from her eyes. 'Yes . . . I should've thought of that myself,' she said simply.

He was vaguely aware that they were standing still and the people walking in front of them had disappeared; it didn't trouble him, any more than his companion's hat now troubled him. He knew his sister wouldn't have worn such a thing, but it only seemed to emphasize this girl's delicate beauty. She flushed because he was staring at her, then suddenly awoke to the fact that the grey stone cottage they had stopped outside was her own home. The door was open, and Hannah Penwarne stood there, waiting.

'Don't hurry yourself,' she said with a snap of irritation at her daughter. 'There's only a score of people here waiting to be looked after, but never let that bother you . . . you just go on dawdling and day-dreaming as usual.'

'I'm afraid it's my fault if we've been slow, Mrs Penwarne,' Tristram said quickly. 'I was talking too much.'

Hannah gestured in the direction of the kitchen at the rear of the cottage and her daughter obediently disappeared. Then Hannah Penwarne's expression relaxed a little.

'It's a busy day for us, Mr Bossiney. You weren't to know that, of course, but Loveday should have remembered.'

She had known him from childhood up, and would normally have called him Tristram. He thought the new formality was deliberate and it increased his feeling of having been put firmly in his place. It reminded him that she had been a schoolteacher before her marriage to William. Old Isaac's younger son – a clayworker in the drying-sheds at Par – was reckoned to have done well for himself. Not only did Hannah speak proper English; she had book-learning, too. Now, perhaps regretting her sharpness, she suddenly smiled at Tristram.

'Come in, do, and have the tea I promised you.'

The rooms inside the cottage were small, and filled with men in stiff, black clothes. They talked in the hushed voices kept for funeral occasions, and nobody laughed. Tristram thought things sounded livelier in the kitchen, where the wives had sensibly segregated themselves among the teacups and the saffron cakes. He smiled at faces he recognized, but felt out of place in the crowded little room, just as he had done in the chapel. He'd known these men all his life but he didn't belong

32

among them. The feeling of clanship here on an occasion like this was almost tangible; the Bossineys of Prospect might enjoy more space and grandeur, but they didn't know how true families lived. It was a relief to see the familiar figure of Uncle Jonathan, talking in a corner with William Penwarne. Jonathan hadn't been in the chapel, and Tristram could imagine him honestly admitting that a Methodist funeral service was more than non-Wesleyan flesh and blood could stand; but it was just as typical of him that he should take the trouble to come here now.

'Not seen you much on the river so far this summer, Tristram,' said a voice beside him. 'Proper wet old days they've been, but that didn't used to stop you!'

William's younger son stood there, looking red-faced and uncomfortable in his best serge suit, but his smile was familiar from all the childhood outings they had shared.

'Only just back from Oxford,' Tristram explained. 'Three glorious sailing months ahead before I go back. When can you come out with me, Charlie?'

''Fraid it won't be till I've time off – Sundays, most like. Walter Jago's taken me on permanently as crew. Proper quarrelsome old toad he is, but he knows where to find herrings and mackerel, and not many other people *do* now.'

It was a sore point with Hannah Penwarne: Charlie had grown to his present age of nineteen without ever swerving from the certainty that he was going to be a fisherman. John, his older brother by one year, was already doing well in the same china-clay company that employed William Penwarne. Hannah frequently informed her husband that John was the clever one; Charlie was more Cornish than was good for him, just as Loveday was.

'All right, Sunday, then,' Tristram agreed. 'By the way, who's the chap talking to your brother? I don't remember seeing him before.'

'That's Daniel. Back along more years'n we can remember, Dad's brother, George Penwarne, went out to dig for diamonds in South Africa, because he said mining was

33

finished in Cornwall. His son, Daniel, was born there but of course he came home to fight in the war.'

Tristram saw nothing to query in Charlie's statement – without ever having seen Cornwall, Daniel Penwarne would still have been taught that it was where he belonged. Instead, he pointed out something else. 'The war ended a year ago – isn't your cousin going back to the Rand?'

'No . . . says he's not Cornish enough to enjoy spending his life in a hole in the ground! Knows a lot about engines, though, does Daniel.'

'Well, that's pretty Cornish too,' Tristram acknowledged. 'Is he going to stay here now?'

'Think so – he's going to set up on his own and make a fortune . . . he says it's time someone in the family did!'

Tristram stared across the room at the Penwarne he didn't know. There was a faint likeness to his cousins, but although they were both solidly built, there seemed to be altogether more of *this* young man. He was broad as well as tall, and energy that his body could scarcely contain seemed to leach out of the large hands that were illustrating some mechanical point to John.

'I doubt if he'll make a fortune here,' Tristram said after a moment or two. 'Fowey's a bit of a backwater now . . .'

He forgot what else he might have said because Loveday Penwarne was following her mother into the room, carrying a laden tray. The hat had been removed now, and he could see the plaits wound about her head in a shining black coronet. Her cheeks were faintly flushed, because the day had been momentous in a number of ways, and she smiled at Jonathan Bossiney with a sweetness that Tristram doubted even his dear uncle deserved.

'I don't reckon Daniel will stay very long,' he heard Charlie muttering beside him, 'just long enough to get started, and mebbe wait for the little maid to grow a bit more.' Tristram's blank stare caused Charlie to explain a little more. 'Daniel's very stuck on Loveday, but she's too young for marrying yet – leastways, that's what my mother says. I reckon Lizzie Tregear wasn't more'n sixteen when *she* married . . .'

Tristram heard no more; Lizzie Tregear could have married at six or sixty for all he cared. He was still staring at Daniel Penwarne's dark, determined face when Hannah pushed a cup of tea into his hand for which he forgot to thank her. He did remember afterwards to say goodbye to her and to William, but of their daughter, presumably kept busy in the kitchen, there was no more sign.

He stepped out of the dimness and heat of the cottage with a sigh of relief. The late-afternoon light lay richly on everything, painting the grey town with splashes of vivid colour – flowering valerian, the Pride of Fowey they called it, overhanging a wall in a shower of deep pink, a slice of blue water glimpsed at the foot of stairs enamelled with the brilliant green of lichen. Schooldays apart, he'd lived at Fowey for all his nineteen years, but suddenly he was looking at the town as someone might who'd never seen it before.

'Tristram . . . *wait*, for pity's sake, dear boy. I can't gallop along at your speed.' Jonathan Bossiney's voice made him spin round, frowning at the interruption to his thoughts. His likeness to his mother was suddenly strong, reminding Jonathan of Lavinia's own moments of displeasure. At such times he remembered that her Norman ancestors had helped rule the West Country before even the Rashleighs and the Treffrys were heard of, much less the Bossineys – not hauled out of merchant status until 1847 with the baronetcy that had followed Queen Victoria's visit to Fowey. Lavinia never referred to this elevation – simply, Jonathan always thought with amusement, because to a St Clyst it scarcely seemed worth mentioning!

'Your first Methodist funeral, I expect,' he said now. 'They're grim affairs . . . no leavening of Irish jolliness, I'm afraid. No wonder you're looking solemn!'

'Was Isaac Penwarne a patient of yours, Uncle?'

'Whose else? My worthy colleague likes to deal with the citizens who can afford to pay his fees. He's a dandy, up-to-the-minute chap, I'm sure, but I have the small merit of being more generally available!'

Tristram grinned but persevered. 'Loveday Penwarne reminded me of something I'd forgotten – her grand-father wasn't a native of Fowey.'

'By no means. Like many others, he was driven here by the failure of the western mines – homesick for St Just, but thankful to be taken on at the great Caradon mine at St Cleer. Conditions by the 1880s were a good deal better than the appalling hardships he'd survived when he was young, but tuberculosis was bound to kill him in the end. He was lucky, even so – thousands of other young miners died before they were thirty. His sons followed him below ground, of course, but William eventually found himself a more congenial job at Par instead. Isaac never quite forgave him for it, even though he finally agreed to come and live here with William and Hannah. Men who've spent their lives digging metal out of the bowels of the earth despise those who merely wash it for china-clay.'

'Isaac's other son stayed a miner, I gather – in South Africa.'

'Yes, George became another "Cousin Jack". There was – still is, for all I know – a whole colony of them out in the Rand, swapping every bit of news they got from home, living and dying under an African sky the Cornishmen they'd once been bred.'

Tristram adjusted his long stride to Jonathan's shorter legs but walked for a while without saying anything. Then he spoke again. 'George's son was there this afternoon – did you meet him?'

'Yes – quite an impressive chap; built like a navvy, but I think his future will be "schemey, not louster", as old Isaac would have said!'

Tristram nodded, feeling unaccountably depressed. It was his impression, too, that Daniel had brains as well as brawn to help him get what he wanted out of life,

36

his cousin Loveday included. 'According to Charlie, he's going to be the first Penwarne to make a fortune.'

'I shouldn't be at all surprised – he was dealing with those newfangled tanks out on the Western Front . . . Insists now that a motorized age is just around the corner. A pity if he's right – I prefer horses myself!'

Jonathan smiled at his nephew, and parted company with him on the corner of the little lane that led to his own pleasant, white-washed house.

Tristram walked on towards Prospect, along the lane that kept the river company on its way to the open sea. But instead of letting himself in through the gate on the lowest level of the gardens, he skirted the sea-wall, went on past Readymoney Cove and St Catherine's Castle, and climbed up on to the headland beyond. He flung himself down on the rough turf, staring out at a view that sometimes threatened to break his heart with its splendour – on his right the mass of Gribben Head nosed out into an indigo-coloured sea, and far beyond it, purple with distance, he could see the even grander mass of the Dodman. On his left, across the sparkling water of the Estuary, the grey and white cottages of Polruan climbed the hillside behind St Saviour's Point.

It had never looked more beautiful than on this sunlit early evening, but for once he was absorbed in the pictures that filled his mind's eye: a girl's tear-wet face, and shining smile, and black silken coronet of hair; a man's determined face and large, possessive hands. He shivered violently, and sat there for a long time with his arms wrapped about his knees. The colour of the sea faded to silver, and when he finally noticed it and ran all the way back to Prospect, he was still very late for dinner.

3

The tray of brilliantly coloured specimens in front of him should have been enticing enough to make him forget the morning's quarrel, but for once even a newly arrived Painted Lady failed to give Sir Julian comfort. He was seriously ruffled – still indignant with Lavinia, but still uneasy as well. A wife was not supposed to question her husband's judgement because, knowing nothing of business matters, how could she possibly be right? But what if she were not entirely wrong?

From his study window he could see her outside in the garden – probably considering some new instruction that would upset old Simeon yet again. Even out there she couldn't let well alone and do what other wives did – merely walk about the garden when the weather was suitable, looking mildly interested. He didn't make a habit of thinking about his marriage, but there were moments – this was one of them – when he was confronted by something that felt like failure. In some way he couldn't understand, Lavinia had eluded him; she was still the aloof, independent creature he'd first met in her cousin's London drawing room. It wasn't *his* fault that he could see, unless it came from choosing a wife from the aristocracy; it was well known that they didn't expect to behave in the conventional ways other people accepted. He liked conventional ways himself, but he recognized that there was a price to be paid for a woman who was so clearly out of the ordinary.

He watched her now, oblivious of gardening apron and old straw hat, greeting a friend who had climbed up through the ascending terraces of the garden. The visitor was their most distinguished neighbour, Sir Arthur Quiller-Couch, now Professor of English at Cambridge University. Julian quite enjoyed having a neighbour so urbane and famous, but found the pseudonym he used of 'Q', a tiresome affectation.

'Good morning, and welcome home,' Lavinia was saying. 'We miss you when Cambridge claims you during term-time.'

He bowed over her hand, ignoring with his usual grace the fact that it was grimed with earth. 'Charming of you to say so, dear lady, but I'm afraid Julian, at least, prefers it when I'm not here. He suspects me of observing my neighbours with a hunter's eye, in search of literary material!'

She allowed him to settle his long, elegant frame on a garden seat before firing a sudden question at him. ' "Q", would *you* call me a very overbearing woman?'

Their friendship was of long standing but it didn't normally deal in personalities. Something, he thought, had occurred today to unsettle her.

'Not overbearing, surely, but I might say forceful,' he ventured cautiously, having considered the matter.

'Old Simeon is less tactful. "Proper old dedicai her leddyship do be" – that's how I overheard him describing me to the new garden boy the other day! He thinks I interfere too much out here.'

Her friend doubted whether it was the gardener's opinion that had prompted her question, but if she now regretted it he must allow himself to be switched on to a different track.

'You interfere with inspired results, at least. I can remember what it was like twenty years ago – straight lines of red tulips in spring and of red salvias in summer, all kept firmly in place by still more straight lines of dreadful privet hedges; an offence to God's idea of what a garden ought to be.'

Lavinia stared at the mosaic of colour all round them. 'Julian *likes* straight lines,' she said pensively. 'He agrees with Simeon – dog-violets and foxgloves and willow-herb have no place in any self-respecting border. My husband is a very orderly man. He likes things kept where he thinks they belong.' She smiled suddenly at her friend. 'That goes for people too, of course. Wives, especially, should know their place!'

'And you don't know yours?' 'Q' enquired gravely.

'Well, I fell from grace this morning by provoking a quarrel – Julian hates getting angry; thinks it's unworthy of him. I'm afraid I rather enjoyed it.'

She tried to sound lightly amused, but couldn't conceal the tension that kept her long fingers gripped together in her lap.

He realized that they had now reached the matter that had shocked her out of her usual reticence.

'Julian has agreed to let Chivers sell the last of our ships – to some marauding Estonian over here looking for bargains,' she burst out. 'I told him he was a traitor to generations of Bossineys who had been part of the mercantile history of Fowey. He was very irritated, but not persuaded to change his mind, unfortunately.'

The professor saw no help for it – in the interests of justice he must venture on to ground he suspected of being dangerous. 'As the elder son, Julian inherited responsibility for what happens to Bossiney's, but is it quite fair to exclude Jonathan completely from blame? He didn't want to be a shipowner any more than Julian apparently does.'

'Jonathan has something even more important to do,' Lavinia said coldly, for once disappointed in her visitor's understanding. 'Julian merely has his butterfly collections.'

'And his responsibilities in the town, which he doesn't shirk.' Arthur Quiller-Couch smiled disarmingly at his irate hostess. 'You won't thank me for saying so, my dear, but the truth is that it was already too late when Julian took over.'

'Because our competitors had already switched from sail to steam. All right, but we might have *tried*, not made things easy for them.'

'It isn't easy for anyone,' he corrected her. 'The post-war boom is over, and trade everywhere is dwindling. Even the coastal traffic that Bossiney's might have depended on now goes by rail.'

'So we fold our hands and bewail the fact that modern life is too difficult? What is the *matter* with us? Our granite moors are still rich in tin and copper if we could exert ourselves to mine them profitably. There are still fish in Cornish seas, but because our boats are old we have to watch while *foreigners* come and catch them. Why can't we fight any longer?'

'Lavinia dear, you hanker after more rumbustious days, when the gallants of Fowey made a habit of fighting *everyone*, and lopped the ears off the king's unfortunate messenger sent to reprimand them!'

Fierceness faded from her face, leaving it regretful. 'Stirring times to have lived in, at least. I hate tameness.'

He thought of the cross of Cornish granite recently unveiled in the Churchyard, commemorating the fact that forty-two of Fowey's young men hadn't survived the war. His own precious son had been wounded and subsequently died. Surely, recent times had been stirring enough?

Lavinia saw the desolation in his face and quickly apologized. ' "Q", I'm not forgetting the war, but if we're ever to achieve Lloyd George's promised "land fit for heroes", we shall have to do something about it ourselves – especially here. Cornwall has always been forgotten by the government in London.'

'*Now* I agree with you. Make a politician of young Tristram so that he can go to Westminster and fight the cause of the Cornishmen!'

Lavinia shook her head. 'I thought *he* might take up doctoring too; when he was small he loved going out with Jonathan in the jingle, on what he was pleased to

41

call "errands of mercy"! But the ambition has changed; he's dazzled by the idea of elegant foreign chanceries and elegant secret diplomacy, and plans to become one of His Britannic Majesty's ambassadors!' Her face relaxed suddenly into a luminous smile. 'I hope you're *not* going to point out the weakness of my argument with Julian. If his only son can't wait to escape abroad, who are we struggling to preserve Bossiney's for, allowing that we struggle at all?'

'It doesn't have to be Tristram. There's a woman in the House of Commons now and female emancipation is in the air. Why shouldn't Jenifer run things for him here?'

'One reason is that my daughter is *not* another Nancy Astor! Another is that *she* can't wait to get away from Fowey either. She enjoys nothing about her life here, and that includes the very suitable and respectable man Julian is hoping she'll marry.'

The professor almost spoke the thought that was in his mind, but remembered in the nick of time that writers inclined to observe other human beings had even less right than friends to pry into what didn't concern them. It was surely the truth that Lavinia herself had been the victim of just such a marriage, but there had been little choice in the days when Victoria was still on the throne. It was no longer necessary now, but even it if were, he thought she would reject the same stultifying fate for her daughter.

'What will Jenifer do instead?' he asked eventually.

'Marry someone who *isn't* suitable and respectable, I expect. My daughter has more than her share of beauty, but less judgement than anyone I know. It's a perilous combination, don't you think?'

His actual thought was that they might have been discussing some slight acquaintance whose future scarcely mattered to her. He would have found such cool detachment repellent in any other woman, but it didn't spoil Lavinia Bossiney for him. He'd realized long since that her feelings were strong but carefully hidden from the world, and he thought he even knew the reason for this reticence. She watched him watching her, and the faint smile twitching the corners of her mouth reminded him that they sometimes played the same game.

'How fortunate for you to be able to observe our little quirks and foibles,' she remarked blandly. 'Small sins, large stupidities, and an occasional dash of pain to give interest to the mixture! Where would you novelists be without us to provide material for you?'

'Forced to imagine you, my dear . . . so much more exhausting! And speaking of exertion, I must now drag myself away to a meeting of the Regatta Committee. My apologies to Julian for not stopping to see him.' He smiled, bowed with his usual exquisite courtesy, and descended the garden steps. It had been a revealing conversation with Lady Bossiney and he thought that she might even now be regretting having given rather too much away.

At luncheon later in the day Julian seemed to have recovered from their quarrel. It was, Lavinia supposed, one of the things about him that other people would say was likeable – a refusal to remember unpleasantness for very long. He punctiliously asked after their neighbour's health, and she as carefully responded with 'Q's apologies. All was going peacefully until Bartlett interrupted them with an envelope brought over by a groom from Lanhydrock. Lavinia frowned over it, told Bartlett that the servant must be asked to wait, and went on calmly eating until he'd left the room.

'The note was from Jenifer,' she said then, without looking at her husband. 'She's been invited to stay on for some special party over the weekend . . . Wants more clothes sent over.'

She waited for the moment or two Julian would require for the message to sink in.

'This weekend?' he enquired carefully. '*This* very weekend?' and saw his wife nod.

'Then in the excitement of hitting tennis balls about she's forgotten that the Vincents are coming here. You must tell her to come home instead, my dear.'

Lavinia shook her head faintly at Tristram, in case he should think it necessary to point out that his sister would have forgotten nothing concerning Lionel Vincent. Then she looked at Julian, thinking how typical it was of him to issue an instruction without the slightest thought for whether it could be carried out or not.

'I'm not sure how I can compel her to leave Lanhydrock if she's made up her mind to stay.'

Julian wouldn't allow himself to shout, but she saw the flush of angry colour in his face. 'She's your *daughter*, Lavinia; brought up, one would hope, to pay some attention to your, or at least to *my*, wishes. Don't send her clothes – then she will be obliged to come home.'

'And we shall have humiliated a girl who considers herself grown up in front of her friends. I doubt if we shall increase her liking for Lionel Vincent by doing that.'

Lavinia's cool, dispassionate voice was like water thrown on blazing coals. After the morning's altercation it was too much to bear. Julian pushed back his chair, and banged the table with a force that made the china rattle.

'All right – have it your own way. But if Lionel gets tired of being ignored by a wayward child who doesn't know her own mind, don't blame me. And if his father backs out of a scheme to take over our empty boatyards, don't blame me for *that*, either. You must decide who you would rather humiliate – your daughter or me.'

He strode out of the room, banging the door for the first time in his life and leaving silence behind. She thought it was also typical of him to beat her with a weapon she didn't know he had – his business discussions with Arthur Vincent.

'Vincent's pleasant enough,' Tristram ventured after a while, 'but he's twelve years older than Jen; she looks on him as practically middle-aged.'

'She looks on him as the last man on earth she wants to marry,' Lavinia said tartly. 'However pleasant he may be, he's losing his hair and has a wart on his chin which, though small, is noticeable.'

Her son's strained face relaxed in a grin, then grew sober again. 'What did Father mean about the boatyards?'

'I don't know – but no longer having any ships, presumably we don't need yards either. Mr Vincent must have a scheme for converting them into something else. If he is hoping to build a glossy new hotel beside the river I shan't mind if it does fall through.'

Tristram rather agreed with her, but at the age of twenty it was hard not to see things mainly in the light of how they might affect *him*.

'I got a lecture the other day about not being extravagant up at Oxford. Father didn't quite say that he couldn't afford to keep me there, but it almost came to that. If I'd said I didn't really want to go back, he'd have jumped at it . . . So now I feel guilty about *not* saying it, especially if Jen's mucked up some business arrangement with Mr Vincent.'

She didn't answer immediately, and the sadness in her face prompted him to walk round to her side of the table and put his arms round her neck. She was usually cool and brisk, but he understood better than his sister that she was the lynchpin on which they all depended, and he loved her very much.

'I'm sorry, Mama,' he muttered. 'Jen's being difficult, and I'm not helping by wanting a career outside Cornwall. It's not that it isn't lovely here, but the only part of Fowey that belongs to the real world is what's discreetly hidden upstream – the ugly quays for loading the china-clay. The rest is still Sir Arthur's "Troy Town" – tea-parties and regattas and suffocating "cumeelfo"!'

His mother's rare smile chased weariness from her face at the reminder of her friend along the esplanade, and the affectionate fun his novels poked at Fowey. '*You* want a town that's fallen asleep looking at its own long history

45

to wake up; and "Q" accused *me* this morning of wanting it to forget modern life altogether and go back to the buccaneering past! Perhaps, in different ways, we're saying the same thing.' She looked at Tristram's earnest face and realized that the guilt he'd referred to remained.

'If you are still worried about your father's lecture, don't be; it's bound to be given to all young men who stray away from home! We live on the brink of financial ruin, apparently, but I shall believe it when expensive rarities stop arriving for his collections.'

Tristram let out a sigh of relief and gratitude. Her cool wisdom had never failed him, and now it seemed to remove most of the unpleasantness of that scene at the luncheon table.

'What are you going to do about Lanhydrock?' he asked suddenly.

'Send Jenifer her clothes, of course. I expect she'll be able to persuade her father to forgive her when she gets home.'

Tristram watched his mother walk out of the room, and only as he settled in a quiet corner of the garden with the Stendhal novel which combined pleasure and what he called his 'serious' holiday reading did the unspoken ending to their conversation occur to him. Julian Bossiney would eventually forgive his daughter, even though she was the cause of spoiling an important guest's visit to Prospect, but it was less likely that he would forgive his wife.

The weekend was the penance that he foresaw, because with Jenifer not there, it fell to him to entertain Lionel Vincent. Once they'd established that Lionel preferred watching cricket to going sailing, and read newspapers when he read anything at all, there was nothing to do but fill the hours somehow between meals. Tristram could understand his sister's objection to someone so hopelessly dull, and promised himself that not one home truth would pass his lips when she came back to Prospect.

The resolution held for the first evening, but not the following day when she followed him up to the headland, to interrupt his reading.

'Enjoyable weekend with the jolly Vincents?' she asked brightly, settling down beside him with the air of someone determined to stay whether she was welcome or not.

'No, but you didn't imagine it would be,' Tristram answered. 'Instead of a decent sail with Charlie over to Polperro, I tacked sedately up and down the river with your friend, who found even that a little too much for his weak stomach.'

She gave the little trill of laughter that always irritated him. 'Not intrepid, I'm afraid: still, he's a more suitable companion for you than a fisherman like Charlie Penwarne.'

'I like fishermen,' Tristram said coldly. There were times when she sounded remarkably like his father, and he might have said *that*, too, but something else about her caught his attention. For once she was looking excited and happy, not dissatisfied.

'You *knew* about the weekend party at Lanhydrock,' he stated with sudden conviction. 'You only went with tennis things to pretend that you weren't going to stay.'

She still smiled, although colour rose under her usually pale skin. It was all she needed for absolute beauty. She'd avoided Lavinia's deep-set eyes and long, thin nose by inheriting her father's finely chiselled features. The dark and fair colouring of both parents had combined in her to produce rich auburn hair that glinted with gold where the sun caught it.

Tristram didn't even notice the picture she made, sitting on the grass and making a chain of daisies; he was used to the way she looked and hadn't finished what he needed to say. 'All right for *you*, enjoying the social whirl at Lanhydrock, but Mother had to put up with a filthy scene because of it. I suppose that doesn't bother you.'

She was too busy to answer and his mixture of resentments suddenly merged into blazing anger. 'Jenifer,

47

stop playing with those damned daisies and *listen* to me.'

'I am listening,' she shouted back, brushing the flowers off her lap on to the grass. 'Father was angry because I wasn't there to be paraded in front of Lionel's parents like a prize cow! I'm sorry he was unpleasant, but . . .'

'. . . you only do at all times what happens to suit *you*,' he finished for her hotly.

Jenifer sometimes remembered that she was grown up, and tried for haughtiness when she fell out with her brother. This morning she could only remember the weekend just past; her own family had become shadows, almost invisible compared with the man who dominated the bright, sunlit picture in her mind's eye.

'You're a fine one to talk . . . Sneering about my occasional social whirl while *you* escape to Oxford. Think what it's like for *me*, stuck here with nothing to do, and nothing to look forward to except an annual visit to Mother's stiff-backed relatives in London. They take me to chamber music concerts and meetings at the Royal Geographical Society.'

The despair in her voice was real, and his anger against her died as suddenly as it had blown into flame.

'Sorry, Jen . . . I suppose it *is* dreary for you here all the year round,' he said awkwardly. 'I know you're not keen on Vincent but don't forget that a lot of the chaps you might have married were killed in the war. At least he could lavish his father's wealth on you . . . give you a different sort of life.'

She shook her head, smiling again because Tristram wasn't hostile now and she could return to the pictures in her mind.

'It doesn't matter about Lionel any more. I've met someone who *does* matter – that's why the weekend was so important; *he* was going to be there.'

'You've played tennis with a stranger, danced with him a couple of times, and established that you both

48

prefer China tea to Indian. Is that enough to make him important?'

'He wasn't a stranger this time; I'd already met him at Menabilly.' Her face was flushed again, this time with the memory of a man quite unlike anyone else she'd ever met. It was hard to be certain whether she preferred the joy of talking about him to the secret pleasure that came from hugging the thought of him to herself.

'His name is Christopher O'Meara,' she confessed in a rush. 'He lives with an uncle in County Kerry . . . admits it's rather tumbledown, but beautiful all the same. As soon as the horses he breeds and trains begin to make pots of money it will be beautiful *and* well cared for.'

Tristram put his head in his hands and groaned. 'If O'Meara admits his home is tumbledown it's probably a total ruin, and I expect he forgot to mention that racehorses are the chanciest creatures on God's earth for making money. He probably imagines that Father's as rich as the people you were staying with.'

Her eyes were bright with anger, but she spoke so quietly that he was impressed, because it was unlike her to be self-controlled.

'He *doesn't* think that. I know you can't bank on horses, but they must sometimes win as well as lose. If his house is a mess I shall have something worthwhile to do, making it beautiful for him again.'

Tristram stared at her face, seeing in it signs familiar since childhood. Her mind was made up, and the matter was serious.

'My dear Jen, Father won't agree. I'm almost sure of that.'

She stood up and carefully brushed grass off her skirt. 'I don't care. Sooner or later I shall marry Christopher; if I have to, I'll live with him in glorious sin until I'm old enough to do what I like.'

He watched her walk away, moving with the graceful free stride permitted women by their present fashions. She disliked her home, hated Fowey, and took no part in any of the pleasures it offered. If O'Meara's doubtful alternative seemed preferable, she must be desperate to get away. Tristram remembered the entranced expression on her face when she spoke his name, and acknowledged to himself that he was being unfair. She was in love with the Irishman, and wouldn't give in until she got her own way. He couldn't blame her when he was just as determined to fashion for himself the sort of life *he* wanted.

The book in his hands remained unread. He watched, without seeing, the waves that made a ceaseless assault on St Saviour's Point across the estuary. They would gather, curl over, break and fall back, only to repeat the same unwearying pattern over and over again. But not even winter storms had been able to wash the point away, and all his father's huffing and puffing would fail to blow away the vision of happiness that Jenifer held in her hands.

Tristram got up and walked slowly home, wishing that the summer were over. October and Oxford seemed an eternity away, and the next two months would be ruined if she was determined to fight her battle with Father before he left. He would have to join in, but he hated rows, and still felt sick inside when he remembered his father's congested face at the luncheon table. Their life at Prospect had always jogged along, coolly but pleasantly enough, and it was disconcerting to feel so certain that it was no longer jogging now. Instead, like the Fowey river in spate, they were rushing over all kinds of submerged and dangerous rocks. *He* was bound to help Jenifer, but he spent the rest of the walk home trying to decide on which side his mother would hoist *her* flag – because *that* would be what counted in the end.

4

Loveday was enjoying herself, being 'lent' to her Eliot grandparents at Polruan. She'd been sent to provide help, but they were so loath to accept it that the week had become an unlooked-for holiday. That was a treat in itself but, most of all, she liked living in their little house beside the ferry. Just by leaning out of the parlour window she could chat to anyone coming on or off the boat, and at night she lay in bed and watched the reflections painted on her bedroom ceiling by the water outside.

Granny Eliot was supposed to be resting after a fall that had broken her right wrist, but 'thou shalt not rest during the hours of day' might have been her eleventh commandment. *She* contrived with one hand to accomplish most of what normally needed two, and Grandfather Tom was hard to help as well, being modestly certain that a sea-faring man could do anything he had a mind to. Loveday was allowed to cook their midday meal; after that he would consult the weather and his compass, and suggest each day the direction she should walk in.

Today his 'west by south, my dearie' had brought her out to St Saviour's sunlit headland. The little drawing-block Charlie had given her was on her lap, but the sketch was incomplete because she could see no end to the view spread out before her. Small, near things were more manageable, like a cluster of wild berries in a hedgerow, or delicate sprays of fuchsia hanging over an old stone wall.

The afternoon light was so clear for once that she could see every detail of the house across the water where Tristram Bossiney lived. She tried *not* to think of him, because the memory of the funeral afternoon long ago was still painful. *He'd* made her feel like a grown-up lady but her mother had treated her in front of him like a naughty child. All the same, there was a picture of him in her mind. She remembered the way the light had caught his fair hair in the chapel. He'd stood there very straight, like a soldier saluting her grandfather, and she'd liked *that* about him, too.

She put her unfinished sketch aside, and sat in a trance of stillness, with her eyes half-closed against the dazzle of sunlight on water. Then a flash of colour ahead of her on the edge of the headland made her open them wide, scarcely daring to breathe. The next moment silence and stillness were both destroyed, and the bird she had glimpsed dived away below the cliff edge in an agitated flurry of black and red.

Climbing the hillside more slowly than his noisy dog, Tristram saw her stand up but offer no welcome to the friendly labrador. She didn't smile at *him*, either, just stood there instead, looking tragically disappointed.

'I'm sorry if we disturbed you,' he felt obliged to say.

'You frightened away a chough. I'd never seen one before, and p'raps that was the only chance I'll ever have.'

It was so little what he'd expected her to say that he was almost betrayed into a grin; not quite, because he remembered just in time why the matter might be serious.

'I'm sorry,' he said again. 'I'm afraid Wilkins doesn't understand that choughs are rare and precious.'

Her eyes, shadowed by the drooping brim of an old linen hat, surveyed them both sadly. 'Never mind; it's gone now.' She sat down again, apparently disinclined for further conversation.

Tristram struggled with himself. Pique at such a cool dismissal advised leaving her there, lonely on the turf; the pleasure of seeing her again recommended swallowing wounded pride. He sat down at a little distance, thinking that even if they could find nothing to talk about, he would at least enjoy the picture she made – notwithstanding another dreadful hat. Jenifer would say that the long-skirted white dress spread out around her was hopelessly old-fashioned too, but he found it graceful and becoming to the old-fashioned girl who wore it.

'You know Merlin's spirit is waiting inside a chough, don't you,' she said quietly 'until it's time to awaken the great king? Grandfather Isaac told me about it; he said we'd go together to Tintagel one day, and Castle-an-Dinas, and Dozmare Lake where Sir Bedivere sank Excalibur.'

The certainty in her voice entrapped him. Not even to save his life could he have shattered it by pointing out the truth – that if the hero of Celtic legend had existed at all, he'd been alive five hundred years earlier than even the medieval monastic remains found beneath Tintagel's unarguably *Norman* castle.

He stared at her absorbed face instead, and thought her as lovely as the name she'd been given. Jenifer and her friends were modern and bright and very shrill; this was a gentle maiden who might have strayed off the pages of a missal and laid her spell on the legendary unicorn.

She looked up suddenly, but even when she blushed to find him staring at her it was impossible to look away, because he wanted to discover why she was so different from all the other girls he knew. It had something to do with the fact that she was elusive in spirit, but more to do at the moment with her startling beauty. Her arms were faintly tanned, and so was the triangle of bare flesh at the base of her throat. He could see the small, firm swell that her breasts made beneath the flimsy material of her dress, and felt ashamed and fever-ishly excited at the same time by the knowledge that he would like to touch them. It was a new and terrible idea, but second by second it took hold of his mind. Would it be such an unforgivable thing to do, provided he didn't hurt or frighten her?

He was only saved by Wilkins bounding up to offer him a stick. He forced himself to take it, and saw that his hand was shaking.

'I didn't expect to find you on this side of the river.' The need to say something made him sound unfriendly, as if he wouldn't have come himself if he *had* known she'd be there. 'Of course, I'm very glad you *are* here,' he added quickly. Oh, God, *worse* – patronizing now; Sir Julian's son being pleasant to a tenant's daughter. His brown hands dug themselves into Wilkins' coat so that she shouldn't see them trembling.

She rescued him, by assuming that he'd meant simply what he said.

'I'm only here to help Granny Eliot while her wrist's mending. Leastways, I'm supposed to help, but Grandfather sends me out every afternoon – to "taste the air", he calls it!' Her mouth tilted at the corners, revealing white teeth that were slightly uneven. 'I think the truth is he prefers the parlour window to himself! He's always settled there with his spy-glass before I'm even out of sight. He can recognize every ship that comes upstream, knows where its home is, and the cargo it carries.'

She sounded proud of her grandfather, and Tristram's fear that he had made a fool of himself suddenly died. He was certain instead that Loveday Penwarne wouldn't take amiss anything that he felt like saying because somehow they understood one another.

'I know Captain Eliot, of course, and I met old Mr Penwarne once or twice. Your grandfathers have been more interesting than mine; in fact their lives are part of Cornish history.'

She nodded, accepting it as a truth she already knew. 'A sea-captain's stories are about places far away, of course; I 'spect that's why I always liked best to listen to Grandfather Isaac. He could remember things other people are forgetting now – stories *his* father told him.'

Her eyes darkened at the memory of them. 'Do you know how it was in the mines back along all those years ago? They were made to run down ladder after ladder, all slimy and broken, till they got to the very bottom of the bal – sometimes carrying children on their shoulders

54

who were too young to manage the ladders alone. A bit of hempen candle stuck to their hats with clay was all they had to see by. Then, when the long core was over, the ladders had to be climbed again. They crawled out into the cold air of night soaked with sweat, and *still* had to find strength enough for the long walk home.'

Her quiet voice made no accusation against families like his own; he doubted whether she even intended to remind him that Isaac and his descendants were on the other side of a line that divided them from the kind of people who'd got rich on so much intolerable misery.

'They were brutal times, Loveday,' he agreed slowly, 'but not only in Cornish mines, I'm afraid. Perhaps we've learned to be a little bit more humane since then.' She didn't seem to notice his use of her name; perhaps it seemed as natural to her as it did to him. 'What will you do when Mrs Eliot's wrist has mended?'

'Go home, of course. Father'll be pleased. He mopes with me not there, Charlie says.' Her eyes were now fixed on the horizon, as if searching for somewhere unimaginably far away. 'Charlie says you've to go back to England, to a place called Oxford.'

'Yes, to New College – only it's not new at all, of course, but so old that it seems to have grown out of the gardens that lap its walls. It's very beautiful, and I've only got one more year there.'

She turned to look at him, hearing the note of yearning in his voice. 'T'wouldn't seem right to me, to keep leaving here; but I can see it does to you.'

'Yes,' he said again, 'but it's not till October. There's still the rest of the summer left, and the regattas to look forward to. Let's hope we do better than last year.'

'We shall,' she informed him, again with a touch of pride. 'Cousin Daniel says so. He's been learning to row in the four-oar races, and he's so strong that Looe and Par and Polperro won't stand a chance—'

'—Charlie says!' Tristram finished for her, with a grin. She nodded but didn't smile, and he thought he'd made

55

a mistake in teasing her. He wasn't to know, and she couldn't explain, about the nervous awe she felt for Daniel Penwarne; he wasn't someone she was able to smile about.

She got to her feet suddenly, as if to say that the conversation was over; he jumped up too, then stooped again for the pad she'd forgotten.

The unfinished sketch caught his eye – delicate, precise, and recognizable. He was about to say he hadn't known she could draw so beautifully; stopped himself because it would have sounded patronizing again, and absurd when there was so little that he *did* know about her.

Loveday looked disconcerted for the first time, but he didn't realize why.

'You can't miss Prospect,' she said with a touch of defiance, in case he wondered why she'd been drawing his home. 'It does stick out so.'

'Like a sore thumb,' Tristram agreed. 'I'm afraid that's the point – my great-grandfather *meant* it to be seen in all its Victorian ugliness.'

'T'isn't ugly exactly . . . it's . . .' If she had another word for it she changed her mind about offering it. 'Still, if you think it is, you'd be bound to love it more – things that aren't beautiful need *more* loving, I reckon.'

She took back the drawing-block and turned to go, so quickly that he had to call after her.

'Which direction will you be going in tomorrow to taste the air?'

'I don't know – it depends on Grandfather!' A ravishing smile illuminated her face under the drooping hat-brim, and then she was gone, running across the turf with the freedom of a wild creature.

He could have caught up with her easily enough; didn't, because it had been her choice to go, but the headland felt strangely empty now, as if in going she'd taken with her all the legendary people who kept her company in her imagination. He felt sad to be alone, but happy as well, because tomorrow he would find her again. He whistled the dog and plunged down the hillside towards the river, and home.

But she wasn't there the following afternoon, nor anywhere else that he looked. He tried to tell himself it was better so – she was temptingly lovely but what did he have in common with a girl whose ambition was never to leave Cornwall, and whose imagination had been fed by little more than Isaac Penwarne's mixture of legend and fantasy?

All the same, he remembered what she'd said about his home, and found himself surveying it to see if he could guess the word to describe it that she'd decided not to use. Prowling about the gardens as usual, his mother caught him in the middle of this exercise.

'You've lived here long enough to be accustomed to *all* Prospect's excesses, I should have thought,' she said dryly. 'What were you doing – counting every last one of your great-grandfather's stone knobs and battlements?'

Tristram grinned but shook his head. 'I was trying to make up my mind about it – vulgarly Victorian, would you say . . . middlingly, perhaps even downright, hideous . . . or appealingly quaint?'

'Never *quaint*,' Lavinia said with unexpected force. 'Nothing strongly built of honest Cornish granite could smack of such gimcrackery.'

She sounded so nearly offended that he couldn't resist teasing her.

'Such heat, Mama! I think I always had the idea that you rather disliked Prospect . . . the house, I mean; not the gardens.'

She did what he had done – turned to stare along its grey, turreted length tucked into the hillside. Twenty years ago it had looked cold and bare. Nowadays, creepers of every kind – camellias, clematis, honeysuckle, and flowering myrtles – flung a web of colour and scent over the naked stone.

'It frightened me when I first caught sight of it,' she admitted slowly. 'Compared with my childhood home, it seemed so unwelcoming that I couldn't imagine I should ever feel that I belonged. Now I pray that I can spend the rest of my life here.'

Tristram smiled at her with great affection. It was always a pleasure to him when his self-contained mother gave something away. He hoarded her small revelations like a miser hoarding gold. 'I met someone the other day who feels about *her* home here the way that you now feel about Prospect. She spoke of Oxford as if it lay at the other end of the world.'

'Who? Do I know her?'

'Charlie Penwarne's sister, Loveday.'

'For her it might just as well be, don't you think?' The blankness in his face made her add, 'The other end of the world, I mean.'

'Yes, I suppose so,' he agreed, and after a moment walked away.

There were two regattas again – Town and Yacht Club – reinstated after the war, and for as long as they lasted during the month of September the haven of Fowey came alive again. The old tea-clipper, *Cutty Sark*, was sailed up from Falmouth to serve as Committee ship, and boats converged on the haven from ports and fishing villages all along the coast.

Even Jenifer forgot her boredom and groaned with the rest of them when her brother and Charlie Penwarne were beaten on the line in the Royal Fowey Yacht Club's special 'Troy Class' race. Tristram bore disappointment with the best grace he could manage and forced himself to cheer Fowey's victory in a thrilling four-oar contest against the men from Looe. Loveday had been right about Daniel Penwarne. Graceful oarsman he was not, but power and determination were what drove a boat through the water to be first at the finishing line.

When the racing was over the excitement had scarcely begun. There was still the carnival procession, headed by the St Blazey Silver Band, and the travelling fair that arrived to cram itself somehow on to the Town Quay without anyone falling into the harbour. Tristram escorted his sister on a tour of side-shows and merry-go-rounds, not even admitting to himself that he was still looking for Loveday Penwarne. He found her when it was too late, and the long hectic day was ending in a blaze of glory. The traditional firework display staged from a barge moored in mid-stream was judged 'best'n ever yet', but Tristram took home with him only the memory of Loveday's entranced face gazing up into starlit darkness, and Daniel's arm heavy and possessive round her shoulders.

He went back to Oxford three weeks later without seeing her again. By the time Michaelmas term was over he was inclined to think that he'd forgotten her. In any case there would be Christmas festivities to attend in neighbouring houses, and sophisticated girls to laugh and dance with who didn't patiently wait for the awakening one day of great King Arthur. Even the discovery that his father had invited Lionel Vincent to spend the festival at Prospect didn't ruin all hopes of enjoyment; but Jenifer managed it with a sudden announcement of her own.

'I've invited someone, too. His name is Christopher O'Meara, and he's an old friend of the Agar-Robartes boys. He would stay at Lanhydrock, but the house is full and there isn't a spare bed for him.' She glanced at the expression on Tristram's face, then smiled beguilingly at her father. 'Dear Papa, *don't* say I shouldn't have offered to help – you *know* you always insist that *we* have a duty to be hospitable, and there's masses of room here. Everybody likes Mr O'Meara apparently, so I dare say he and Lionel will get on like a house on fire.'

Tristram listened to this masterly speech with the feeling that he had seriously underestimated Jenifer. His father looked undecided – inclined to like the idea that Prospect could offer what Lanhydrock could not, but disinclined to have anything interfere with this final attempt to make Vincent acceptable to his daughter.

'It would have been courteous to consult your mother first,' he pointed out with reason, 'still more courteous if the Agar-Robartes had done so.'

'I know, but it's all my fault – they *would* have done but when they sounded so desperate, I rather jumped in.' She turned to the other end of the table. 'Am I forgiven, Mama? Will you let him come?'

'It scarcely seems that we have much choice,' Lavinia said calmly. 'Where does this paragon come from, whom everybody likes?'

'Oh, Ireland somewhere, I believe.' She sounded no more than vaguely interested in their unexpected guest, but her eyes were fixed on Tristram again, imploring him to be her friend. He gave her a little nod and, after their father's unenthusiastic permission had been given, tactfully diverted attention by asking what had been happening in the town while he'd been in Oxford. It only occurred to him afterwards that Jenifer would almost certainly give herself away once O'Meara was staying in the house, but when he pointed this out to her she merely smiled and danced away.

By Christmas Eve both their guests had arrived and Tristram found himself obliged to feel sorry for Lionel Vincent. Against the darkly romantic good looks of O'Meara Lionel had no chance at all. How were sober worth and wealth to compete with Irish gaiety and charm? Even Sir Julian, lulled by the smiling deference with which he was treated, seemed to be enjoying Christmas more than usual. It was pleasant to have a fourth man in the house to play billiards with, and he even warned Tristram off all tactless reference to Irish republican activities, although he deeply disapproved of them himself and was normally vocal on the subject.

It was Jenifer who provoked at last the scene Tristram had been anticipating all the holiday. As soon as Lionel, rejected by her as usual, had followed their other guest to the station, she heaved an exaggerated sigh of relief and smiled cajolingly at her mother.

'Now admit it, Mama, aren't you thankful to have had Christopher here? We should all have died of boredom without him, and even Papa *liked* him.'

'Because he wasn't aware of the shabby little trick the pair of you had played on us,' Lavinia said coldly. 'It was pre-arranged between you that he should come here, even if they'd had a dozen empty rooms at Lanhydrock.' She saw Jenifer open her mouth to protest but swept straight on. 'Don't bother to deny that you knew him before this visit – it was apparent every time you looked at each other. Apart from the deception, I resent being thought so stupid that I shouldn't be aware of it.' Her voice bit like a whiplash and Jenifer's colour rose under it, but she seemed to Tristram, watching them both, almost eager to be quarrelling with her mother.

'All right, I *did* know him,' she admitted defiantly, 'but it wasn't arranged between us, Christopher thought he'd been invited – he wouldn't have come otherwise.'

'So you were being devious all round! Is that really how you've been taught to behave?'

Tristram was torn between a cowardly longing to escape from the room and the fear than one of them – he wasn't sure which – might need him before the battle ended.

'I *had* to be devious,' his sister cried. 'Unless you saw Christopher you'd never understand why I'd die rather than marry Lionel Vincent.'

'My dear girl, there *are* other alternatives.' Lavinia watched the expression on her daughter's face and knew the alternative had already been decided upon. 'Am I also supposed to understand that you *would* marry Mr O'Meara?' She saw Jenifer nod, and when she spoke again her voice was suddenly gentle. 'Have you considered for a single moment what that would mean – living among people whose habits, interests, religion even, are different from your own? You positively dislike horses, you're bored by country life; and your father could give you very little to help prop up the young man's crumbling inheritance, even if staying here has convinced him otherwise.'

'He knows that, but *you* understand *nothing*. Can't you see that I shan't mind because they'll be *his* horses and *his* country life? He won't always be poor, but it doesn't matter if he's never rich, because we love each other.'

She saw a strange expression flicker across her mother's face and thought she knew the reason for it. The resentment that had smouldered in her heart for years burst into sudden flame, burning up everything but the need to shout what she knew at her mother.

'You *ought* to know what it feels like to be held in a man's arms – not Father's, of course. *Much* too dull to be in love with your own husband, or to care about your own children. But you know what Uncle Jonathan's arms feel like – I saw you together once, and it made me feel sick.'

The silence in the room was a palpable thing, holding Tristram rooted to the spot when he wanted to fight his way through it. He knew now which of them needed him, but it was a physical effort to reach his mother and put his arm round her shoulders. She patted his hand by way of thanking him, but moved away so that she could face them both. Her face was chalk-white, and so was Jenifer's now; he thought it was how they would look if they were bleeding to death internally.

'My marriage began in Queen Victoria's reign,' Lavinia said eventually, in a low but perfectly composed voice, as if they had asked for a lesson in family history. 'Poor, ignorant creatures that we were, we were taught to hope at most for kindness and respect – *passion* was not to be expected in a lady's marriage. Kindness and respect I have had from your father; passion I might have found with his brother, but it was too late. I was already married.' She looked across the room at Jenifer. 'Jonathan held me *once*, the day he was leaving for France; it's as much as I know about the joy of physical loving.' Her hands gripped themselves together so tightly that her rings bit into fingers, because the most painful confession of all was still to be made. 'I don't believe that I have ever hurt your father, but I'm terribly afraid that I may have hurt *you*, by not showing you both how much I love you.' A smile of transfiguring sweetness broke the stillness of her face. 'Perhaps I can do better now!'

Tristram bit back the words on his tongue, knowing that it must be Jenifer who spoke – he looked at her, willing her to speak, and at last she did.

'Mama . . . I'm sorry . . . very s. . . sorry.' Tears began to stream down her pale cheeks, but all she could find to whisper was that one word, 'sorry', again and again.

Lavinia walked across to her, holding out the hand-kerchief that Jenifer didn't seem to possess. 'It's all right, my dear; it was time to be honest with each other. Now, if you're convinced that you'll be happy with Christopher O'Meara, I shall try to persuade your father that he would like an Irish son-in-law!' She kissed Jenifer's wet cheek, smiled again at both of them, and walked out of the room.

After a moment or two Jenifer glanced at her brother's stern face. 'Don't say it,' she begged. 'I know you want to rend me limb from limb, but Mama's already reduced me to the size of a worm . . . and that's pretty re . . . remarkable when you come to think that she's the g . . . guilty one.' Tears overflowed her eyes again and, from wanting to hit her a moment ago with a violence that shocked him, Tristram was suddenly obliged to feel sorry for her.

'Don't weep, you silly mutt – it's all *right*; Mama said so. I didn't think so when you were shouting the odds about Uncle Jonathan, but now I suddenly realize that it might be a tremendous relief to Mama to know that *we're* in the secret, too. It *is* a secret still, by the way. If you ever said anything to Father I'd push you off the top of Gribben Head.'

Jenifer nodded and mopped her wet cheeks. 'Poor Father,' she said mournfully, all the same.

Tristram stared at her, irritated by such mistaken sympathy. 'Why? *He's* perfectly happy. Feel sorry for Mama

63

and Uncle Jonathan – trapped here, forced to keep meeting each other . . . and having to make do with *us*!' His sister's pale, woebegone face made him relent enough to smile at her. 'Cheer up, Jen . . . I expect *you'll* get what you want in the end; but for the Lord's sake make sure that O'Meara's what you really want before you plunge.'

5

Lavinia's efforts to interest Julian in the idea of an Irish husband for his daughter met, first of all, with an astonished stare, and then a flat refusal when he realized she was in earnest. It was difficult to continue an argument in which she privately agreed with him, but the memory of Jenifer's expression when she spoke of Christopher O'Meara forced her on.

'She's been dissatisfied and restless here for a long time, Julian. It will be much worse from now on, because she's convinced that her only chance of happiness lies with O'Meara. If we deny her *that*, she thinks she'll be fated to end up old and grey and slightly mad in Fowey, like one or two of the elderly spinsters she knows here!'

'Rubbish, Lavinia . . . the girl's nineteen. How can she be happy with a penniless, Catholic horse-breeder, who probably has republican sympathies, for all that he kept very quiet about them when he was here. There are plenty of other, *suitable* men – let her choose one of them.'

'She'll never choose Lionel Vincent, if you still have *him* in mind. She can't bear him anywhere near her, and actually touching her would be out of the question.'

Julian fidgeted with the paperknife on his desk, made uneasy by even that slight reference to the idea that a woman might hope to enjoy the physical rituals of marriage. Lavinia struggled with a sudden and, as usual, ill-timed longing to give way to amusement. If she laughed now, he would never forgive her, and if she said that their daughter expected to find nothing less than rapture in a

65

lover's arms, he would probably die of heartfailure.

'There's nothing wrong with Lionel that I can see,' he muttered, 'and a link with the Vincents would have been very useful.' His wife didn't answer, and unfortunately there was nothing he could object to in her silence, a fact that irritated him still further. 'Times are damned difficult, Lavinia. Our income shrinks steadily, and there's still the expense of keeping Tristram at Oxford.'

'I know,' she agreed gently, 'and I'm sorry if your dealings with Mr Vincent are going to fall through. Can't Chivers suggest some other way of helping our shrinking income?'

'There *is* a scheme he wants to talk to me about,' Julian admitted. 'I suppose I shall have to find the time to listen to it.'

Lavinia took a deep breath and reminded herself that he took his civic duties seriously – an elected alderman of Fowey had much to think about nowadays. Julian had strongly disapproved of the building of the new, mechanized jetty above Caffa Mill, even though it was well out of sight of Prospect – let Par and Charlestown, not Fowey, smear themselves with the dust of china-clay. But he was much concerned with other improvements. The railway was bringing more and more summer visitors to the town: it needed a less medieval water supply, electricity instead of old-fashioned gas-lighting, and the demolition of its more scabrous and insanitary cottages perched on oozing rock for the past four hundred years.

'Will you also find the time to talk to Jenifer, or shall *I* tell her that you won't agree to her marrying Christopher O'Meara?'

The quiet question offered him an escape if he wanted it, but Julian couldn't allow her to think him a coward.

'I shall tell her myself, of course. Depend on it, my dear – in six months' time she'll have forgotten him.'

Lavinia thought he was wrong, but saw no point in saying so. She was the more certain of it when he reported with the air of a man who'd been right all along, that Jenifer had accepted his decision with very little fuss. She was suspiciously docile, in her mother's opinion – in fact so apathetically quiet that Lavinia was forced to write to Tristram in Oxford, imploring him to bring some lively fellow undergraduate home with him for the vacation. When he replied that he would invite a German friend, Kurt Winkler, Lavinia sighed over the choice – she wasn't ready for Germans yet. But she confided only to Jonathan Bossiney that both her children seemed to have a rare talent for destroying her peace of mind.

Easter approached in an explosion of colour as bright as the sound of the trumpets about to proclaim that Christ was risen. Across the estuary, streams of golden gorse flowed down the hillside above Polruan, and in every scrap of garden in the town daffodils 'took the winds of March with beauty'. Fowey was at its best, and Tristram looked forward to showing it off to Kurt when he arrived from paying a brief visit to his own parents in Germany. There was less to be confident about at Prospect: the atmosphere at home seemed more strained than usual, and his sister was giving an excellent impression of a Victorian maiden in the last stages of decline. When Lavinia enquired hopefully whether his German friend would be able to take Jenifer's thoughts off Christopher, Tristram was forced to admit that Kurt was clever and nice, but serious-minded.

It was a relief to escape from Prospect and visit his uncle at Salubrious House, even though it was hard to look at Jonathan now without remembering his mother's confession. In the event, embarrassment was forgotten, because he was hauled outside to admire his uncle's new 'toy', and share in a christening ceremony that named the Austin 7 'Rosinante'.

'I never thought I should prefer the internal combustion engine to a friendly horse,' Jonathan admitted, 'but there's something to be said for *this* lady when a new baby decides to arrive at an outlying farm on a filthy wet night.'

Tristram allowed himself to be driven back and forth along the lane above the doctor's house, and duly admired her paces. 'Very impressive,' he agreed, grinning at his uncle. 'What happens when something goes wrong? I suppose you climb back into the jingle and get wet after all!'

'Certainly not; I consult our efficient new mechanic, who puts it right. Didn't you know that we now have such a wonder? You ought to – because he bought up some of your father's empty boatyards and converted them into a workshop and garage.'

'I didn't know – Father doesn't discuss matters of business with me,' Tristram said slowly. 'I don't suppose I know the mechanic either, if he's new.'

'Well, you know *of* him – he's William Penwarne's nephew, Daniel.'

In a way he couldn't have explained the news came as no surprise to Tristram. When he thought about it afterwards it was as if he'd known, ever since the day of Isaac's funeral, that whatever Daniel Penwarne did would have its effect on *him* as well.

'Charlie said he was going off to make his fortune,' he murmured.

'I expect he thinks he can begin here. He's a clever, hard-working chap . . . I rather like him myself,' Jonathan said consideringly.

Tristram discovered with a force that shocked him that he didn't like Loveday's cousin at all. He remembered her watching the Regatta fireworks, and Daniel holding on to her as though she already belonged to him. If he also remembered telling his mother that Fowey needed modern enterprise he wasn't going to mention it now.

'I can't see that we want workshops in the middle of the town,' he burst out resentfully. 'Why can't he set up his business where the rest of us don't have to look at it.'

It was Jonathan's turn to look surprised. 'Ask him, dear boy. I expect he'd say that Fowey did rather well out of commercial activity in days gone by, and could do with a bit more of it now.' He stared at his nephew's disgruntled face and felt obliged to chide him a little. 'Oxford's dreaming spires spoiling you for our workaday life, lad? Remember that nothing is made easy for people like Daniel Penwarne. They have to carve out their own place in the world.'

'Sorry if I sounded like Father,' Tristram said shortly. 'Of course Penwarne must do as he pleases. It's just that, like everyone else who goes away, I always want to come back here and find it unchanged.'

Jonathan nodded, and had the tact not to say that something more than a general dislike of change had upset his nephew. Tristram himself was already changed – seeming more adult and self-possessed after a couple of years at Oxford, but also more vulnerable – as if in him, at least, Bossiney emotions that were usually so well under control, now lay too near the surface for comfort. Jonathan thanked God for middle-age. Being young was the very devil, even for someone whose family life was easier than Tristram's was at Prospect.

'Come and learn how to drive Rosinante if the weather's too bad to get your boat in the water,' he suggested. 'Or are you going to tell me that a diligent undergraduate's vacation reading is never done?'

'I'm not as diligent as all that, and in any case I've got a friend, Kurt Winkler, arriving soon.' He hesitated for a moment and then spoke again. 'I don't suppose I shall ever set my sights on making a fortune; but there's no reason why Daniel Penwarne should be the only one to become successful. I'm thinking of having a shot at it myself.'

Jonathan's face broke into a broad smile. 'Said like a Bossiney of old, dear boy. Your great-grandfather is probably applauding in his grave!' It was time for his evening surgery, and they parted company at the front of the house, but the doctor watched his tall, fair-headed nephew walk away down the hill out of sight before he went inside and closed the door. Tristram hadn't seemed interested in wordly success before, but for a reason that was left undisclosed, he was interested now.

At the cottage in Fore Street, Hannah and William were engaged in what she liked to describe as 'talking matters round'. He knew from more than twenty years' experience that his role was to listen while Hannah talked. Her mind would have been made up on the subject before she began and the object of the exercise was, more accurately, to talk *him* round to her point of view. Usually he was happy to agree. She was the clever one, and he knew as well as everyone else in Fore Street that he'd been lucky to get Hannah Eliot as a wife. It had been a nibby-gibby thing – he'd almost lost her to a flashy school inspector who kept finding reasons to visit Fowey's elementary school. Fortunately his visits had so irritated Hannah in the end that she'd forgotten to be flattered and married William instead.

It wasn't often that he queried her opinions, but this morning the talking-round procedure wasn't going smoothly.

'The maid's too young,' he said stubbornly for the third time. 'There's no call for her to be married off for years yet.'

'I know that, but Daniel will be happier for being sure something's fixed between them.'

'Tis Loveday I'm thinking of. S'pose *she's* not happy with the fixing.'

'Tell me what she *is* happy with,' Hannah snapped, 'apart from mooning about with a sketching-block and her head filled with your father's tales about the past. She's only content at the school when she's drawing pictures for the infants and stuffing *them* full of old legends about Cornwall. It's not what a junior assistant is supposed to be doing.'

''Twon't do the children any harm,' said William defiantly.

'Maybe not, but Mrs Nicholls employs her to help teach them to read and write.'

He could see that this was true. It was his own opinion that Loveday wasn't suited to school work, but he could also see far enough ahead in the argument to know that Hannah would find some way of using it against him. He was still wondering what it *would* be safe to say when she landed on the subject herself.

'Even if Mrs Nicholls doesn't lose patience with her dreamy ways, Loveday's never going to make a good teacher. You don't want her to work in a shop, so what else is she to do? Answer me that, William.' The knowledge that she'd managed to silence him now made her ready to be gentle. 'Truth is, my dear, you don't want to lose her to *anyone* – you'd have her always stay here.'

He smiled sheepishly but found a point on which his ground was strong. 'Nothing wrong with Daniel 'cept that he'll take her away when he gets too big for Fowey. 'Twouldn't be what *she'd* like – leaving here.'

Hannah heaved an exasperated sigh. 'I suppose you'd rather see her with one of the Tregear boys, or a fisherman like all Charlie's friends seem to be. Daniel will take good care of her, William, and *you* won't always be here to do it.'

She was right about that; he knew it, and now had to make the best terms he could.

'All right, then – something fixed between them if you like, but no marrying for another year at least – not till she's eighteen.'

Hannah nodded, and decided not to mention that his nephew was inclined to be an impatient man. She had done the best she could for Daniel. If he found another year too long to wait for a wife, it was up to *him* to convince Loveday that she would like to marry him sooner.

It was a point of view that had already occurred to Daniel himself. He'd been in Fowey more than two years and made it plain from the moment he clapped eyes on his cousin that *she* was the girl he was going to marry. There were plenty of others who'd have come running if he'd crooked his finger; but Loveday was different. Far and away more beautiful, of course, but that wasn't what attracted him so strongly. For one thing, she was unexpectedly unimpressed at being the one he'd chosen; for another, although she seemed not unwilling to be caught, she always evaded capture. It wasn't a state of affairs that he could allow to go on much longer, but he liked challenges and had rather enjoyed her little bid to keep him waiting. He might have been more impatient if he'd been less busy, but in any case there was no danger of losing her.

The day when this suddenly changed started like any other. Even though it was Easter morning he didn't avail himself of Aunt Hannah's invitation to attend the chapel in North Street, but he went as usual to eat the midday meal she always offered him on Sundays. Loveday smiled at him when he arrived, but he couldn't help noticing that she smiled just as warmly at her Eliot grandparents, rowed across from Polruan by Charlie to share in the Easter celebration. If he'd remembered that they'd be there he might have stayed in his own lodgings. Tom Eliot was, in their Cornish phraseology, a powerful opinionated old man, and Daniel was tired of hearing his views on the stupidity of burning coal to drive ships along. God Almighty had provided winds for that purpose, Tom was happy to point out whenever he saw Daniel.

It was Tom who irritated him again today by disapproving of the use the Bossiney boatyards were now being put to – their proper function was to house good timber, canvas, and Manilla rope, not broken-down bits of machinery.

'Saw young Tristram looking round yesterday,' the captain said next, 'and *he* didn't seem too happy either.

We had a proper nice old chat about the Bossiney ships he could remember.'

Daniel was watching Loveday and saw the little smile that lifted the corners of her mouth. She knew nothing about ships and, as far as he was aware, she knew very little about Tristram Bossiney, so she must be enjoying her grandfather's sly dig at an enterprise he didn't approve of. It was another irritation, because she wasn't supposed to laugh at the man who intended to marry her.

When the meal was over and her tasks in the kitchen were done he suggested that the day was mild enough for a river outing.

'Anywhere you say,' he offered pleasantly, 'provided you don't suggest we row all the way up to Lostwithiel and back!'

'Tide's falling,' Charlie pointed out. 'You'd get stuck, anyway.'

Loveday considered the matter. 'Castle Dore, then,' she said inevitably. 'That won't be too far.'

She went away to dress herself in a warm jacket and scarf, and Daniel found his aunt beside him.

'I spoke to William,' she murmured. 'He's agreeable to Loveday being *promised* to you, Daniel, but he doesn't want her wed for another year. I dare say he might change his mind if *she* should seem ready to marry, though she doesn't seem ready to at the moment, I'm bound to say.'

Hannah smiled at her nephew and walked away, unaware that she had just filled his cup of irritation to the brim. No, Loveday did not seem ready, and it was time she did.

The journey upstream was enjoyable enough. She was very knowledgeable about wild flowers and birds. When he could take his eyes off the river, he liked looking at her sitting in the boat, and didn't mind listening to her instruction in the art of recognizing redshank from sanderling and oyster-catcher (sea-pie, Grandfather Tom called *that*, she said, to confuse him still further). He

73

noticed again that on her own ground she was perfectly self-possessed – even confident enough to tease him because he called all seabirds gulls. They left the rowing boat tied up at Golant and walked up from the hamlet to the earthworks that scholars identify as the site of King Mark's Castle. To Daniel it was marginally interesting – anywhere inhabited long before its progress could be written down was worth a glance, if only to decide what had brought human beings there in the first place. But Loveday's total silence as they wandered about was beginning to pall; he expected her to make more of a contribution to the afternoon than simply looking beautiful.

'You've been quiet for the past quarter of an hour,' he said eventually. 'Does that mean you're happy, tired, or bored with the remains of iron age forts?'

Her expression, entranced when she turned to stare at him, changed at the sight of his own half-mocking smile. She wasn't much concerned with iron age remains, but this was sacred ground. 'How could anyone be bored here?' she asked almost angrily. 'Don't you know *anything* about Cornwall? This was King Mark's citadel, where his nephew, Tristan, had to bring him a bride chosen from Ireland. But on the journey here poor Tristan and Iseult fell in love.' Loveday pointed to where they could see the river winding beside St Sampson's Church at Golant. 'Before the church was built there was a chapel there; that's where Iseult used to hear mass.'

She might have been describing something that had happened the day before yesterday. Daniel had been in Cornwall long enough to accept the fact that past still cohabited with present, not only in its landscape but in the tribal memories of the people who lived there. Even so, Loveday's capacity to drift out of the real world into an imaginary one she seemed to prefer became a threat that he hadn't properly understood until now; it was *this* habit, he could suddenly see, that was directly linked with her other habit of eluding him. Fear made him rough for the first time; if he couldn't break her of it, he might lose her in the end.

'It happened fifteen hundred years ago, if it happened at all,' he shouted. 'Forget Tristan and Iseult, and try thinking about *us* for a change.'

His last sentence almost passed her by because she was so shocked by the first one. 'Of course it happened – you can feel them here . . . *See* them, almost.'

It was as far as she got before his hands fastened on her shoulders, shaking her into a different awareness.

'All right – they *were* here. Two men wanted the same woman, and by all accounts *she* knew as much about passion and lust as they did. Isn't that roughly the story?'

His eyes, and the strength in his hands, might have warned her to be careful, but she was beyond noticing.

'No, it isn't – Iseult knew about *love*. You just make it sound wicked and . . . and horrible.'

Daniel was aware that nothing had changed. She was shaken out of her usual tranquillity, but not because she was there alone with him. That damned legend, and all the others Isaac had taught her, still absorbed her *mind*, while every particle of flesh and blood and bone in his *body* clamoured for possession now, so that she might be taught the difference between legend and reality. Even if he had remembered Hannah's careful warning it would have been ignored. He could wait another whole year and still find Loveday living in her dream world. The lesson must begin now.

His hands unbuttoned her coat, fastened round her, and pulled her against his own hard body. His mouth brushed hers gently, almost tantalizingly, at first. It required huge self-control, but when he felt the unexpected quiver of response in her, fear gave way to confidence. She was reachable, after all. It was going to be all right, as long as he was very patient with her.

'Sweetheart, I'd be the first to agree there's nothing wicked or horrible about love. I'm all for it myself!' His face was very close to hers; she stared at it trying to recognize in this smiling, ardent man the Daniel Penwarne who had often impressed her and occasionally frightened her. His hands on her body were warm and gentle; their effect was exciting in a way she couldn't understand, but she could feel the same excitement in him, glowing like a flame.

'I've been very patient, little maid, but I can't go on waiting,' Daniel murmured against her cheek. 'I want to love you – like this, but more . . . Oh, a lot more.'

She was mesmerized by the soft sound of his voice, his nearness, and his hands that seemed to be asking her body to merge with his. She was going to marry him . . . no, she was Iseult, learning to be loved by Tristan. When Daniel's mouth covered her own again it wasn't gentle now; her lips were forced open, but she still wasn't frightened. Her body seemed to recognize, even to want, what was happening. When he lifted her off her feet and laid her on the grass, she smiled. His body was heavy, but warm; without protest, she even let his hands unbutton the bodice of her dress and chemise. But the breeze blew coldly on her bare breasts, making her open her eyes, and the expression on his face was frightening. He was the Daniel she had always been careful to escape, after all; *she* wasn't Iseult, but Loveday Penwarne, trapped in a waking nightmare that must end in disaster.

'Stop, Daniel . . . please, please, don't touch me again.' Her hands tried to push his shoulders away from her. 'Please . . . I want to go home.'

'Sweetheart, we *can't* stop now.' He smiled, but it didn't lessen the terrible naked hunger in his face. 'I'm only going to love you a little; then we'll go home.'

She began to struggle, with the strength born of terror and desperation, but it was like being buried alive under Cornish granite. She was suffocating under his weight . . . dying. Until, mercifully, a respite came. Daniel lifted his head, and turned to stare at something behind them. In the same moment that *he* swore violently, she heard something else as well – the sharp, excited barking of a dog who, pleased with himself for having found them, now squatted on his haunches waiting for praise. 'Wilkins' – she couldn't be sure whether the name appeared because her mind held a distant memory of the cream-coloured labrador, or because the name had just been shouted.

She felt Daniel's heavy body roll off her but, before she could sit up, Tristram Bossiney appeared from the other side of the grassy bank. She saw his face change as he caught sight of her still lying there – clothes pulled off her shoulders, and bodice still gaping open.

'Take your dog and go,' Daniel said quietly. It cost him a huge effort not to shout, but the fever in his blood had died and he was in control of himself again. Even if she had known that, it would have made no difference. She was dying of shame, but Tristram Bossiney musn't leave her there alone with Daniel.

'Take me, too, please . . . please.' The agonized whisper barely reached him but her face held him rooted there, torn between embarrassment, anger, and the sickening fear of having blundered into something that didn't concern him.

'No need for *you* to trouble yourself,' Daniel said more sharply. 'I shall see her home.'

Loveday's next move took them both by surprise; she was suddenly on her feet, clinging to the dog as if her life depended on it. 'I won't go with you, Daniel. I'll walk all the way instead.'

Her voice still trembled, but it held a note of finality that he recognized. The moment became suddenly unendurable – his own frustrated longings, Loveday's public rejection, and Bossiney's obvious mixture of embarrassment and disgust.

'Do what you like – I don't care.' The shout seemed to echo back at them as he walked away down the hill towards the river, leaving silence behind.

Loveday mechanically fastened up her clothes, and wrapped herself in her coat as if she would never feel

77

warm again. She stared at the ground when she spoke to Tristram.

'I just needed Daniel to go – you don't have to . . . to trouble yourself; I know the paths all the way home.'

'It's miles on foot,' Tristram said awkwardly. 'In any case Wilkins is a very simple-minded fellow; he'll get confused if you go in one direction and I go in another.'

She bent down to hide her face against the dog's silky fur. Thanks to Wilkins, she was still free to choose what became of her; by now, without him, she knew that she would have belonged absolutely to Daniel. The thought made her shiver, but she stood up and spoke, still without looking at Tristram. 'All right – I'll go with *you*.'

They walked slowly, each knowing that Daniel must be given time to reach the river well ahead of them. Tristram racked his brain for a subject safe to talk about, found nothing, and glanced sideways at Loveday to find tears pouring silently down her face. He saw her smearing away the tears with the back of her hand so that he wouldn't notice them and the little gesture stabbed him with a sudden shaft of pain. When he held out his handkerchief her huge, drowned eyes met his for the first time.

'You did that before – after we'd buried Grandfather Isaac,' she said slowly. He'd taken her arm then, too, but he wouldn't do that now; she remembered the expression on his face when he'd seen her lying on the grass.

He still didn't find anything to say, and they were both silent until he'd led her to a rowing boat tied up at Golant Quay. She sat facing him, with her hand resting on Wilkins' broad head. The dog licked her face, and in the warmth of his friendly kiss the frozen lump of humiliation inside her melted into a kind of grief. She'd been desperate not to have Daniel take her, but *he* had been hurt as well; she knew that, and felt sorry for him.

'We were going to be married some time – Daniel and me,' she said in a low voice. 'We shan't now, though.' She was quite certain about it; all the months of knowing

78

what was in his mind and *not* knowing what was in her own were over now.

'What . . . What will you do instead?' Tristram asked.

Loveday heaved a small sigh. 'Stay at Mrs Nicholls' school, I s'pose, if she'll keep me on. I'm not a very good junior teacher, but I like drawing pictures for the little ones.'

'I should think *they* enjoy that, too.'

She heard the kindness in his voice, and, because when she looked at his fair, serious face she saw pity but no disgust there now, it was suddenly possible to go on talking to him.

'It wasn't Daniel's fault, what happened – it came of b . . . being at Castle D . . . Dore. For a moment or two I was Iseult . . . not m . . . me at all. Then the dream turned into a nightmare, but Wilkins came and rescued me.'

If he laughed at her it would be more unbearable than anything that had gone before. Instead, he nodded as if what she'd just said was perfectly reasonable.

'It wasn't just Castle Dore, Loveday; it comes from being Cornish. When I sit in my little study at Oxford I often feel the past jogging my elbow – the room is still inhabited by the ghosts of students who've been in and out of it for the last few hundred years! I don't dare tell anyone else that, though, in case they think I'm mad.'

A quiver broke the tragic stillness of her face. He understood, and nothing was unbearable now, not facing Daniel again, not even facing her mother.

'Penwarne didn't . . . didn't hurt you this afternoon?' Tristram asked gently, and saw her shake her head.

He fixed the oars in the rowlocks and manoeuvred the boat out into mid-stream. 'Hang on to Wilkins for me. He's apt to take exception to any other boat with a dog in it – he's got no manners at all, I'm afraid.'

'I don't care – he's . . . handsome.' She selected the Cornish word after some thought, then smiled faintly; yes, it was just right for Wilkins.

Tristram began the long pull home, grateful that she wouldn't expect him to row and talk at the same time. She had found some reserve of strength and dignity that was holding her together again, but his own thoughts were chaotic. Penwarne wasn't the man to accept defeat, so she would probably marry him in the end. The thought made him feel sick, but she couldn't spend her youth and beauty drawing pictures in an infants' classroom, and what else was she to do? He was no nearer solving the problem by the time they were alongside the steps at Town Quay, nor any nearer finding something else to say. Loveday thanked him gravely for bringing her home and then jumped out of the boat. Before he could even ask whether she would like him to walk with her back to Fore Street, she was gone, and the strange, disturbing episode was over.

6

The haven was filling with boats for a day of Eastertide racing – it wasn't really part of the normal regatta calendar, but any excuse would do to begin the joyful business of getting boats into the water again. Barometers, consulted and compared, were high and steady; for once so early in the year the weather was set fair. Still, for the first time that he could remember, Charlie Penwarne wasn't looking forward to a day spent afloat with Tristram Bossiney. Other times they'd spent together were coloured golden in his memory, however mucky the weather might have been. They'd set off time and again with a pasty or two in their pockets as a stay-stomach and nothing to do but make Tristram's little boat dance over Lantic or St Austell Bay. They'd talked when they felt like it, laughed when they got soaked, and listened to the wind playing in the canvas above their heads. Now, something had changed and although Charlie didn't blame Tristram, he thought the change was in his friend. Two boys hadn't bothered about the difference between Town school and the handsome old place Sir Julian's son had been sent to; but between a Mevagissey fisherman and a young man home from Oxford who was going to become something important abroad, there'd opened a gap too wide, Charlie reckoned, for them to step across now. The new foreign friend Tristram had staying with him seemed to sum up the change – old friendships sometimes had to be allowed to fade when children grew up.

Charlie didn't intend to air these views at home, but the subject of the regatta was raised by William Penwarne when they were at the tea table the day before racing began.

'Daniel not rowin', then, tomorrow?'

'No . . . says he's got better things to do,' Charlie reported briefly.

'I should think he has, with a business to run here and one in Lostwithiel, now, as well. It stands to reason he's busy,' said Hannah. It rankled with her deeply that Loveday had suddenly made up her mind she wasn't going to marry Daniel. William had, with unexpected firmness, said that the maid wasn't to be badgered into taking her cousin, but Hannah still regretted the best opportunity she thought her daughter was ever likely to have.

'Doesn't matter; we can manage without Daniel if we have to,' Charlie said in answer to the grin on his brother's face.

'I'd like to know how – we'd have been nowhere without him last year; he practically won for us single-handed.' John passed his plate for another helping of pudding and thought of something else that would irritate Charlie. 'Mr Tristram Bossiney will want you to win *his* race for him with that fancy German friend of his looking on. Then, if you're lucky he'll remember to say thank you before they both disappear into the Yacht Club and leave you outside.'

Charlie stared down at the food on his plate – figgy-duff, his favourite, this roly-poly pastry stuffed with bits of fig, but tonight it seemed to be choking him. The difference between a fisherman and Tristram Bossiney wasn't something they could do anything about, but John had jabbed a nerve and it hurt.

'I don't care about the old Yacht Club, nor about Daniel rowing, either,' Charlie muttered. 'In fact, if he can't say good morning like a Christian to Tristram's friend, I hope he stays away from the quay altogether tomorrow.'

'Why *should* he be polite to a bloody German – tell me *that*,' John shouted. 'We were fighting them back along a few years ago.'

'That's *enough*.' Hannah suddenly intervened, and when she spoke in that tone of voice both her sons still listened to it. 'If you *must* quarrel, go outside and do it.'

Charlie got up from the table and went outside – not to continue the quarrel, but simply because the cottage – Bossiney-owned – seemed too cramped for him, and his family no help to him at all. John was like their mother, ready with an opinion about everything under the sun, never troubled by the doubts that bothered him. His quiet, gentle father wasn't troubled either, but only because he was content to accept things. 'To do justly, and to love mercy, and to walk humbly . . .' That was enough for William, just to try to follow His Lord's teaching; but Charlie would have liked to steer some middle course between walking humbly and squaring up to everyone he came across, as John and Daniel did.

He walked down to the quay because he could think better in a boat afloat on water, but the noise and bustle made him row across the river to the peacefulness of Penpoll Creek. No regatta excitement there, just the quietness of a golden spring evening. If he sat very still he might soon hear a sand-jar give its low, churring call, but already the oyster-catchers were busy in the shining mud left by the tide, and an occasional heron stood motionless, humped among its feathers, considering things.

It was the sort of evening that he often shared with Loveday. She knew even more about river life than he did, and was usually the one to spot things first. But among the things that troubled him nowadays, she was included. She didn't talk about herself, but he knew she wasn't happy at Mrs Nicholls' school. She wasn't going to marry Daniel, either, but he didn't know why. Charlie gave a sigh, and began to row home across the river. Taking things all round – what with Daniel being awkward, and Tristram's foreign friend, and John stirring up things better left unsaid – he'd be glad when the old regatta was over.

Kurt Winkler saw Charlie set off across the river and

recognized him as a friend of Tristram's. It might have been pleasant to call out and be taken aboard for an early-evening row, but he was also enjoying his solitary walk before it was time to go back to Prospect to dinner. He was beginning to understand what Tristram had often tried to explain. Cornwall *was* almost a separate island, nearly severed from England by the Tamar river, and everywhere else pounded, lashed, lapped, and cradled by the ever-present sea. He could see now why the Cornish might be a different breed of men.

Being a serious student, Kurt knew quite a lot about the place he had come to visit; he read about its burial chambers, quoits, and stone circles that were the visible remains of a past too ancient to be recorded otherwise; knew that its ruined stacks and roofless engine-houses spoke of the wealth and misery of more recent times. All its desolate beauty was clear to him. But the people he had come to visit were a puzzle to someone whose life's work was to be the study of human nature.

Sir Julian and Lady Bossiney, for instance: they seemed to meet only at meal times, and were then as polite to each other as strangers placed by chance at the same table. Their neighbour along the Esplanade, whom Kurt knew to be a most eminent Cambridge don, seemed to be more concerned here with yachts than the finer points of literature; and Tristram's sister confused him most of all. She was beautiful to look at, but she ignored *him*, her brother's guest, completely. Instead, some inner excitement occupied her, even to the exclusion of her own family. Kurt put the problem aside because his walk had brought him to the war memorial in the churchyard of St Fimbarrus. He was standing bare-headed in front of it when he recognized Tristram's uncle in the man who had stopped beside him.

'Good evening, *Herr Doktor* – are you thinking that I of all people should not be standing here?' he asked gravely.

Jonathan shook his head. 'My thoughts would be the

84

same whoever was here – that this commemorates a more senseless slaughter of life than the human race has ever managed to perpetrate before. Those four years achieved nothing, except a map of Europe redrawn in ways that are certain to cause more trouble in the future.'

'More trouble? Perhaps, sir, you forget the League of Nations?' Kurt suggested diffidently.

'To which Germany and Russia don't even belong? No, I don't forget it, my friend.' Jonathan put aside a League in which he had no faith and returned to the beginning of their conversation. 'May I ask if you *have* been made to feel unwelcome in this country?'

'Never in Oxford; only once, a little, here in Cornwall. Tristram's friend, Charlie, tried to introduce me to a cousin of his, but the man walked away. It is understandable, of course; the war ended such a little time ago.'

Jonathan's smile approved his nephew's taste in friends, but quickly faded again. The boy in front of him made light of the incident but no doubt it had been painful at the time, both to him and to Tristram.

'I suppose the cousin in question was Daniel Penwarne,' he said slowly. 'He fought in some of our bloodiest battles on the Somme. Forgive him if you can, as he must learn to forgive you.'

'I understand.' A grin suddenly routed Kurt's serious expression, making him look his true age again. 'There are things I don't understand about the English, of course, but Tristram tells me that this isn't even England at all.'

'You'll believe him after dining at the Yacht Club, where we still solemnly toast the Duke of Cornwall! What does it matter to Cornishmen that everyone else knows him as the Prince of Wales?'

Jonathan consulted his watch and gave a little sigh. 'I would stay and enlighten you further, dear boy, but for the ailments of a lady called Lizzie Treloar. Don't ever take up the practice of general medicine if you wish to call your time your own.'

'I shall take up the practice of psychiatry, *Herr Doktor*.

85

I believe people's minds to be more interesting than their bodies.'

A gleam of amusement shone in Jonathan's eyes but he answered with careful gravity. 'The two are not altogether unrelated in my experience. *Auf wiedersehen*, Kurt. Observe our quirks and oddities as much as you please, but don't take them too seriously!'

The regatta got under way the following morning, in conditions that were pronounced on all sides as 'proper 'andsome' – bright sunshine to make the town look its best, and enough breeze to make the races exciting. Julian took his seat on the terrace of the Yacht Club beside his neighbour – 'Q' resplendent in blazer and yachting cap for the occasion. Jenifer chose to lead their guest into the crowd shouting itself hoarse on Albert Quay.

When the hubbub died down between events she offered him the cool smile he'd come to expect, if she smiled at all.

'Something wrong? You didn't seem to be watching the race. If it upsets you to be here rubbing shoulders with the hoi polloi you can always go and join my father.'

'And leave you alone? I don't think so, *gnädige Fräulein*,' he answered gravely.

'Not fitty, as we say here? Not what a German gentleman could bring himself to do? Shall I let you into a secret, Herr Winkler? I don't care a damn whether things are fitty or not.'

To provoke and shock her brother's friend made her feel sophisticated and worldly-wise. He was so serious and courteous and kind that it was pleasure to behave badly. He was so often watching her when he thought she wasn't looking that it was exciting as well to run the risk of having him guess more about her than she wanted him to know.

'I think you have *other* secrets but it is natural that you don't wish to tell me about them,' Kurt said quietly.

When she swung round to look at him her face was

vividly bright for the first time in his acquaintance with her. She was very lovely, with a smile on her lips and the breeze ruffling her hair; but there was derision, not warmth, in her smile, and he could see no glow of friendship in her eyes.

'You're right – in fact, I don't wish to talk about anything at all, or to go on standing here. I shall take a walk instead. I'm sure you know your way back to the house by now.' She nodded a cool goodbye and disappeared into the crowd. Kurt hesitated, made up his mind, and then followed her. When they were clear of the press of people by the riverside and climbing Custom House Hill he caught up with her again.

'Where are we walking to?' he enquired pleasantly, ignoring the angry flush of colour in her cheeks.

'*We* are walking nowhere, my *gnädige* friend. I don't feel obliged to entertain my *brother's* guest and *you* don't have to dance attendance on me.'

'Both statements are true; nevertheless I shall continue to go with you. We can talk, or walk in silence – whichever you prefer.'

She came to an abrupt stop and stood staring at him, fighting a strong inclination to swear in sailors' language overheard along the quays of Fowey.

'Look – I prefer to walk by myself. I do *not* want you with me. I'd say it in German if I could, to make it more clear.'

'It is entirely clear,' Kurt said cordially. 'What is not clear is why you dislike me so much. Is it because I belong to a country that fought yours? Remember that you won in the end, and that our people still suffer much hardship as a punishment for the sins of their leaders.'

The gentle confession made no excuses and sought no pity. She might have been disarmed by it if she hadn't reminded herself that he was Tristram's friend, almost part of the family that cruelly refused to allow her to be happy. It was easier when she was angry with them all to think only of Christopher and of the joy she was missing.

'I don't much care about your people or your leaders,' she said candidly, 'and I don't know of any reason why I need like *you*.'

'Nor I,' he agreed. 'Tell me instead why you don't even seem to enjoy this lovely place you live in.'

They had turned without her being aware of it into Bull Hill, and Kurt stopped to lean on a convenient stone wall. A sweep of his hand indicated the view spread out below them. Gull-lined roofs dropped down in terraces to the crowded quays, and sunlit river; beyond it a hyacinth-coloured sea stretched to the horizon, and met a sky for once rinsed clear of clouds.

'I hate this "lovely" place,' Jenifer said deliberately. 'So might you if you spent a few winters here, either muffled in grey mist, or listening to the rain and the seagulls crying.' She turned to stare at his quiet, gentle face, and its very difference from the face she needed to remember made her want to hurt him again. 'In any case, it's people who provide enjoyment, not places. I don't expect *you* to understand that, of course. Like my brother, all your learning comes from books. The lusts and longings of the flesh aren't allowed to trouble you in sleepy college quadrangles!'

The jibe had an even more gratifying effect than she bargained for, because he swung round and grabbed her painfully by the shoulders. She was dragged so hard against him that she could feel the thudding of his heart.

'You are mistaken, *Fräulein* – it's not a monastery we live in,' he said fiercely. She opened her mouth to protest, but his lips fastened on hers, proving that not quite all his learning had come from books. When he finally released her he was breathless and pale, and she was trembling, but trying to smile.

'My . . . my apologies to Oxford,' she murmured. 'I underestimated it!'

Kurt wiped an unsteady hand across his mouth, as if to brush away the longing to kiss her again that must some-how be resisted – but dear God, it was hard when she was beginning to smile properly at him for the first time.

'I'm sorry, Jenifer . . . It is *I* who must apologize,' he muttered with difficulty.

Also for the first time in his acquaintance with her, she looked at him with warmth and charming amusement in her face.

'We're back to where we began, I'm afraid – you think it wasn't fitty to kiss me! I asked for it, and I'm grateful to you for helping me make up my mind. I've been stupid, not realizing what I must do.'

She began to walk in the direction of the Esplanade and, although he now understood her even less than before, she talked only of trivial Fowey matters all the way home. They were entertaining enough, but had nothing to do, he felt sure, with what really occupied her mind.

At Prospect afterwards, Lavinia noticed gratefully that her daughter now treated Kurt as if he were actually there. It was a pity that he and Tristram would be leaving so soon to return to Oxford for their last term just when Jenifer was looking more cheerful than she'd done since Christopher O'Meara's Christmas visit. Even when they'd gone and the house suddenly felt too quiet again, she remained good humoured, if slightly preoccupied. Julian noticed the change in her, and couldn't resist pointing it out to his wife – had he not said all along that a brief infatuation would be forgotten soon enough?

The shock was all the greater when it came. Jenifer went to Lanhydrock for an overnight visit, but instead of re-turning the following day arranged for a servant to deliver a note to her father. It said briefly that she couldn't wait any longer for him to change his mind. She was already on her way to Liverpool, and the night boat for Dublin.

Lavinia knew from the expression on Julian's face what the note contained even before he handed it to her. She wondered whether it was safe to say that they should have known better than to let Jenifer go to Lanhydrock at all, since all her wrong-doing seemed to be plotted there. But she decided that he was too hurt by his daughter's sudden departure to be asked to see it as anything but a scandalous disgrace. Genuine anxiety for her was the worst part of his distress, but there was the shame as well of having it known that his daughter had run away.

'She . . . she said something just before going to Lanhydrock . . . something about O'Meara getting tired of waiting for her,' he confessed wretchedly. 'God forgive me, I didn't think she meant it.'

His desolate face prompted Lavinia to gentleness. She took back the note that he was now holding again in shaking fingers, and covered his hands with her own warm ones.

'There's nothing to blame yourself for – I'm sure this was planned well ahead; it's why Jenifer has been so cheerful recently.'

'I said "no" again – that's what drove her to run away.'

'Perhaps, but any father is entitled to try to stop his child making what he thinks is a disastrous mistake. You did no more than that.' It was the only comfort she could give, but Julian looked grateful for it. He stared at her, suddenly struck by something he hadn't noticed so far.

'For a woman whose only daughter has just behaved with scandalous impropriety, you seem remarkably calm, I must say.'

'I can't help thinking that she's also behaved with quite a lot of courage,' Lavinia astonished him by pointing out. 'If O'Meara *is* necessary to her happiness, perhaps she was right not to accept the waste of two more years until she could do as she pleased.' She almost smiled at the expression of offended surprise on his face, but remembered in time that he never dealt with life's crises by trying to treat them lightly. Instead, she did what she could for her daughter.

'My dear, write to Jenifer – she was thoughtful enough to include Christopher's address! She'll be unhappy until she hears from you. Give them your blessing, and do whatever else you can for them.'

Gloom settled on Julian again. 'I don't know that I can do *anything*. I keep saying that we grow poorer year by year, but nobody listens to me. Chivers won't hear of us selling property, but it will come to that in the end. Thank God this is Tristram's last term at Oxford.'

Lavinia agreed, with her rare, charming smile, that they were all a great trial to him. The first shock was wearing off and, although he would miss Jenifer at Prospect, if he could discover that the O'Mearas had some blue-blooded connection, she thought he would eventually become reconciled to his daughter's marriage.

7

Tristram left Oxford for good at the end of Trinity term. It was another milestone passed. He was happy – of course he was – to be setting forth, fully adult at last and with the likelihood of an honours degree to prove it, on the next stage of his journey. Immediately, that meant joining Kurt Winkler on a walking holiday in Bavaria before going to stay in Paris for three months. After that, there was the Foreign Office entrance examination, which he intended to pass with flying colours. The future was mapped out in his mind, clear and full of promise for someone who now prided himself on being a cosmopolitan, a true European, for whom national boundaries and differences were nothing but a dangerous threat to everlasting peace. He and Kurt had agreed on this in many serious late-night discussions, and he had no doubt that it was true.

They were to meet up in Munich in a fortnight's time, but first he must take back to Prospect the mass of books and belongings accumulated over the past three years at New College. He settled himself in the Paddington to Penzance train, with a feeling of regret that he wasn't already travelling down to Dover with Kurt. But as each remembered name on the Great Western line flashed by, cosmopolitanism died a little more. Perhaps being a European could wait a little longer after all, while he took one last sail across St Austell Bay, and watched sea and heavens merge from his favourite vantage-point up on the headland above Prospect.

Jonathan Bossiney was waiting for him at Lostwithiel with Rosinante in the yard outside.

'She can manage a suitcase or two, dear boy, but your

trunk will have to come by the carrier,' Jonathan explained as they shook hands. His face looked tired under the battered straw panama, well-known as 'Doctor's' summer headgear, but his smile was as warm as ever. Tristram returned it with a sudden rush of affection – there was nothing wrong with being a native Cornishman if it meant being like this wise and charming man.

'You're feeling a bit torn, I expect,' Jonathan remarked above the characteristic rattle of Rosinante's starting-handle as he threaded his way out on to the Fowey Road. 'Not sure whether you feel more excited than sad, or the other way round?'

'Something like that,' Tristram agreed. 'How is everything at home? I know Jen's married now, of course, but she hasn't found time to write to me.'

'Nor to me, but I can report via her occasional letters to your parents that nothing mars her Irish bliss – her home at Mount Merrion *is* a trifle shabby, but in the grand Irish way that makes shabbiness more desirable than luxury; her uncle-by-marriage, Patrick O'Meara, is everybody's friend, and her husband all that a husband should be.'

Tristram took note of the hint of grimness in his uncle's pleasant voice, but decided not to comment on it. 'A bit sad for her to get married without the rest of us there,' he said instead. 'I thought weddings were supposed to be family affairs.'

'*Her* choice, was it not? She could have invited her parents at least; but my own opinion is that she revelled in the drama of it all – plucky bride ignored by her heartless family!'

'You're not being just a trifle harsh?' Tristram suggested diffidently.

Jonathan's expression relaxed into a smile. 'Probably, dear boy; but it might have occurred to her that your mother and father would be hurt at *not* being asked; I can't abide thoughtless unkindness.' It was all he intended to say on the subject, and Tristram was obliged instead to answer questions about his future that saw them the rest of the way home.

Apart from his sister's absence, nothing else seemed to have changed at Prospect. Events in the country at large – the widespread industrial unrest that had culminated in the bitterness of Black Friday and the failure of the Triple Alliance to support a coalminers' strike – seemed to be mostly ignored at Prospect, as in the rest of Cornwall; more important *there* was the steady decline of fishing and agriculture, and the virtual death of Cornish mining. The official toast of the county – 'Gentlemen, I give you Fish, Tin, and Copper' – had a despairing ring to it nowadays. Tristram would have liked to ask his father about these things, and even more about how their own family concerns were surviving, but Julian took refuge in much cheerful talk about local matters. What a mercy that St Catherine's headland had been saved from the clutches of bungalow-builders and given to the National Trust by Mr Stenton Covington; what a boon that Town Quay had been greatly extended by the demolition of some ancient cottages; and what a mixed blessing that large china-clay boats could now be loaded in a single day from the great new jetty above Caffa Mill.

Tristram accepted his father's obvious reluctance to talk about Bossiney affairs, and also his mother's careful conversation about plants when they were out in the garden together, until she stopped in the middle of what she was saying one day and smiled ruefully at him.

'I'm sorry, my dear. What on earth does it matter to *you* whether or not that useful but common yellow jasmine is smothering my precious viburnum fragrans? I'm sorry Kurt Winkler couldn't come down with you – it's boring for you with not even Jenifer here.'

Tristram shook his head. 'I'm not bored, and I shall be seeing Kurt soon enough, but I'm very glad you learned to like him: you weren't terribly keen to begin with,

I thought, on the idea of a *German* friend!'

It was lightly put but she answered with the honesty that he realized was the bedrock of her character. 'No, I wasn't keen at all. Individuals like Kurt I can learn to love; but if you insist that I must admire the whole German race, I shall still disappoint you. The past is too much with us yet for that.'

'But that's just what has to be forgotten if we're ever to make any progress,' Tristram said earnestly. 'That's what makes me feel a career in diplomacy's so worthwhile, instead of staying here and helping Father run things. No more arguments settled by bloodshed in future, simply peaceful negotiation – with justice for everyone concerned.'

It sounded so wonderful, and his belief in the reasonableness of human nature was so touching, that she would have died rather than say she couldn't share it however much she tried. Instead she tucked her hand inside his arm as they walked along and agreed that she approved of his chosen career.

'All the same, I have the feeling sometimes that I *ought* to have stayed here,' Tristram confessed. 'Cornwall might not be in the depressed state it's in now if young men like me hadn't been leaving it in droves for the last hundred years.'

'True, my dearest; but even to help Cornwall you wouldn't want to be a fisherman or a farmer.' She didn't say, because she didn't know, what *was* required to help the depressed affairs of the Bossineys. Instead, she changed the conversation by pointing out to him the grand new mansion that now crowned the hillside above the town.

'Fowey Hall, it's called. Vulgarly ostentatious, your father thinks, but perhaps we should take heart from an emigrant like Charles Hanson, who returns with a fortune made in Canada. I think we could do with more such Cornish sons and, according to Jonathan, we may get one in the person of young Daniel Penwarne.'

*   *   *

Tristram had set off for Germany by the time one of Jenifer's infrequent letters arrived, announcing that she was expecting a child. It ignored, as usual, their invitations to the O'Mearas to visit Prospect, and still failed to offer *them* an invitation to go to Mount Merrion. Apparently horse-breeding was an arduous, full-time business.

So, too, was Jenifer's pregnancy. As the autumn dwindled into winter she began to sound so querulous that even Julian noticed the change of tone.

'Something wrong, do you suppose?' he asked Lavinia anxiously.

'Nothing that the birth of the child won't cure. She's probably bored with her present inactivity – most young mothers-to-be are.'

'Yes, but can we be sure she's being properly taken care of? They're a feckless, backward lot, the people she lives among.'

'Perhaps, but since she refuses to come here, we must trust Christopher to take care of her.'

Julian relapsed into silence, then aired another anxiety. 'It's odd that she doesn't mention his business affairs. You'd think by now we'd have heard that his horses were beginning to make a name for themselves.'

Lavinia was merciful, and forbore to add to his worries by pointing out what seemed obvious, but she was as relieved as he was when, in May of the following year, Jenifer's daughter, Morwetha, was safely born. The choice of an old Cornish name for his granddaughter so pleased Julian that he was tempted to suggest they paid a surprise visit to the baby's christening. But Jonathan reminded him in time that it would be a Catholic ceremony. Wesleyan dissenters were bad enough to a staunch Anglican; a church full of Papists would be intolerable.

Jenifer sounded thankful that the tedious and painful business of childbirth was over, but her letters in subsequent months didn't get any more cheerful. Lavinia's

96

anxiety grew but Julian was in his usual civic bustle of helping to run the town, and instead of sharing her worries with him, she took them to Salubrious House.

'It's not uncommon for women to feel depressed after the birth of a child,' her brother-in-law pointed out. 'There's nothing sinister about it.'

Lavinia nodded, remembering clearly enough a time when her own unhappiness had seemed most desperate and she had actually begrudged Julian his daughter. Even so, the conviction remained that things were not well with Jenifer.

'She's young and healthy and loves her husband,' Lavinia said slowly. 'In normal circumstances I'm sure she would have recovered from the birth of Morwetha by now. It's more likely to be money that is troubling her, but Julian was as generous as he could afford to be when she and Christopher married. Even if I asked him to help again, I doubt if he could; it's hard enough to manage here.'

Jonathan watched her long, thin fingers gripped together in her lap. She looked tired and anxious, and anger burned deep inside him that his brother, fussing about his civic duties, was too busy to notice. Given the right, *he* would have spent his life shouldering her problems and kissing away the little frown that worry always set between her brows. Lacking the right, he was allowed to make her laugh occasionally, and offer the services of a friend. He had found his niece a tiresome child and a not very likeable young woman; the offer he made now was not for *her* peace of mind, but Lavinia's.

'I'm not exactly rich, but I could do something to help, my dear. Write and find out if money *is* the problem . . . I mean it, so please do as I ask.'

She was touched almost to tears by his kindness, but tried to smile at him. 'How *could* you be rich, when half the time you don't charge your patients at all?'

'Well, I ask a lot of those who *can* afford to pay,' he

explained solemnly. 'It's the coming thing – socialism in action! Now, having dealt with Jenifer, how's my nephew getting on?'

'Swimmingly . . . Loving the work, and quite finding his feet in London. He is also, much to my astonishment, still staying with Julia in Green Street. When I suggested it as a temporary measure while he found lodgings of his own, he looked horrified. Now, he seems quite content to stay there. What are you smiling at?'

'Your astonishment, my dear! Consider what Julia offers: a Mayfair address, a brother who's now the Earl, and a husband who happens to be a Governor of the Bank of England. Tristram's right to stay there as long as he can – it's *just* the sort of background the Foreign Office likes its acolytes to have!'

Jonathan's rich chuckle made her smile but she shook her head. 'He's not nearly so cynical as you are. Julia has obviously mellowed with the years, and makes him feel welcome.'

'And her trio of ghastly daughters don't object to a personable young man living in the house!'

'Not all of them are *entirely* ghastly,' Lavinia pointed out fairly. 'I agree there's no hope for Elinor; but Charlotte is harmlessly devoted to good works; and Victoria has grown quite attractive, despite a tiresome fondness for Beatrice Webb – but Tristram says he hopes to wean her from that!' Amusement chased the tiredness from her face as she remembered something else. 'He regards Julia now, if you please, as faintly pathetic; I quote – "a Victorian dinosaur left stranded by the receding tides of twentieth-century life"! It strains the imagination to think of Julia as pathetic, but I suppose he *could* be right.'

The note of doubt in her voice made Jonathan give a shout of laughter, but after a moment he suddenly grew sober again. 'I don't know why I'm laughing – he probably sees us as two more relics of the same unlamented age. Dammit, no . . . Lavinia, I refuse to have *us* be anything of the kind. If not immortal, you and I shall at least be forever young until we die!'

Her transfiguring smile accepted a suggestion which, certainly as far as it concerned Jonathan Bossiney, seemed entirely reasonable. Only judged by the strict measurement of time, and a waist-line assaulted over the years by Mrs Trago's potato cakes and pasties, could he be reckoned middle-aged.

Jenifer took a long time to answer her mother's carefully worded offer of financial help from Jonathan, and when she did reply sounded so apathetic about the future that Lavinia's mind was finally made up. She waited for Julian to say there was no need for them *both* to go to Mount Merrion, forgetting something that he unexpectedly remembered.

'St George's Channel in late November? My dear, you must be more worried than I realized.' She then was reminded of the rough crossing that had begun their wedding journey – they hadn't left England together since. He didn't refer to it again, but agreed with a lack of fuss she was grateful for to ask Chivers to make their travelling arrangements. They were within two days of setting out when a letter finally arrived from Jenifer. The journey need not be made after all because she was already on her way to England with her eight-month-old daughter.

They arrived three days later, in a hired carriage from the station. The sleeping child was handed over to the nursemaid recruited in a hurry by Bartlett's wife, and Jenifer – scarcely recognizable now as a tired and tragic-faced woman dressed in black – was installed by the fire in the drawing room. Julian hurriedly prescribed a restoring glass of wine and Lavinia a restoring rest. Jenifer accepted the wine but insisted that she'd recovered sufficiently from the nightmare of the journey to talk to them.

'The maid only came with me as far as Liverpool. It

was as much of England as she could stand, apparently.' She took another sip of wine, frowned over the memory of a servant who had been insolent, and then launched without warning into her story.

'Christopher was killed a month ago. He was thrown from his horse out hunting, and was brought back to the house dead.' She gave no sign of having noticed her parents' shocked faces and went on in an expressionless voice that might have been recounting a stranger's tragedy. 'It was bound to happen sooner or later – the biggest gate, the widest ditch, whatever anyone else couldn't or wouldn't tackle, my husband had to be the first over.'

Lavinia found her voice with an effort. 'My dear, I'm so very sorry,' she murmured.

'Of course . . . of course,' Julian muttered distractedly. 'Still, a husband and a father – he should have had some thought for *you*, my poor girl, instead of behaving like a . . . a carefree bachelor.' He'd been about to say 'lunatic' but changed it just in time.

Jenifer stared at her father, as if surprised that he still didn't understand. 'Christopher only thought about horses. During the winter months, of course, he thought only about *hunting* with horses.'

The calm statement left a silence that they didn't know how to break. Jenifer watched the flames leaping on the hearth as if she had told them all that needed saying. Lavinia watched her daughter's face and wondered what its pale mask concealed – heartbreak, bitter resentment, or perhaps something of both?

'Christopher's uncle must be very upset as well,' she suggested gently, when the silence seemed to have lasted too long.

Jenifer gave a little shrug. 'I dare say, but he has other nephews. In any case, he's largely to blame – he encouraged Christopher to take the risks he could no longer manage himself.'

'My dear girl, we were worried about you,' her father suddenly remembered. 'In fact we should have been in

Ireland by now if your letter hadn't arrived in time. It doesn't matter now you're here, but you need a good long rest. We shan't let you go hurrying back home.'

Jenifer sipped her wine, still staring at the fire. 'I'm *never* going back – I hate Ireland.' The words echoed round the quiet room, confirming for Lavinia the knowledge that, though her daughter might be grief-stricken as well, she was certainly resentful.

'I can't tell you what it was like,' Jenifer burst out suddenly. 'Dogs everywhere and dirt that they never seemed to notice . . . and people coming at all hours to drink and talk . . . they *never* seemed to stop drinking and talking. I thought I should go mad.'

Julian patted her hand and vowed to himself that he would *not* say he'd been right all along about Christopher O'Meara; nor would he ask for a long time yet what had happened to the settlement he'd made them at the time of their marriage.

'It's over now, my dear,' he said earnestly. 'Prospect is your home, and Morwetha's too. There's nothing for you to worry about.'

The nursemaid engaged by Mrs Bartlett didn't stay long; nor did her replacement, found by Lavinia. Handmaiden number three survived for almost a week before announcing that she'd made a mistake in coming. A hitherto smoothly running household was being reduced to total dislocation by one small infant when Jenifer indirectly solved the problem by fainting at the breakfast table one morning.

Jonathan, summoned to Prospect by the garden-boy, pronounced her to be pregnant again. Liking babies himself, he was disappointed by Jenifer's silent acceptance of the news, and by Lavinia's appalled expression when she was told that she was to be a grandmother for the second time.

'My dear, I *know* it's sad – a fatherless child always is. But Morwetha will have a companion, and for Jenifer there will be this last precious gift from Christopher to look forward to.'

'If you're thinking of saying that to my daughter, I wouldn't recommend it, Jonathan,' she said dryly. 'Jenifer finds one such gift rather more than she can cope with at the moment.' She regarded her fingers pensively. 'I expect you're about to suggest that we get help – an efficient nursemaid accustomed to dealing with a child even as full of . . . of *character* as my granddaughter. Such paragons come but, alas, they also go. At the moment the rest of us are doing our best – even Julian, I'm bound to say – but we lack whatever it is that Morwetha misses.'

Jonathan grinned at the familiar dryness but soon grew serious again. 'I got the impression from something Jenifer said that she doesn't want to go back to Ireland. I can understand that it's too painful for her at the moment, but surely O'Meara's relatives will feel they have the right to be acquainted with his children?'

'I don't think that she will care *what* they feel. It's what Jenifer wants that matters, and she wants never to see Ireland again. Marriage and motherhood haven't changed her very much as far as I can see.' She made a faint grimace of self-disgust. 'I'm sorry if that sounded cruel about a newly widowed girl not yet twenty-one. We never did manage together very well, she and I, but now I can't get near her at all. She's insulated by anger, and I can't even make up my mind whether she was more angry with Christopher alive than she now is with him dead!'

'Well, if she and her children are here to stay you *must* have some reliable help,' Jonathan said firmly. 'I shall go home and consult the oracle. If a good, kind nursemaid is hiding in the nooks and crannies of Fowey, Mrs Trago will know where she is to be found.'

The oracle's suggestion when it came surprised him, and surprised Lavinia still more; but, obedient to his instructions, she set out for Fore Street one morning to call on Hannah Penwarne. Jonathan had arranged the interview aware that in doing so he was taking a real risk. The ladies concerned were well-matched when it came to holding and expressing points of view: if Mrs Penwarne should be truculent, not liking the proposal, his dear Lavinia would probably mount her high horse, and no good would come of the meeting at all.

In the event Hannah was forthright but polite. 'What you suggest – it's not what I intended for Loveday,' she said straitly. 'Meaning no offence, Lady Bossiney, I wanted something better for her.'

'I understand that, but if she isn't happy working for Mrs Nicholls and has no other future in view . . . ?' Lavinia allowed the question to trail delicately away because Hannah was frowning over some past memory.

'She *had* a future – we thought it was all arranged a year or two ago. She was to marry . . . Well, no matter, now, who it was to be, because she took against the idea and would never even say why. Loveday's very soft-seeming, but there's a streak of Cornish granite in her that we break our toes on now and then – it comes from old Isaac Penwarne, I dare say.'

Lavinia was interested in the marriage that hadn't come off, but returned regretfully to the matter in hand. 'If she doesn't enjoy schoolwork, would she mind looking after a small child?'

'No, it's a classful of the bigger ones she can't manage. She's good with little children.'

'She would need to be,' Lavinia said honestly. A charming smile warmed her face, taking Hannah by surprise. 'Three nursemaids have been defeated so far, and my granddaughter resists all *our* efforts to make friends with her!' She chose her next words carefully. 'Did Dr Bossiney tell you about my daughter?'

'He said she was expecting another child, and that her husband was killed in an accident recently. I'm sorry, your ladyship – it's a very grievous thing.'

'Yes, it is,' Lavinia agreed slowly. 'Would Loveday

understand that grief sometimes makes people behave unreasonably? I have to ask that because my daughter is not easy to live with at the moment. If our arrangement were to fail, Loveday might feel herself to blame, but the failure of kindness is more likely to be *my* daughter's, Mrs Penwarne.'

There was a little silence while the two women looked at each other. Jonathan would have rejoiced to know that there was no awkwardness in their silence and no hostility – they understood and even liked one another. Perhaps more important, Loveday liked the idea of getting away from Mrs Nicholls, Fore Street and occasional awkward meetings with Daniel Penwarne in her brothers' company. By the time Tristram returned from London for the Christmas holiday, she was already living and working at Prospect.

Lavinia hadn't seen her son for long enough to notice a change in him. His life in London was having its effect and he was now a pleasantly self-possessed, charmingly mannered young man – surely the very stuff of which budding diplomats were made! She was slightly amused to find that she felt so proud of him.

'Has Jenifer got over the shock of Christopher's death, do you suppose?' Tristram asked when they were alone together. 'She *seems* very calm.'

'As a frozen pond is calm,' his mother agreed sadly. 'It isn't her natural state, but Jonathan says it's much too soon to expect her to come to terms with what has happened. He's a great help and best of all, I suppose, he found us Loveday Penwarne.'

Tristram found it disconcerting that he should remember so vividly the girl who was now living in his home. All the same, of course, he'd quite outgrown the sick anger that possessed him whenever he thought of her with Daniel Penwarne. And now that she was a sort of servant at Prospect, he could regard her as he did Bartlett's wife, or the maids who cleaned the rooms.

'Was it so hard to find a competent nurse?' he asked

grandly. 'I should have thought that Fowey was full of them.'

'It may be, my lofty young friend – but finding one who was prepared to endure my grand-daughter's tantrums and her mother's unpredictable moods was *much* more difficult, I promise you.'

'I stand corrected, Mama,' he muttered, looking slightly pink. 'How did Miss Penwarne survive this baptism of fire?'

'By sheer kindness of heart,' Lavinia said unexpectedly. 'I could swear that Jenifer's tragedy has become *hers* – she forgives any rudeness, any fit of temper, because nothing is unforgivable in a pregnant young widow and a fatherless child. In the face of such sweetness, even Jenifer capitulates.'

Tristram almost said that it wasn't a surprise. To a girl who'd been capable of imagining herself into the role of Iseult, becoming Jenifer O'Meara wouldn't be difficult; but the words already forming in his mind sounded ungenerous. He said instead, 'I seem to remember that there was talk of her marrying Daniel Penwarne – presumably she won't be staying here for very long?'

'The arrangement fell through – much to Hannah Penwarne's regret, I fancy. Loveday seems happily settled here, and it's hard to know how we should manage without her. Now, it's time to be introduced to your niece; I warn you she'll require your entire attention and enslavement.'

A few moments later he saw what she meant. A dark-eyed infant stared up at him, gravely making up her mind whether this was another human being to be spurned, or accepted. When he obligingly squatted down to make the inspection easier, she smiled a ravishing smile, reminding him poignantly of her dead father. Poor Christopher O'Meara . . . poor fatherless scrap . . . and poor lonely Jenifer. Tristram's heart ached for all of them.

'You're honoured,' his sister commented coolly.

'Morwetha normally refuses to accept people without a struggle.'

He thought she might have been speaking of herself – between her and the rest of the world, including even her own child it seemed to him, there was now some kind of barrier; they were visible to each other, but no contact could be made.

'Thank God you had Father and Mother to come back to, and Prospect,' he said impulsively.

'Yes . . . there's always Prospect,' she agreed without enthusiasm.

He remembered that her longing had always been to escape from the place she lived in. She was still young, still beautiful when she wasn't looking bitterly disgruntled, but what hope did she have now of escaping again? When she looked at Morwetha he had the shocking impression that she resented even her own daughter – perhaps resented still more the child alive and growing inside her when her husband was dead.

He took hold of her hands in a sudden longing to give her warmth and comfort. 'Jen, I'm better able to offer you a lecture on the works of Racine and Goethe than to explain how to cope with grief; but I'll do my best to help if you'll let me – I'll even learn how to entertain very small nieces like this one!'

A quiver of some emotion he couldn't identify broke the rigidity of her expression but she didn't smile until the door opened and Loveday Penwarne walked into the nursery. He thought he'd remembered her, but felt the weight of her beauty now like a blow over the heart. She wore her braids coiled on the nape of her neck, but tendrils of silky black hair still framed her perfect face. Eyes as deeply blue as the sea off Gribben on a summer afternoon confessed that she remembered *him*.

She wasn't going to marry Penwarne, his mother had said – well, of course, the idea was unthinkable. He tried to work out how old she was now . . . eighteen, perhaps, to his twenty-two.

'I expect you remember my brother,' Jenifer was saying. 'He's just been rash enough to offer to entertain Morwetha for us while he's at home.'

Loveday smiled, and Tristram understood something else his mother had said. She was content to be at Prospect, and she was kind enough even to absorb Jenifer's bitter dejection. Perhaps it was *that* that made her different from any other girl he'd ever known.

8

On a day just after Christmas when the Bossineys were to dine at Fowey Hall the symptoms of a heavy cold that Lavinia had woken with grew steadily worse. There was no question of her going but no question either, as far as Julian could see, of making an excuse not to go himself. He had always been courteous, but being the cousin-by-marriage of an earl required extra care in ensuring that his neighbours should never feel slighted. To Fowey Hall he would have to go, even though he found the house and Sir Charles Hanson's hospitality overpowering. It came as a surprise when Jenifer suddenly offered to take her mother's place and go with him.

'Are you sure you . . . you feel up to it, my dear . . . I mean . . .'

'You mean, shouldn't I remember that I'm recently bereaved? Papa, think of uneven numbers at the dinner table! I'm taking pity on Lady Hanson. In any case, I don't foresee an evening of unbridled gaiety that a widow ought not to indulge in – do you?'

Looked at in this light, he agreed that it was reasonable and, above all, considerate; they would go together, and a little outing might even be good for her.

The outing was as dull as she'd assumed it would be until she took her place at the table beside a man who'd arrived too late for the pre-dinner round of introductions. Of all the guests there he was the one who seemed nearest to her in age, and the one who seemed most alive and vigorous. He was also teasingly familiar but if she'd ever known his name, she was unable to recall it.

'You're either trying to remember who I am, or wondering what the devil I'm doing here if you *do* remember,' he said, calmly investigating the array of silver in front of him. 'If my second guess was correct, you can have the pleasure of telling me when I go wrong with all these knives and forks!'

Jenifer acquitted her hostess of deliberate malice; as the youngest woman guest she'd simply been landed with the least important male – whom she now recognized.

'I remember,' she said smoothly. 'You distinguished yourself once in the regatta – all rowed fast, but none rowed faster than Daniel Penwarne! Why *are* you here, if it isn't a rude question?'

She was disappointed to see the barb slide off him, doing no injury. He was tough and self-possessed and she needn't fear that he would treat her with the wearying solicitude everyone showed her at home. Without knowing him at all, she was quite certain of that. Daniel drank some of the wine that had been poured into one of the many glasses in front of him, and gave a considered reply to her question.

'I suppose because I'm on the way to becoming a successful man – a self-made one like our host. I can't match Charles Hanson's achievements yet, but I *shall* do; and being a generous Cornishman, he's letting me benefit from rubbing shoulders with the gentry – very beautiful shoulders they are too, if a self-made man is allowed to say so.'

His glance at her was deliberately mocking, but it nevertheless took in the contrast she made to the other women present. It wasn't just a question of youth; she was the finished article, with her burnished hair, delicately chiselled features, and beautiful skin that gleamed pearly-white against her black taffeta gown. She made the others look dowdy, and he was tired of their well-meaning efforts to pretend that they enjoyed seeing him there. The girl next to him made no such effort at all, but he doubted if there was anything personal in her hostility; she looked to be at odds pretty well with the rest of the world, although he didn't know why.

'What a gentleman might or might not do needn't trouble you; you have your *own* rules, I dare say,' Jenifer suggested after a moment or two.

Daniel observed the wedding ring on her hand. 'I see your father here, but not anyone who looks as if he might be your husband. Is he left behind in . . . in Ireland, wasn't it, that you went to?'

'Yes, he is left behind,' she agreed matter-of-factly. 'He was killed in a riding accident six weeks ago.' She had the satisfaction at last of knowing that she had disconcerted him. 'I'm only here because my mother is unwell and I am taking her place. She will be sorry to have missed making your acquaintance.' It was almost total rout, but she had one final shot in her locker. 'Now it's time for you to talk to the lady on your right, Mr Penwarne; otherwise she will begin to feel neglected.' She gave him a sweet smile and turned to listen to the elderly guest sitting on her own left.

It had been an exhilarating few minutes after so many endless days and nights of not feeling alive at all; but now she was tired of a game that suddenly seemed as pointless as everything else – the long elaborate meal, the pleasant, boring people she'd left to escape from, the slow procession of years ahead in which she would grow old in listening to their same, interminable chatter. The buzz of conversation in the room re-echoed in her head like the sound of hell itself, the faces of those pleasant, boring people became St Fimbarrus' grinning gargoyles, jeering at her journey down into damnation. She bowed her head, fighting the panic that made her feel both feverish and deathly cold. Then a quiet voice spoke beside her.

'It's very hot in here. Sip some wine – it will make you feel better.' A glass was slid into her shaking hand and held until she could grip it safely. She did what she was told, and the demons faded into the crimson flock paper of Sir Charles' dining room. When she turned to Daniel Penwarne his expression was thoughtful and no longer mocking.

'Thank you for, for noticing . . . I'm all right now,' Jenifer muttered.

'I've been away for weeks – only got back here last night; otherwise I might have known about your husband. I'm sorry – it wasn't intended to hurt you.'

'But it was *my* intention to make you feel uncomfortable.' The confession was necessary, but she resented it as much as she resented him knowing that she'd needed help a moment ago. Now, no doubt, he would offer some conventional dose of sympathy that she could reject; being ready for it, she was irritated when the sympathy didn't come.

'You're making a visit to your parents, I take it – going back to Ireland before long?'

'No – Prospect *is* my home now, and my small daughter's. Perhaps you also don't know that your cousin is with us too, as Morwetha's nursemaid?' The frown on Daniel Penwarne's face jogged a memory of his past connection with Loveday. 'If you feel concerned about her, you needn't be,' Jenifer added sweetly. 'Even my brother, home from London at the moment, noticed at once how happy she seems to be, working for *us*.'

Daniel's frown changed to a glinting smile as dangerous as a rapier blade, but she was made reckless now by success; for the first time in months she was aware of fully occupying the attention of a man, and this one's very different kind of attraction had no power to remind her of Christopher. She reverted to what he had said earlier.

'Tell me why *you* are going to be so successful, Mr Penwarne, when everyone else seems to have settled for hopeless decline.'

'Everyone else you know has,' he corrected her gently, 'people who've lived richly in the past off industries that are now dying. They've had their time, and no amount of pious hope or wasted effort will give them back everlasting life.'

She wasn't sure whether he was pronouncing death on the traditional Cornish industries or on families like her own – both, probably. Her father would say that he was one of the new socialists, determined to pull down the old ordering of society about their heads.

Across the table, Julian Bossiney listened to his neighbour's flow of small talk, and 'Q' was defending himself from a militant dowager's charge that he avoided lecturing to lady students at Cambridge. They were two courteous survivors who, according to the man beside her, didn't deserve to survive much longer.

'What do you propose to do instead?' she said angrily. 'Build cheap boarding houses and fairgrounds, I suppose, for the visitors who are gulled into thinking Cornwall a summer paradise – "Q"'s "delectable duchy"! He must wish by now that he'd never invented the damned phrase.'

Daniel shook his head. 'I'm a mechanic, not a builder, and we're now living in a mechanized age. I've got a long way to go still, but one of these days my businesses will stretch from London to Land's End.'

It wasn't an empty boast, though in any other man she knew it would have sounded like one. She was impressed in spite of herself, and aware that, whatever he might become, he was already remarkable. The son and grandson of miners and seamen hadn't needed any guidance from her after all in getting through the long, elaborate meal, and afterwards he helped to hand round coffee-cups as though Lady Hanson's drawing room was his natural habitat. Jenifer decided that it even amused him to play the harmless social games of people he despised – because he could not only do what they did, but much else besides. He made no further effort to talk to her, and she went back to Prospect with her father feeling piqued and faintly disappointed.

'Extraordinary of the Hansons to invite that fellow, Penwarne,' Julian said predictably on the short journey home, 'and not quite fair, perhaps to throw him into the jaws of Fowey society.'

'You've got it the wrong way round, Papa,' Jenifer pointed out coolly. '*He* is the basking shark . . . *we* are the poor fish waiting to be swallowed whole.'

Julian turned to look at her with an expression of genuine astonishment on his face. 'Surely not, my dear – I know things have changed for the worse since the war, but people like the Penwarnes still know their place, I assure you.' He patted her hand in case reassurance were needed on this crucial point, and she didn't know whether to weep or burst into laughter that would deeply offend him. 'Pious hope' wasn't going to be nearly enough to prevent the dawning of the new age, and the people who would inherit it would be Daniel Penwarne and his like, not gentle, scrupulous men like her brother.

Tristram found himself unexpectedly enjoying a Christmas visit undertaken out of a sense of family duty. It had been a sore temptation to accept Kurt's invitation to go skiing in Austria, but he'd turned it down knowing that his mother, especially, would be thankful to see him at Prospect. He wasn't sure if he'd achieved much in the way of helping Jenifer, but now and then she'd smiled at something he'd said, as if she'd really been in the room listening to *him* instead of to some echo of past talk in other places. With his niece, though, he fancied *he* had made progress. She now welcomed him to her presence with a toothy smile, and consented to ride on his back round the nursery floor. Her nursemaid had been welcoming, too, but she was very little more talkative than Morwetha, and he supposed that embarrassment about the past made her shy. After the merciless onslaught of 'clever' conversation that cousin Julia's daughters engaged in, being with Loveday Penwarne was like being in the peace of a woodland glade after the Sunday morning hurly-burly of Speakers' Corner in Hyde Park. Even Morwetha responded lovingly to her, inspiring Tristram to wonder how soon even infantile human beings were able to understand that what they looked upon was beautiful and good.

The new year of 1923 dawned in the noisy bluster of a south-westerly gale that flung slanting sheets of rain against the windows of Prospect, and piled the incoming tide into their little cove in a muddled, heaving mass of dark-green water. Then the tempest rampaged on eastwards into Devon, leaving silence and mildness behind.

On his last afternoon at home, Tristram climbed to the cliff edge above St Catherine's Castle without the danger of being blown out to sea. After the turbulence of the past few days the ocean still heaved and fretted against the rocks below him, but in the sheltered hollow he still thought of as his he could sit and watch the gulls planing above his head, then dropping through the air to rest on a convenient wave.

It was a very Cornish sort of day, and he blamed on *that* the knowledge that he was reluctant to go back to London. With no-one else about to share the vast, empty view with him, it was also a rather lonely sort of day until he saw a solitary girl begin to climb the hillside below him. With her head downbent, she was unaware that he was there, but it didn't surprise him to recognize her. Without knowing it, his thoughts had been full of her the whole time he'd been there – she was bound to have come, sooner or later.

When he stood up, she stopped abruptly, uncertain whether to walk past or turn back. Tristram settled the matter by waving her with a little bow to his hollow and the mackintosh he'd spread there.

'Consider yourself captured by a Fowey gallant and taken into port!' he said, smiling at her. 'I was beginning to think there was no-one left in the world but me.'

Loveday tried to smile back, but it was hard when she was trembling inside with the mingled pleasure and pain of finding herself alone with him. Of course, it amounted to no more than her frequent meetings with him at Prospect during the past week or so, except that then he'd really only come to keep Morwetha amused – now, there was just *her*, and he was too kind not to pretend to be glad to see her. She remembered that she hadn't felt awkward with him in the past, but things were different now – she was his mother's servant, and something called the Foreign Office employed *him*. The name conveyed very little to her, but what he did sounded important, setting him far apart from Charlie's fishing boat, and John returning to Fore Street each evening with china-clay dust still white in his hair and fingernails.

'I promised myself I'd get as far as Gribben Head after being cooped up indoors for days,' she explained, pleased with herself for sounding calm. 'I shan't manage it by sitting here; it'll be dark in another hour.'

'I was longing for someone to talk to – won't you let Gribben wait until another day?' Tristram asked quietly.

She nodded by way of answer and they sat for a while without speaking. The gunmetal sea crested with white seemed to engage all her attention, and he was free to look at her. For once she wore no dreadful hat, and the damp air had crinkled the little tendrils of hair that always escaped her braids. Her face had grown thinner since he'd been away; the faint hollows at temple and cheekbone – he hadn't remembered them before. The braids seemed too heavy for her slender neck. He wanted suddenly to loosen them and run his hand through a cloud of silky black hair. Oh God, what he *did* remember was how she'd looked that afternoon at Castle Dore, lying on the grass waiting to be possessed by Daniel Penwarne.

He gripped his hands together and made a desperate grab at self-control. Conversation was the thing . . . it didn't matter *what* they talked about; anything would do to keep his mind off the frantic knowledge that he wanted above all things to make love to her.

Loveday glanced quickly at his bowed head and remembered what her mother would say – it wasn't fitty to leave one's companion all the work of finding something to say.

'Will you be glad to go back to London? Or a bit wisht at leaving here?' she asked suddenly.

He looked up and smiled, calmed by the knowledge that she hadn't been aware of the thoughts whirling in his head.

'I'm glad, *and* wisht, at the same time. Have *you* ever wanted something, and *not* wanted it with equal longing?'

'No,' she said after considering the question gravely. 'If you know you're not going to get what you want, you don't need to not want it as well.'

He heard a note of regret in her voice, and hated the idea that occurred to him – that it might have something to do with Daniel Penwarne.

'I thought you liked being at Prospect . . . enjoyed looking after Morwetha and being kind to my sister.' It came out more accusingly than he'd intended – as if the job of nursemaid was as much as she had any right to expect, and she ought to be satisfied with it. Different words came tumbling through his brain that he couldn't collect into order enough for his tongue to speak – she *must* enjoy living in his home . . . he wanted her to, because it was where she seemed to belong . . . and above all, she must *never* think of marrying her cousin . . .

'I love looking after Morwetha,' she said firmly enough for him to hear above the confusion in his mind, 'and I expect I shall love the new baby when it's born. My mother hoped I'd become a schoolma'am or . . . or do something else; but Father's happy because this way I can still get to see him in Fore Street each week. I 'spect he misses me a bit at home.'

Tristram thought she'd steered deliberately off a subject she didn't intend him to pursue. Whatever it was she wanted but hadn't got, she didn't intend to let him know.

'Is it very important . . . what you do in London?' she asked suddenly.

He thought of his cubbyhole, shared with someone as insignificant as himself, and the ladder of officials above him stretching halfway to heaven. He tried not to smile, failed to stifle a chuckle, and began to shout with laughter in which she was finally forced to join – not understanding why they laughed, but glad that some of the tension she'd sensed in him had disappeared.

'Sweet Loveday, th . . . thank you,' he gasped when they were more or less serious again, 'but I'm still just about the least important m . . . minion the Foreign Office owns!' He reached out suddenly and took hold of her hands, and she was conscious of another change in his mood; conscious, too, that their hill-top was still lonely, and that he'd called her by a name she'd never forget.

'I'm not always going to be as insignificant as I am now,' he said earnestly. 'It will take a few more years to really start climbing the ladder, but I mean to get to the top in the end.'

'An . . . an ambassador, I've heard her ladyship say,' she agreed, trying to smile. 'I've seen pictures of *them* in one of Mother's books, wearing handsome clothes, and chatting to His Majesty!' It didn't occur to her that it could be otherwise, but when it happened she wouldn't be there to see. It was a sudden pain in her heart, so sharp that she gave a little gasp and tried to hide it by scrambling to her feet.

'I must go back – it will be past Morwetha's teatime.' She smoothed down her coat, and then gave it up because her fingers were trembling. She would be late, but it still wasn't quite possible to walk away for as long as he stood staring at her as he was doing now.

'If I wrote you a letter sometimes from London, would you write back to me?'

She nodded, unable to speak; then he leaned forward to leave a kiss on her mouth, and it was heart-breakingly soft and sweet.

'That's to . . . to say goodbye,' he said unsteadily. 'I shall have left tomorrow before you and Morwetha have finished breakfast.'

She stared at him for a moment, then broke the stillness that held her and started to run down the path towards Prospect. He let her go, remembering another time when she'd run away leaving him as lonely as he felt now.

He was untalkative at the dinner table that night, but Lavinia made no comment on his quietness; much as he enjoyed his life in London, she understood that it was a wrench when the time for leaving came. He excused himself from coffee in the drawing room on the ground of packing to be done, and went upstairs to his own room. Ten minutes later Jenifer knocked on the door and walked in. She settled down in his only comfortable armchair and accepted the cigarette he offered her. He supposed that sadness had driven her upstairs, or perhaps boredom – Father was probably holding forth again on the Whitehall government's meanness in refusing to give Cornwall new roads.

Jenifer looked at the glowing end of her cigarette and then began casually on what she'd come to say.

'I had to speak to Loveday quite sharply when she came back from her walk this afternoon. She seemed to have forgotten that Morwetha has her tea at four o'clock, not four-thirty.'

'It was entirely my fault, not Loveday's,' Tristram said quickly. 'We bumped into each other up on the headland and I . . . I expect I talked too much . . . about this and that.'

Jenifer gave a little shrug, as if what they'd talked about could scarcely have been important enough for him to remember now.

'Her name cropped up at the Hansons' dinner party. I had the dubious pleasure then of sitting next to her cousin. As Father rightly says, times are changing!'

Tristram stared at his sister's expressionless face and thought that she intended him to put his next question.

'Do you intend to tell me what was said about Loveday?' he asked curtly.

'Oh well, it wasn't anything much; but I rather got the impression that Daniel Penwarne doesn't like her being here. I should hate to lose her, of course, because Morwetha's almost human when she's around, but I'm sure Mr Penwarne still wants to marry her . . . and since he informed me that he's going to become *very* successful, it certainly wouldn't be fair to stand in her way.'

Jenifer stubbed out her cigarette, and got heavily to her feet. 'Don't tell Mother about that – she disapproves of me smoking. Thank God I shall be looking normal by the time you come down again. I hate and loathe being pregnant.'

Tristram looked at her pale face, and felt deeply sorry for her. Grief was *not* the ennobling thing that Romantic poets loved to sing about; for most people, his sister included, it was destructive and embittering.

'Life *will* get better, Jen,' he said compassionately. 'Just give it a bit more time, and wait till the new baby's born – you'll feel differently then.'

'Very true, brother dear. I shall have *two* little mill-stones round my neck instead of one.' She gave a faint, derisive grimace. 'I'm more like Mama than I knew . . . definitely *not* your natural, born mother!'

'That's not fair; in fact it's bloody *unfair*, if you ask me – just because she's never poured syrupy affection over us by the bucketful. She suits me the way she is, and it wouldn't hurt *you* to feel grateful to her, and to Father, too.'

Jenifer's colour rose under a reprimand that she knew was justified. 'Sorry – I must try to stop snivelling.' She walked to the door and smiled at him from there. 'In exchange for your advice, I'll give you some of my own. Don't make a habit of bumping into Loveday when you're down here. She was looking quite distrait when she came in, and I've a feeling Daniel Penwarne wouldn't like it!'

She closed the door behind her, leaving him staring into space for a long time with his packing still not done. The warning she'd come with had been delivered, but it made no difference to his intention of writing to Loveday. He wasn't at all clear why he wanted to do this so much, except that it might keep her from the terrible mistake of being persuaded to marry Daniel. Beyond that, his thoughts were as chaotically confused as the water that tumbled in and out of Prospect cove.

9

Tristram addressed his first letter to Loveday's home, aware that it might cause her embarrassment at Prospect. It would have caused more comment than it did in Fore Street if Hannah's attention at the time hadn't been distracted by the bothersomeness of both her sons. John so sensible and steady as a rule, had taken to disappearing from the cottage every evening. When she complained about this one day on a visit to her parents across the river at Polruan, Captain Eliot scratched his head and looked thoughtful.

'Think I can tell you where he goes, my dearie – I sometimes call in at the Old Ferry Boat Inn upstream at Bodinnick, and I had it from the landlord himself. Seems young John is powerfully taken with the daughter of the house.' He smiled at Hannah's expression and tried to pour oil on troubled waters. 'It's not often she's serving behind the bar there . . . only now and then.'

It was no comfort at all that she could see, and nor was William's gentle reminder later in the evening that their Lord had seen fit to eat with publicans and sinners.

'Well He may have done,' she said crossly, 'but it still doesn't make me want a barmaid for a daughter-in-law.'

Her anxiety about Charlie didn't involve girls – he was shy of them, and they rarely shared his passion for being out in a small boat in rough weather. His only error, and it was a serious one in his mother's opinion, was to have his face so cussedly against learning to do anything but sail a boat and fish. Where was the future in *that* nowadays? She was fretting over the problem one afternoon when Daniel called in unexpectedly. They saw less of him now that he was more often in Lostwithiel than Fowey and she was pleased to find him at the door; he was one of the few men she had unqualified admiration for. Jonathan Bossiney was another, but Daniel was William's kith and kin and that meant quality for once could be claimed within the family.

'There's only me here,' she said smilingly, 'but maybe you were passing and felt like a cup of tea!'

'The tea would be welcome, Aunt Hannah – I was too busy to eat at midday; but I came to see you.'

He followed her into the kitchen to avoid being shown into her parlour with its precisely arranged furniture and lace antimacassars to keep the chairbacks clean. He had a horror of those little bits of material draped over everything.

She put the tea in front of him and a generous helping of heavy cake, whose name belied it because it was deliciously stuffed with currants and lemon peel, and not heavy at all. He was allowed to eat and drink in peace, and reckoned that by now almost any other woman he knew would've had to ask what he'd come about. Hannah Eliot was different – so it was no surprise her daughter was as well.

'I've been over to Polruan this afternoon,' he said when the cake had been disposed of. 'Now that old Caleb Holman's dead, with no son to follow him, there's a boat-repair yard going cheap. I had a fancy to get it if I could.'

'And did you?' she asked as a matter of form, knowing that if he wanted Caleb's yard he would have made sure of getting it by now.

Daniel nodded and went on. 'Last week I was in Mevagissey looking at a yard there. A lot of fishing boats have been laid up – is Charlie still working for Walter Jago?'

The anxious frown returned to Hannah's face. 'Yes, but we don't know for how much longer. Walter's getting too old to go on struggling, even if his boat were proper match

'– which it's not – for all the drifters coming from the East Coast and the Continent.' She stirred her tea reflectively, thinking of times past. 'The great days were over even before Charlie was old enough to handle a net. You weren't here then, of course, but it was something to see . . . the pilchard shoals used to arrive as regularly as the swallows in spring, and as soon as the watchers gave a shout, the men would trap them in the Seine nets close in-shore, thousands at a time. Now the drifters have to go far out to find any at all.'

'And I suppose the railway line to London turned out to be no boon in the end,' Daniel commented. 'It put a huge market within reach of our fishermen, for anything they could catch, but attracted all the fleets from outside as well.'

Hannah nodded – a scarcity of fish, and too many anxious men seeking what there was; it was the problem in a nutshell.

'If fishing's dead or dying, would Charlie like to work for me?' Daniel asked suddenly. 'That's what I really came to find out. I'm going to need more help at Polruan, and I'm prepared to invest in making a mechanic of him – he already knows a lot about boats.'

'I can't speak for him,' she said with obvious regret, 'but if he's got a grain of sense he'll take your offer, Daniel. Only trouble is he's a cussed boy . . . might think he'd to stay with Walter till the fishing gives up.'

'Well, tell him to come and see me, Aunt Hannah. I can't wait, though – if he's not ready to start learning, I shall have to find someone else.' He finished his second cup of tea and then said casually, 'I gather Loveday's working at Prospect. How is she getting on?'

'She seems happy enough working there, though I fancy Lady Bossiney's daughter mayn't be easy. Still, there's some excuse – the poor girl lost her husband and she's still to bring another fatherless child into the world.'

'She didn't tell me *that*,' Daniel said slowly. 'I met her a few evenings ago up at Fowey Hall. Unlike the other women present, she was honest enough to ask why our host had invited me. I didn't know then about her husband, either, so it gave her a real chance to trip me up – she enjoyed doing that!'

'Proper quarrelsome she sounds, poor creature, but I'm bound to say her ladyship warned me about that before Loveday ever went to Prospect.'

'What about the rest of the family – are they as bad?'

'Lady Bossiney's very well regarded, I'd say, and there's no harm in Sir Julian; he's not one for rubbing shoulders with his tenants, but he's busy enough sitting on boards and committees for the town. His brother's different – everybody loves the Doctor.'

'Charlie's friend isn't here now?'

'Tristram? No, he works in London.' Hannah frowned again, remembering something that other anxieties had pushed to the back of her mind.

'He's taken to sending letters to Loveday, and she has to write back, telling him how Mrs O'Meara is, and the little girl. I don't see there's anything wrong in it, but Loveday's face went as red as a rose when she had to mention Tristram Bossiney's name. I suppose the truth is I wish she wasn't there at all, getting used to people she's not born to.'

Daniel smiled at his aunt but didn't comment on what she'd just said. 'It's time I went. Don't forget to ask Charlie to come and see me – he can find me at the workshops on the quay most evenings.'

Hannah closed the door after him, for the moment not thinking about his offer. He hadn't said so, but she should've remembered that *he* seemed to be getting even more used to people he wasn't born to – eating dinner at Fowey Hall and mixing with the gentry. She sighed over the teacups that needed washing. Ten years ago she'd have been glad to see Daniel getting on so well, ready to cock a snook at everybody and change the way of things. But that was before the war had come to blow the world they knew to bloody, mangled pieces.

Looked back on, the years before 1914 seemed sunlit and carefree and orderly . . . it was probably why she felt differently now about changing things.

Loveday laboured over her replies to Tristram, conscious of having little to say that would fill a page, however large the hand she wrote – it didn't matter to him in London that Morwetha had walked the length of the nursery on her own; that Charlie had gone out in the Fowey lifeboat on a day of dreadful storm, or that February primroses were out, golden as butter, in the roadside hedges. She persevered, because that had been their bargain, even though she doubted whether he found the time to read her offerings at all. *His* letters, sometimes one a week, sometimes scarcer if there had been too many receptions and parties and theatres to attend, she carried back to Prospect to read in the privacy of her room. There was nothing in them that her family couldn't have seen, but they were the private treasure no-one else possessed, the only precious things she owned. It didn't occur to her to hide them away; in any case she liked to see the little pile growing on her window-sill. Sometimes when she looked at Jenifer O'Meara's bored, unhappy face she felt guilty about her own blossoming contentment, but she never mentioned Tristram's letters. His sister was usually pleasant enough, but she wasn't friendly; Loveday knew she wouldn't think it fitty for him to be writing to her daughter's nursemaid.

Although she was unaware of it, the correspondence *was* known about. She was out with Morwetha one morning when Jenifer had to go into her room to investigate a banging window that had slipped its catch. The envelopes on the window-sill, written in her brother's unmistakable hand with the greek letter E he always used, caught her eye immediately. Beside them lay one addressed to him, waiting to be posted. She adjusted the window and left the room again, but the resentment that had kept her company for months had become the more pleasurable

125

glow of righteous anger. Tristram was a fool to ignore well meant advice and complicate his life so thoughtlessly; Loveday Penwarne was an excellent servant, *not* a fit choice for an ambitious young diplomat. But the servant was also very beautiful and Tristram was kind as well as foolish. Jenifer didn't underestimate the danger.

The problem was almost welcome – it gave her something to think about on the tedious daily exercise recommended by her uncle. After a week of grey sea-mists, a late-February morning dawned mild and clear enough to tempt her to walk on the other side of the river for a change.

She crossed over on the ferry and plodded up the long slope to St Saviour's Point. It enabled her, at least, to stare at the sea from a different angle before completing the walk down the hill again. She turned to leave, caught her foot in an unseen bramble lying across the path, and pitched forward head-first on to the wet turf. It seemed a long time that she lay there, listening to the thudding, unsteady beat of her frightened heart. She wasn't sure that she could move, was too afraid to discover that she couldn't if she tried, and terrified of what she might have done to the five-month-old child she carried within her. She hadn't wanted it at all, but now to lose it would be more than she could bear. She remained where she'd fallen, unaware that the wetness on her skin came from the tears trickling down her face. It wasn't uncomfortable, lying there . . . no-one would think of looking for her; she could die in peace and escape her burden of misery at last.

'Where have you hurt yourself?' The voice sounded a long way off, then more sharply in her ear as the question was repeated, insisting on an answer this time. She lifted up her head and found herself staring at Daniel Penwarne, crouched down on the ground beside her. Rather than consider whether she was hurt or not, she wanted to ask what he was doing there, then had a vague memory of having asked him that once before.

'*You* can go away,' she mumbled crossly. 'I'm staying . . . I *like* it here.'

'I'm sure you do, but the grass is very wet and it's going to be raining before long. I think we'll both find shelter if you don't mind.' She fully intended to object, but his hands gently turned her over on to her back and a moment later she was lifted in his arms and he was on his feet. He shook his head when she started to protest.

'Thank God it's all downhill, but I shan't have breath to carry you and argue as well.'

She was still very slight, and he was a more than averagely strong man, but he was thankful to arrive at Captain Eliot's front door and have Jane Eliot waste no time. He was led upstairs to a small, neat bedroom and there allowed the exquisite relief of laying down a burden that seemed to be dragging his arms out of their sockets. He retreated downstairs, thankful to be able to leave a woman to take charge.

Jane reappeared, looking concerned. 'Tom, you'll have to send Benjy for Doctor. There's no knowing what that poor creature might have done – she's five months gone and it's no time to be falling over.'

The captain was out of the door as she spoke, roaring down to the ferryman getting ready to push off at the end of the slipway.

'Hold it, Albert – need to send Benjy over with a message.'

'She's Dr Bossiney's niece,' Daniel was explaining to Jane.

'I know, she told me. You sit with her, Daniel, while I make some tea. I fancy she's hilla-ridden, poor thing, lying up there on her own.'

Jane had much in common with her daughter, he realized; her orders were quietly given, but they were orders for all that. He meekly climbed the stairs again and went into the bedroom. Jenifer's sheet-white face and frightened eyes seemed to confirm that she *was* in the middle of a nightmare.

'The captain has sent a messenger for the doctor, Mrs Eliot is making tea, and I am to keep you company until it arrives,' he said matter-of-factly, sitting down on a chair that looked too small for him.

'I know who she is,' Jenifer muttered. 'You and your family are being very . . . very k . . . kind.'

'And it hurts you to have to say so? Never mind – it needn't stop you despising us.'

The terror in her face retreated a little under his brisk treatment. 'Mrs Eliot wouldn't think much of your bed-side manner,' she said resentfully; 'you're supposed to soothe the patient . . . not goad her.' The protest faded into something that was unmistakably a sob, and Daniel was alarmed to see tears on her cheeks again.

'For God's sake don't weep – Jane Eliot will rend me limb from limb.'

The ghost of a smile touched Jenifer's pale mouth, but the tears continued to brim over her eyelids and trickle down her cheeks.

'It's not your fault – it's *me*,' she whispered. 'I've been such a mess for months – even since before Christopher was killed. I made a mistake, you see . . . but instead of admitting that it was entirely my own, I just got angrier and angrier, as if everyone else was to blame. I even managed to convince myself that I didn't want this baby. I deserve to lose it, if that's what I've done.'

Daniel pulled out a handkerchief, inspected it for engine oil, and handed it over. 'Wait until you've heard what the doctor says, and remember that you fell on very soft ground; there may be nothing to worry about after all.'

The rattle of china outside the door made him get up thankfully. Jenifer O'Meara was in a chastened mood but only for the moment. He doubted how long it would last, and afterwards she'd remember that he was the last person on earth she'd have chosen to make her confession to.

Downstairs he explained to Tom Eliot that in case the Bossineys were already getting anxious about her, he'd go over to Prospect and tell them where she was. After that, the doctor and her own parents could look after her.

Half an hour later he was being shown into a book-lined, firelit room whose huge window faced across the estuary, the very spot where he'd found Jenifer. A tall, thin lady received him politely, but with a faintly wondering air that made him appreciate her daughter's malice at the Hansons' dinner table. He could see that Lady Bossiney would have been astonished, not pleased, to meet him there.

'I came to tell you that Mrs O'Meara is being looked after by a relative by marriage of mine – Mrs Eliot, at Polruan,' he reported briefly. 'She'd had a fall up on St Saviour's Point. I found her there and carried her down to Ferry Cottage. Dr Bossiney's been sent for – in fact he's probably there by now – but I thought you might be getting anxious. She doesn't *seem* to have damaged herself, and she's in good, kind hands.'

'I'm sure of it,' Lavinia said quickly, 'but how grateful I am to you, Mr Penwarne, and to Mrs Eliot. I think I must go over to Polruan myself, when I've spoken to my husband, but perhaps you'd like to stay and have tea with your cousin? I expect you know she looks after my granddaughter here.'

'Yes, I do know, but I can't stay, thanks – I have to be on my way.'

She accepted the graceless refusal calmly and led him out to the hall. A servant waited to open the door, she offered her hand with a charming smile, and recommended the garden route as the quickest way back to the Esplanade.

He leapt down the descending flights of stairs pursued by his own anger. For once self-confidence hadn't been enough against someone whose composure was effortless because it was inbred. He forgot the warmth of Lavinia Bossiney's smile and thought instead of his dislike of a family that continually managed to catch him wrong-footed – no doubt Sir Julian would have completed the pattern by offering him a tip for rescuing his daughter.

He was probably being treated even now to her ladyship's account of a Penwarne who'd thought himself above taking tea with his cousin in the servants' room. That – he could hear the baronet saying – was what came of letting the lower orders get above their station; they never knew afterwards where their proper place *was*. God, he hated the lot of them.

Jenifer was left to stay overnight at Ferry Cottage after Lavinia and her uncle had gone back to Fowey. She didn't mind being there . . . didn't mind anything now, because Jonathan had said the baby was all right. It was peaceful lying in Jane Eliot's spare room watching, as Loveday had done, the lights reflected on the ceiling from the river outside. She lay awake late into the night only because there was a lot to think about; her mind drifted from one thought to another like Mrs Bartlett's tabby cat at Prospect, trying to find the right spot in which to settle. Gradually the spot chose itself and she recognized what had happened to her. Somehow the anger that had been bottled up inside her for months had been washed away by her tears up on St Saviour's Point. She felt empty of everything but a huge relief – light-headed enough to dance round the room if Jonathan hadn't ordered her to lie still for twenty-four hours. Still smiling at the thought of being found by Captain Eliot waltzing about in Jane's best crochet-trimmed nightgown, she finally fell asleep.

Fetched home by her father the next afternoon, she was only half-joking when she told Jane and the captain that she wished she could have stayed for ever. She recognized another unfamiliar feeling – real concern in case the Eliots should misunderstand her father's ornate manners and think themselves patronized. But he was graciousness itself and she decided that, if anything, they were privately amused by him.

The problem she'd taken with her on her walk to Polruan had retreated to the back of her mind, but it soon elbowed its way forward again. A letter from Tristram announced that he would be home for Easter, and she presumed that Loveday had been sent this information, too. No-one could be so patient with Morwetha's tantrums who hadn't some inner fund of happiness to draw on.

Jenifer was still debating whether or not to share the problem with her mother when another letter arrived from London. Julia Haddenham wrote to hint, not very delicately, that an invitation to travel down to Prospect with Tristram would fill her daughters, Charlotte and Victoria, with joy.

'Elinor too?' Julian asked his wife, without much hope of being wrong.

'Apparently not. We are to be spared Elinor.'

'Well, there's no need to look so glum,' Jenifer said brightly. She coloured under her mother's astonished stare, but soldiered on. 'I think it will be nice to have . . . to have some company for Easter – a good thing for Tristram too.'

Lavinia resisted the temptation to remind her that she'd loathed her Haddenham cousins from the very first moment that she'd learned to recognize them. There was a change in Jenifer so welcome that nothing must be allowed to discourage it. If it made her happy to see Julia's daughters at Prospect, Lavinia was even prepared for Elinor to come as well.

'You're quite right,' she said thoughtfully. 'Who cares that neighbours like "Q" will be bemused by Lottie's William Morris art and craftiness and astounded by Victoria's membership of the Independent Labour Party. Let them broaden their views, I say!' She smiled at her family and left the room to compose her letter of invitation.

Tristram escorted his cousins to Cornwall a fortnight later with all the stylish care that a rising young diplomat was bound to provide, whether he wanted to or not. Lavinia noted a new air of confidence about him now that his Foreign Office cubbyhole had been exchanged for a room of his own. The future ahead of him was beginning to look full of promise, and the vision that he saw *she* could see too, with pride and great contentment.

Charlotte Haddenham, perhaps deterred by the cool weather of early spring from going barefoot in disciple sandals, looked pleasantly plain, and quite normal after all. Victoria, the same age as Tristram, was more lively, and so pretty that Julian was very pleased with her until she fell from grace.

'Be careful whom you invite to dinner, my dear,' he said feelingly to his wife. 'Some of our usual guests might not enjoy being told that the working class must be mobilized in the fight against capitalism – she's damn nearly a crypto-communist! God knows what Julia and Richard are thinking of to permit it.'

'Like us, they probably sometimes feel themselves incapable of dealing with their children. Speaking of which, do *you* find a change in Jenifer? I'm almost afraid to mention it in case you say I'm thinking wishfully. She may not be happy still, but she isn't locked away in some lonely, private misery that we aren't allowed to share.'

Julian considered this for a moment, and then nodded. 'I dare say it's a good thing having Lottie and Victoria here. They're company for Jenifer and *she* won't care if Beatrice Webb thinks state ownership is our only hope of economic salvation.'

It was true that Jenifer didn't care; she found it more worrying that Tristram hadn't lost his habit of visiting his niece in the nursery. Loveday was always there as well, but since she was employed to look after Morwetha it would have been unreasonable to expect her not to be.

'You've got guests here,' Jenifer tried reminding her brother. 'Shouldn't you be entertaining *them* instead of playing havoc with the discipline we're hoping to persuade my daughter she'll like if only she gives it a try?'

He grinned at the echo of Lavinia's familiar dryness, but shook his head. 'They're Prospect's guests, and I have all the opportunity I want in London to hear about free milk for schoolchildren and syndicalism versus pure socialism! In any case, it's good for *you* to have to be sociable.' He studied his sister's face before continuing more diffidently. 'Things *are* a bit better, aren't they, Jen? I seem to get that impression.'

When she finally answered, it seemed as if she'd ignored his question. 'I went to Ireland chasing that thing you think is real but doesn't exist.'

'A mirage?' he suggested.

'That's it. Happiness was to be sharing Christopher's life, for ever and ever, amen.'

'You weren't to know his life would be such a short one – that was just terribly bad luck.'

Jenifer shook her head. 'There was nothing to share, even when he was alive. Over here our love affair was enjoyable and exciting, but in Ireland he didn't need me at all. He liked his dilapidated house the way it was, and horses and friends were all he wanted to fill the waking day. I was only useful at night, and *he* didn't mind if it meant we eventually filled the whole house with children – they'd be something to keep me occupied.'

'No wonder you seemed to be seething with rage when you arrived back here,' Tristram said compassionately.

'It wasn't rage against Christopher, so much as rage against myself. I'd been too blinded by vanity to see the mistake I was making. Mama knew, of course, and it made matters worse that one day I'd have to admit that she'd been right all along.'

There was silence in the room while he found words for the only comfort he could offer. 'It's not *all* waste. Morwetha and the new child that's coming prove that it wasn't entirely a mirage after all.'

Jenifer's sudden smile acknowledged the truth of what he said. They'd wandered far from where the conversation had begun, but she could see no tactful way of leading back to its starting point. He was a brother kinder than most, but a grown man now, with dignity to preserve and no relish for well meaning assaults on his privacy.

'Not all waste,' she agreed at last. 'Still, take a lesson from me when your turn comes – let your head get a look-in as well as your heart!'

He agreed that it sounded good advice, and there she had to let the matter rest. To prove that he'd listened to it, he politely escorted his cousins to dinner with the Treffrys at Place, attended the Easter service at St Fimbarrus with the rest of the family, and went with them to lunch at The Haven and listened to 'Q's reminiscences of the Fowey of thirty years ago. It was the time-honoured pattern of holidays at home – familiar as the fresh, salt smell of tidal water, and the plaintive sound of seabirds crying from the roof-tops. But he listened to the gulls knowing that Loveday would believe they housed the spirits of sailors drowned at sea. In the moment of thinking about her he knew what made the pleasant luncheon party seem such a pointless waste of time.

Duty done, he was free to please himself afterwards. A fast, fierce tramp to Gribben Head brought him back eventually to the headland above St Catherine's. He caught a distant glimpse of someone already there . . . felt irritated that *his* place should be occupied . . . and then began to run, because he knew who it was sitting there.

Loveday scrambled to her feet as he came towards her, about to explain that she was in the habit of coming out while Morwetha slept during the afternoons. The words were never said. Tristram opened his arms and she went into them, as naturally as a bird finds its nest. They didn't need words – theirs was perfect happiness, shared only by the little wind that brought them the scent of flowering gorse. When he loosened his grip enough to look at her, she smiled because he did, even though the moment seemed the most solemn she'd ever known.

'Your letters aren't nearly as long as mine,' he complained.

'But they take more writing,' she pointed out truthfully. 'You know all about what happens here . . . I don't know anything about London.'

The wind blew tendrils of dark hair across her mouth. He smoothed them away with gentle fingers and then, because it was inevitable that she should be kissed, leaned near to cover her mouth with his own. Her lips opened under his, like flower petals responding to the sun. Tenderness merged with passion and then got lost altogether in a leaping wave of desire. His hands pressed her down on to the grass and she was lying beneath him, flushed and trembling but unafraid. Nothing mattered but to give him pleasure, and to know that she was loved. The moment wouldn't last, but for as long as it could be made to, joy was theirs, entirely. She gave a little moan of pleasure when he unbuttoned her dress and touched her breasts with his mouth. The sound was faint, but it made him lift his head.

'Don't stop, Tristram,' she whispered. 'You don't have to.'

'Sweetheart, I'm afraid I do, while we still can,' he said unsteadily.

'But I'm *me* this time, not Iseult.' Her flushed face was beautiful, and her smile promised him that the gift of herself was offered with a generosity that asked nothing in return. It was exactly what made it impossible to accept.

'What you are is almost too much for me,' he said hoarsely, 'but you must listen, my little love, and understand. I've made a good start in London but there's a long way to go before I can support a wife, and Father isn't well enough off these days for me to even think of asking him to help.'

The sudden pallor in her face told him what was in her mind before she found anything to say. 'I wasn't looking for you to . . . to marry me, Tristram. Prospect isn't . . . isn't where I properly belong to be.'

'You belong *with* me, as soon as I am able to marry you, sweetheart; but it may mean waiting a year or two. Will you mind that?'

Mind . . . when the Holy Grail of happiness in front of her was shining with a thousand points of light? Her smile was radiant but she put it into words as well, in case he should be left in any doubt. 'No, I shan't mind waiting.'

He fastened up her dress and smoothed her tumbled hair, left a butterfly kiss on her mouth and then pulled her upright. Even in the midst of such a swell of happiness, the first rock of anxiety was poking its head, warning of danger . . . because where was her waiting to be done?

'Can we let things be till . . . till we're ready, Tristram? There's no call to tell anyone else yet, is there? I have to take care of Morwetha, and there's the new baby coming . . .' She sounded anxious now, as if she'd recognized danger, too.

He wanted to insist that they run all the way back to Prospect with the news, and dance and sing for the joy of it. But then she wouldn't be able to be employed as his niece's nursemaid, and what else was she to do? At least at Prospect he could be sure that she was safe and happy while he toiled for promotion in London.

'All right, my dearest one,' he agreed slowly. 'It's our secret now, but only for the time being.' They turned in the direction of Prospect, walking hand in hand, but finding nothing more to say. The outside world that had floated away over the horizon was all around them again, and the wind blew more coldly now that they weren't holding each other. They walked slowly, unaware of anyone else, but Lavinia became aware of *them*. She could see them clearly from the terrace, coming down the hill towards her with clasped hands and tranced faces.

She went indoors before they'd reached the boundary gate, and went upstairs to her own room. After long thought, she sat down at her desk and began a letter to Julia Haddenham.

IO

Tristram realized more clearly than Loveday that concealing their changed relationship was a strain they might not be able to bear very long. It worried him, too, that his share of the strain, away in London, would be a great deal less than hers. The secrecy they were trapped in was wrong – and in some way that he understood instinctively – dangerous as well. This conviction grew stronger each day, but Loveday's glance on him pleaded for nothing to change as long as he had to leave her behind at Prospect.

In the end he went back to London with their secret still intact, telling himself that it could do no harm to wait until he came down again in late summer. But between now and then he would apply himself so diligently to studying H.M. Government's diplomacy that his masters were bound to recognize the promise of their protégé, and promote him accordingly.

Even so, it was nerve-racking to find himself one evening sharing Lady Julia's dinner table with the man who presided most distantly over his fortunes, the Marquis Curzon, Secretary of State for Foreign Affairs, former Viceroy of India and not so much man as god to minions like himself. The god looked benign enough drinking Richard Haddenham's best burgundy, but Tristram prayed for invisibility. His lordship's handling of the Turks at the conference in Lausanne had been masterly but, in the humble opinion of a very junior assistant, some other negotiations were more questionable. He stayed safely out of range afterwards in the drawing room until Julia Haddenham selected him to take the great man his coffee. It was delivered with a praiseworthy bow and no mishaps. He had almost turned away when Richard tactlessly explained that the coffee-bringer was a budding member of the Foreign Office staff.

Lord Curzon stared for a moment at his unknown slave. 'Indeed. And which area of the globe is fortunate enough to engage your attention?'

'I'm posted to the European desk at the moment, sir.'

'Ah, so you are aware of the French occupation of the Ruhr. Do you agree with the British government's acquiescence in this move?'

Tristram saw the pitfall in front of him: he was probably damned whether he agreed or not. In the end he plumped for honesty. 'Perhaps we could do nothing to stop Monsieur Poincaré, sir, but I wish we had protested more forcibly.'

'You don't think France suffered enough in the war to deserve the reparations due to her from Germany?'

Whatever else the marquis excelled at, Tristram reflected, he was a pastmaster at asking the unfairly loaded question.

'She suffered hideously and deserves all she can get – but not at the cost of reducing Germany to economic collapse and destabilizing Europe all over again.' A little silence followed, and Tristram suspected Richard Haddenham of holding his breath.

'I must find an opportunity to acquaint the French premier with your views, Mr Bossiney,' Lord Curzon said affably. The slave was dismissed with a cool nod, and allowed to hide himself at the far end of the room. He smiled a good deal, spoke when spoken to, and inwardly debated his chance of an early switch to whoever had charge of the Galapagos Islands or sundry uninhabited Pacific atolls; his brief career was almost certainly at an end. The expected move came two months later, but when it came it took his breath away. He was to get ready for his first posting abroad at the end of the summer – a two-year stint as Third Secretary in the Embassy in Paris!

His letter to Lavinia about it coincided at Prospect with the birth of Jenifer's second child – delivered after a long and difficult labour, and with so much anxiety attached to it that his promotion seemed only a happy postscript to the news that she and her baby son were both going to survive, after all.

Loveday, too, had only the night-time hours in which to think about the news Tristram had sent her. She was monopolized during the day by a small, jealous girl who resented being displaced by a newcomer at the centre of the household's attention. Loveday's patience was tried, but she sympathized with Morwetha. Her own inclination in the privacy of her room at night was to weep for a similar feeling of abandonment, but there was no-one to tell *her* sadness to. Tristram must work in London – that she knew; but it had never occurred to her that separation wouldn't stop there. At home in Fore Street she consulted her father's little globe that they'd been allowed to twirl as children. *There* was the great mass of land they called the continent of Europe. Beside it, how tiny England looked, and how separate. Fowey, apparently, didn't exist at all.

The baptism of Petroc Julian O'Meara was timed so that Tristram could act as a godfather during his last visit to Prospect before going to France. Lavinia felt obliged to mention the baby's Irish relatives but was rewarded with a blunt refusal to invite them.

'Both children can visit Ireland when they grow up if they want to,' Jenifer said stubbornly. 'Until then, the less they know of the O'Mearas the better.'

'All right, but it's customary for a boy to have two godfathers. Who is to be the second one?' Lavinia waited to hear the name of one of their Lanhydrock friends, or perhaps that of Jonathan Bossiney. But the answer was unexpected when it came.

'I've asked Tristram to invite Kurt Winkler,' Jenifer admitted with a trace of defiance. 'Don't you think he'd do rather nicely?'

'Very, if he accepts,' her mother agreed after a moment's thought. 'He's a Christian Jew, so religion won't be a difficulty, and I'm certain he will take his duties very seriously.'

'Victoria is threatening to support Lottie through the ordeal of being a godmother. Interesting to confront Kurt with *her*!'

'Oh, I agree! If he needs convincing that women should have been left unemancipated, Victoria is *just* the girl to do it, I fancy.'

Jenifer smiled and didn't explain that the confrontation she had in mind was her cousin's provocative looks and ways versus Kurt's Germanic seriousness of mind.

But in the end Tristram and Lottie arrived without Victoria. They brought with them instead a friend of the Haddenhams – a stranger to Prospect, whom Julia Haddenham had decided should see Cornwall before leaving England for good. She was a relative of the Belgian Ambassador in London, about to begin a course of studies at the Sorbonne. Cécile Sabatier sounded intellectual enough to appeal to the most sober-minded fellow-guest. Lavinia had high hopes of her as a congenial companion for Kurt, even if she wasn't likely to be decorative enough to take Tristram's mind off Loveday Penwarne. Still, *that* brief little attraction hadn't come to anything. Loveday's time was entirely occupied by Morwetha, and Tristram would be just as fully occupied with his guests. By now, in any case, Paris must be beckoning as the greatest excitement of his life, swamping all other pleasures.

A day or two after the visitors arrived she had to confess to Jonathan that, as usual, life never went quite according to plan.

'You mean Kurt and the charming Cécile don't conveniently take to one another?'

'Well, he's polite to her, of course; he always is. But if he notices her whenever Jenifer is in the room, I should be very much surprised.'

'*Jenifer*? Good God! You're not, I hope, going to ask me to believe that *she* is equally aware of our serious observer of the human race?'

'My dear Jonathan, she's *intensely* aware of him,' Lavinia snapped, irritated by such blindness. 'She seems to be a different creature . . . charming, considerate, even patient with Morwetha! It's remarkable, but it's also very worrying.'

Jonathan looked thoughtful. 'I'm afraid I have to agree, if she has the slightest hope that Kurt will marry her. Of course he appreciates her beauty, and her gaiety when she's happy – he'd have to be a bloodless stick not to. But he's much too intelligent not to realize that they haven't a thought in common. Passion spent, their marriage would be a disaster.'

Lavinia gave a long sigh. 'Yes, of course it would be, but it means that she's going to be hurt all over again. I have so *prayed* for her to find happiness before it's too late.'

With no comfort to offer on the subject of a girl who would never, in his opinion, make a sensible stab at happiness, Jonathan reverted to the beginning of the conversation.

'So it's Tristram who has to occupy himself with Mademoiselle Sabatier. I don't imagine he finds *that* a hardship.'

'No, and at least it's *something* to the good that she should be so attractive. She will be in Paris in the autumn, so he'll know someone there, and her diplomatic connections are excellent for a young man in a strange city. I have great hopes of Cécile!'

As if the word had gone round that Tristram was soon leaving for France, the house constantly swarmed with visitors. Neighbours dropped in to wish him well, and friends scattered over the rest of Cornwall all seemed suddenly inspired with the single idea of calling on the Bossineys in Fowey. He would have enjoyed the social bustle if it hadn't isolated him from the one person he needed to see. Remote from the rooms in which guests were entertained, Loveday might just as well have been walled up in a nunnery. If he prowled the nursery corridor waiting for a servant to go downstairs, Jenifer would appear, bringing someone to admire her children. And when everyone else failed, Morwetha was certain to be there, demanding Loveday's entire attention. It was an intolerable situation, made worse by the fact that he was scarcely able to tell her so.

Several days dragged by before it occurred to him that she was deliberately making matters worse. She was actually *clinging* to the role of nursemaid. There was nothing wrong with the clothes she wore for looking after the children, but he would have liked Kurt to see her at her most radiantly beautiful, not tired, or bedraggled after bathing Morwetha. He wanted her sweet, quirky goodness to shine, not be overshadowed by the sophisticated, elegant charm of a girl like Cécile Sabatier.

He had no idea that, torn by a frustrated longing that matched his own, Loveday's only defence was to be *more*, not less, of what she was there to be. She smiled at anyone who came to see the children, but said very little about anything else because she couldn't guess what they expected her to say. She was stiff with Tristram for fear of giving herself away, and sometimes for the worse fear of not being able to recognize him at all. He *looked* familiar, but he spoke to Kurt Winkler in one strange language, and to Charlotte Haddenham's friend in yet another – at such times he became a stranger moving confidently in a world that was unknown to her. On her afternoon off when she was bound to visit Fore Street, she hoped he might be waiting for her when she left the cottage, but he wasn't there, and she couldn't know that he'd been trapped into taking Kurt, Charlotte, and Cécile to visit Menabilly.

She did know about the birthday ball at Place they were all to attend the evening after Petroc's christening. While they were getting ready for it her task was the usual evening one of persuading Morwetha that she would like to go to bed. The same rearguard action was fought every night by a stubborn small girl who reckoned that there were more interesting things to do with her time than sleep. She gave in at last and Loveday crept thankfully into the day-nursery next door. Jenifer O'Meara was there, dressed and ready for the ball, looking very beautiful, Loveday thought ungrudgingly. A gown of turquoise satin became her to perfection, but she was happy again as well, and vividly alive.

'Success at last?' she asked Loveday.

'Yes, but not without I'd drawn every animal in Mr Barrow's farmyard for her!'

For once Loveday's voice sounded tired, even discouraged, and Jenifer felt a stab of compunction. It was an unequal world, in which some got more than they deserved, and others much less. Loveday might treasure the letters she got from Tristram, but they were a poor substitute for the young man of her own kind that she ought to belong to.

'Morwetha will be better when everything settles down again,' Loveday was explaining. 'She enjoys it when all these visitors come to see *her*, but they make a fuss of Petroc as well and then there's trouble.'

It was true that the visitors unsettled Morwetha, but she knew that *she* resented them as well. She only mentioned these other people in the house because she was driven to it by the pain bottled up in her heart, and it wouldn't even help when they went away because then Tristram would go too. She felt ashamed of her discontent – he loved her, and that was more happiness than she had any right to expect, but the Lord who could see into her heart knew how hard it was to smile when she had to watch him being charmed by another woman.

Jenifer looked at Loveday's downbent face and chose her next words carefully.

'The only person Morwetha's always on her best behaviour with is "Uncle Trissam". What a pity we shall scarcely see him for the next couple of years! Still, it's the most tremendous luck for *him*, of course, getting Paris as his first foreign posting – it might have been some dreary legation in Patagonia or Peru.'

Loveday tried with all her aching heart to think only of Tristram. If Paris was nicer for him than these other places she had dimly heard of, then she would be glad for *him*; but this was only the first posting. There would be a lifetime of journeys to the far corners of the earth. That was what being a diplomat meant, although she hadn't properly realized it until now. It seemed a very dreadful way to live to a girl who asked nothing better than to spend her life in Cornwall.

'I hope he won't be lonely,' she murmured.

Jenifer smiled at the strange idea. 'Scarcely that! A young, attractive bachelor is so welcome in embassy life that he can go to a different party or reception every night if he wants to.' She hesitated, but finally decided to go on. 'It's helpful for him, meeting Miss Sabatier here. She's been mixing with embassy people since she left the schoolroom, and she's going to be in Paris at the same time as my brother, studying at the university there.'

Loveday moved about the room, collecting the toys that Morwetha had scattered during the day. In a moment or two she must go downstairs to share the Bartletts' supper; she must smile and talk while she tried to imagine the life Tristram would lead in Paris. All she could be certain of was that it would bear no relation at all to the way her own life was spent – a daily round of tasks, repeated yet not boring, because Morwetha, and Petroc too, changed a little every day; the same surroundings of grey town, river, and sea, dearly familiar yet always changing too, because the seasons and the Cornish weather brought their magical variations. The only link between this world of hers and the one that Cécile Sabatier knew was Tristram himself, whom she loved more than life itself but scarcely ever had the chance to speak to, even when he was there.

The thought of him seemed enough to make him materialize in front of her. She was unaware of having stopped to stare out of the nursery window until he walked out on to the terrace below, dressed in the evening splendour of white tie and tailcoat for the Treffry ball at Place. The last rays of sunlight caught his fair head, reminding her of the first time she'd been vividly conscious of him – in the chapel at Grandfather Isaac's funeral.

She saw him smile and thought for a heart-easing moment that he'd seen *her* standing at the window. But he was watching his German friend, and Charlotte Haddenham, who now walked outside as well to join him. Loveday scarcely noticed them. They were kind and pleasant people – she found she could talk naturally to *them* when they came to see Morwetha; but she waited now for the girl *they* waited for.

Jenifer had come to stand beside her at the window and appreciated, as Loveday did not, that Cécile's late arrival was deliberate. Her entrance was finally made in a flurry of filmy white skirts; her apologies were offered in charming broken English, in the confidence of knowing that she must be reckoned worth waiting for. Her face was exquisitely made-up, and she was continental allure personified, but Loveday's attention was riveted on what she wore – a dress so fragile and beautiful that it might have been spun out of seadrift or moonbeams. Wearing it, the Belgian girl was lovely enough to match the young man who bowed and held out his arm to lead her down through the garden. It was the highest tribute Loveday could offer her, and the most painful.

Jenifer abstained from the cruelty of pointing out that the two of them made a perfect couple. Instead, she said the first trivial thing that came into her head.

'A blessing for everyone that it's a fine, warm evening, but especially for Miss Sabatier – she doesn't realize yet that it's more usual here to arrive at a party blown about by the wind and soaked with rain, with her dancing shoes in her coat pocket!'

Loveday's sad face suddenly broke into a smile luminous enough, Jenifer thought, to dent even Cécile's self-confidence if she could have seen it. 'I didn't remember that,' she said softly. 'She knows a lot of things, but not the Cornish things *we* know.' The important things, she might have said, except that it would have sounded boastful: like curtseying to a solitary magpie, and never whistling in a boat, and being sure to leave a few crumbs from one's pasty for the Little People. Tristram understood that these small duties were crucial, because he was as much a part of the stream of Cornish history as she was herself, and as generations of Bossineys and Penwarnes had been before them. When she remembered *that* it was easier to wish the girl beside her a pleasant evening and mean it. It even became possible to swallow her own hateful jealousy and go downstairs to watch without feeling sick as John Bartlett demolished his favourite giblet pie.

But when her fingers happened to touch the material of her cotton dress she gave a little sigh. Mrs Bartlett would have liked to know why, but she didn't ask, nor even comment on the food still left uneaten on Loveday's plate.

The house party at Prospect broke up the day after the ball. While Charlotte took Cécile back to London via her uncle's castle at St Clyst, Tristram borrowed Rosinante to drive Kurt to Lostwithiel station. After a separation of two years they'd had a lot to talk about, but he thought they were both aware of reticences there hadn't been a chance to overcome. They arrived at the station with time in hand, and settled themselves on the platform. It was quiet and peaceful after the noise of Rosinante's progress, and suddenly Tristram wanted to talk about Loveday. He didn't know how to begin, but Kurt made it easy for him.

'You'll be glad to go to Paris. It's . . . what do you call it in English . . . a "plum", *nicht wahr*?'

'Yes, it's that all right. I hope it's been earned, though, and not dropped into my lap through Mama's august connections!' Tristram's grin faded, and when his face was serious it seemed older than its years. 'Nothing is perfect, though that posting *almost* is, because it means leaving Loveday here for two more years. I'm going to marry her, Kurt, but no-one else knows that yet.' He stared at his friend's face, slightly disappointed that it looked unsurprised.

'I wondered,' Kurt admitted slowly. 'You were so very stiff and formal, my friend, that it could only mean that you wished to behave to her quite differently!'

'Never underestimate a psychiatrist,' Tristram said ruefully. 'I hope my family doesn't have your powers of deduction! It's better for Loveday to stay at Prospect while I'm away; but it's damnable to leave her behind. It's also rather damnable when I'm here not to be able to acknowledge her properly.'

'Yes, I see that.' Kurt narrowed his eyes against the brightness of sunlight on the metal track in front of them. He could see those parallel rails in his imagination, stretching across Europe to Berlin. It seemed painfully far away.

'Do you remember how we liked to pride ourselves on being good Europeans – no nationalistic idiocies for *us*, and no chance of anything ever going wrong again in future?'

Tristram looked surprised at a question which seemed to have nothing to do with what they'd been talking about. 'Of course I remember. We "tired the sun with talking and sent him down the sky", and in the process settled most of the world's problems!'

'Do you still believe it? Imagine the unimaginable for a moment, Tristram – suppose that our politicians or military managed to be stupid enough to embroil us in another war. Being a good European, would you refuse to fight for England, or expect me to refuse to fight for Germany?'

'I should refuse if England seemed to be an unjustified aggressor; of course I should. But it's too remote a possibility to contemplate – we're not warlike people.'

'All right – what if she were attacked or felt obliged to help defend some other country?'

'Then I should have to fight,' Tristram said slowly. 'I imagine the same applies to you and Germany.' He stared at Kurt's sombre face and shivered suddenly although the late-August morning was very warm. 'It won't happen – you're forgetting the League of Nations, as well as a lot of other people who think the same way as we do about another war.'

'Your uncle has no faith in the League of Nations – and there are many people who share that opinion of his.'

The London train was signalled at last and Kurt stood up, gathering his luggage together. 'If you have to wait two more years for Loveday, Tristram, at least you can look forward to happiness after that. Pity me a little, my friend. After *twenty*-two years I shall still be a German, and the girl I'd give my soul to marry would still suffocate in present-day Berlin for lack of English air. That's why I can't ask your sister to marry me.' He grimaced at the astonishment in his friend's face, gave him a quick hug, and then climbed into the train that had now arrived. Not until it began to move was Tristram suddenly jerked into running along the platform beside it.

'Don't be a bloody fool – *ask* her,' he yelled, against the noise of the engine's gathering speed and piercing whistle. Even if Kurt heard, it was too late for him to answer. His dark head at the window was cut off from Tristram's sight by a curve in the track, and there was only the empty station left and the melancholy feeling always induced by having just waved someone goodbye. He drove Rosinante slowly home, distracted for once from thinking about his own problems. His attention had been concentrated on them, but even so he'd been aware of some change in his sister. She'd looked happy – *that* had been the change. He shivered suddenly, knowing the unyielding cast of his friend's mind when a principle he believed in was at stake. Kurt was the stuff of which martyrs were made; happiness would be renounced if he thought it had to be, and even if he grew to hate present-day Berlin he would be unable to convince himself that he didn't belong there.

At Prospect, Tristram found his mother in the garden as usual, but the heat had deterred her from working and for once she was sitting under a sunshade, reading. She smiled when he walked towards her and put her book aside – *Chrome Yellow*, he noticed with slight surprise.

'I'm *not* working, as you can see, but neither am I enjoying myself. If a writer as clever as Mr Huxley is supposed to be can only be brilliantly cynical about modern life, it's a depressing prospect for the rest of us poor idiots trying to muddle our way through.'

She expected Tristram to leap to the defence of a literary idol, but he seemed disinclined to abandon his own train of thought – and that was as depressing as her choice of novel to judge by the expression on his face.

'I expect you're sad to see all our visitors go,' Lavinia said gently. 'Your father certainly is, and Jenifer was so desperate for a distraction that she's gone over to Polruan to show Petroc off to Mrs Eliot. Actually it's quite a nice idea, because Jane Eliot was very kind to her when she had a slight accident over there. Morwetha refused to be left behind, of course, so she and Loveday have gone too.'

Tristram nodded and found for the first time in his life that it was hard to keep a conversation going with his mother. There were so many subjects that seemed dangerous until he could get Loveday to release him from a promise that was becoming more and more unbearable. But the thought of his conversation at the station filled his mind and had to be shared with someone.

'Just as the train was leaving Kurt said something that I very much disagreed with, but there wasn't time to argue with him.' Tristram relapsed into silence, frowning over the arguments he might have used.

'You haven't yet told me what was said,' Lavinia reminded him after a while.

'Oh, well, he seemed to think that two people with very different backgrounds, different outlooks, cultures even, could never marry and be happy – *shouldn't* marry, because it wouldn't be fair to the one who had to make the most adjustments. Do *you* agree with that?'

Lavinia recognized the moment as being one of those few in life that are suddenly crucial. What she answered now might safeguard or ruin Tristram's future, but the moment had come upon her unawares and she was ill prepared for it.

'*Every* marriage is a constant process of adjustment,' she replied eventually. 'Apart from that, I agree with Kurt. The less well matched the couple, the harder the adjustments are – or the more is unfairly asked of one of them, Kurt would say.'

Tristram sat so still that a butterfly landed on the top of his shoe, mistaking it for a stone. He felt vaguely sick, and shockingly aware for the first time in his life of a longing to shout at his mother. The calm certainty in her voice threatened more than his argument, and he doubted that her judgement would change even if she knew that it was his happiness they were talking about.

'You and Kurt forget something,' he muttered. 'If two people love each other, it must be wrong to miss the chance of being together, just for want of a little courage.' He looked up and saw a moment's desolation in his mother's face before she caught his eye and managed to smile instead.

'I'm damned either way if you remember a conversation we had long ago. Condemned by Jenifer for being unfair to your father, and by you for not being brave enough to throw my bonnet over the windmill and run off with Jonathan! As it happens, he never asked me to – another sad want of spirit, you'll say! But our little chance of happiness didn't seem enough to set against the ruin of his brother's life and his own obligation to care for the sick and needy here.'

Tristram realized that he'd expected her to agree with him *because* of her own wasted chance. It was maddeningly unfair to have it used against him instead. 'We were talking of a general principle,' he said stiffly, 'not about you and Uncle Jonathan.'

'Were we? I thought we were carefully *not* mentioning Kurt, who accepts that Jenifer is not transplantable to Germany . . . and *you*, who would rather not accept how different Loveday Penwarne is from you.'

He watched a lone gull settle on the balustrade in front of them. It picked its way deliberately along the warm stone, found nothing of interest, and took off again in a single, graceful sweep of wings. Now there was nothing left to concentrate on except the thing his mother had just said. In the maelstrom of emotions inside him relief seemed almost uppermost – she knew after all, without being told.

'Loveday's grandfather was a tin-miner, William washes china-clay – is that what makes her different?' he said fiercely. 'If so, the standards we use to judge people by are not only rotten but ridiculous. I simply won't accept them.'

Lavinia wondered how it was that she could feel intensely irritated by her son's stupidity in the very same moment that she felt intensely proud of him. She struggled to sound calm and almost succeeded. 'Loveday is beautiful, kind, and loving – that ought to be enough for society; if it isn't, then society's an ass.'

'Well, you *agree* with me then,' he almost shouted.

'Yes, but you forget that I also agree with Kurt. My dear, think what you'd be asking of a girl who would feel exiled just to cross the Tamar into England. Morwetha is persuaded to go to sleep at night listening to the legends of the Little People and the Idylls of the King. These aren't fantasies to Loveday – they're as real as the birds and flowers that live along the banks of the Fowey, and just as precious. Ask her to live among people who don't even know that Cornwall exists and *you* would have to be enough to make up for everything else – the foreigners she can't understand, the mystifying formalities of embassy life, and all the loved, familiar things that she would have to leave behind.'

It was on the tip of his tongue to insist that, just as he realized society *would* be enough of an ass to undervalue her, so she already realized and accepted these things. But the fear that it might not be true held him silent. Did she really have the slightest idea of what her life with him would be?

'How did you know? I thought I'd been very careful not to give myself away.'

'You couldn't help looking at her; it's not surprising – she's well worth looking at.' Lavinia prayed for him not to tell her that some understanding had already been reached with Loveday, because it would mean that his life was ruined before it had properly begun. But she had watched Loveday too and found her as serene and even tempered as usual; it seemed safe to hope that Tristram had at least retained some vestige of sense and kept his infatuation to himself.

Now, finding nothing safe to say about his own predicament, he reverted to his friend's instead.

'I hope you're right to agree with Kurt that marriage to a girl who couldn't settle happily in Ireland would be a disaster in Germany. And I hope to God that Jenifer agrees with both of you.'

He went back inside the house, leaving Lavinia with the certainty that in the worst adversity he had known so far she had bitterly disappointed him.

Late that afternoon, when even Morwetha was overcome by the excitement of the visit to Polruan, he managed to find Loveday alone in the nursery at last. He closed the door behind him, took out of her hands the piece of material she sat stitching, and pulled her up into his arms.

'Someone might come in, Tristram,' she murmured nervously.

'Let the whole bloody world come – I don't care!' He tried to smile in case she thought his anger was for her. 'Sweetheart, if I'm not allowed to kiss you now I shall burst with frustration. That would be far worse than having Mrs Bartlett walk in on us.'

Her body felt slighter than he remembered; she'd grown thinner, and her beautiful mouth looked sad when she forgot to smile. But it offered itself to him with such sweetness that he could put aside for a moment all the things that troubled him. His mother and Kurt were wrong . . . the only thing that mattered was the chance to love each other. They clung together in their feverish need to wipe away fear and loneliness, kissed and murmured small, meaningless words of love, and kissed again, until Tristram lifted his head and tried to sound rational.

'Listen, my heart . . . I came to talk seriously to you; sternly, if need be!' Her lips curved into a smile that required kissing again, but then he put her away from him and pushed her gently back into the chair she'd been sitting in.

'Stay there, and try not to look so beguiling that I have to hold you again. Loveday, my dearest dear, we made a promise. May I break it now and tell your family and mine that we're going to marry as soon as I can offer you a decent home?'

Radiance died out of her face, leaving it very pale, but she spoke calmly. 'I don't care what you can offer . . . I don't need very much; anything would do if you said we could be married tomorrow.' She knew the answer before she saw him shake his head, and smiled to show that she hadn't really expected him to agree. 'No, I can see it's not possible, of course, when you've to think about going to Paris. So we must let the promise be as it is, my dear, so's everything can go on as before until you come back . . . *Please*, Tristram.'

He wavered on the brink of confessing that his mother knew about his own feelings, though not about hers; wavered on the very edge of saying that somehow they would marry before he went away and be damned to all the problems that commonsense piled up in front of them. But Lavinia's words still clung to his mind, and sharper than fishbones swallowed inadvertently were all the things she *hadn't* said because he knew them already.

'All right . . . we'll leave the promise intact,' he said on a long sigh. 'In two years' time I shall be an old man of twenty-five and you will be twenty-one; we'll be more than old enough then to please ourselves. Every night and morning of these accursed two years will you promise never to forget how much I love you?'

She nodded slowly but had no chance to answer in words because Morwetha's voice floated in from the room next door.

'Lowdy . . . where are you? I'm all finished with sleepin' now.' In case there was any doubt about it, the bars of her cot were thumped vigorously to prove that, being wide-awake, she required company.

'I'll have to go or she'll disturb Petroc,' Loveday said, caught somewhere between tears and laughter. She reached up to leave a little kiss on Tristram's cheek, and then walked away from him trying not to feel that in some way she didn't understand she had just said goodbye to happiness.

He left the following day, looking so unhappy that even Julian noticed and asked his wife to tell him why a young man launching on his chosen career should appear to be going to his execution. Unable to explain, she said crossly, 'For the same reason, I suppose, that Jenifer seems to be contemplating suicide – they think they want what life hasn't provided for them.'

11

The turn of the year, into 1924, brought changes. To Julian Bossiney there seemed the shocking likelihood of a Labour government for the first time in Whitehall – the Tories had done little enough to help Cornwall, but at least they were gentlemen who knew how to behave. William Penwarne didn't take much account of goings-on in London, but he was unhappily faced with his elder son's decision to abandon the drying-sheds at Par to go and work for Daniel.

'You're used to going off with John each morning,' Hannah pointed out. 'The trouble with you, Will, is that you don't like anything to change. We'd still be back in the Dark Ages if everybody thought like you.'

'The trouble with me is that I don't altogether know where I am with Daniel,' William said truthfully. 'There's something about him that I don't understand.'

'It's called ambition,' his wife told him. She'd never regretted her marriage, because only a fool would regret a husband who was good and kind, but if she'd been married to a man like Daniel she wouldn't still be living in a poky, rented cottage that didn't even belong to them. She relented a little at the sight of William's anxious face and spoke more gently.

'No need to fret, my dear – look how well it's worked out having Charlie in Daniel's workshop at Polruan.'

That was true, William's nod conceded, but his anxiety about John remained. He couldn't put it into words, and he knew it would have irritated Hannah if he'd tried, but it was the difference in their two sons that troubled him. Charlie accepted what happened to him but refused to be changed by it. Working for Daniel wasn't as good as being out all day in Walter Jago's old boat, but at least he was still as near the water as he could get. He dealt expertly with machinery now, accepted the internal-combustion engine as a powerfully useful thing, but mourned in his heart the lost glory of the sailing ships that, fully-rigged, had floated downstream to the open sea. What William couldn't explain to Hannah was that Charlie still remained himself; John would try to copy Daniel, and probably fail because he wasn't as sharp as his cousin. William didn't set much store by success; he just wanted his children to be happy, and thought that Hannah, who wanted happiness *and* success for them, was likely to be disappointed.

John was so confident of his future in Daniel's garage businesses that he tried to light a spark of ambition in his brother.

'Daniel says you're real schemey when it comes to fitting engines together,' he reported generously, 'but there's no sense in staying over at Polruan – motor-cars are the coming thing.'

'I prefer boats, and I like Polruan. It means I can keep an eye on Grandfather, too; he's much too lively still, and inclined to forget he's getting on.'

'You mean he forgets the times he's told his stories before, about Bossiney schooners racing all the others across to Dordt and Elsinore and St Petersburg!'

'I like the stories as well,' Charlie said stubbornly. 'They get better with telling.'

'I hope he's never hanging around the yard when Daniel comes over to see you. It's the future that counts with him; stories about the past wouldn't do, even if they didn't concern the Bossineys.'

'Why *doesn't* he have a good word to say for Tristram's family? They've not done *him* harm, unless he still reckons Lowdy might've married him if she hadn't gone to work at Prospect.'

John scoffed at the idea. 'It was years ago that Daniel

had a fancy for Loveday. He can take his pick now. There's girls in Lostwithiel and Par he could have for the asking.'

'Well, I notice he doesn't marry any of them.'

'Time enough – he isn't thirty yet, and he says a wife's a drag on a man with a long way to travel.'

'If he says it at home, Mother will fetch him a scat round the ears . . . Not that you could call Father a man who's been held back from travelling! He just wants to stay quiet where he is.' Charlie stared at his brother before risking a delicate question.

'Is that why you stopped going to Bodinnick to see Mary Tucker – because Daniel said to forget about her?'

'I don't do everything Daniel says,' John answered hotly. 'I'd go soon enough if I wanted to, but she kept dropping hints – when were we going to see vicar? Seemed to me *I* was the one to say that, not her.'

Charlie abandoned the subject without pointing out that it was exactly the reply his cousin would have given. 'Seen Loveday lately? Seemed to me she did a lot of smiling at Christmas-time, but looked wisht when she thought no-one was watching.'

'Getting too grand for Fore Street, p'raps. We don't run to dinner at night, nor a room called a library and our own private cove when we want to go swimming. I reckon Mother should never have let her get used to living at Prospect.'

'She's there because she's a servant – nothing very grand about that.' Charlie corrected John more sharply than he meant to, because there was a chance that his brother was right. Loveday wouldn't ever think herself above *them*, but he could see it wouldn't be easy running up and down the scale that stretched from a miner's cottage to Prospect House.

She would have agreed with him on both counts. It didn't occur to her that she no longer belonged in Fore Street, but she remembered with a sense of shame the first time she noticed that her home seemed cramped and

157

airless after the spaciousness of Prospect. Her mother took for granted the busy, narrow street outside the parlour window, but now it had become noisy and unprivate to someone grown used to looking out on gardens, sea and sky. Charlie was right about something else as well. It had been hard to go to chapel with her father on Christmas morning and rejoice in the birth of little Lord Jesus when Tristram hadn't come home at all for the festival. Somehow she'd counted on seeing him, and the disappointment was bitter when he wrote to say that it would be tactless to refuse an invitation to join a skiing party in Austria. She was becoming familiar with the words 'tactful' and 'tactless'. They cropped up so often in his letters that the thing called tact seemed to rule his life in Paris. To be sure that she understood why it was so important she looked the word up in her mother's dictionary at home – 'the faculty of saying or doing the right thing in dealing with others . . . so as to avoid giving offence, or to win goodwill'. The dictionary didn't explain, she thought, how Tristram was to win goodwill in Paris without giving hurt to those who loved him in Cornwall.

In the week after Christmas she went back to Prospect disappointed in another way for the first time. There hadn't *not* been a letter before even if sometimes it had been brief and hurried, but she walked home reminding herself of his kindness in finding the time to write at all. Paris was at the centre of much European diplomacy in the post-war years, he'd explained to her often; the staff of the British Embassy there led responsible and busy lives.

She learned by accident a little more about the Christmas skiing party, only because Charlotte Haddenham came on to Prospect to check on the progress of her godson after spending Christmas at St Clyst.

'Victoria didn't come down with you?' Jenifer asked when Charlotte was ensconced in the nursery, with Petroc on her knees.

'A quiet family party is *not* my sister's idea of pleasure. Didn't Tristram mention that he was going to collect her off the boat-train in Paris? They were going on to the Arlberg together.'

Loveday sat nearby, drawing pictures for Morwetha until it was time to give her her tea. She didn't know Victoria Haddenham, but imagined her to be a younger version of this brown-haired, gentle-faced woman whom she liked very much indeed. Tristram *hadn't* mentioned her, but they were cousins – of course they were likely to share a holiday.

'Cécile was in the party, too,' Charlotte said next. 'In fact, I believe she was the instigator of it. Kurt Winkler was to make all the arrangements and join them from Berlin.'

'We didn't know about Cécile, either,' Jenifer said meaningfully. 'My dear brother has been *very* secretive about his Christmas pleasures!' She strolled to the door, smiling at Charlotte. 'It's Mrs Bartlett's afternoon off, so I'm superintending tea. Loveday will take over here when you get bored with my son!'

The little silence that followed was broken by Morwetha's indignant voice. 'Lowdy . . . wake up . . . you's sleepin'!'

Charlotte looked across the room at the white-faced girl who stared at the paper in front of her but had ceased to draw the menagerie Morwetha required. She wasn't asleep, but Charlotte felt sure that her thoughts had been absorbed by a vision so painful that she had been unaware of the rest of them.

'How does one ever get bored with a child?' she asked quickly. 'There must be something different to watch in these two every day.' The baby's eyes were held by the gleam of her gold bracelets, and his small fat hands suddenly made a grab at them. He chortled so loudly with pleasure that Loveday was jerked out of her trance of stillness into the knowledge that some conversation was required of her.

'You can see he's Cornish,' she said. 'Fascinated already by metal, and the more precious it is, the better!'

Once started, it was easy to go on talking to this friendly woman – and more bearable by far than thinking about Cécile Sabatier flying like a bird down a white mountainside. Loveday felt certain that this was how the Belgian girl would perform if she ski'd at all – not for her the humiliating falls that would beset other people.

'My grandfather was a miner,' she explained suddenly with a rare touch of pride, 'but he was looking for the lodes of tin, of course, *not* gold. I remember every one of the stories he used to tell me, and when Petroc's old enough to understand I shall tell them to *him*.' She frowned with the effort of putting into words for someone else the kind of thought she normally kept to herself. 'I s'pose we're all searching for something; but at least Grandfather Isaac knew what he was looking *for*.'

'It's happiness the rest of us mostly try to find, don't you think?' Charlotte suggested diffidently. 'Such very precious metal that it's no wonder we're often disappointed!'

They smiled at one another, conscious that more than liking was shared; some experience of sadness was also common to them both, putting them on equal terms. Charlotte came often to the nursery after that for as long as she stayed at Prospect, and Loveday instinctively knew what her sadness was – this woman loved children but was beginning to fear that she might never have any of her own.

She left for London halfway through January and they settled into their usual winter isolation. There was little visiting to be done while south-westerly gales drove rain-clouds and high tides in from the Atlantic. Perched on its rocks out of reach of even the most menacing seas piling into the mouth of the river, it was as if the house welcomed the onslaught of wind and rain. Watching the tumult from inside, it seemed to Loveday that she was part of the outer wildness, and part as well of the Cornish stone and slate that so stubbornly resisted it. She belonged in Tristram's home . . . which made it strange that she was beginning to realize, more and more certainly as the weeks crept past, that she didn't belong in his life.

She still wrote to him regularly of their small happenings – Charlie's rescue of a drowning cat, Morwetha's daily discovery of some new word, Petroc's triumph in hauling himself upright unaided. These things gave her pleasure, and in any case they were all she had to write about. Tristram's replies – haphazard since Christmas – had become, she noticed, brief, polite comments on what *she* had written. He no longer described what filled his own days and nights, because she was part of the Cornish life he'd left behind and couldn't be expected to understand what was all-important to him now. Through long, slow winter afternoons she sat by the fire in the library, half-listening while Sir Julian told Morwetha the names of his beautiful butterflies, or Lady Bossiney read to her granddaughter the exploits of Badger, Mole and Ratty – written while their creator stayed with his friend, 'Q', along the Esplanade. She could have waited easily for two years in this house for Tristram to come home. But the truth was slowly dawning. He would *never* come home, and a wife who knew only Cornish things would be of no use to him.

The winter wasn't quite over when Jenifer returned from a visit to friends at Bodmin complaining of a heavy cold. It developed into such severe influenza that Jonathan had to be called to Prospect, and she emerged eventually from her bedroom thin and listlessly disinclined to pick up the threads of daily living again. As usual, Lavinia took the problem to Salubrious House, undeterred by an afternoon of Cornish weather when the wind seemed to be blowing from all four quarters of the compass at once.

She arrived breathless, and dishevelled enough to shock the doctor's housekeeper, who reckoned that ladies, being made of frailer clay than most, should behave accordingly.

'My dear sawl, tesn't no day for a spriggan to be out, much less your leddyship.'

'I rather enjoyed the battle, Mrs Trago, but it will have been wasted if Dr Bossiney isn't at home.'

'In his study-room, jest as usual; you go along in there while I put the kettle on.' She bustled away, congratulating herself on the foresight that had prompted her to bake a fresh supply of splits for Doctor's tea. Thin as a rail Sir Julian's lady was – in need of plumping up, to Mrs Trago's way of thinking.

Jonathan laid aside the medical journal he was reading as Lavinia walked into the room, and smiled charmingly at his visitor.

'My dear, what an unexpected pleasure. You'd have sent for me if necessary, so there's no emergency and I shall simply say that a walk in a high wind becomes you!'

She went to the mirror over the fireplace to tidy her hair, and smiled back at him in the glass. Passion was spent after twenty-five years. Free of its destructiveness now, she thought they both enjoyed the ease that came of deep, abiding affection.

'Mrs Trago didn't seem impressed. Ladies aren't supposed to arrive looking as if they'd been dragged through a hedge backwards! What's a spriggan, by the way?'

'A branch of the Little People – the malicious kind who specially enjoy making trouble for travellers. If that's what you came all the way to find out, Loveday Penwarne could have told you.'

'No, I came about Jenifer. She isn't ill any longer, but she seems determined not to enjoy anything ever again. I hoped you might be able to suggest a remedy. Julian isn't much help because he assumes that everyone else must be contented as he is. He's splendid when it comes to something practical, like Fowey's antiquated sewage system, but other people's problems are a mystery to him.' She watched Jonathan's face and answered her question for him. 'You think Jenifer's old enough now to deal with her own problems; forgive me for bringing them to you, when you have to listen to everyone else's as well.'

Jonathan knelt down to poke the fire with unnecessary vigour, then turned his head to smile at her. 'Don't apologize for a visit that gives me nothing but pleasure.'

She didn't have to answer because a thump on the door was followed by the entrance of Mrs Trago, carrying a laden tea-tray. When she'd talked herself out of the room again he sat, watching Lavinia pour the tea. The leaping flames of the fire lit her thin face, and he wondered how old and dim-sighted he would have to grow before he lost the contentment that came from looking at it.

'I *am* sorry for Jenifer,' he said slowly, 'just as I'm sorry for anyone who makes a mistake that can't be unmade. But there are young widows far worse off than she is – women who must earn the means to keep their children alive, as well as come to terms with grief and loneliness.'

'I know, and she *has* tried since Petroc was born; but she isn't naturally maternal, and the children can't fill her life. Instead, they chain her to Prospect. Without them, she might have been brave enough, as she was once before, to set off in pursuit of happiness. But even Jenifer sees the impossibility of landing uninvited on Kurt Winkler's doorstep, clutching two small children.'

Lavinia stared at the glowing fire for a moment, then went on speaking almost to herself. 'I shook Tristram's confidence in me by saying that Kurt was right to go back to Germany alone. Now, I think he *wasn't* right to go without an explanation that might have been some comfort to Jenifer.' She looked up and smiled at the man watching her. 'I speak from experience, you know! There *is* joy in being told that one is loved; she hasn't been given that by Kurt.'

Jonathan laid his hand on hers for a moment, then released it, and tried to think only of Jenifer's problems.

'No point in being mealy-mouthed about it – she's still young and beautiful, and she needs a man to love her. Fowey isn't, as far as I know, going to be able to supply an alternative to Kurt, so we must cast our net wider, that's all. Why not get Tristram to invite her to Paris for Easter? At the very least a change of scene will help.'

Lavinia considered this gravely for a moment. 'You're right. Paris in the spring might in itself be enough to convince her that life is still worth living. It means we shan't see Tristram here, but that's a disappointment Julian and I will have to put up with.'

'When she comes back, there's *one* young man occasionally here who might be able to make an impression on her. I've dined in his company a couple of times at Fowey Hall, and so, I think, has Jenifer. Brave my brother's displeasure and invite Daniel Penwarne to Prospect.'

Lavinia shook her head reluctantly. 'I think not – Julian would be flummoxed and Mr Penwarne uncomfortable. Besides, there's Loveday to consider. How could we have her cousin here as a guest when *she* is not? No, my hopes are pinned on Paris, and I shall now go home and write to Tristram.'

She touched Jonathan's hand by way of farewell, and began the boisterous walk home aware that for once she hadn't been completely honest with her brother-in-law. The strongest argument for sending Jenifer to Paris was just that it *would* keep Tristram away from Prospect. Lavinia felt almost certain that his infatuation with his niece's nursemaid was fading with every day that kept them separate; but it must continue to fade. She wasn't unaware of the sadness that Loveday now struggled to contain, and felt deeply sorry for her; but it still didn't occur to her for a single moment that anything but disaster for both of them could come of so unthinkable a marriage.

By the time Jenifer returned from Paris, Loveday had already made up her mind to leave Prospect. The decision was taken before she had to listen to accounts of Tristram's hectic life, of his close friendship with Cécile, of the Belgian girl's unfailing ability to charm ambassadors and, even *more* usefully, ambassadors' wives. Cécile Sabatier would not only make the perfect helpmate for a rising young diplomat, said Jenifer with certainty, but she was also clearly head over heels in love with Tristram; really, it was an ideal arrangement.

Loveday listened, smiled when a smile was called for, and prayed to the Virgin Mary, Queen of Heaven, to help her escape from Prospect with pride. It was very clear to her – the rock to which she clung amid the swirling waters of despair – that she must leave proudly, not slink away in the tatters of defeat. But she could still see no way of doing it, nor even the way to go at all, when Charlie walked back with her to Prospect one evening after a visit to Fore Street. A recent shower of rain inspired a blackbird in a nearby ilex tree to start singing and Charlie walked beside her imitating his whistling song. He broke off, grinning at her, when the blackbird climbed too high for him.

'Seen anything of Daniel lately?'

Loveday shook her head, but didn't say that he seemed careful to stay away from Fore Street when she was likely to be there. All she knew of him nowadays was that he was talked about as doing very well, and that both her brothers had reason to be grateful to him.

'Seems to me he's doing handsomely down here, but he reckons he's not moving fast enough – England's the place to be. John's going to be left in charge at Lostwithiel, seeing that he's got a proper old sharp head on his shoulders, while Daniel goes off to London to open his garages there.'

'Won't that cost a lot of money?' Loveday ventured.

'Mebbe, but I reckon he's got enough by now, even without his father's help. Uncle George's been poorly out in South Africa for a long time; when *he* goes round land any time now Daniel will have more what he calls "risk capital". I'd buy a boat if I were him,' Charlie said wistfully.

'Perhaps he'll become rich enough to set *you* up as a fisherman one day,' she suggested, always glad to offer hope.

'Mebbe,' Charlie said again. He glanced sideways at his sister, noticing that she looked pale and tired. 'You all right, Lowdy . . . Those children not getting you down?'

Loveday tried to look as if nothing was getting her down. 'No, I'm all right; but first Mrs O'Meara got ill, and then she went to France. Morwetha didn't like her mother being away, and she believes in letting everyone else know when she's unhappy!'

Charlie stopped at the gate of Prospect, smiling at his sister. 'Rather you than me looking after her – I should reckon Tristram's glad to be away too! See you next week – Mother's birthday, don't forget.'

She nodded and let herself in through the gate, stabbed by pain – Tristram *was* glad to be away, but sooner or later he must remember that he had parents who needed visiting. It was very necessary to be out of Prospect before he came.

A week later she walked into the cottage, carrying an armful of flowers for her mother – a tall, slender girl whose white skin and darkly blue eyes seemed a perfect match for the colours of the irises she carried. Daniel hadn't seen her since she went to live at Prospect. He hadn't forgotten that he'd wanted her, but hadn't remembered quite how beautiful she was. When he got to his feet, for once not ready with something to say, she smiled as if she was happy to see him there, dwarfing the small parlour.

'It's kind of you to remember Mother's birthday, Daniel – at least, I s'pose that's why you're here?'

Her voice was still soft, but there was a difference about her now. He realized that living among the Bossineys had taught her things she hadn't known before. She was self-possessed – for the moment more so than he was. He didn't know whether that pleased or irritated him.

'I'm just leaving, but I came to bring Aunt Hannah my good wishes, and your father a bit of news. I'd have stayed to see him, but I must be back in Lostwithiel this evening.' Loveday waited, not sure that she was to be given the news as well until Daniel spoke again. 'My father is very ill, dying in fact; but he's made up his mind to die on Cornish soil, and sailed from Cape Town ten days ago, apparently. I haven't seen him for almost ten years.'

'When you left South Africa to come to England and fight for the king.' He could only have been a boy of nineteen, she thought, but didn't say it out loud.

'When I came looking for adventure!' Daniel corrected her with a faint smile. 'I dare say my father preferred your version, though.'

He spoke matter-of-factly, but she thought he didn't *feel* matter-of-fact about his father's return. If he could have managed it, he'd have said that it was the act of a fool for a sick man to embark on a sentimental journey of six thousand miles. But he *couldn't* say it, any more than he could admit to the sudden compulsion that had taken him into Fowey church that morning. He didn't know how to pray, but had stayed there in the quietness for a while, willing his father to survive the voyage.

'*My* father won't have seen Uncle George since they were boys growing up at St Just,' Loveday said slowly. 'Even a little time together again will be something for them.' She glanced at Daniel, then quickly looked away again because he was watching her, but his face had made a clear impression on her mind's eye – there was no softness to it, provided either by expression or by an ounce more flesh than was needed to cover its bones; she'd seen desire there once, but no tenderness. She went on at random, confused by the direction her thoughts had taken. 'Charlie said something about London.'

'Yes, I've got it planned for the future, but it will have to wait a bit now.' He moved towards the fireplace to inspect Hannah's collection of china dogs arranged there with care. Loveday trembled for them, but his fingers touched them with surprising gentleness. 'What do *you* plan to do? Stay buried at Prospect for ever, being graciously allowed to relieve Mrs O'Meara of the job of looking after her own brats?'

'They won't need me for ever,' she pointed out, 'but I need to find something else to do soon – before I get too fond of them and forget they don't belong to me!'

She smiled to show that she meant it as a joke, and Daniel was aware of another compulsion as rare as the one that had taken him into the church. This time he didn't give in to it, but he wanted to put his arms round Loveday Penwarne and hold her close . . . for her comfort, he realized with astonishment, not for any pleasure of his own. Her smile had been beautiful but sad and, for some reason he didn't enquire into, its sadness seemed to entitle him to hate the Bossineys even more than before.

Silence *seemed* safe, but the little room hadn't space enough to contain her cousin, talking or silent. Loveday struggled to stay calm, but she could feel the spark of tension in the air. It was a huge relief when her mother walked into the room, ignored the electric atmosphere, and accepted her daughter's gift of flowers. Daniel left soon afterwards and she didn't see him again until the day of his father's funeral – because George Penwarne didn't quite manage to see Cornwall again after all. He died in London, too weak to be moved from the hotel where Daniel had taken him from the docks at Tilbury. William made only the second railway journey to London of his life to visit him there, and returned to Fowey with Daniel and his brother's body.

The funeral seemed to Loveday to complete something begun four years earlier. This time Tristram was missing from the small congregation. There was no shining, fair head to catch the light, no gentle smile and charming apology for his father's absence. The unreal vision of knightly grace that ever since then had merged for her with the real Tristram Bossiney had now to take its place with the other lost dreams of her imagination.

Instead, Daniel needed her help. She could see him struggling with grief and, for the first time in his life, a sense of failure. Without being told, she knew that her uncle's death in London had become *his* failure, because he'd set his heart on bringing George Penwarne back to Cornwall alive. She thought he seemed grateful for the small gathering of Penwarnes and Eliots at the cottage after the service. His plan to leave Cornwall altogether would surely materialize, but the body of his father lying beside Isaac's in the churchyard would always link him now with the rest of the family, and she sensed that he was glad this was so.

She handed round tea but left the menfolk to talk to him, Grandfather Tom valiantly avoiding all mention of steam versus sail, and scarcely shouting at all in his daughter's small parlour. Only when Daniel was about to leave did she find him in front of her, not quite sure what to say now that he was there. She smiled and held out her hands to say goodbye.

'Don't be wisht about your father, Daniel,' she said gently. 'He's where he did belong to be . . . that's the important thing.'

He wanted to shout that it wasn't the important thing for *him*, and that blurring the fact with childish Cornish folklore made it worse, not better. But her shining belief in the comfort she was offering defeated him; what she'd just said even became true. He bent down and kissed her cheek, and then walked quickly out of the room.

12

It was a strenuous year for anyone involved in European diplomacy. Tristram shared his father's objection to a Labour government at home, but one fact was undeniable: Ramsay MacDonald was having more success abroad than Lloyd George, or either of his Tory counterparts. Acting as foreign secretary, as well as prime minister, MacDonald was helping to solve one of the worst problems bedevilling Europe since the war.

Tristram explained this to Kurt Winkler when they met in Paris, in the wake of a medical meeting his friend had come to attend. Kurt observed him across the café table where they sat drinking beer.

'You've got thinner – too much energetic tennis? Or too many embassy balls, and nights without proper sleep?'

'Too much *work*,' Tristram protested. 'While you slumber in your peaceful laboratory, we toil like bees in a hive – telegrams, agendas, reports, tactful soundings of foreign colleagues. It's never ending!'

'And does it achieve anything besides the wearing-out of its devoted slaves?'

'As a matter of fact, it does,' Tristram insisted seriously. 'Largely thanks to our prime minister, who's the most persuasive honest broker we've managed to produce for years, the whole frightful argument over reparations looks like being settled. France will reasonably accept what Germany can reasonably be expected to pay – assuming,' he added as a hurried afterthought, 'that you agree she should be asked to pay anything at all.'

Kurt's wry glance met his across the table. 'We don't see each other very often, but that doesn't mean we no longer know each other's views. Germany started the war – of course she must pay, within limits that are bearable.' He took another sip of his beer, then changed the subject of conversation. 'I've been to Italy since I saw you last. What do your people think of Signor Mussolini?'

'That, despite his past history, he's to be encouraged on the whole – methods of gaining power questionable, benefits to that chaotic country considerable, is roughly the verdict, I believe.' He saw Kurt's expression and asked abruptly, 'Don't you agree?'

'I have no opinion to offer, my friend. But the people I talked to *had* – no benefits at all, and eventual disaster was their prediction!' He shrugged off the memory of those disturbing conversations and smiled instead. 'Forget politics; tell me about Cornwall, and your family and Miss Penwarne instead.'

'Well, they're all much the same as when you saw them last. Father's trying to pretend that he doesn't want to be mayor; Mother's trying to persuade old Simeon that, at the age of seventy-five, it's time he gave up gardening; and Loveday reports that Jen's children get more interesting every day.' He hesitated and then added. 'Jenifer wasn't very well earlier in the year; spent Easter with me here, as a matter of fact, and I was sad to see her looking so pulled down.'

'I'm sorry,' Kurt said expressionlessly. He took a long time to light a cigarette and blow a smoke ring into the air. 'Give her my . . . my best wishes, please.'

Tristram looked at his friend's withdrawn face, was on the point of saying 'Go to Prospect and give them to her yourself', when Kurt spoke again, deliberately changing the subject. 'You've been in Paris almost a year – what happens when you finish here?'

'I've no idea – back to London, maybe, but I'm hoping for another continental posting; Berlin, if I'm very lucky, and the powers-that-be remember that my German's fairly good!'

'I hope Loveday would enjoy that,' Kurt said politely.

A glance at his watch confirmed that it was time to leave, and he went away promising to try to join Tristram at Prospect before the end of the summer.

Left alone, Tristram made an effort to concentrate on what Kurt had said about Italy, but his mind insisted on returning to worries nearer home. It would have been a relief to admit to how hopeless it was becoming to think of marrying Loveday, but he'd baulked at confessing to such a huge mistake. And Kurt had carefully *not* enquired about the very different girl who seemed to share more and more of his friend's life in Paris. Tristram saw clearly that he was being unfair to both Loveday *and* Cécile, but had no idea what to do about it.

Loveday's letter arrived a week later, saying with complete finality that their understanding was at an end; it had been a mistake, for which she seemed ready to take all the blame. It would be another mistake, apparently, to stay much longer at Prospect, and she would leave when someone suitable to look after the children had been found. Tristram read the brief letter over and over again, determined to find something that didn't seem to be there – a hint that she'd sensed some of his own confusion? There was no such hint at all. A trace of pain or heartbreak? Certainly not. A suggestion that she was the least bit jealous of Cécile? Not a trace of it. In fact, it was damnably cool and calm, when *he* was plunged in a chaotic mess of anger, relief and aching loss.

Anger seemed the thing to fasten on. If their poor little love affair was to be stillborn, it was for *him* to do it, not Loveday Penwarne. But he was ashamed of the thought the moment it came into his head. No, better to accept that she had faced the future more honestly than he'd done – a future that for her would always be in Cornwall, while his would scarcely ever be in England. As a couple they were infinitely more ill-matched than Kurt and his poor English Jenifer. Altogether Loveday's letter was an immense and heaven-sent relief. His mind fastened on the phrase and wouldn't let it go. He walked alongside the river and found himself repeating it out loud, until a passer-by's astonished stare jerked him into remembering that he was going to be very late back in the Faubourg St Honoré.

Fowey in mid-summer was full of visitors. They came in trainloads, now, from London and many of them stayed in the splendid Fowey Hotel along the Esplanade. Cornwall needed this new holiday industry, apparently, and the visitors from across the Tamar spent their money freely. All the same, Charlie preferred not to watch whenever one of his friends went by. It didn't seem right to him that in order to feed their children men who'd once been brave and skilled fishermen should now have to row cargoes of 'foreigners' on sightseeing trips up and down the river.

Charlie reckoned himself lucky to be working for Daniel. The boatyard was always busy, even with the two extra boys who'd come as apprentices from Town School. They all had to work hard, but Charlie didn't mind that. He didn't often get a sail across the bay now, though sometimes he went to help on the professor's yawl. But when the long day's stint was over, the river and its creeks and inlets were always waiting for him, free of visitors at eventime, and beautiful. He quite often called in at Bodinnick, too. John was a fool to have given up the landlord's daughter; Charlie was beginning to like Mary Tucker very much indeed, but he hadn't said so yet at home.

He hadn't seen Loveday since the day of his uncle's funeral, until she rowed herself across the river one hot, still afternoon, and after a call at Ferry Cottage walked into the yard.

'Good time to stop for a "coozey",' he said, smiling at her, 'while I'm waiting for a coat of paint to dry.'

'Granny said you'd be hungry as well by now – so I've brought you one of her saffron cakes.'

'Well, I can eat as well as talk. There's a bit of a breeze down by the water.' They perched themselves on the end of the sea wall, and while Charlie munched his cake Loveday watched an oyster-catcher examining the mud left by the ebbing tide.

Her face, shadowed by an old sun hat, looked withdrawn and sad, and when she turned towards him he saw that her eyes were full of tears.

'What's up, Lowdy? Something bothering you at Prospect?'

'Only the need to leave it,' she said miserably. 'Charlie, I've got to find another job, before Tristram comes home. I thought there was plenty of time, but Lady Bossiney heard from him this morning. She told Morwetha that "Uncle Trissam" would be here in time for the regatta.'

'That's only a month from now, maid.'

'I *know*.' Her voice trembled on the edge of being suspended altogether, but she swallowed the tears clogging her throat. 'I meant to ask Mrs Nicholls if she'd take me back again at the school, but she won't want anyone till holidays are over.'

'You hated the school, and you weren't much good at it,' he pointed out honestly.

'I know,' she said again, 'but don't you think I might do better now I'm older? Doesn't matter what it is, long as I'm away from Prospect before Tristram comes home.' She tried to smile, but it did nothing to lessen the desolation in her face, or the tension that kept her hands locked together.

Charlie thought confusedly of the worst that might have happened. Couldn't have, he decided thankfully; Tristram hadn't set foot in Fowey since he went to France a year ago. She read her brother's mind and shocked him by putting his own thought into words.

'I'm not bearing his child,' she said bleakly. 'I just don't want to see him, that's all. Mother will have to know I'm leaving, but there'll be less fuss at home if I can say I've got another job to go to.'

'Well, you could ask the minister – no, better still ask the vicar; they're richer folk who go to St Fimbarrus

174

– more likely to be able to afford a nursemaid. Best of all, go and see Dr Bossiney.'

'And tell *him* I'm trying to avoid his nephew?'

'Reckon you could tell him anything – he's powerfully good at understanding,' Charlie said stubbornly. 'Any case, *he* sent you there, so he's just the chap to get you away again.'

Loveday was by no means sure that she agreed with her brother's reasoning, but it was certainly true that the doctor knew more about Fowey than anyone else. She kissed Charlie goodbye, assured him that he'd been a great help to her, and rowed herself back across the river.

It didn't occur to her that his greatest help was still to come, and that the next time she set out to walk from Prospect to Fore Street, Daniel would catch her up fifty yards along the Esplanade.

'It's too fine an afternoon for Aunt Hannah's parlour,' he said lightly. 'I've got to go up to Lerryn – why not come with me?'

Loveday hesitated, but couldn't help agreeing with him; even if Lerryn hadn't been lovely, anything would be better that having to sit in the cottage pretending to her mother that life went on just as usual.

'All right, but I'm expected at home,' she pointed out. 'I'd have to just stop and say I'm going with you.'

Hannah looked surprised at the sight of them together, but raised no objection. Five minutes later, jacket and tie removed, Daniel was rowing upstream through slack water that shone like silver in the afternoon sunlight.

Loveday trailed her hand in the river, apparently not conscious of the man who sat facing her. She was trying not to be conscious of anything at all. For as long as she could stay in this little boat, feeling the heat of the sun on her face and the coolness of the water slipping through her fingers, time past and future didn't exist. There was nothing to regret, and nothing to fear.

But even without looking at him, she couldn't quite blot Daniel out of her mind's eye – she supposed there was altogether too much of him for that. His sunburned arms and thick, dark hair cut very short to keep it from curling, and the shuttered expression that hid his feelings from the world – she could visualize these things clearly, and be thankful that they made him an entirely different man from Tristram. He rowed without attempting to talk as well, and she told herself there was no reason for her sudden feeling of nervousness – his mind wasn't on her at all. She held up her hand to watch the water-drops fall off it in prisms of coloured light and a moment later the boat bumped gently against the jetty at Lerryn. She jumped out on to the steps and caught the rope he threw her. An old man sat there hoping for someone to talk to, and she smiled warmly at him.

'I'll wait here till you're ready to go back,' she said to Daniel.

'Why? I've nothing to do except take a walk with you. Which direction do you fancy?'

His faint smile confirmed that there was no business deal to be struck, no derelict premises to be inspected – a walk *was* all he'd come for. A faint tingle of alarm ran along her nerves, but she managed to answer composedly.

'St Winnow's then – it's lovely there.'

'All right, show me.'

They walked in silence until the little church and grave-yard were in front of them, lying by the water's edge. 'It's old and beautiful,' Loveday said suddenly, 'and it always reminds me of a line in a poem I once read – about a place where "peace comes dropping slow". Seems to me that's what it does here.'

Daniel didn't reply, but followed her without protest into the church – blessedly cool after the heat outside, and dim except for an unexpected blaze of light through beautiful old stained-glass.

'Father used to bring me here to look at these windows,' she explained. 'He said they outlasted the destruction of the Civil War only by the hand of God Himself, who'd made sure that something so glorious was left intact.'

Daniel's dark eyebrow sketched a query. 'I thought staunch chapel men like William were supposed to disapprove of such things – far too extravagantly Papist and sinful!'

Loveday's serious expression relaxed into a smile. 'Well, he wasn't ready to disapprove of St Winnow's.' She watched Daniel inspect a memorial plate inscribed with the names of two men killed in Victoria's Zulu wars – one of them having earned her highest medal. 'Does that make you homesick for South Africa?' she asked gently.

'No, it only reminds me of the bloody futility of most wars.'

Outside again, he chose a convenient gravestone, spread his handkerchief on it for Loveday, and invited her to sit down. 'I can see why you like this place. It ought to be where all good Penwarnes come when they die, instead of that miserable chapel graveyard.'

A motor engine disturbed the peace around them and he waited for it to fade as it left them behind. 'Charlie said you've got it in mind to leave Prospect soon.'

Without making a question of it, he seemed to be waiting to be told the reason, but she wasn't ready with a convincing lie.

'It's . . . it's not that I *want* to leave Morwetha and Petroc, but—'

'—you don't want to get too fond of them; I know – you told me *that* before.'

'There's nothing else to tell,' she said more firmly. 'It's time to leave, that's all.'

'And you've got another job to go to. You'd better tell me what it is – I'm a very good judge of whether Aunt Hannah will approve or not.'

He *knew*, she was almost sure of it, that the job remained to be found; she was painfully aware of being outmatched in this sort of game, but she didn't know how to be devious and in the end could only answer with the truth.

'There *isn't* another job yet, and no-one knows I'm

going, except Charlie and now you. I don't know why he had to tell *you*,' she added with a spurt of resentment that made him smile.

'Well, it's all in the family . . . I expect he thought I'd be interested!'

She bit her lip, confused by him in this mood and only certain that he wasn't as harmless as he sounded. 'We ought to be getting back – the tide will be on the turn by now and you'll have to row against it.'

'I dare say I can manage that when I have to, but I've something to finish here first.' He propped himself against the gravestone beside hers, folded his arms, and watched her carefully.

'Do you remember how it was years ago, when I first came to Fowey? William said you were too young to marry, but we all seemed to be agreed – you included – that we *would* marry when the time came.' Again he seemed to be waiting for her to say something, and she had to murmur, 'Yes, I remember.'

'And you probably haven't forgotten that I got impatient and frightened you off the idea.' He waited again, and this time she merely shook her head, with colour flooding her cheeks.

'After that you hid yourself at Prospect in the home of your handsome Castle Dore rescuer. Tristram Bossiney must have seemed all the things that I *wasn't*. Still am not, if it comes to that, and won't ever be. You have to be clear about that, Loveday, because I can't change, even for you.'

She found the courage to stare at him and discovered that his face was serious, and almost gentle.

'Why do I need to be clear about it?' she asked in a low voice.

'Because I'm hoping you'll wake up from your pretty little dream about Bossiney in time to marry me. But it has to be soon because I'm going to London.'

'It wasn't just *my* dream.' The words were wrung out of her because pride insisted on the truth. 'No-one else

178

knew, but we were waiting till Tristram could afford a wife. Only . . . it was a *Cornish* dream, you see; I think he woke up from it once he went away.'

'Yes – I see,' Daniel agreed after a while. He stepped towards her and crouched down so that they were face to face. 'Listen, Loveday: if you can forget Bossiney and bear to have *me* touch you instead, leave Prospect and come with me. I'd have to take you away from Cornwall now, but it needn't be for ever; I'd look after you with all my strength; I'd make some mistakes, I dare say, but I wouldn't let anyone *else* hurt you. Do you think that might do instead of the Cornish dream?'

She had no idea whether it would do or not, though in its own way it sounded a great deal. If he'd talked a lot about love, and said she must love him back, she'd have had to say no; but he hadn't asked her to. With Tristram lost to her, what else was there to do but find other families with children to be looked after, down through all the empty years ahead? She'd dreamed of children of her own, and some kind of home that she could make beautiful. They were what she was being offered now, but it would mean taking Daniel as well; she trembled inside at the thought of him as a husband.

'I'll need to think about it,' she said at last.

'All right; I'll give you till next week. Thinking too long never helps, and in any case I have to be in London by the beginning of September – none too much time to get things arranged with "Passon" if we need a wedding ceremony!'

He took hold of her hands to pull her towards him, and the next moment she felt his lips on her own, gentle but firm, and in no hurry to end a kiss that she didn't find frightening. She had no idea of the iron self-control that prevented him from making love to her there in the peaceful, empty graveyard. He'd waited a long time for her – but he could still wait a little longer, especially if it meant winning over Tristram Bossiney in the end.

His hands cupped her face, forcing her to look at him.

'I think we'd do quite nicely together, Loveday,' he said, half-smiling at her. 'But if I'm not to prove it to you here and now, I'd better take you home.'

She was pulled to her feet, aware of feeling vaguely let down. It hadn't been necessary, after all, to steel herself to accept without fuss the lovemaking that hadn't come. It was true she had to remind him to pick up his handkerchief that she'd been sitting on, but she didn't notice that his hand was trembling.

The row back to Town Quay against a flowing tide was hard work, but Loveday pretended to stare at the birds along the riverbank. Daniel watched her face, wondering whether for the first time in his life he was over-reaching himself. She still fancied she was in love with Bossiney, and he had reason to fear the strength of her fancies.

He refused Hannah's offer of tea more brusquely than he meant to, and went away. She looked at her daughter's preoccupied expression, and regretfully abandoned the little glimmer of hope she'd been blowing on all the afternoon.

Tristram came home a little later than planned, having waited in Paris in the hope that Kurt might arrive and they could travel to England together. But the illness of his father, that had delayed Kurt in the first place, ended in Professor Winkler's death. Kurt's English holiday had to be cancelled, and Tristram came back alone. For the first time that he could remember, he didn't want to arrive at Prospect. Replies to Loveday's letter had been written but not sent. Better, he decided in the end, not to write at all, but wait and at least persuade her that it would be the height of foolishness to leave Prospect when there was absolutely no need. No-one had known of their engagement; no-one would have to know that it was at an end. Thought about calmly in Paris, the interview had seemed sane and feasible; with every spin of the locomotive's wheels now it became more impossible to visualize.

At Fowey nothing seemed to have changed in the year

he'd been away. Alfie at the station reported that a proper cantankerous old summer it had been; mebbe Paris had been better; and, yes, the lad could bring the luggage to Prospect on the station handcart. Tristram was free to walk home through a rain-soaked town that seemed ridiculously small and confined after the city he was used to. The shower had ceased by the time he let himself in through the postern-gate, and soft September sunlight lay over the garden. He could see his mother waving from the terrace above him and he raced up the steps, suddenly swept by a wave of longing for all the things he'd thought he could do without.

'Dearest, how *lovely* to see you,' Lavinia said when she emerged from a fierce hug. 'Such a long time it's been.' Her face was lit by the transfiguring smile he remembered, and he could see no change in her. It wasn't her opinion of *him* – his face looked older, and more disinclined than before to show what he was feeling; but she supposed that it was one of the things they taught young diplomats.

'You'll have to make do with me for the moment,' she told him. 'Your father is attending a town council meeting, for *once* reluctantly, but he'll be here soon. I'm afraid you won't see Jenifer and the children until tomorrow. They were committed to attending a birthday party at Lanhydrock and staying overnight.'

Tristram smiled, made suddenly cheerful by the reprieve – no children, no Loveday to face. 'I think I can wait until tomorrow! In any case they'll have forgotten me.'

'Morwetha hasn't. She's been very fractious recently, but we're hoping that you'll make a sufficient distraction!'

'Distraction from what?'

'From losing Loveday Penwarne, of course,' Lavinia said, surprised that he should need telling. 'You must surely remember that Morwetha regarded Loveday as belonging exclusively to *her*. She took it very unkindly when the time came to say goodbye.'

Tristram shaped words even though his lips felt stiff,

but no sound came and he had to try again. 'You mean she's . . . she's left? So suddenly?' His mother nodded. 'You might have written and told me,' he muttered.

'Loveday asked me not to. She didn't say why, and I couldn't see that I had the right to enquire.' Hadn't wanted to enquire, Lavinia knew she should have said; but Tristram didn't challenge her – he was struggling to identify the turmoil raging inside him. Relief was there, and anger with Loveday, and beneath all that the throbbing ache of grief. He knew why she hadn't wanted him to know; he hadn't bothered to answer her letter, and didn't care about her.

'I'll have to call in Fore Street,' he said at last, 'just to . . . to wish her well.'

'She isn't there. Her marriage to Daniel Penwarne took place a fortnight ago – they've gone to live in London.'

'Why didn't you *stop* her, for God's sake,' Tristram shouted. 'She belongs *here* . . . Couldn't you *see* that? You *did* see it – told me she'd never survive away from Cornwall. That's why I knew in the end it would be terribly wrong for *me* to marry her.'

Lavinia's heart ached for his unhappiness but she couldn't help thinking that Hannah Penwarne's daughter had behaved with more courage and commonsense than her son was showing.

'Loveday was employed here,' she said coolly. 'If I'd known that she was more than that, I might have felt justified in interfering, but you hadn't seen fit to confide in us. As it was, she seemed very certain of what she was doing, and even content with the prospect of going to London. Nor is there any doubt that the man she married will make her an excellent husband.'

The flush of colour had faded from Tristram's face, leaving it ashen pale. He had himself under control again and spoke quietly. 'You're right to blame me for making a mess of things, but wrong about everything else. Loveday will *hate* London, and Daniel Penwarne is the last man on earth to make her happy.' He bent down suddenly to kiss Lavinia's cheek. 'Sorry I shouted. Now I'll take a little walk till Father gets home.'

He managed a faint smile, and went on through the garden, and let himself out on to the hill path leading to the once-familiar headland. He stayed there a long time, slowly coming to terms with things, accepting the price to be paid for the life he'd chosen. He'd lost the place where Loveday would say he did belong to be; never mind, with a little more time and experience, he was going to become a true citizen of the world, instead of a dyed-in-the-wool Cornishman. Much, much worse, he'd lost *her* for ever; but his shy, unsophisticated dreamer of dreams and believer in legends wasn't the stuff that citizens of the world were made of. If he clung to *that* firmly enough, he could bear the thought of her beauty and sweetness being possessed by Daniel Penwarne. He would write to her at last when he got home – offer his sincere good wishes for her future happiness, and do his damnedest after that never to think of her or Daniel Penwarne again.

By the time he finally walked back to Prospect, his father was at home. He smiled cheerfully at Lavinia to show that his little attack of anguish was over; now there was nothing to do but enjoy his leave, and keep them entertained with a spirited account of the strains and diversions of diplomatic life.

The calm façade was only threatened for a moment when Jenifer returned with the children and the new nursemaid the following day. Morwetha stared at him uncertainly for a moment, recognized him, and ran into his arms when he stooped to catch her.

'Uncle Trissam . . . my Lowdy's gone away.' Sobs began to shake her small body, but for once they were caused by grief, not rage, because when he lifted her up her huge dark eyes were drenched with tears. 'Ask her to come back for me . . . *you* ask Lowdy, please.'

He held her tight, until he was sure that he could trust himself to speak.

'Sweetheart, I'd give her back to you if I could, but I

can't. If *you* weep about it, though, I shall want to weep too, and gentlemen aren't supposed to go round bathed in tears!'

She stared at him, only half-understanding what he said but fully aware of some sadness in him that matched her own. Her sobs dwindled to a hiccup or two and he was allowed to mop her wet cheeks with his handkerchief.

'I expect you've got a nice new friend to look after you,' he said gently. 'You'll soon love her as well.'

Morwetha shook her head. 'She doesn't know Merlin's stories and . . . and she can't draw *nuffin*.'

Tristram conceded defeat in the matter of the new nursemaid. 'Never mind. Come and see what I've brought you home from Paris.'

He didn't mention the name of Loveday to her again, and nor did Morwetha mention it to him. It seemed to be a precious secret they shared.

Lavinia was equally careful, and inclined to think as the days of Tristram's holiday went by that it wouldn't be long before they could all forget Loveday's impact on the family. By the time he was back in Paris, immersed in the work and the social life of the embassy, her image would be fast fading from his mind.

Six months later she knew she'd been right. He returned to England the following Easter to be married to Cécile Sabatier at the Brompton Oratory in London. Their wedding reception afterwards at the Belgian Embassy in Belgrave Square was attended by the cream of the *corps diplomatique* and of London society. Julian Bossiney smiled proudly on a daughter-in-law whose poise, charm, and family connections amply outweighed her handicap of belonging to the Church of Rome. Lavinia watched Tristram's smiling face and prayed that he would be happy.

His best man, arrived from Berlin for the occasion, spent no longer talking to Jenifer O'Meara than courtesy demanded, and much longer apparently enjoying a conversation with Charlotte Haddenham. But it was a merciful relief to find himself at last standing beside someone he knew, who seemed content merely to observe the people all around them.

'Have you ever visited the London Zoo?' Jonathan Bossiney enquired. 'If not, I can tell you that there's a remarkable resemblance between the inmates of the parrot house and the guests at a fashionable wedding!'

'And the higher the fashion, the stronger the resemblance, I suppose, in terms of extravagant plumage and meaningless noise,' Kurt observed.

'Exactly!' Jonathan cast a quick glance at his friend's face. 'You don't feel inclined to follow my nephew into matrimony?'

Kurt's eyes rested for a moment on a slender, auburn-haired girl talking in a quiet corner of the room with Julia Haddenham.

'I might feel *inclined* to do all sorts of things, *Herr Doktor*, but we are supposed to be rational, thinking creatures, *nicht wahr*? We have not to listen to what the heart whispers.'

Jonathan smiled a little sadly. 'More's the pity, dear boy. As a clever student of human nature, can you tell me why we always learn too late that it's the only thing worth listening to?'

13

Loveday's first child was born four years after she arrived in London with Daniel. It seemed a long time to wait for something that would justify what she had done. She measured the years by *this* anxious expectancy, not by the crawling passage of time since she'd been where she belonged. When Daniel went to Cornwall to check up on his businesses she never went with him. For as long as she didn't cross the Tamar or hear the soft West Country speech that seemed to belong to a different language from the one she heard every day, she could manage very well. If she didn't remember Fowey at all she could accept the dingy, uniform streets of Hounslow, mournful under winter rain or erupting into little bubbles of hot tar in summertime. If she never thought of the quiet, secret places of the river and the empty sea stretching to the horizon, she could make do with the strips of London sky glimpsed between endless rows of houses.

Loveday had prayed for the son Daniel wanted, but when the longed-for child came at last it was a girl, born reluctantly after a long and difficult labour. Still, he managed to look pleased when he came to visit her, and smiled at the black-haired scrap held up for his inspection. She came closest to loving him *then*, when he stood looking at his daughter.

'I thought of a name for her on the way here – two names, in fact. If she grows up hating one of them, maybe she'll fancy the other one better.'

Loveday's tired face broke into a smile because it sounded so exactly like him. The principle of what he called ahead-thinking governed his life. It didn't protect him from *every* accident that Fate unfairly used to trip a man up, but it brought much more success than failure. Without knowing the ins and outs of his business ventures, she knew that they were increasingly successful.

'You haven't said what the names are,' she reminded him.

'Polly, for *us*, and Jane for your granny at Polruan, mostly to spike Tom Eliot's guns! Miss Polly Jane Penwarne – nothing too fancy, but I think it has a firm, friendly sound to it.'

Loveday thought the name-choosing was typical of him too; he'd made up his mind on the way to the hospital, and any more discussion would be a waste of time.

'All right,' she agreed, 'firm and friendly let her be!'

Daniel bent down to kiss his wife's cheek. It was cool and petal-soft, and smelled of the faint flower scent she always used. Desire stirred in him, as it always did whenever he was near her – not so much because she was beautiful, but simply because she still eluded him. She was the only aching failure of his life, and in rare moments of despair he glimpsed the certainty that he would never possess her completely. Even when his body demanded and got total surrender, the victory was empty; her spirit wandered in some region from which he was always excluded. His only pride was in hiding from her the fact that he knew.

'The starched harridan outside says you must stay here for another week,' he muttered. 'Polly's all right, but you've got to rest.'

Although there was no criticism in his voice, Loveday felt obliged to apologize. 'I'm sorry, Daniel. It sounds silly, and I'm sure I could come home sooner. Other women have babies without needing a rest afterwards.'

'Some of them don't have any choice. In any case, it works out very well to have you being looked after here. I'm going to be very busy for the next week.'

She knew what it meant, and accepted without any more argument the gift of seven whole days and nights shared only with her precious daughter. He was certain to be getting some new venture started, and the pattern was becoming familiar to her now. Eighteen hours out of every twenty-four would be devoted to it, and he would have no time for a wife who needed help or attention. Each new enterprise removed them further from the struggling days of their first arrival in London. Daniel's inheritance from George Penwarne had bought his first garage on the Great West Road leading out of London to Bath, and another on the A30 taking motorists to the West Country. Ahead-thinking showed him where the best opportunities were; after that, hard work and single-minded concentration on the task in hand did the rest. Loveday understood by now that it wasn't money for its own sake that attracted him – only what it represented in possibilities *he'd* realized that other men had missed.

When visiting time was over and he'd gone away she allowed herself to think about the week ahead. It shone in her mind, as golden and empty as the days of her childhood. Every moment of the past five years had been coloured by the presence, real or felt, of Daniel. His personality filled the small rooms of their rented house even when he wasn't there; only in the little back garden, that held no interest for him, could she become Loveday Penwarne again, instead of Daniel's wife. She refused to remember the gardens at Prospect, but in her own little patch dug and planted what she could, unaware that she shared the need that Lavinia Bossiney had felt, to create something beautiful out of error and loss.

When the week was up and Daniel came to take her home she sensed in him more excitement than he could quite contain.

'The new venture, whatever it is, is going well,' she said smiling at him. 'I can read the signs by now.' She also knew that he drove hard bargains. If he had won, someone else had probably lost – it was one of the reasons why she didn't want to be told about his business affairs.

'I think it's going *very* well,' he agreed, 'but I shan't know for certain for a little while.'

The route he was taking from the hospital was unfamiliar to her, but she didn't query it; he knew London by now, far better than she did. Only when he stopped outside a strange house in a strange street did she ask what they were doing there.

'If we're visiting someone, Daniel, we can't stay long. Polly will need feeding soon.'

'You can feed her whenever you like,' he said, and strode up the path to the front door.

Loveday followed with the baby, struggling not to feel angry. He was always high-handed, but she'd grown used to accepting that *he* chose the pattern of their married life. It hadn't mattered until now, when there was Polly to be considered as well. Still without understanding, she saw him unlock the front door instead of knocking; but the sight of furniture, *their* furniture, piled up in the sitting room, suddenly told her that this was where she was now expected to live. For the first time in her life, rage exploded inside her, running through her body like a flame.

'You didn't think to mention that we were moving?' Her trembling voice took him unawares, signalling a situation unknown so far. It was unexpected, but not worrying; his gentle, compliant wife wasn't recovered from the unsettling business of childbirth.

'It was meant to be a surprise,' he said calmly. 'How could it be that if I mentioned it?'

To Loveday it seemed the last straw that he should stand there half-amused, half-disinclined to take her seriously.

'I'm not a child to be given surprises, Daniel,' she shouted. 'I'm a woman grown, and we're supposed to talk things round *together*. If I don't like this house *you've* chosen, I shan't live in it.' She didn't stop to consider what alternative she had – the carefully buried pain of years refused to be ignored a moment longer. It couldn't be told even now, but anger was a safety valve releasing some of the anguish inside her.

Daniel stared at her flushed face, torn by a muddle of emotions of his own. Brought to life by rage, she seemed more vividly beautiful than ever, and more achingly desirable. He wanted her there and then, would have pushed her to the floor and taken her, but for the child in her arms. Frustrated longing made his own voice rough.

'You'll live where I live. You're my wife, remember?'

Loveday's mouth sketched a faint, bitter smile. 'I hadn't forgotten – you make sure that I don't.'

It was like a goad to a maddened bull. With a huge effort of self-control he still didn't touch her, but he made sure of reaching her in another way. 'I'm *entitled* to remind you that you belong to me, now and always. Whatever dreams and fantasies you indulge in when I'm inside you, it's *me* there, my dear, not Tristram Bossiney.'

The taunt drove the colour from her face but she was suddenly too sickened by what was happening to answer. It didn't need a small protesting sound from the child in her arms to remind her that she and Daniel were solely responsible for a helpless human being. She might feel like weeping, for his grief as well as her own, but Polly didn't know or care about the snare her parents were caught in – she simply demanded to be fed.

Loveday looked around the jumbled furniture, found an empty chair, and sat down to unbutton the bodice of her dress. The baby's contented sucking noises made a strange echo to the tension that lingered in the room. Loveday clung to the knowledge that her daughter was real. The bitterness and hurt that had torn at them a few moments ago would have to be made to seem unreal if life was ever to be bearable again.

'Where can Polly sleep afterwards?' she asked, not looking at Daniel.

'Her cot is ready upstairs.' He walked to the window and stood staring out at the neglected back garden. 'This is Barnes, by the way. You can't quite see it from here, but the Thames is very close by. I had the stupid idea that you might like to be near a river again.'

Something in his voice made her look at him. More than ever she wanted to weep, but the tears might never stop if they once began to well out of the sadness in her heart.

Daniel misunderstood her silence, and sounded harsh when he spoke again.

'It's time to come to terms with life – you've done nothing but run away from it since the day I married you. The things you can't have – Fowey, your family, the Bossineys – don't cease to exist just because you pretend they do. Come with me to Cornwall sometime and find out.'

'I *can't*, Daniel . . . truly, I can't.' It was a cry of pain that reached him even through his own unhappiness.

'Then let your family come here . . . Be normal about it, for God's sake. The other house wasn't big enough, but this one is.'

'Is *that* why we're here? You should have said so. I imagined it was because we'd got too successful for Hounslow, and neighbours who keep racing pigeons and eat cockles for tea on Sundays!'

The gentle irony, more effective in its way than her anger had been, was another reminder of a change in her that couldn't be mastered by brute strength. Perhaps she'd been changing for a long time and he'd been too busy to notice. He spoke as quietly now as she had done, so as not to disturb Polly.

'We moved for several good reasons, one of them being that we can afford something better than Hounslow now. I hope we shall be worth something better still before I've done. But I didn't buy a house in Castlenau just to prove that I could – I hoped you might miss Cornwall a little less, being here.'

Her eyes examined his face, and saw no mockery there. 'Then I'm sorry I didn't seem more grateful, Daniel,' she said gravely. 'Please don't uproot us again as a surprise, because there's Polly to consider now, as well as me, but I dare say we shall grow to like living in Barnes.'

A sudden gleam of humour lit his face, making him look his true age again – for a moment she'd reminded him of Hannah Penwarne, putting a saucy schoolboy firmly in his place. Instead of saying so, he picked up the suitcase he'd left on the floor and moved towards the door.

'When you've finished with Polly, you can tell me where you want all this furniture to go – I knew that whatever I did with it would be wrong.'

Loveday nodded, because what he said was true. He was a brilliant mechanic, and a clever businessman; he also rowed a four-oared boat to win, but she hadn't yet discovered what else he could do. When he'd left the room she calmly transferred Polly to the other breast, but she was still shaking inside from the closeness of their brush with disaster. It lay in wait for them, like a pit of still, black water beneath a fragile cover. For Polly's sake they must never risk shattering the cover again. She smiled at her sleepy daughter and then deliberately chained her mind to an easier problem. The room in which she sat seemed twice the size of her previous sitting room, and presumably the rest of the house had the same space and dignity. Much better still, where Daniel had been standing, she could see a windowful of hazy sky, instead of the drainpipe-festooned backs of another row of houses. She was ready to admit that, to the very marrow of her soul, she'd hated Hounslow.

In time the house they now owned and the garden she slowly reclaimed from a wilderness of ground-elder and willow-herb provided, with Polly, more contentment than she had ever expected to find outside the place where she belonged. She secretly prayed that Daniel would lose the restiveness that drove him on – it seemed kinder than asking heaven for his enterprises not to prosper. But a year after their move to Castlenau a calamity three thousand miles away began to affect their lives. The Wall Street crash in America sent its shock waves through the rest of the world, and an ever-deepening depression left behind a trail of havoc – mounting unemployment, hardship and despair. Daniel clung on grimly to what he'd achieved so far, but for the moment there was no more talk of ambitious schemes to put the name of Penwarne into every town between London and the West Country. Barnes looked to be where they'd stay for good, after all.

In the summer of 1933 Tristram thankfully boarded the night train for Paris and heaved a sigh of relief as the express slowly pulled out of Rome station. In thirty-six hours, barring hold-ups along the way, he'd be sitting on the terrace at Prospect with a damp westerly breeze blowing in his face, and the greenness of Lavinia's garden and the silver coolness of the river to rest his eyes on. It seemed an eternity since he'd last been there, with nothing more to worry about than the four-year-old twins' determined uproar whenever it was time to evict them from the paradise of Prospect Cove. That had been two years ago. He hadn't been back since, and he hadn't seen either his children or his wife for the past two months. He didn't blame Cécile for wanting to escape from Rome – the heat had been unbearable, and the twins had grown fractious and unwell. But he'd missed them very much, and he was sick at heart for other reasons.

It was raining when the boat-train steamed into Victoria Station – soft English rain that brought the smell of wet grass through the open window of his cab when it skirted St James's Park. Julia and Richard Haddenham were away, but Charlotte welcomed him to the house in Green Street for the night. A servant led him to a room he recognized; it was the one he'd been given when he first came to London, and for a moment the past took him by the throat.

When he went downstairs again Charlotte was waiting for him in the drawing room. He had to guess her age – thirty-five, perhaps, now; all those years lived in the shadow of her forceful mother. He thought she'd deserved something better.

'Poor Tristram, how tired you look,' she said gently. 'Has it all been very tiresome in Rome?'

The adjective, so typical of her, made him smile because it was inadequate and apt at the same time.

'Yes, rather tiresome, and very hot, and extremely lonely without Cécile and the twins. To think I once found the embassy's social round exciting!'

Charlotte put sherry in front of him, wondering whether loneliness or fatigue accounted for all the strain she sensed in him. 'I expect you know my father sits in the Lords now. He comes home disgusted with some of his fellow peers of the realm – dotty, elderly fools, he calls them – who persuade themselves that Fascism is the salvation of Italy. Is that how it strikes you in Rome?'

Tristram frowned at the golden wine in his glass. 'Scarcely, although it's still the official view we're supposed to take of the régime. In some superficial ways I suppose the country *is* more efficiently run; but in all the ways that really matter, the outlook seems lamentable to me.'

The charming smile that Charlotte remembered suddenly chased weariness from his face. 'When I got into the train last night and saw myself reflected in the window I laughed out loud because I looked so bloody miserable! My fellow-traveller obviously feared that I was mad, but I was remembering two absurdly idealistic young men who prided themselves on being true cosmopolitans. Ten years on I'm so sickened by what's happening that I shall soon be thanking God as fervently as my father does for the Channel that keeps England separate from Europe!'

'It didn't keep us separate enough to avoid the Great War,' Charlotte pointed out thoughtfully. 'Has the other young man's view changed as well?'

'I suspect so. Kurt must know better than I do what a nightmare present-day Germany is. It's been caught more viciously than the rest of us in the undertow of the Depression, and it's a breeding-ground for any ideology that offers a way out of chaos.'

'Is Kurt well in himself . . . happy?'

'I don't know about his happiness,' Tristram answered, 'but he's certainly doing well professionally – *Herr Doktor* Winkler now, and he'll be a Professor in another year or two.'

He put aside memories of the past and smiled at his cousin. 'I hope you'll be coming down to Prospect while I'm there.'

'Well, I went recently so probably *not*, I think; it was Petroc's tenth birthday. No doubt all godmothers are biased, but he seems an especially nice child to me. Morwetha is inclined to possessiveness – it's *her* home, *her* cove, *her* sea, which she'll share with the twins if she's feeling generous. Petroc takes the trouble to play with them, and curbs his sister when she gets too bossy.'

'How was Cécile?' Tristram asked casually.

'Looking just a *little* bored, I thought – missing you, of course.'

'And not in the least interested in Father's butterflies or Mother's garden!'

'She did seem to find *something* lacking in the evening conversation,' Charlotte acknowledged with a twinkle. 'Try as we would we couldn't discuss the dream theories of Dr Freud or the Cubist school of painting!'

She was glad to see Tristram grin, and hoped that, having done sufficient justice to the subject of his wife, she could now talk of something else.

'Speaking of modern art, I stumbled on a strange co-incidence the other day. I was in a part of London I scarcely ever go to and found myself passing the window of a shop selling the usual jumble of old furniture and rather bad paintings. But one of them, a watercolour of an old stone house sitting on a bluff above a river, caught my eye because it reminded me of Prospect.'

'Is that the end of the coincidence?'

'Not quite. I couldn't read the signature so I went in and asked the owner of the shop. He said that a lady called Mrs Penwarne had brought it in and asked if he could sell it. I remembered, of course, that Loveday moved to London with Daniel Penwarne, but I never knew that she could paint – rather exceptionally well if this picture is anything to go by.'

'You . . . you didn't buy it, I suppose?' Tristram asked in a voice that sounded unlike his own.

'Yes, I did. It's hanging upstairs in my bedroom.' Charlotte left the room and returned a moment later with a small framed picture that she put in front of him. It was a delicate, tranquil thing, in shades of grey and silver – Prospect for sure, against a Cornish sky, with the river quiet on a still day in winter.

'The man said he'd had others – some of them the same subject seen at different seasons of the year. They'd all sold quite easily, apparently.'

'Did he say where Mrs Penwarne was?'

Charlotte shook his head. 'I don't think he knew; she just calls in occasionally.' Tristram still stared at the painting, unaware of yearning in his face that his cousin found too painful to watch.

'Take it if you'd like to,' she said impulsively. 'If it *is* Prospect you have a better right to it.'

Tristram got up with the painting clasped in his arms and kissed her cheek. 'Dear Lottie . . . in case I've forgotten to mention it before, you're almost the nicest woman I know.'

She smiled and looked almost beautiful. 'My godson was kind enough to say that too. At the time it seemed such a tribute that I nearly wept, but I shall soon be getting used to it at this rate!'

Cécile was waiting for him at the station. He hadn't seen her for two months, and he was struck as if for the first time by her unique sense of style. In Paris or Rome she held her own among more sheerly beautiful women – here, in dark-blue linen slacks, striped cotton sweater, and a bandeau round her shining hair, it was inevitable that everyone should stare at her.

He kissed her on both cheeks, and smiled for the happiness of seeing her there. She was his charming wife, the mother of his children – what more did a man need than that?

'Dearest, let's go home at once – you're causing havoc here! Even the poor engine driver is too bemused to remember that he hasn't yet finished his journey!'

Cécile accepted the embrace and the compliment calmly, and led the way outside.

'Uncle Jonathan's got a new model, so I've been allowed to borrow Rosinante – not the most dashing thing in motor-cars, but it's better than nothing.'

'*She*, not it. Rosinante is a lady; slightly middle-aged, and therefore all the more susceptible to having her feelings hurt!'

Cécile smiled perfunctorily, having no taste for the whimsical English humour she sometimes detected in her husband, but more often missed noticing altogether.

'You didn't bring the twins?' he said with a slight note of disappointment. 'They would have enjoyed the ride.'

'But I should not have done. In any case they're perfectly happy where they are.' She didn't invite Tristram to drive; knowing herself to be a competent motorist when few other women were motorists of any kind was something she enjoyed. But she waited until they were clear of Lostwithiel and on the road back to Fowey before she launched a topic which she knew would upset him.

'The children are *so* happy here that I think we should leave them at Prospect when we go back to Rome.'

In general, when Cécile began a suggestion with the words 'I think that we should' he accepted it in the knowledge that she was usually right and that in any case, right or wrong, her mind was made up. This time, with the twins at stake, he couldn't give in without a fight.

'Pull in to the side of the road,' he said with sudden, rare anger. 'We can't possibly talk like this.'

She was tempted to ignore what he said, but the subject must be thrashed out, and perhaps better here than at Prospect.

'Very well, my dear Tristram – we are stopped, as you insist; and I have said what I think would be best. What would *you* like to say?'

'That I think it's a perfectly appalling idea, and I won't agree to it for a moment.'

Her hands tightened on the steering wheel. The refusal was blunter than she'd expected. She didn't try to interfere, as some diplomats' wives did, in matters that didn't concern her; but *their* life she believed that she *did* have the right to order, because she could arrange it better than he could.

'For whom don't you agree?' she enquired coldly after a moment or two. 'The children, your parents, or perhaps yourself?'

'All of us,' he said with feeling. 'My parents have had to accept Jenifer's children but there's no reason on earth why they should be saddled with ours as well. In any case, the twins belong with us, and *they* know it even if you don't.'

Cécile swallowed the angry riposte that would only make him more stubborn. 'Boxing clever' was an English expression someone had once explained to her. She'd remembered it ever since; discovered, in fact, that she was rather good at it. Now abandoning the steering wheel, her hands sketched a little gesture of pleading to accompany a reproachful sigh.

'*Mon cher*, if *you* won't consider what is best for the children, I *must*, *n'est-ce pas*? Rome in summer is unsuitable enough, but your next posting could be a good deal worse. Before long they must start school – let it be here where they already feel at home. Otherwise soon we move them from whatever they begin in Rome, we move them again later on, and then yet again. What sort of a life is that?'

It was the argument he should have expected her to use. No colleague that he knew had avoided separation from his children, except at the cost of remaining in a menial job in London. What sort of life was *that* for a career diplomat?

'Well, they don't have to go to school just yet; they can come back with us and share a governess for a bit.' It was the beginning of retreat, he knew; already he could taste the bitterness of defeat in his mouth.

Cécile smiled at him forgivingly. 'We must try not to be selfish, my dear. In Rome they are bored and naughty; here they are perfectly happy, and only a *little* spoiled! On the whole your mother is quite sensible with them.'

Tristram bowed ironically. 'I must tell her that you're pleased, but it may not be enough to persuade her that she wants more grandchildren here permanently.'

Cécile had an answer even for this. 'She will get pleasure from doing anything that helps *you*. But *we* also can do something to help. Your father talks freely to me, Tristram, and he is anxious about the future. If Luc and Lisette are here, *we* can take on the burden of a new governess and the existing nursery staff – it is not help he will accept otherwise.'

She was right about that too; he was miserably aware that she was right altogether.

'Well, I suppose it must be discussed with my parents,' he muttered finally, and was rewarded with a look of such melting tenderness that he felt worst of all for having misjudged her; she would miss the children as much as he did if they decided to leave them behind.

From then on, certain of getting her own way, she was at her excellent best – charmingly affectionate to all his family, a devoted mother to the twins, and a willing partner at night who seemed determined to make him forget their occasional, lacklustre lovemaking in Rome. She even joined in the unexciting social life of Fowey and transformed *that* by some special alchemy of her own.

They went one evening with Jenifer to dine at Fowey Hall, and the Hansons were clearly charmed by a guest so sophisticated and delightful. For Tristram the evening didn't recover from the discovery of another guest who happened to be visiting Fowey from London. He had no wish to meet Daniel Penwarne anywhere, much less at a shared dinner table.

'You've got very snobbish,' Jenifer said under her breath. 'Stop glowering at the poor man just because you think he has no right to own a dinner jacket and a black tie.'

'Don't worry . . . I shall smile and smile and smile.'

He did, with some success, and Daniel smiled back until, expecting to give pleasure, Cécile referred to the picture she had come across when she unpacked Tristram's luggage.

'Do you have an artist in the family, Mr Penwarne? I'm sure I deciphered that name on a painting my husband brought down from London. The subject seemed familiar too.'

An expression she couldn't pin down flickered across Daniel's harsh features and was gone. 'My wife, I expect; she dabbles in watercolours – I believe that's the right expression!'

'But not quite adequate in her case,' Tristram said stiffly. 'The painting is beautiful.' Conventional behaviour insisted that he be courteous when with every fibre in his body he wanted to wipe the smile off Penwarne's face.

'Strange that you of all people should find one of Loveday's little efforts,' Daniel observed.

'My cousin found it, but gave it to me. She guessed, rightly, that *I* should value its worth.'

Their glances met and held across the dinner table. Observing them, Cécile realized for the first time that Daniel Penwarne and Tristram hated each other. She didn't understand what Daniel was saying but Tristram did – one of them owned the painting, the other owned the wife.

14

The twins remained at Prospect, as Lavinia realized her daughter-in-law had intended all along that they should.

'It's for their own good,' she explained to Jonathan after Tristram and Cécile had gone back to Rome. 'A devoted mother has to take these agonizing decisions when the welfare of her children is at stake.'

There was no inflection in Lavinia's voice, and no expression on her face that Jonathan could read. 'Does Tristram have nothing to say in the matter?' he asked cautiously. 'Or you and Julian?'

She gave a tired little shrug. 'I think it broke Tristram's heart to leave them behind, but he can't help seeing that Prospect is a healthier place for small children than the capital cities of Europe. Julian doesn't in the least mind the twins being here – he likes children in the house and says they're company for Morwetha and Petroc. In any case, Cécile has the gift of charming him – whatever *she* decides is right.'

'But you don't have the same faith in her judgement?'

'She often *is* right,' Lavinia admitted ruefully. 'In fact, she's the perfect wife for a man in Tristram's position and I, therefore, am a silly old fool!'

Jonathan didn't pursue the subject of what troubled her; if she wanted him to know, she would tell him. 'I'm bound to say that I wouldn't want a child of mine growing up in Fascist Italy,' he confessed instead. 'Mussolini's programme for his countrymen includes the complete indoctrination of their children – that's a sinister development if you like.'

'And Kurt's letters don't sound any happier about what is happening in *his* country.'

'I should think not, with *their* new chancellor in the saddle. Herr Adolf Hitler still has something to learn from the Duce about how to play the game of European politics, but he's word perfect already in the role of apparent saviour of a humiliated, desperate nation.'

'We live in "interesting times",' Lavinia observed thoughtfully. 'No wonder the Chinese wish *that* on their enemies as a curse!'

Her strong private wish was that Tristram would never find himself posted to Berlin, but it happened two years later when his extended tour of duty in Rome finally came to an end. He had now an even better ring-side seat from which to watch the unholy alliance at work – Führer and Duce each encouraging the other's mad ambitions. Germany was to avenge past defeat and take back within its borders every German excluded from the Fatherland by the wicked Treaty of Versailles. Italy was to achieve an empire again, by the simple method of helping itself to the colonies of other nations.

Tristram hated Berlin, but it had one saving grace – he could see Kurt regularly and share with him as the hectic months passed the dreadful fascination of watching a megalomaniac take possession of an entire people.

'He's not insane yet, though I think he will become so,' Kurt said one day. 'Before that happens he'll have run rings round your government and the French, but you won't understand that until it's too late.'

'We can't face the idea of another war . . . prefer to pretend that if we treat dangerous lunatics as sane and civilized men, *that* is what they will become.'

'So you pretend also that Hitler and Mussolini don't meddle in the Spanish Civil War and make it worse just to get a training ground for their own troops and bombers.'

'Oh, there's no limit to what we can pretend,' Tristram agreed sombrely. He took a long time to light a cigarette before he spoke again. 'Cécile's going home, by the way – back to London; the poor girl's bored here. She's been left a small inheritance by a relative – enough to buy a flat in London. It means she can make a home for the children again, although I fancy they'll hate leaving Prospect.'

'And you will be lonely here without her. I'm sorry, my friend.'

Tristram met his friend's compassionate glance and answered honestly. 'I've been lonely for years, if you want the truth. It isn't Cécile's fault . . . I'm always up to my ears in work, and I can't blame her for getting sick of the same old dreary round of cocktail parties and receptions.' He stared at the glowing end of his cigarette for a moment. 'Kurt – go with her, please. Get out of Nazi Germany while you still can.'

'And leave everything behind?' Kurt asked slowly. 'My patients who depend on me, my family, my . . . my identity even?'

'Your professional standing protects you at the moment, but it won't for much longer. To the people who run this unfortunate country now you're a Jew, not a German at all.'

He saw a rueful smile touch his friend's mouth for a moment and fade again. 'And you would like to say that it is *I*, now, who refuse to see what is under my nose! I see it clearly enough, but even if I could leave everything else, I couldn't abandon the sick people who need me.'

'You're a bloody fool . . . do you know that? Can't you stop being so damned noble?' Tristram wasn't aware of shouting until the heads of other people in the café turned curiously in their direction. He glared back at them but lowered his voice. 'What help can you be if you don't stay alive yourself?'

Kurt ignored that question, because his thoughts dwelt on the past. 'You called me a fool once before, I remember. There have been times enough when I've agreed with you, but now I thank God every day of my life that Jenifer isn't here, to have her loyalties torn in two.

You English are peace-loving people but sooner or later you're going to have to fight or let the Fascists swallow Europe whole.'

He was proved right, although it took longer than he expected. Czechoslovakia had to be dismembered, and Poland invaded by German armies before the British government's efforts to go on supping with the devil were seen to be futile. On 3 September 1939 Neville Chamberlain finally declared war on Germany, and France followed suit. The Union Jack was hauled down the flag-staff outside the embassy in Berlin for the last time, and Tristram and his colleagues got ready to leave for London. Until the very last minute he begged Kurt to travel with them, but when the train steamed out of the station Dr Winkler was still standing bare-headed on the platform, waving goodbye.

Tristram stayed for a long time alone in the swaying corridor. It seemed likely that he would never see Kurt again and that was grief enough, but there was something almost worse. He was coming to terms at last with a truth too painful to be faced until now. It had taken him fifteen years to discover that diplomacy was an expensive farce after all; he would have done better to spend the time in Cornwall, helping to keep the shaky fortunes of his family afloat.

After Berlin the sights and sounds of London seemed blessedly calm and normal, apart from the scattering of silver barrage balloons floating in the sky. Even the children, hung about with name-tags and gas-masks, waiting to be evacuated at Victoria Station seemed unconcerned about escaping mortal danger; more worrying was the idea of being sent to some unknown quantity that people called 'the country'.

Across the city, at Paddington, Loveday waited with Polly for a train to Penzance. She had turned down the idea of going when Daniel first broached it, and didn't change her mind even when an air raid warning sounded immediately the prime minister's broadcast declaration of war.

'It's a false alarm,' she pointed out calmly. 'Listen – there's the all-clear signal already.'

'It *may* be, but there'll be other warnings soon that mean exactly what they say – German bombers in *our* sky trying to blow London to hell. If you still can't bring yourself to go back to Cornwall, then *I'll* have to take Polly down to Fowey.'

Loveday recognized in his expression the signs of a subject no longer open to discussion. With or without her help, their daughter was to leave London. 'Very well, Daniel . . . I'll go with Polly, but I shan't stay. As soon as she's settled with her grandparents I shall come back.'

His dark eyebrows sketched surprise. 'Wifely devotion, or cockney loyalty to London? Both are slightly unexpected!'

'This is my home,' she insisted quietly. 'It seems wrong to be driven out of it, that's all.'

It wasn't quite all, and he regretted a jibe that she didn't deserve. He knew perfectly well what it was that would draw her back to London – a grave in the churchyard half a mile along the road. Their only son, Robert, was buried there, dead of diphtheria just before his third birthday. He would have been eight now, two years younger than Polly. There had been no more children – only more businesses begun for Daniel, more wealth achieved and social hurdles vaulted over; and for Loveday the need to translate into paintings the pictures she saw in her mind's eye. Daniel didn't mind her doing it; she ran his home perfectly, and had learned to be the sort of hostess his circle of acquaintances required; apart from that, she could do as she pleased.

'Come back when you like,' he said more gently, 'as long as Polly understands *she's* got to stay down there. She's an independent-minded little cuss – takes after her grandfather Eliot too much, if you ask me.'

'She takes after *you*,' Loveday pointed out truthfully,

'but I'll resort to bribery if I have to – a new box Brownie for her to play with when she's got different places to take photographs of.' It might still not be enough, she realized, for a child who knew her own mind with almost more than adult certainty. Polly was fascinated by the idea of 'taking pictures' with the press of a button – much better, she reckoned, than her mother's slow labours with a paintbox; all the same, even a new camera wouldn't weigh for long against being separated from Daniel.

When the time came to leave she was intrigued enough by the idea of a long train journey to make no fuss about going, although she took the precaution of making things clear to her father.

'We'll be back before you've had time to miss us – it's just a little visit.'

If he'd thought there was a chance that she'd forget what he said, he'd have taken the coward's way out and agreed. But he still remembered breaking a promise to her once, when an urgent business meeting had seemed more important than watching her in a school gymnastics display. She hadn't sulked or wept afterwards, but her disappointment in him had been made so clear that he'd never made that mistake again. His difficulty now was that if he admitted she was being sent away for the duration of the war, she'd refuse to go at all. The only option left was a show of parental authority.

'I may miss you, or I may not; either way you'll do as you're told for once, and stay till I say you can come home.'

She smiled at him with a huge affection that forgave him for the bluff. 'I won't promise,' she said prudently, 'in case me and Fowey don't take to each other.'

'Why *shouldn't* you like it when you're Cornish right through? You should've been taken long before this to the place your forebears belong to.'

She didn't say that what she knew already of Cornwall was a worry to her, even though her father went there 'on business' without them and always returned safely.

It was connected with a memory left in her mind from years ago when she was still small.

She'd been aware of something different about the house, although she didn't understand then that it was because her little brother had died. The rooms were full of strong-smelling flowers and people in black clothes. To escape them she struggled up an unfamiliar flight of stairs and wandered into a small, dim room that she discovered was full of treasures. When Loveday came looking for her she was sitting on the dusty floor, engrossed in the drawing book on her lap. She smiled at her mother from beneath another find – a large straw hat trimmed with faded artificial roses.

'Mum, what's this place? It looks as big as the house the king lives in.'

Loveday stared down at a pencil sketch and was suddenly transfixed by a shaft of pain. 'It's . . . it's not a palace,' she said unsteadily. 'Ordinary people live there. I knew them when I was a little girl. It's a long way from here – the place called Cornwall that your father sometimes goes to.'

She'd tried never to say the word. It was a key unlocking the door slammed shut on memories, and now they came pouring out, drowning her in waves of sadness. Polly had never seen her mother weep before. She crept close and cried too, and always afterwards connected Cornwall with the sound of her mother weeping. But from then on things changed. She listened at night to stories she didn't properly understand, but they lodged in her memory; and it was then that her mother began painting pictures, often of the house that wasn't quite a palace – Prospect, she called it.

Now that they were actually going there at last Polly felt anxious but curious as well. She liked the names of the stations they passed – Exeter St David, Liskeard, best of all Lostwithiel, where apparently Uncle John lived; but it was another uncle – Charlie, a friendly, soft-voiced man, who came to meet them at the station. Fowey was a disappointment – an up and down, higgledy-piggledy sort of place that looked as if it might tumble clean off the hillside and fall into the water. Polly was glad she hadn't made any promises about Fowey, especially when her grandparents' house looked so little like her home in London that she hesitated about going inside.

'I dare say it's not quite what you're used to,' Charlie said gently beside her. 'We like our houses small and grey, Polly – that way the wind blows over them without noticing that they're here! We have a powerful lot of wind in Cornwall, you see.'

She rather liked the idea, but wasn't ready to say so. 'We don't have to bother about the wind in London,' she pointed out grandly instead, but his smile was so kind that she fell off her high horse with a rush. 'I expect I'll get used to it, though.'

There was a lot to get used to. She took to her grandfather William at first sight – a gentle-faced man who rarely stirred from his armchair by the window; but Grandma Penwarne looked a harder nut to crack.

'It shouldn't have taken a war to bring you home,' she was saying to Loveday, 'or to give us a sight of our granddaughter.'

'I know . . . I'm sorry.' Loveday blinked away the tears her mother would despise and tried to smile instead. 'Nothing's changed – I might never have been away.'

Hannah thought she couldn't say the same of this slender, elegant woman who no longer looked or sounded as if she belonged in Fore Street. Daniel had prospered, of course; they all knew that. But she hadn't expected quite such a transformation. 'I wonder Charlie recognized *you*,' she said.

'Well, I'd have known Polly, at least,' he insisted. 'Apart from having Lowdy's eyes, she's the dead spit of Daniel.'

'She's very thin,' Hannah said critically. 'Small for her age, too. She'd better be fed up a bit while she's here.'

Polly detected a note of complaint that she was inclined to resent, but when the frail man in the armchair

209

gave her a slow, deliberate wink she suddenly felt better. All the same, she was glad when Charlie offered to take her down to the river and back – just to get her bearings, he suggested smilingly.

'All right, but don't be long – tea'll be on the table by the time you get back.' Hannah sounded sharp as usual, unaware that her eyes were full of love as she watched them go. 'Your brother doesn't change,' she muttered to Loveday. 'He can't stay away from the water any more now than he could when he was a child.' She saw her daughter's sudden change of expression, and put out a hand in a small, rare gesture of affection. 'I'm sorry, my dear. Talking of Charlie as a boy . . . that was thoughtless of me when I dare say you've never stopped grieving for little Robert. We *wanted* to go to his burial, but your father was very poorly at the time. Dr Jonathan wouldn't hear of him trying to make the journey, and I couldn't leave him.'

Loveday went to kneel down beside her father's chair. 'I'm sorry I stayed away so long,' she said simply. 'It was only in case I wouldn't be able to leave again if I ever came back.'

'I thought it might be that, Lowdy. Doesn't matter now. You're here, with Polly. She looks a proper little Cornish maid.'

'I'm afraid *she* thinks she's a proper little Londoner! Don't mind too much if she says Fowey's a poor place compared with what she's used to. She won't mean to be hurtful but, like Grandfather Eliot, she has the habit of speaking her mind!'

William simply smiled and sat holding his daughter's hand while Hannah bustled about, getting the tea ready. There was a lot of talk when Charlie and Polly came back, and she had to wait for a quiet coozey with him until her parents and Polly were in bed.

'I'm sorry you never came to London with John,' Loveday said.

'It doesn't need two of us, and he's the one in charge

down here. In any case, I'd get lost up there for sure.'

'You mean you'd rather stay here! How *are* things, Charlie?'

'Much better than they were. A lot of men were laid off work during the bad years, Father included, but the china-clay business has picked up again since then. The haven isn't exactly booming even now, but we get the bigger boats that can't load at Par or Charlestown. We get holidaymakers too, and *their* boats. The Yacht Club's still choosy, although I'm let in nowadays, but the shopkeepers like the extra trade.' Charlie's blunt-fingered hands stuffed tobacco carefully into the bowl of his old pipe. 'Now, just as we're doing quite nicely along comes another troublesome old war to muck things up again.'

'But *you* won't be called up, surely?'

'Mebbe not called up exactly, but I reckon I might still get back to sea. They'll be needing men of my age in the Merchant Fleet before long.'

When ships started being sunk and crews lost, Loveday realized what he meant. 'That makes the war seem real,' she said slowly. 'It didn't feel like that in London, despite the air-raid shelter in the garden and the barrage balloons overhead. Daniel even had to talk me into bringing Polly here.'

She looked at her brother's brown, weather-beaten face and saw for the first time a likeness to Daniel; she'd never noticed it when he was young. He was nearly forty now, and suddenly she could have wept for all the years that she'd chosen to stay away from him and the rest of her family.

'I've been stupid about a lot of other things . . . perhaps I'm wrong about this unreal war as well,' she admitted after a while.

'It'll get real soon enough, Lowdy, and that's not just my idea. Dr Jonathan says the same when he comes here sometimes of an evening to play chess with Father.'

'Do you . . . do you see the rest of the family?'

Charlie grinned suddenly. 'It's hard *not* to see Sir Julian in Fowey – he's still a powerful busy gentleman! Her ladyship mostly stays at Prospect these days, being a trifle stiff in the joints, poor lady. The two you looked after are still there with their mother, but nowadays while Tristram's in foreign parts his children live in London, so I'm told.'

Loveday knew that Tristram's wife lived there as well. Under her married name of Cécile Bossiney she had become very fashionable – the expert in interior decoration that everybody who had money but no taste of their own wanted. It was as much as Loveday wanted to know about Cécile.

'Morwetha must be seventeen now,' she said instead. 'Would I recognize her?'

'I expect so. Although she's not as pretty as her mother was – talkative though, and very opinionated!'

'She always was, I remember. What about the baby?'

'*Petroc*, you mean? Maid dear, you've been away a long time. He's six feet high, and already handles a boat as well as I do! Mostly he's away at school, but holiday-times like now he and I sail a bit together, just as I did back along with Tristram. You'll see him around, I expect; a tall, thin lad with black hair and a smile that doesn't come too often. Still, you're bound to go and call at Prospect.'

Yes, she was bound to, but she knew she wouldn't be going just yet. It had been hard enough coming back at all; she must get used to being there before she felt brave enough to walk along the Esplanade and call on the Bossineys.

Polly got there first, by accident. She arrived wet, bedraggled, and very cross, having been hauled across Prospect Cove by a tall, black-browed creature who'd shouted at her.

She'd set out with her new camera, explaining to her grandparents that she liked walking alone. The streets seemed small and squashed up after London, but she was beginning to understand her uncle's liking for the river. With the tide out, she could wander along the wet sand, trying to take pictures of seagulls that, stupid things, took off in a huff whenever she got near them. The sand gave way to rocks, but she enjoyed the scramble. Feeling pleasantly adventurous, she struggled on, enticed by another sandy place ahead of her. Above it a long, grey house surrounded by greenness seemed part of the grey rocks it stood on. She stared at it, slowly realizing why it seemed familiar – she'd seen it before in London, in the pictures her mother painted.

The cove below the house was sheltered and peaceful. She sat there for a long time, wishing that her father were there to tell her the names of the birds she didn't recognize. He might be able to explain as well why she was beginning to feel so lonely and sad. It had to do with the immense view in front of her – empty grey-green sea stretching as far as an empty blue-grey sky. She couldn't bear to look at it any longer, closed her eyes against it, but still the sadness seemed to become unbearable.

She got up to go home, brushed sand from her legs, and looked for the rocks she'd clambered over. They were nowhere to be seen. The cove itself had shrunk without her noticing it, and the water that was steadily swallowing it up now poured over her route home in a foaming, white cascade. Sadness was lost in the first faint prick of fear. She was conscious, too, of a change in the weather – the wind was picking at her hair and skirt, and she remembered what Charlie had said – they had a lot of wind in Cornwall. He'd said something about the tides, as well. 'Always stay above the water-line, Polly love, when the tide's on the flow; that way you'll come to no harm'. The water-line must be above where she stood because the next wave suddenly gathered strength enough to fling itself over her sandals and bare feet.

She stared from the water-strewn boulders she'd come by to a worse sight on her right – a huge lump of rock guarding the far side of the cove that now lifted its head out of swirling green waves. It would have to be the boulders after all. She tucked the precious camera into the front of her jacket and splashed her way towards them. Spray fell coldly on her as she started to clamber up, and above the flat level of the sandy cove the wind blew stronger. The next wave washed over her legs, and suddenly she was very frightened indeed. She hated Cornwall . . . almost hated her father for sending her; she'd tell him so the first chance she got, but now she wanted him to be *there*. He wasn't, though, and she must try a different prayer. 'Heavenly Father help me instead, because I can't see which way to go.' It wasn't the right way . . . water poured over her, leaving her blinded.

She still clung, sobbing, to the rock she was on, unable to go on or back, when an angry voice sounded behind her.

'You stupid idiot! What's the point of sitting up there?'

When she turned her head she saw a boy standing up to his knees in water down in the cove she'd so laboriously crawled away from.

'You won't do any good *there* for at least the next three hours . . . you'll have to come back *this* way.'

'I don't want to.' She was made defiant by the sight of another human being. If she could have managed it she'd have said that she *liked* being there, but her fingers were sore with gripping sharp rocks and she was soaked all over. She saw him turn away, and bravado drowned instantly in the next cold douche of spray.

'I *can't* move,' she sobbed desperately. 'I'm stuck here.'

Now she couldn't see him at all, and even God in His heaven had deserted her. But the next moment the boy was beside her; she was lifted off the rock and slung over his shoulder.

'Try not to strangle me, and don't wriggle or we'll both finish up in the river.'

She hated him as much as she hated the place he belonged to, but it was hard to say so when she was hanging upside down. Instead, she watched his bare brown feet picking a way over the streaming rocks. A moment later they were back in the cove, splashing through the water.

'I can walk now,' she muttered.

It made no difference; still upside down, she was carried up a flight of stone steps cut almost invisibly in the rock at the back of the cove. A veil of greenery at the top was brushed aside, and at last – she felt sure of it – they were above Charlie's water-line. She had an impression of brilliant colour that would have pleased her at any other time as the boy climbed the different levels of the garden; then he walked through an open door and she was finally set on her feet in front of a tall, thin lady.

'There you are, Gran – one little drowned rat for you! She seemed to think she was a mermaid.'

Polly was aware of not looking her best. Water trickled down her face, and a pool was forming about her feet; but even though the boy had rescued her, he was hateful. 'I think *you* are an impudent *pig*!' she shouted furiously.

Lavinia Bossiney held up her hands, suspending hostilities. 'You can continue exchanging compliments when you're both dry. Petroc, go and change your clothes; *you*, child, come with me.'

Polly went, meekly. There was something about this lady that ruled out argument. She was delivered into the hands of someone plump and white-haired who smiled kindly at her, and clucked over the scratches on her hands and legs. Free of the cold, wet clothes that clung to her, she was wrapped in the comfort of a huge towel. Afterwards, dressed in borrowed clothes, and pleasantly conscious of being the heroine of a real adventure, she was taken downstairs again.

Her new friend – Mrs Bartlett, she'd said her name was – walked slowly, and there was time to see that this house was as different from her own home as Grandma Penwarne's cottage was. If not the palace she'd called it years ago, it was large and rambling, and grand, and her borrowed shoes made too much noise when she stepped off rugs on to stone-flagged floors. The room she was led into made her stand stock-still. Books lined the walls from floor to ceiling, and they were even piled on tables as well. Untidy, Granny would have called that, but Polly could see the sense of it – why not keep them within reach? A huge, rounded window faced the sea, and she shivered suddenly, remembering more than recent terror; before that there'd been the aching sadness that made her forget Charlie's warning about the tide.

'Her name's Polly, your ladyship,' Mrs Bartlett said in her soft, slow voice. 'Now I'll be sending Gwen in with some hot milk for her.'

Lavinia pointed to a chair, and examined her guest for the first time. A pretty child she was not. A mop of short dark hair was drying in a dark cloud about a face that looked too small for the features it contained. Only her eyes were noticeable – black-lashed and deeply blue.

'Polly what?' Lavinia asked the question, but knew the answer as she did so.

'I'm Polly Jane Penwarne.' It sounded bald; perhaps she should have tacked on the words that Mrs Bartlett had used? She smiled hopefully instead, and saw the lady's severe face change.

'Now I'm *sure* I knew your mother a long time ago – you remind me of her when you smile. Have you both come to stay in Fore Street?'

'Yes, but not for long,' Polly explained firmly. 'I expect we shall go home to London soon.' She sipped heroically at the milk brought in by a girl who seemed not much older than herself. Hot milk, like Cornwall, was something else she didn't like. But this tasted sweet and spicy, and unexpectedly delicious. Perhaps Prospect itself might be a bit like the milk. She'd always hated the idea of it because of the effect it had on her mother, but now that she was there she didn't seem to mind it at all. In fact, she rather liked this quiet lady whose eyes smiled when her mouth was serious. The only thing wrong was The Boy, as she now thought of him, but alas it was he who was sent for when the milk was finished, and told to take her home.

Polly might have argued, but she could see that he disliked the idea as much as she did. Serve him right, in that case.

'Ask your mother to come and see us,' Lavinia suggested as they were leaving the room. 'We'll keep your clothes drying until then.' Then she smiled openly. 'This is my grandson, Petroc, by the way.'

The walk back through the garden and out on to the Esplanade was made in silence. Then, overcome by curiosity, he pointed to the curious bulge in the front of her jacket. 'What on earth *is* that? I remember it sticking into me all the time I was lugging you across the cove.'

'It's my camera . . . I'm going to be a *famous* photographer when I grow up, but I've started already.'

He turned to frown at her, black brows pulled together until they met above his beaky nose. 'So that's what you were doing there – snooping! You were trespassing on private property. If I catch you there again I'll tip your beastly little camera into the sea.'

All the muddled emotions of the morning met in a surge of pure rage. Her eyes flashed blue fire at him, startling him with their beauty. 'I'll kill you if you do . . . I'll find *some* way of killing you.'

'You'll drown *yourself* first if you don't pay attention to the tides in future. This is Cornwall, remember, not some London suburb.'

She stopped in her tracks and stared disdainfully around her. 'I can see the difference . . . you don't have to remind me. Now, *you* can do what you like; I'm going the rest of the way alone.'

Before he could even reply, she was off at top speed, on thin, pale legs almost hidden by the too-long skirts of Morwetha's borrowed dress. She was a tiresome little creature but, for a Londoner, she could run . . . he had to admit that as he turned back in the direction of Prospect.

217

15

Lavinia waited with interest for Loveday's visit, but saw no need for the speculation about it indulged in by her daughter and granddaughter.

'I can just remember that I was upset when she went away,' Morwetha informed them more than once.

'Upset? You screamed with temper for days,' Lavinia reminded her, 'and kicked poor Lucy Jago whenever she went near you.'

Morwetha looked pleased with herself for having behaved with such spirit. 'Well, Gran dear, she *did* sniff all the time and have those hideous red hands! I seem to remember that Loveday was beautiful, but I suppose she'll be quite old by now.'

'In her dotage at thirty-five?'

A lady with youth well on her side at seventeen could almost think so. 'Not quite, but definitely a bit passée . . . and judging by some of the women here, marriage is a very ageing business!'

Lavinia stared involuntarily at her daughter's face and looked away again – perhaps not being married was even worse.

'There's nothing wrong with marriage if you pick a wealthy man,' Jenifer told *her* daughter with a touch of bitterness. 'Daniel Penwarne may not be everybody's choice but he manages to look quite the thing when he dines here with the gentry. Loveday has been lucky, if you ask me.'

'It's funny *she's* never come back before,' Morwetha said slowly. 'I wonder why not.'

'Wonder if you like, but please don't ask; it's no concern

of ours.' Using that tone of voice, Lavinia intended to be heeded, but then she relented a little. 'I liked her daughter, by the way.'

Both Jenifer and Morwetha found reasons for staying in the house the following morning and were eventually rewarded. Smiling with pleasure, old Bartlett announced that Mrs Daniel Penwarne had called. The woman he showed into Lavinia's little sitting room was hatless, and mainly recognizable by the black hair which she still wore unfashionably long in a coronet of plaits about her head. Otherwise she was modern elegance personified, in a well-cut jacket and skirt of cream linen, and pale buckskin shoes that were surely handmade.

Jenifer stared, Lavinia smiled and held out her hand, but it was Morwetha who broke the ice.

'Lowdy . . . it's just come back to me that that's what I used to call you.' She planted a friendly kiss on Loveday's cheek, then smiled broadly. 'Gran says I made a fearful fuss when you went away.'

'So you did once before, when your brother was born. I hope you've grown to like him since then!'

Morwetha stared at the smiling woman in front of her. 'You're still just as pretty . . . I was afraid you wouldn't be.'

Lavinia held up her hands in despair. 'My dear, forgive her, please. Who would believe that my granddaughter was reasonably well brought up?'

Loveday looked from Morwetha's bright face to the woman whose conduct she herself, without realizing it, had tried to copy. Lady Bossiney was little changed – the same upright carriage, even if it required an effort nowadays, neat fair hair mixed imperceptibly with silver, and the remembered face that sprang into warm life only when she smiled.

'I came to thank you for rescuing Polly yesterday,' Loveday murmured. 'Charlie *had* warned her to be careful, and she's so sensible normally that we don't need to worry about her at all.' It sounded inadequate and she was forced to go on in a voice that trembled slightly. 'She's very independent, you see, and it's important not to smother her, but since our little son died six years ago . . .' Her voice died away and Lavinia hastened to fill the silence.

'What a grief for you . . . I'm so sorry.' It didn't explain why Loveday had never come back to Fowey, but it certainly accounted for the air of controlled sadness that now seemed part of her. After a moment or two, Lavinia led the conversation back into an easier channel. 'Petroc was asked to escort Polly back to Fore Street yesterday, but I understand she dispensed with his services. He was distinctly ruffled when he got back!'

Having said nothing so far, Jenifer suddenly leapt into speech. 'Mama, in no time at all Loveday will start to imagine that her courtesy visit has lasted long enough. Before she decides to leave why don't we ask her to dine with us one evening? If she brought Charlie too it would give Petroc someone to talk sailing with.' Pleasantly aware of having done something to take her mother aback, she sparkled a little more than usual. 'Loveday, do say you'll come.'

With only a fractional pause, Lavinia accepted the fait accompli gracefully. 'It's an excellent idea – shall we say the evening after tomorrow, my dear . . . at eight o'clock?' Almost she added that dress would be informal, then remembered just in time that Charlie Penwarne would own a dinner jacket now – he attended the Yacht Club on even its most formal occasions.

Loveday accepted the invitation calmly, wondering what her brother would think of it, and left soon afterwards with the neat parcel her old friend Mrs Bartlett had made of Polly's clothes. Jenifer waited for some comment from her mother but it didn't come, because Lavinia was occupied in more serious thinking. The girl she'd been certain Tristram would ruin himself by marrying had become an elegant, charming woman. His 'perfect' wife now spent her time telling rich, vulgar people what curtains they should choose. Really, at times life was unbearably ironical!

She sent a message to Jonathan, begging him to balance the numbers at her dinner table, and the following morning another ingredient was added to the dinner party Lavinia devoutly wished wasn't happening at all. Tristram and Cécile arrived unexpectedly, almost before she knew that he was back in the country.

'No warning, Mama . . . do you mind?' he asked, smiling at her out of an exhausted-looking face. 'After Berlin, I am allowed a little extra leave by my masters in Whitehall. When Cécile said she could spare the time to drive me down I suddenly couldn't resist the thought of Prospect.'

'Dearest, what warning do we need? We're just so happy to have you here.' She kissed her daughter-in-law as well, and tried hard to sound cordial here too. 'The twins aren't with you, my dear?'

'No, Mère . . . they're staying with schoolfriends, on a rather grand estate in Gloucestershire. I have to collect them on my way back to London; I've really only come here to deliver Tristram.'

The estate would *have* to be grand, Lavinia reflected; Cécile wouldn't dream of calling there otherwise. She smiled suddenly, remembering the evening's dinner party. Her daughter-in-law should have the rare pleasure of being partnered by Charlie Penwarne!

But when the evening came only Julian, it seemed to his wife, was behaving naturally, by looking faintly surprised that it should be happening at all. He enjoyed offering hospitality and was always ready to be affable, but confided to his brother before their other guests arrived that he hadn't ever expected to have a one-time nursemaid seated on his right hand.

'But perhaps you hadn't expected, either, to see the nursemaid as she is now.' Jonathan had an unfair advantage in this, having already met Loveday in town, and he watched Julian when the Penwarnes arrived, so as not to miss his brother's change of expression.

Cécile was, as always, the obvious attraction, in a dress of flame-coloured chiffon that she wore with the confidence of a woman accustomed to being looked at enviously by other women. By comparison, Loveday's slender white silk gown looked starkly simple, and her only ornament was a silver-mounted sapphire hanging from a delicate chain. Tristram understood why Daniel gave her sapphires to wear – the stone was exactly the same colour as her eyes.

He'd bowed and taken her hand, even managed to smile, he thought; but the seasoned veteran of countless diplomatic parties had found little to say. Loveday looked pale but composed, which was irritating when he felt anything but composed himself.

'London seems to suit you . . . I didn't think it would,' he said. Then a tinge of colour came into his thin cheeks in case she took that to mean something else – that he hadn't expected marriage to Daniel to suit her. But he'd forgotten her habit of accepting what he said at its face value – it was a custom rare in diplomatic circles.

'I hated it to begin with . . . could scarcely understand what was said, but now it's my home.' A slow smile lit her face, wiping away all the past long years. 'I should be hopelessly lost among the foreign people you and your wife have to deal with.'

Tristram nodded, accepting a reference to the past that seemed intended to let him know that no sting lingered after fifteen years. It was long over and forgotten, and, to prove it, she moved away from him to talk to Jonathan. He felt strangely blank – detached from the buzz of conversation around him; then Charlie, after a glance at his friend's face, said something a little more loudly for the second time.

'It's a proper long old time since you were here, Tristram. I reckon you can do with a breath of handsome Cornish air.'

'I'm sick for it, old friend. My lungs are still filled with the stench of hatred and hysteria in Berlin!' He tried to speak lightly, failed, and wondered fleetingly if Kurt would say that this was how breakdowns began.

'Come out with Petroc and me,' Charlie recommended. 'I don't tell *him* so, but he'll be a better man with a boat than either of *us* one of these days.'

'War permitting? . . . don't forget the bloody war, Charlie.' He stared across the room at Loveday. 'That's what seems to have brought your sister back to Fowey.'

'Not for long, though. She'll be going back along to London soon. What about you?'

'Washington, I believe. I'm supposed to help convince our strictly neutral American friends that they may be required to lend a hand before long.'

'It looks as if I've got an easier job to do . . . I'm signing on as a merchant sailor!' He smiled without bravado or vainglory – just a simple, ordinary man quietly choosing how best he could serve his country. Tristram prayed to God that there were still many more Charlie Penwarnes around, because he knew better than they did that England was going to need them.

The day after the dinner party Cécile left for Gloucestershire, and then London, where there were a thousand things to do, she explained. Her partner would try to keep the business going, but there were details to be settled, and the flat to close before she sailed with Tristram to America.

'You don't prefer to remain behind this time?' Lavinia asked.

'Certainly not – Washington sounds exciting, and Tristram will tell you that I'm very good with Americans! In any case, the twins will be better off there, don't you agree?'

'Tristram must go because he's being sent; it's his war job. I don't think others should go because they might be better off.'

'Dear Mère – so splendidly patriotic!' Cécile said; so absurdly old-fashioned and quaint, her smile added.

She didn't wait for Lavinia to reply, deposited a kiss

on the air somewhere near her mother-in-law's face and roared away from the lane above the house. Tristram was left to breathe Cornish air in peace for a week or two. It *was* strangely, selfishly peaceful. He'd forgotten just how self-contained his native place still was, even from the rest of England. 'Any man's death diminishes me because I am involved in Mankind.' So John Donne had written, but what did Fowey men like Walter Jago or Will Varco care about the death-agonies of Poland, or about Jews like Kurt singled out for destruction? 'Not a bloody thing,' he told his uncle bitterly.

Jonathan answered with heroic mildness. 'No, they merely fought their way through four years of unspeakable slaughter not so long ago because they were told that England needed them!'

'Sorry . . .' Tristram mumbled after a moment or two. 'Take no notice of my little outburst. Perhaps it's time I got back to work.'

'It's time you relaxed first, and eased the world's troubles off your shoulders for a while.'

His nephew's strained face broke into a smile. 'Morwetha thinks so, too. Petroc, sensible chap, goes his own way but, bless her, she's determined to be a comfort to me! I'm reduced to sneaking out at dawn before she's up.'

In fact he enjoyed more than anything else the solitary walks he took before the rest of the world was astir. Over to the Gribben and back was still a good pre-breakfast tramp calculated to stretch his body; in time it might restore perspective to a troubled mind as well. Whenever he crossed St Catherine's headland he knew that it was still haunted by the past, but it *was* the past . . . Loveday had firmly made that clear. Perhaps, for that reason it didn't occur to him that he would ever find her there, sitting in a hollow of the shelving hillside, staring at the opalescent, early-morning sea and sky.

She didn't move when he dropped down beside her, except to hide her hands in the pockets of her jacket.

'It's very early to go walking,' he pointed out almost irritably. 'I don't normally see another soul.'

'That's why *I* come now,' she agreed. Her delicate profile was tilted up to watch the changing sky. The sun was still below the horizon, but its rays were beginning to colour the clouds with a wash of pink. She was so absorbed in the gradual transformation that he wondered if she would even notice if he got up and walked away. But her expression was sad, reminding him of something his mother had said.

'I'm sorry about your little son, Loveday . . . So *very* sorry, my dear.'

She had to turn around then to look at him, and understood for the first time something about *him*. Whatever else the past fifteen years had done, they hadn't made him a happy and contented man.

'We still have Polly – our pride and joy . . . as your children must be to you.'

He nodded, but didn't pursue the subject of the twins. They belonged to his life with Cécile and for that reason seemed outside *this* unlooked-for interlude.

'I've been away for years,' he went on quietly, 'Paris, Rome, Berlin – exciting, important places where I liked to think I was doing exciting, important work.'

'So you were, surely?'

'I doubt it now; doubt it so much that the years seem to have been completely meaningless. I might have been learning about the things that really matter instead.'

'Like ". . . gentleness, in hearts at peace, under an English heaven"! Shall we listen to the poems of Rupert Brooke in *this* war, do you imagine?'

It was exactly what was in his mind, and the dreadful, cold feeling of isolation that had surrounded him since he got back home melted away. If this one woman understood, it didn't matter if no-one else did. He watched the sun climb over the horizon. The clouds were edged now with a rim of gold, hinting at radiance just out of range.

'I used to try to paint this view in my mind's eye whenever I got really heart-sick . . . Did *you*, when London seemed more than you could bear?'

Loveday shook her head. 'For a long time I didn't dare remember it at all. Then, after Robert died, Polly found one of my old sketching-books, and the dammed-up memories burst open. After that I found that I could tell her the stories Grandfather Isaac had told me, and I began turning the sketches into paintings.'

'I know . . . I have one of them. Charlotte happened to see it, and gave it to me. My wife sees that it's beautiful, because she's clever about such things – but she doesn't know what makes it precious.'

Loveday didn't answer, because there was nothing she could find to say. But Tristram suddenly knew that there were things he *had* to say.

'I'm going to Washington soon, and you will go back to London. This may be the only chance I shall ever have to confess the truth – I should have made you marry me all those years ago. I was a coward, Loveday.'

Her eyes pricked with tears for the sadness in his voice. 'I was frightened, too,' she said gently, 'terrified of not knowing how to behave, of making you ashamed of me. Love might have made us braver, I suppose, but we were afraid for each other most of all.' She smiled at him suddenly, and he saw how beautiful she still was. 'We *meant* well; perhaps that excuses us a little!'

'I shall die still loving you. I've always known it in the secret places of my heart . . . it's a relief to be able to tell you, just this once.'

Her tears brimmed over and trickled down her cheeks. He could bear his own grief but not hers, and if a dozen Daniel Penwarnes had been watching them, he thought he must still have gathered her in his arms. Then, as directly as a child might, she put up her mouth to be kissed. Old tenderness, new longing – he didn't know which it was; perhaps they simply fused together in this overwhelming need to cling together. It was the only chance they might ever have to hold each other and shut out the rest of the world.

'Blood of my heart . . . oh, Christ, help me . . . stop me . . .'

She was held against him scarcely able to hear the muttered words for the sound of her own thudding heartbeats. For fifteen years she'd been denied the joy of looking at him – it was unbearable not to be able to see him clearly now for the tears that blinded her.

As if his mind was inside her own, he wiped away her tears and then cupped her face in his hands.

'Dearest love . . . leave Daniel, please. We've wasted so much time. Surely we're entitled to be happy at last.'

'The years haven't been entirely wasted,' she said in a low voice.

'Are you going to pretend that you love Daniel? I should never believe you.'

'No, although I've tried. Polly is a different matter . . . Daniel adores her, and she him, but I know that she needs me as well. I couldn't hurt Daniel either. He's been good to me . . . done his very best for both of us.' She saw the despair in Tristram's face, and knew that it proved the truth of what she said. 'You couldn't give up *your* children either, even if you could abandon your work and a faithful wife whose religion would prevent her marrying again. *Our* happiness couldn't survive that amount of sacrifice.'

He felt physically sick with the anguish inside him. Of course, living with another man's wife would put an end to his career, but he could find something else to do. Cécile wouldn't be able to marry again, but he doubted if she was a woman who needed a husband – admirers would do. Her self-esteem would be shattered if he left her, but even this damage he might bring himself to inflict. But, as Loveday had said of Polly, the twins were a different matter, because they would stay with Cécile. He knew her virtues by now – she was hardworking, clever, elegant, a charming companion when she set out to be – but her heart was cold. He couldn't allow his children to grow up learning only *her* cynical creed, *her* materialistic values. He smoothed Loveday's tumbled hair, wondering why men were not allowed to weep when heartbreak consumed them.

'I sometimes used to think that I would die unfulfilled because I'd never had the chance to make love to you;' he said unsteadily. 'Now I know that what I shall miss more than anything else in the world is the right to grow old with you. That is what we *should* have done, my dearest dear, grow old together.'

'I know, but knowing it is something.' She reached up to leave a gentle kiss on his mouth. It both accepted what they knew and agreed that nothing could be changed.

Tristram tried to smile at her. 'Years ago we weren't brave enough; now we aren't selfish enough. God knows it isn't because we don't love each other enough. Shall I see you again – just while I'm here, I mean?'

'No, I shall go back to London tomorrow. I *must*, now.'

Without argument he lifted her to her feet; and hand in hand they climbed up to the track that led across the headland; they didn't speak because there was nothing more to say.

Petroc bicycled along the road from Fowey, speculating about his chances of persuading the local Recruiting Officer that a sixteen-year-old schoolboy was old enough to join the Navy. In another week he'd be back at Blundell's, and stuck there for at least another term. He'd cut himself while shaving . . . it might help, or it might not; he wasn't sure.

A small, thin figure became visible ahead of him, interrupting his own anxious train of thought because it was faintly familiar. When he got closer, the doubt became a certainty – it *was* Polly Penwarne, trudging along miles from home, with the dogged air of someone who wasn't just out walking. He came abreast of her and she gave a little gasp, then looked steadily ahead again.

'A brief good morning is generally considered obligatory, though not exactly fulsome; but perhaps you aren't feeling chatty at all this morning.'

'No, I'm not. But I'll say it if you like, then you can pedal on and leave me alone.'

Petroc glanced at her face and saw that it was smudged with tear-stains wiped away by a slightly grimy hand. He didn't know what ailed her, but it was surely something more than just an acute attack of homesickness. She was a tiresome nuisance when he had worries of his own, but he found it hard to leave her to walk by herself.

'Isn't it time you turned back? You've got a long way to trudge home.'

He thought her mouth quivered at the word, but all she said was, 'I'll turn when I'm ready. Goodbye!'

'Dismissed again – you do rather make a habit of it, I must say.' A glimmer of humour touched his long mouth, and for a moment she was reminded of his grandmother. 'All right, Miss Penwarne, I can take a hint.' He gave her a little mock salute and heaved himself on to the saddle again. A few moments later he was almost out of sight, and the road was suddenly empty, and very lonely again.

She plodded on, refusing to think about the great lump of misery pressed down below the surface of her mind. There was a more immediate worry – two, in fact. She mightn't have money enough for the fare home, and perhaps they were told, in any case, not to sell tickets to customers whose heads barely reached above the counter.

Half an hour later she was very tired, but at least sitting on a bench at Par Station waiting for the London train. There'd been enough with ninepence to spare, and a kindly ticket-clerk had made no fuss provided she travelled next to the guard. With all that accomplished, it was hard to keep her mind from worrying at what had sent her headlong out of Fowey. She wasn't ready to think about it, though, and concentrated instead on reading every sign and advertisement she could see.

When they were finished, she started on them all over again.

'You get yourself into some very strange places, Polly Penwarne. What the devil do you think you're doing here?'

It was The Boy again . . . she recognized the voice, and the hectoring tone. He was standing behind the seat when she turned around, hands in his pockets as if he had no intention of going away. Her face went so pale that for a moment he thought she was going to faint, but her eyes were still clear, and bright with anger.

'If it's anything to do with you, I'm going to London, that's all. I hate Cornwall, and I'm never coming back.'

'Going without waiting for your mother?'

'She . . . she likes it here more than I do.'

Petroc had taken the precaution of asking the time of the train. It was nearly due and he knew that he couldn't stave off the moment of truth much longer.

'I'm thinking you'd better come back with me, Polly. Then you can talk to Mrs Penwarne and tell *her* that you'd rather be in London.'

She would have run, but there was only the end of the platform to run to, and he would catch her easily. 'You can't make me leave . . . I'll scream.'

Other passengers were already staring at them curiously. He cursed her in his heart for the embarrassment she was bringing on him, but she couldn't be left there.

'Scream if you like, but listen first, and use your loaf, for heaven's sake. I don't know or care what's sending you back to London like a frightened rabbit, but I assume your father *would* want to know. If I could I'd let you go and arrive at Paddington alone, but I *can't*. You're coming back to Fowey with me, whether you walk through the station on your own two feet or I have to lug you again. Which is it to be?'

She sat glowering at him, stopped from screaming by the one undeniable thing that he had said. Her father wouldn't be put off by the excuse that she hated Fowey, no matter how often she said it. He was a man who got to the bottom of things.

'I'll walk,' she said sullenly. 'But I'll hate you for ever.'

They made the journey back with Polly perched un-comfortably on the crossbar of his bicycle. He didn't think that a sore bottom was the cause of the tears that slipped down her cheeks, but she climbed down outside the cottage without saying anything.

Her face was tragic, and he had the strange impression that it reflected the entire sadness of a world that seemed bent on tearing itself to pieces.

'You went without your camera.' It was a ridiculous thing to say, but all that came into his head.

'I threw it away,' she muttered, and then walked up the path to the front door without saying another word.

1950

'Say, is there Beauty yet to find?
And Certainty? And Quiet kind?
Deep meadows yet for to forget
The lies, and truths, and pain?'
                                    Rupert Brooke

16

Spring comes early to southern Cornwall as a rule. This
year was no exception; already streams of gold ran
down the hillside across the river, where the gorse was
in flower, and the hedgerow grass was clotted with
primroses, luscious and yellow as cream. In another
week the wild daffodils would be out – lenten lilies,
Cornish people called them. In the years before the war,
Petroc couldn't remember ever noticing this unfolding
pattern of the spring – it was just something that
always happened, like the ebb and flow of the tides in
the estuary, and the wild inconstancies of the Cornish
weather, glorious one moment, vile the next. But war-
time convoy duty in a destroyer, shepherding supplies to
Russia and troops to the fighting in the Mediterranean,
had rammed home a number of lessons.

The most important of them, although he hadn't
realized it at the time, had been the need to take
nothing for granted again. Fifty years *was* 'little room
to see the cherry tree in bloom', and the way things
were going there might not even be fifty years to look
properly at everything in God's Creation. Five years into
so-called 'peace', United Nations troops were about to
start fighting in Korea, and Europe – East and West –
was locked in the suspicion and hostility of the Cold
War. Worst of all, the threat of atomic warfare now
hung over them all like the Sword of Damocles. Petroc's
considered opinion was that only politicians had nerve
enough for overviews. He was content nowadays just to
look at nearer things – herons prinking by the river, and
wild daffodils blowing in the wind.

The day was mild – 'lent' from a later season of the year – but still only March; too early for a lady not very far short of eighty to be sitting out-of-doors. He wasn't sure of his grandmother's exact age, but he knew that at the time of her marriage the throne had still been occupied by Queen Victoria. This morning, caught unawares, she looked frail and wistful. Then she heard his footsteps, turned to frown at him, and he decided he'd been mistaken – his dear Lavinia was just as usual, after all. The old black beret she always wore in the garden was crammed on her head; perhaps it was only by chance that it framed her thin brown face and silver hair with such artistry.

'So you've found time to call on me – now nice! I suppose I'm to consider myself fortunate – one of *many* ladyfriends who need visiting.'

'True, but the one I visit first!' He bent down to kiss her cheek, smiling at the same time. The smile turned up the corners of his close-lipped mouth and made him, while it lasted, quite unfairly attractive. She thought it was a good thing for the peace of mind of Fowey's female population that he didn't do it very often; the poor things were susceptible enough as it was.

'I only got rid of my O'Meara cousins yesterday evening – too late by your standards to come calling. They were kind enough to say that I take after *them* rather than my mother's family!'

'Irish flattery,' Lavinia pointed out with her usual candour. 'You're not nearly as good-looking as Christopher O'Meara was.' Then she changed tack abruptly. 'Being convinced Republicans, I suppose they would have liked Germany to win the war?'

'Perhaps, but at least they were tactful enough not to say so. It must be the *only* thing they *didn't* say. God knows how they ever get anything done at home. It will take *me* days to catch up, but I'm glad they came.'

Lavinia nodded, aware that he'd always regretted not

being acquainted with his father's family. But they were wrong about him – he was a Cornishman, first, last and always. And along with Tristram and Jonathan, he was the human being she loved most in the world.

She watched him for a moment, unobserved, because he was frowning at a rooftop visible from where they sat – a Bossiney rooftop, more than likely, if it needed attention. What Lady Bracknell once said about land applied, in Lavinia's experience, to property – there was just as little profit in owning cottages that were always falling down.

'I suppose you think Tristram should come and attend to family affairs here instead of leaving them to you,' she said, misunderstanding his expression. 'So he might if his dear wife would let him come to Cornwall without the devil of a fuss.'

Petroc liked Cécile Bossiney as little as Lavinia did, but it was also his view that his uncle had let Cécile have her own way for far too long; to oppose her in anything now probably required a declaration of war. He knew better than to offer *this* point of view to his grandmother and said instead, 'I'm here on the spot, Uncle Tristram isn't; but I sometimes wish old Chivers had persuaded Grandfather to make a clean sweep of everything when they sold off the ships. I can't see young Luc devoting himself to Fowey in future.'

'Luc? My dear boy, now that he's old enough to do as he likes, he comes to Cornwall once a year for the birthday party your mother insists on arranging for me. I can't think why. She's had time to learn by now that I *hate* birthday parties.'

Petroc was aware that if they'd all agreed to ignore Lavinia's birthday she would have been deeply disappointed and hurt. Altogether, she was in fine, fractious form this morning, but her thin fingers gripped the arms of her chair, giving away some inner tension. He was tempted to ask the cause, but she would tell him when she was ready, not before. It was surely more than sadness about Luc, deeply though she regretted that the war years spent in America had released Cornwall's hold on him – he'd loved Prospect as a little boy.

'It's colder than it seems out here, Gran . . . shouldn't you be indoors?'

She rose like a fish to a choice morsel of bait. 'Why? I'm not in my dotage yet. When I can't stand a little sea-breeze you can shut me up in my box . . . Better still, row me out past Gribben Head and tip me overboard. I'd prefer that to being eaten by worms.'

'Have a heart, dear girl. You *know* that even the river makes the vicar seasick. A fine burial that would be!' Enjoyment of the idea shone in her face, wiping away strain.

'There's plenty of time to change your mind,' Petroc went on. 'Walter Guest stops me regularly in the street to congratulate me on having such a mettlesome piece for a grandmother. Not quite his words, but that's roughly what he means.'

'If the *vicar* has noticed, I must have become even more eccentric than I meant to,' she said regretfully. 'It's a risk when the people of one's own generation disappear. I'm left behind like a Victorian museum-piece; you'll have to put a label on me soon – "species almost extinct"!'

Petroc smiled, but understood her inner sadness. His grandfather hadn't lived to see the ending of the war, and her old friend, 'Q', further along the Esplanade, had died only a few months after Julian Bossiney.

'You're feeling a trifle jaded this morning, love,' he said gently. 'I know things don't look very cheerful, but somehow we shall survive . . . we always do.'

She shook her head. 'I wasn't thinking about *now*; I was remembering how things looked after the other war – the "Great War", we called that. God knows how posterity will decide to describe what's happened since. When that first war ended it seemed as if the world we'd known had gone for ever; but except for the men who were killed and the women who were left to live without them, almost *nothing* altered. The changes that can't be reversed have come this time.'

'No empire, and no reassuring things called gold reserves. Well, never mind, at least we have the Welfare State!'

She screwed up her face in an expression of distaste – what a sickeningly cossetting ring it had to it. Milk for schoolchildren, medicines for the sick, pensions for the old . . . no-one could regret such things. But the idea that personal responsibility was dead because the state alone was in charge, was something she would still find strength to reject with her dying breath. She was about to say so when the rattle of crockery warned them of a new arrival.

Jenifer O'Meara was carrying out a tray and Petroc got up to take it from her. She was huddled inside a thickened, shapeless cardigan – the garment of long-suffering widowhood, Lavinia called it to herself. Her own preference was to wear Julian's old Yacht Club blazer, still bright with brass buttons and embroidered badge.

'Really, Mama, anyone would think it was midsummer – *must* we drink our coffee in the garden?'

'You can drink yours wherever you like,' Lavinia answered mildly. 'I happen to enjoy being out here.' She sipped her coffee, and withdrew from her daughter's conversation which she found uninteresting. When Petroc had reproached her in the past for this habit of removing herself in spirit from what was happening around her, she'd smiled and insisted that it was one of the privileges of growing old – the ancient of days, like herself, were *allowed* to retreat into memories when they wanted to. She was following the conversation sufficiently, nevertheless, to hear a name mentioned that seemed no disturbance of her own train of thought. The Penwarne family had figured in their lives since she'd come to Fowey fifty years before.

'It doesn't seem quite right to me,' Jenifer was saying.

Lavinia had lost count of the things that didn't seem right to her daughter – from independence for India, to the new pavilion in Readymoney Cove, that now brought the noise and laughter of children into their once-secluded beach. Her worst enemy couldn't say of Jenifer now that she was eager to move with the times; she had been once, but life had defeated her.

'Explain to your mother that this is not the year of grace 1910,' Lavinia suggested to her grandson. 'We're in 1950 now, and it doesn't matter a twopenny damn if the regatta is organized by someone who began his working life as a fisherman.'

'True in the case of Charlie Penwarne, at least . . . He'll do it very well,' Petroc agreed, 'and I'm thankful to be unloading the job on him.' He smiled at his mother, hoping to smooth her ruffled feathers. It was hard on both of them – he'd been aware of that ever since he was old enough to realize that it wasn't only children who had problems they couldn't solve. Lavinia loved Prospect, especially now that she had Jonathan Bossiney's company there, but his mother, widowed for nearly thirty years, had been forced to return to a place she'd always hated. The war years had broken the monotony of her life at Prospect; she'd been busy, felt useful, looked attractive again. But that was over now. The American armada moored in the river had sailed for France, and finally for home. There was nothing left to look forward to. He got up to go, kissed them both, and promised to find the time to come to dinner soon.

He ran down the flights of steps leading to the bottom level of the garden and let himself out into the road. It was too early in the year for holidaymakers. For a month or two yet, thank God, Fowey belonged to itself, 'not to any of they' from across the Tamar. Normally in walking along the Esplanade he liked to imagine it when it had been the Rope Walk, with miles of yarn laid out for the ships' rigging. There would have been barques and brigantines and schooners moored alongside Town Quay then, and all the rumbustious life of a seaport that did business in great waters. He wished he could have known Fowey then.

But this morning his thoughts were still with the women left at Prospect. There was no doubt about it: something had happened to ruffle Lavinia; and about his mother there had been an air, not quite hidden, of pleased expectancy for once. In *her* it was rare enough to be noticeable. He felt slightly anxious, but told himself that Lavinia would have had the sense to tell him if the matter was urgent.

On the following Sunday morning – a fine one when he would rather have been out-of-doors – he sat at his kitchen table wrestling with the milk returns demanded by the Min. of Ag. But the view outside enticed him into putting down his pen, recalling the conversation that had shaped the future of his life after he left the Navy. Two years at an agricultural college learning about farm management had been followed by a job in Devon, running an absentee landlord's estate. When he'd been there for eighteen months and was home for a much-needed holiday, Jonathan Bossiney had made his astounding suggestion.

'No point in waiting till I'm dead . . . Have the money now, lad, and get started on your own. It's nonsense to use your best years working for someone else.'

'It's . . . it's amazingly generous of you, but I can't . . . can't possibly accept,' Petroc had stammered.

Jonathan's fluffy white eyebrows had climbed up his forehead. 'Why not, pray? Too proud to accept a helping hand when you need it?'

'Not that, certainly. But even if you don't want to establish a home for overworked, broken-down doctors, there are relatives with a nearer claim on you than me.'

'Tristram, and your mother, you mean? True, but *he* has the Bossiney inheritance such as it is – you don't; and if Jenifer ever needs help, she'll be able to call on you.' The stubborn expression on his great-nephew's face made him take refuge in a little show of anger. 'Dammit, boy, I can do what I like with my own money. Why can't you behave like any sensible chap and accept a little gift without all this unseemly argy-bargy?'

'Because it isn't little,' Petroc had insisted. 'Of course I'd accept gratefully if it were a hundred or two . . . it would buy me a good second-hand car. But you're proposing to hand me the result of a lifetime's work and give up your home into the bargain. How can I possibly take that?'

'Because you're like the son I never had, and because it means that if I leave here I shall finally have an excuse to share Prospect with Lavinia.' A shy smile lit Jonathan's face as he made his confession. 'I wanted to marry her, you know, but I was too late – Julian found her first. We've both been lonely ever since. Apart from that, it would please her more than anything else to see *you* get started on your own.'

No argument was possible after that. Petroc used the money to buy two farms, as different from each other as two holdings could be. His home was now a white-washed farmhouse called Tregenna in the valley of the little Lerryn river. Well-founded shippons clustered round two other sides of a square; on the fourth side grazing meadows dropped down in terraces to the river. It was very beautiful and, for Cornwall, lush. Trebinnick to the north, on the much wilder slopes of Bodmin Moor, was a different proposition altogether – an isolated hill-farm, still primitive by mid-twentieth-century standards. The lonely stone house that went with the land was barely habitable yet, but the shepherd who looked after Petroc's flocks lived contentedly in a cottage just as primitive. Jonathan could see both neglected farms being put back into working order . . . and would die content in the knowledge that Petroc cherished what he owned of Cornwall.

The milk returns were done at last. He heaved a sigh of relief almost at the same moment as someone thumped on the kitchen door. Morwetha stood there, smiling at her brother.

'In time for coffee, I hope . . . it's thirsty work pedalling all the way here.'

'Come in and take a seat. Better still, be housewifely and make us *both* some coffee! Why are you here, though? I thought you'd gone to the Great Wen.'

'I went . . . I'm back.' She set out mugs, put the kettle on, and reflected that there was nothing like service in the Navy to teach a bachelor good habits. Petroc's kitchen was a model of cleanliness and order, but it was a pity, in a way. She'd have liked to see him in need of a wife. 'I'm full of news, as usual,' she said, bringing their mugs to the table.

'Tell me.'

'Uncle Tris has gone dashing off to Zurich, much to the wrath of Aunt C., who required him, of course, to do something else. But for once, according to Lisette, he turned a deaf ear. It seems he's heard of a German living there, by the name of Winkler, and convinced himself that it's his old friend, Kurt. I hope he turns out to be right. You were only a babe-in-arms at the time but I can just remember Kurt Winkler coming to Prospect long before the war . . . a very gentle young man who sang me lullabies in a language I couldn't understand.'

'If it *is* Uncle Tris's friend, remember that he's had to survive Auschwitz – he may be barely recognizable.'

Morwetha nodded, shivering at the horror of what her brother had just said. It was not a particle of good their saintly Vicar preaching Christ's message to her. Father forgive them for they know not what they do. The Germans in charge of the bestialities committed in concentration camps *had* known what they were doing. She had no intention of forgiving them, ever.

'What news of the Haddenhams?' Petroc asked, to remove the shadow from her face.

'Cousin Julia is still going strong, believe it or not . . . raising cain at St Clyst, watched over by patient

Charlotte. The poor wretched earl and his wife have *his* mother there as well as Julia. They must wonder what they've done to deserve *two* such spirited octogenarian dowagers on their hands. Victoria's in New York, where her husband seems to be permanently attached to U.N.O. Elinor has the house in Green Street and uses it as a kind of residential club for former members of the Czech and Polish forces here – the ones who can't or won't go home. They're well-connected members, of course; they're able to kiss her hand very elegantly, and sponge off her with equal grace!'

'*Quite* worthy of Gran,' Petroc said appreciatively. 'You'll be just like her one of these days.'

'I shan't mind that.' Morwetha helped herself to a cigarette from the packet lying on the table. 'By the way, Lisette's threatening to come down for Easter. Luc is *not*! According to Aunt Cécile, he's already an interior designer of near-genius; in another year or two everyone, but *everyone*, else will be copying his work. If you ask me, he's a poisonous mixture of post-American confidence and studied continental "charm"! Not a bit like Uncle Tris at all.' She smiled at her brother in quick apology. 'Sorry . . . I sound acid this morning; perhaps it's because I'm worried.'

'What about?'

'Something Lisette let fall unintentionally. There seems to be a definite movement under way to get Prospect disposed of the moment Granny dies. Aunt Cécile makes it clear that nothing would induce her to move there, and she's got a faithful echo in Luc, for whom life in London is the only life worth living. Lisette doesn't much care, although she likes coming to Cornwall, and would probably feel uncomfortable about turfing Mama out, and Great-uncle Jonathan if he's still alive.'

'You don't say anything about Uncle Tris . . . it happens to be *his* house since Grandfather died.'

'I think he, poor man, is like whoever it was caught between Scylla and Charybdis . . . not wanting to do

244

anything to hurt anyone, but confronted by the facts that Cécile keeps shoving under his nose.'

'Like – fact no. 1: the income from Bossiney property scarcely does more than keep *that* above ground, and certainly doesn't do much to support the running costs of Prospect – I should know, I have the job of trying to balance the books; fact no. 2: since Uncle Tris gave up the Foreign Office and took to publishing, it's probably Cécile's business earnings that enable them to live in the style they do in Pont Street.'

His face looked drawn suddenly, making Morwetha want to give comfort if she could.

'Don't get too alarmed, love . . . it may only be Lisette liking to make a mountain out of a molehill. In any case, Gran's not "goin' round land" for years yet; and spiking Cécile's guns must give her more to live for than anything else!'

Petroc smiled at his sister, nodded, and invited her to inspect two new foals in the paddock outside. But when she'd bicycled away, his face looked sombre again. Her Pont Street gossip explained the change of atmosphere he'd sensed at Prospect the other day. Lavinia had got wind of something – probably because his mother had received a hint from Cécile that *she* wouldn't have to end her days at Prospect after all – expulsion would seem like a merciful release to Jenifer O'Meara. Lavinia would know that she had nothing to fear for herself – Tristram would never evict her, even to please his wife – but Prospect represented more to her than the roof and four walls that sheltered them. It was part of Fowey's history and the home of the Bossineys – the place where they belonged to be. Petroc agreed with her, and he'd be damned if he'd let his Belgian aunt-by-marriage win *this* fight without a struggle.

17

The weather in London had turned unseasonably cold. There'd even been a fall of sleety snow overnight – just enough to rob the park of its familiarity. The thinning veil of white on grass suddenly evoked a memory from years so long ago that Polly stopped to pin down what it was – the lace of spindrift left behind in Prospect Cove when a wave ran back into the sea. Ridiculous to think of that now in the middle of Hyde Park; in fact, ridiculous to be here at all, when her fingers were numb with cold, trying to catch the effect of black winter trees against a covering of snow and a low, grey, London sky.

When the stream of Knightsbridge traffic allowed her to cross, she headed towards Wilton Mews and the house that was the present home of the Penwarnes. There had been so many changes of address in recent years that she sometimes found herself stopping to remember where it was she had to go. Now, with a leap across Grosvenor Place and a scramble over a high wall, they could be in the gardens of Buckingham Palace itself. She hoped this proximity to royalty might be enough to keep her father happy – not because she particularly liked Wilton Mews; but she was very tired of moving.

On the way home she stopped at one of her usual dawdling-places – a picture gallery of the discreetly expensive kind that never treated passers-by to more than one picture at a time. Its proprietor clearly favoured modern art, and Polly's daily pleasure lay in thinking how absurd most of it was.

This morning one picture was displayed as usual, signed by an artist called Lowry. For once, she didn't smile, but stared for a long time instead, with her nose almost touching the cold plate-glass. It was a very simple painting – a pale wash of sky, a deeper band of colour for the ocean, and in the foreground one small figure of a man looking over a sea-wall. Nothing remarkable about it at all, but for the second time that day she was catapulted back into the past. The wave of yearning sadness that swept over her was recognizable; she'd felt it once before, ten years ago. The noise of the traffic behind her became the steady thump of waves against rock, and a car's horn the sound of a seagull crying. She was inside the picture with the man, staring at the empty sea, sharing his need for something unidentified but desperately longed-for.

Then the strangeness of the moment faded. She was back in a London street again, and she could see the proprietor watching her from inside the gallery, curious to know what kept her standing there in the cold. She saw reflected in the glass the image of what he saw – a thin girl with short dark hair ruffled by the wind; scarcely pretty, with a wedge-shaped face that was broad across the temples, pointed at the chin. Thick, straight brows drew attention to the eyes beneath, but they would have been noticeable in any case – black-lashed and deeply blue; her only claim to beauty.

She started walking again, trying to think about the work waiting for her in the little darkroom she had rigged up at the top of the house. Her photographs were beginning to be known, and she was proud of a series of London street scenes just being published by *Picture Post*. Work finished for the day, she was being taken to see *Swan Lake*, danced gloriously by Margot Fonteyn and the rest of the Sadlers Wells Ballet. Life might still seem unfairly austere to people resentful of the rationing and restrictions left over from a war they were supposed to have won, but at nearly twenty-one, Polly insisted on finding it exciting to be alive in London. The city might be shabby still, but it was where she belonged. She'd seen it bombed and burning, but never doubted that it would survive; she was content as she was, and that strange hankering outside the gallery window had been the dying flicker of a dream.

At breakfast the following morning, Daniel Penwarne seemed disinclined, for once, to hide behind his newspaper, even though it contained an item of particular interest to him.

'I saw the headline,' Polly said, smiling at him. 'Petrol's coming off the ration at last. The age of mass motoring is about to dawn, and Penwarne garages are braced for the first rush!'

'They've been braced for far too damn long. An allowance of ninety miles' motoring a month hasn't exactly made garage-owners rich.'

'No, but that wouldn't have troubled Sir Stafford Cripps. You ought to know by now that he's very much agin capitalism!' Polly glanced at her father's face, looking for a gleam of humour that for once wasn't there. Something other than the subject of petrol-rationing clearly occupied his mind. 'Anyway, we don't need more money,' she added firmly. 'We're rich enough.' She had no idea whether it was true or not; but it didn't matter anyway if he would only work less hard.

'*I'll* decide when we're rich enough. But that wasn't what I was going to say.' He poured more coffee in his cup, but sat watching it grow cool. 'I called in at Thurloe Square on my way back last night to see the Gallaghers' new house. They've had it done over in some nineteen-thirties style: Art Deco, they called it – squashy white sofas, and tables made of glass.'

'Sounds *very* vulgar to me,' Polly commented, 'but I can see the Gallaghers loving it, especially when everyone else is still having to make do with Utility.'

His mouth twitched but he sounded severe. 'I shouldn't have sent you to that fancy school – it's made a snob of you.'

She smiled, knowing that he was too sharp to have missed her dislike of his Irish friends. They, and others like them, drank his carefully hoarded whisky and boasted of the fortunes to be made in post-war London by those sharp enough to see the loopholes in government restrictions. Polly judged her father to be hard but honourable in his business dealings; she had no such confidence in Patrick Gallagher and his cronies.

'You keep interrupting,' Daniel said unfairly. 'I'm trying to tell you that two unusual things happened yesterday. First off, I called on Kirkmichael, who charged me ten guineas for the privilege of looking wise and telling me it was time I took a holiday.'

'Is that all he told you?' she enquired carefully after a moment.

'Not quite – slight heart murmur; nothing that a couple of pills a day and a little rest won't cure, so you needn't get het up, if that's what you're thinking of doing.'

She knew that he would refuse to be fussed over, just as he refused to fuss over her, but their love for each other was what warmed their lives. Attachment had gone on deepening since the day five years ago in the closing stages of the war when Loveday Penwarne had been killed by one of the last V2 rockets to fall on London. Polly knew that since then, too, her father had abandoned almost everything in life but work. It wasn't wealth that he pursued so single-mindedly; only the next brilliant idea, the coming opportunity that other men failed to see because they allowed themselves too many other distractions. There were very few in Daniel Penwarne's life, Polly being the only one that mattered to him.

'So there's nothing to worry about,' she said in a voice she didn't allow to tremble. 'All I want to know is when you leave for your holiday.'

A sudden grin disturbed the lines carved into Daniel's face, making him look less weary for a moment or two. 'When I'm ready! Now, hold your tongue and listen to yesterday's second happening. Mary Gallagher had also invited the woman who redesigned the house for them. Guess who *she* turned out to be? Someone you've heard your uncles talk about – Lady Tristram Bossiney! Her son Luc was there as well, wearing a lot of black in the hope that someone would notice him, I suppose, against all those white sofas.'

Polly had no interest in a couple she didn't know, and scarcely stopped to consider the strangeness of three of Mary Gallagher's guests being linked with the same small corner of a forgotten county at the other end of England. Only one question penetrated the haze of anxiety about her father's health.

'If she's Lady Tristram Bossiney, does it mean that old Lady Bossiney is dead?'

'Far from it, according to her daughter-in-law. She's still living in that barn of a house at Fowey, with her widowed daughter. *You* wouldn't have met them there. The Bossineys didn't make a habit of calling on the Penwarnes – still don't, as far as I know.'

'As it happens, I *did* meet Lady Bossiney once – by accident. I liked her,' Polly said slowly. 'I bumped into her other grandson there as well . . . But he was a bossy, objectionable schoolboy at the time.' The encounter was still vivid in her memory, and so was the house she'd been taken to. 'Mummy must have . . . have known Prospect very well; it's in a lot of the pictures she painted.'

Daniel stared at his cup, emptied it in one quick gulp and put it down too hard on the saucer again.

'Of course – she lived there as your objectionable schoolboy's nursemaid.'

Silence filled the room but it was full, too, of the presence of a woman who had never been there. Loveday's gentle ghost had kept them company ever since she was killed, and Polly sometimes wondered if it was what her father had tried to escape from each time they moved. There were echoes in her own mind of the legends she'd been taught by Loveday. Seagulls housed the unquiet spirits of sailors lost at sea and thus denied Christian burial. No such ceremony had been needed for her mother, either, trapped in the path of a descending rocket-bomb.

No-one had released her spirit into eternity with grave, beautiful words of comfort. The knowledge was the cause of a recurring nightmare that Polly had never shared with her father. To make up for this secrecy she *had* admitted to her refusal to accept the rest of Isaac's legacy of fact and fantasy. She was a Londoner born and bred, and proud of it; had no need of Celtic mysteries; they were as alien to *her* as the ghost of Hamlet's father had been to the soldiers on the battlements at Elsinore.

Daniel never spoke voluntarily of his dead wife. A line seemed to have been drawn round her memory, forbidding entry. Polly supposed that she'd stepped over the line this morning because his reference to the Bossineys came so closely on the heels of her own vivid recollection of Prospect, outside the gallery window. She shivered, remembering that her mother would undoubtedly have said that the coincidence was 'meant'.

'No good thinking of going abroad,' Daniel said suddenly. 'The currency allowance we're doled out at the moment wouldn't do more than buy us a couple of meals. I think we'll go to Cornwall instead – hire a house for a few weeks, maybe; I hate living in hotels.'

Polly's gasp made him stare at her, and he misread the expression on her face.

'No need to look so horrified – we'll hire a housekeeper as well.'

'*You* hire a house and housekeeper; it's you who need the rest. I'm going to stay here.' When disagreeing with her father she was usually careful to be gentle. This fierce rejection of his scheme not only irritated but puzzled him.

'What's wrong with Cornwall, for God's sake? You belong there.'

'I don't . . . I won't. I refuse to belong anywhere but here, and I *specially* refuse to be Cornish.' She was afraid of sounding childish or hysterical, but didn't care. Instinct urged her to trample on logic, and avoid a place she *knew* to be dangerous.

Daniel registered her sudden pallor, and the tension that locked her thin hands together. She was often stubborn, but rarely unreasonable. Whatever the objection she had to revisiting Fowey, it was real to *her*. He could still remember her coming back with Loveday from that brief war-time stay – silent and strangely sullen for a child who'd got her own way about not being left behind down there. He'd never discovered the reason, and she'd never explained it afterwards, but now the memory made him unusually patient.

'Listen, maid, you had a bee in your bonnet last time you went there – the war was starting and you had some silly idea you didn't want to leave me behind in London. On top of that, Cornwall's not an easy place to get to know. It's secretive, and glad to be different from anywhere else. But, like it or not, all the blood in your veins flows from there. Give it another chance and come with me.'

He saw resistance still strong on her face and resorted to cunning of the lowest kind – even managed to look wistful. 'I'm supposed to be taking my holiday in peace, not worrying about you left alone here. And it would have been a treat for your grandparents to see you again – they're getting very old now. Still, if it's too much to ask . . .'

'Oh, all *right*,' she shouted. 'I'll come, but don't think I'm going to fall for all that Cornish stuff about Merlin and King Arthur, and dancing maidens turned into blocks of stone, and Little People banging around underground, because I'm *not*!'

'No need to believe a word of it,' Daniel said largely. 'I don't myself.' He smiled, and the knot of fear inside her loosened a little. 'I've had an idea, though. There's plenty there that's *real* to photograph – ancient things, as well as derelict chimneys and engine-houses, and ivy-covered remains of tinners' shacks on godforsaken bits of moorland – art studies, don't they call them? If your photographs are any good we'll get them published in a book.'

'Good or not, they're scarcely going to be cheerful, by the sound of it. Ruins seldom are,' she said crossly.

'Cornwall past *and* present, then. That would only be fair, and a bit more lively,'

She nodded, aware that his suggestion might even make the visit bearable. Her father was generous, and the pair of pre-war Leicas he'd found for her were almost as precious in their own way as Loveday's sketch-books that held pride of place among her private treasures. He was quite proud to see her name beneath published photographs, but he had no idea whether her work was good or bad. His genius was for practical things, and *her* gift for 'seeing' beautiful or telling images had come entirely from her mother. She was aware of it, but aware, too, that it was something else she didn't discuss with Daniel.

'I expect I shall be busy keeping my eye on *you*,' she said gravely at last, 'but I might manage to take a decent photograph or two as well.'

'We'll leave in a week's time, then – have Easter there.'

Leave in his allotted time they would, whatever strains it put on his overworked staff, and however much she had to do herself. Busy as she was, she was reluctant to accept an invitation which arrived halfway through the week. Cécile Bossiney apologized for its lateness, entreated them to come, and Daniel – not a cocktail party man as a rule – said, to Polly's surprise, that it would look churlish not to look in at Pont Street.

She had worked out the family relationships and allowed herself to be introduced to Luc and Lisette Bossiney with an ear cocked for the arrogance she remembered in their cousin. Luc, more startlingly handsome than her father had thought to mention, bowed gracefully over her hand. Stately as a duchess, Polly bowed back, then grinned when he'd moved on, because the performance had been so ridiculous.

'You're not supposed to laugh at Luc,' a voice said beside her. 'He *aims* to be different. I'm his twin, Lisette,

253

by the way. Maman says *you* hail from Cornwall, too.'

She was recognizably related to Luc Bossiney, though not an identical twin – small and beautifully curved, with a mane of reddish-gold hair, bright hazel eyes, and a mouth that smiled easily. Recognizably, too, she was the daughter of the woman who stood talking to Daniel. But whereas she had the artless friendliness of a puppy, Cécile Bossiney was the elegant, finished product of much time, thought, and money. Polly stared at her for a moment, appreciating the overall effect, then smiled at Lisette.

'I was laughing at myself as well. Does your brother always dress in black, and try to behave like a Spanish grandee?'

'It makes people remember him . . . so it's very good for business! He and my mother decorate houses together, you know. I've been away in Paris, learning to cook. It shows, I'm afraid – good cooks have to keep tasting things!' She cast a wistful eye over Polly's slenderness. 'I can see it isn't what you do.'

'No, I take photographs – outdoor things, mostly, so I get a lot of exercise. If it's any comfort, my father probably approves of *you*. He thinks women *should* be nicely curved and feminine.'

Lisette smiled happily. 'I expect he enjoys good food, too – we're made for each other!' Her amusement vanished suddenly. 'Oh, God – now I've remembered . . . been tactless *again* . . . I'm sorry.'

Polly shook her head, liking Lisette Bossiney more than she'd expected to. 'I haven't met *your* father – isn't he here this evening?'

'No, he's in Switzerland, looking for an old friend. Maman was a bit miffed about that – hence the party! I dare say he'd have found an excuse not to be here anyway – he doesn't much care for my mother's parties. He'd rather be at Prospect, but she doesn't care for *that*. I don't think I shall ever bother to get married – why spend your life doing things *you* don't want to do, or making someone else do what *they* don't want to do?'

As a viewpoint born of Lisette's observation of her parents' relationship, it was certainly discouraging, but Polly didn't say so. 'I believe there's usually considered to be a bit more to marriage than that,' she suggested cautiously.

'You remind me of my grandmother – Lavinia's got the same trick of sounding solemn when her eyes are smiling.' Lisette stared a moment longer, then made up her mind about her mother's guest. 'I wish you'd come to Cornwall sometimes. You obviously never do, because I'd have seen you there . . . Fowey isn't big enough to hide a flea in.'

'I went once, but didn't stay very long,' Polly said briefly. 'As it happens, though, I'm going again soon with my father, and we shall be there for a few weeks. Our kind, clever doctor has finally frightened him into taking a holiday.'

'And I've already invited myself to Prospect for Easter . . . *what* a good thing!' Her smiling face darkened suddenly. 'You're bound to meet my cousin Petroc; perhaps I should warn you about him.'

'No need – I met him by accident ten years ago; we didn't take to each other, even then.'

'Well, that's all right,' Lisette said with satisfaction, 'because I've adored him for years – ever since the days when he used to regularly half-drown me in his beastly little dinghy; but he's got a lot more attractive since then! He belongs entirely to me, although I'm not sure he *quite* realizes it yet.'

'I shouldn't beat about the bush if I were you,' Polly advised gravely. 'Make the situation clear, in case he imagines he's still free to choose.'

She smiled suddenly because Lisette was looking thoughtful, and the smile startled Luc Bossiney into changing his mind about Mr Penwarne's daughter. With her face sparkling with amusement, she was intriguing enough to lure him out of the clutches of one of his mother's rich but undeniably boring clients.

Lisette frowned as he came over to them, not wanting a conversation with her new friend to be interrupted just as it was getting interesting. 'Go away, brother dear . . . *you're* supposed to be charming the middle-aged ladies while Maman does her stuff on all the elderly men! Only *I* am here to enjoy myself.'

Polly felt a twinge of pity for him. Lisette might be an entertaining companion but she must be an embarrassment to her family. Being with her was like the childhood pleasure of being allowed to share someone else's doll's house – each room she let you peer into gave away another secret of their life that wasn't intended for public viewing.

Luc smiled charmingly at Polly. 'I can't imagine why we've never met in Fowey – it's such a tiny place.'

'Your grandparents live at Prospect, mine in Fore Street – there's a certain distance between them!' she reminded him bluntly. 'It's true that I strayed into Prospect Cove one day, but it was made very clear to me that I was trespassing.'

Lisette pounced on this with glee. '*That* was when you met Petroc! It sounds just like him . . . he's very dynastically minded. What's ours is ours, and blow the rest of the world!'

'Then I should be grateful he didn't leave me to drown, I suppose. But your grandmother probably sent him out to fish me off the rock I was clinging to . . . I don't think he rescued me from choice.'

'Well, this time I shall *invite* you to Prospect,' Lisette said kindly. 'I can't say I'd want to live there for ever, as Granny and Aunt Jen have done, but I love brief visits. I must have got Pa's Cornish genes when they were shared between us, and Luc got all the Sabatiers' continental ones. He never goes near Prospect if he can help it.'

Polly regretfully bit back the question on the tip of her tongue . . . What would happen when it became his turn to inherit the old grey house that kept watch on the tides flowing in and out of the river mouth? Lisette would almost certainly give her a full and indiscreet answer but, however unEnglish his genes, it was doubtful if Luc Bossiney would welcome their family affairs being discussed with a stranger. She saw her father across the room, looking bored in the company of one of Lady Bossiney's elderly admirers; it was clearly time to rescue him and go.

'Until Easter then,' she said, smiling at Lisette. 'I'll show you the rock in Prospect Cove on which a small but highly promising photographer nearly met her watery end!' She nodded at Luc, giving him no chance to deliver another elegant bow, and walked away from them both with a slight feeling of relief. Like Lisette's opinion of Prospect, the company of the Bossineys was enjoyable in small doses.

She said this to her father as they drove away, expecting him to growl that the visit hadn't been enjoyable at all. He didn't answer immediately, but when she turned to look at him she realized that she'd been mistaken. A faint smile hung about his mouth, signalling to someone who knew him very well that he had found the evening worthwhile.

'You seemed to be getting on very well with Lisette Bossiney, and I dare say young Luc improves with acquaintance,' Daniel observed with unusual tolerance.

'I doubt it, because he's got continental genes – Belgian ones inherited from his mother! Mummy took me to see Grandfather Eliot at Polruan one day, and *he* was of the opinion that nothing good had ever come out of Belgium. Still, we must assume that he never had the chance to meet Lady Tristram Bossiney!'

Daniel took time to consider the matter. 'They'd be well matched, I'd say . . . the irresistible force being her ladyship, and the immovable object Captain Tom! You know, maid, I'm quite looking forward to our little Cornish jaunt.'

It was all he would say on the subject, and Polly was left to wonder to herself why the thought of a holiday he would normally abhor should be giving him so much pleasure.

18

Tristram led his companion to the most sheltered spot
he could find, behind the hull of a slung lifeboat. But
even here the wind blew round them with the cutting
edge of a knife, and outside Calais harbour the waves
were being whipped back on themselves in ominous,
dirty-white crests – it was going to be the worst kind
of March crossing. They could have been home by now,
but Kurt had rejected the idea of flying, as definitely as
he'd shaken his head a moment ago at the offer of the
saloon's smoky warmth down below. Frail as a skeleton,
pale as a ghost, he seemed nevertheless determined to
avoid contact with other human beings. His gaunt face
was turned towards the sea, giving nothing away, and
Tristram was left to wonder yet again whether it had
been right to bring him to England.

There'd been no difficulty in recognizing his friend.
After a moment's rigid stillness, Kurt had known him,
and smiled. But Tristram's horror had grown gradually,
throttling him with pity and anguish, and the knowledge
that his own life must seem to have been intolerably easy.
Kurt's face had the greyish pallor of someone who lived
too much indoors on too little food. When he put out a
hand the number tattooed on his thin wrist stood out
lividly still, like a brand of the damned. Pinned to the
lapel of his coat was the tiny star of David – cloth emblem
of Jewishness that prisoners like himself had been made
to wear, though he wore it now from deliberate, proud
choice.

'Dear friend . . . I didn't think to see *you* ever again.'
'You damned nearly didn't.' Tristram managed to

swallow the sick, helpless anger that made him want to shout. 'I hadn't anything to go on when I started looking for you. Why couldn't you have written to me? You knew where *I* was likely to be.'

Kurt examined his hands, and seemed surprised to find that they were trembling. 'You and everyone else I loved belonged to the past,' he explained slowly. 'Then came the war . . . and now this.' His gesture indicated the comfortless room that was now his home in a Swiss boarding house. 'Three separate lives . . . three different men, whose only connection is that they have shared the name of Kurt Winkler.' A fit of coughing interrupted him, but he went on when it was over. 'What was I to write – that a man *you* never knew now lives at No. 7 Lindenstrasse, Zurich?'

'You live here instead of in a comfortable apartment in Berlin. You support yourself God knows how, but probably *not* as a professor of psychiatry. Otherwise, to me you're the same man – the oldest and dearest of my friends,' Tristram said steadily. 'Come back with me to England, please. If you refuse I'll know for sure that you're the same stubborn devil I first met at Oxford. Where will your case be then, Professor?'

A faint smile touched Kurt's mouth, then faded again because remembering was painful. 'I'm afraid that *that's* how they taught you to argue at New College, my friend . . . *I'm* out of practice now!' He gestured again, this time to a table pushed up to the room's one small window. 'You can see what I am now – a woodcarver. I'm getting so much better at it that someone who lives downstairs manages to sell things for me occasionally. But I'm not worthy yet of the man whose tools I use. They belonged to an Austrian – a very gentle genius, who couldn't survive what was done to him. When I tracked down his widow after the war, to tell her that Hans was dead, she insisted on giving me his beautiful chisels. They are my only precious possession now.'

Tristram blinked away the tears that pricked his eyelids

and stared at the small wooden creatures in front of him – animals and birds – that seemed to have come to rest on Kurt's table. They had been shaped from memory because no wildlife was visible from this miserable room, but surely only in the carver's opinion were they not yet worthy of his Austrian friend. Tristram fingered them gently, half-expecting them to move when he touched them because they seemed so full of life.

'They're beautiful, but you need real models to work from. We can find you those in Cornwall. Come with me, please. I can't leave you cooped up here.'

'And *I* can't be among people any more,' Kurt explained quietly. 'You are very kind, my friend, but I'm happy now on my own. I've grown selfish, you see . . . and also rather cowardly. Cooped up here, as you put it, I feel safe.' His voice suddenly shook, and in his eyes was the desolation of a man whose faith in humanity had almost been destroyed by the sight of too much evil. Unable to put comfort into words, Tristram simply wrapped his arms round Kurt's shoulders and stood holding him until horror had loosened its grip.

At last he spoke again, slowly and deliberately, to be sure that Kurt understood. 'I'm not offering you very much – only a lonely, primitive, little house on Bodmin Moor. It belongs to my nephew, Petroc, but he doesn't live there. A tenant would be good for it, so you'd be doing *him* a favour, and you could watch animals and birds practically hopping round the door – what more could an industrious woodcarver ask?'

'Only an occasional buyer for his wares – otherwise he would be unable to eat at all!' Imagining that the objection would put an end to an idea that, just for a moment, had glowed as brightly as a lamp in darkness, Kurt put it aside and asked a different question. 'Your family no longer live at Prospect?'

'My father died before the war ended, but Mother, Uncle Jonathan and my sister are still there.' Tristram regretted the mention of Jenifer, and hurried on. 'My niece is sometimes there as well. Do you remember her? A bossy, self-willed little creature who smiled enchantingly and thereby turned away much wrath. She hasn't changed! During the summer she has a shop at Polperro, displaying the work of local artists. Visitors flock there and she makes sure they buy something before they leave.'

'She sounds alarming; but I am not a "local" artist to be supported by her endeavours.'

Tristram shrugged the objection aside. 'It isn't what she set her heart on doing. Very early in the war she'd met and married a charming, kind man called Peter Kendrick. They'd run Prospect eventually as a home for handicapped children. But the life of a fighter-pilot in the RAF wasn't worth much; Peter was killed in the closing stages of the Battle of Britain. So, now, she chooses to look after struggling artists instead.'

Kurt relapsed into silence, looking back over the long and dreadful lapse of years. He didn't want to think about Jenifer O'Meara; it was less painful to remember a small, bright-eyed child who *had* indeed smiled entrancingly.

'What will happen to Prospect now?' he asked eventually.

'Nothing until my mother dies. After that, heaven knows. The only certain thing is that Cécile will never agree to live there.'

'Perhaps she will change her mind when you retire.'

'Diplomacy already manages without me,' Tristram said dryly. 'I left the foreign service at the end of the war. Now I'm a publisher in London. Cécile and Luc, my son, run a successful interior-decoration business there. *She* is rather well-known – a feature of the London scene; I am not!'

Kurt had lost the habit of conversation, but not the acuteness of his ear for the concealments that others felt obliged to take refuge in. He avoided people now for that very reason – there was no more grief that he could bear to share.

'Your uncle is at Prospect you say?' he murmured to break an awkward silence.

'He sold his own house when he gave up doctoring and moved back into Prospect with my mother and sister.' Tristram put down the wooden squirrel he found he was still holding. 'There's only one other person to mention whom you would have remembered – Loveday Penwarne,' he said abruptly. 'She was killed almost at the end of the war, by one of the last rocket-bombs to fall on London. Cécile and the twins and I were still in Washington at the time. My mother sent me the news, but I didn't need telling – I already knew that something very dreadful had happened.'

There was another silence in the room, broken at last by Kurt's quiet voice.

'Tristram, I think after all, that I should like the little house on Bodmin Moor.'

Three days later they were huddled in the lee of the lifeboat on the cross-Channel steamer – one of them looking ill and withdrawn into the loneliness of spirit in which he now seemed to feel at home; the other racked by anxiety. Tristram knew that his urgent telephone call to Petroc would have ensured that, somehow, the house would be made habitable; but nothing could be done to change the fact that Trebinnick was isolated and primitive. It had been the act of a madman or a fool to think that it was the place for a man in Kurt's present condition, much less to imagine that he might find peace of mind there.

While Petroc went to the station to meet his uncle and their unexpected guest, Morwetha finished what preparations they had been able to make. The house was as clean as scrubbing and polishing could make it; rugs and pieces of furniture hastily purloined from Prospect took away its emptiness; lamps were filled with oil, the fire was laid, there was food in the larder. At last, tired and worried, she finally closed the door and drove home to Fowey. If her uncle had been there she would have told him what he'd been telling himself ever since he left Zurich. Instead she told her grandmother.

'Trebinnick on a fine spring day, with a breeze to chase the clouds over the hills, and the gorse blazing, is all very well; on a day of mist or driving rain it might be bearable to a contented man with a brave, frontier-spirited wife. Kurt Winkler is *not* such a man, and driving rain and loneliness are what he's likely to get. Uncle Tris has taken leave of his senses.'

Lavinia was far from sure that she didn't share Morwetha's opinion, but she had no intention of saying so. 'You're very tired, my dear; things can easily look hopeless then – *quite* unnecessarily.' She stared at her grand-daughter's pale face and offered the comfort she had been clutching to herself.

'Kurt was very happy here as a young man – that might help, don't you think?' She frowned over another memory, intrusive and less comforting, and was dismayed to hear Morwetha put it into words.

'Did he really fall in love with my poor dear Mum? She's been in a complete twitter ever since we knew he was coming, with lots of dark hints being dropped about some highly romantic affair.'

Lavinia sympathized with her grand-daughter's faint air of disbelief, but felt obliged to insist that even the middle-aged had once known painfully what it was to be young.

'Your mother was newly widowed at the time, and rather beautiful; Kurt was a charming, clever, young man – too clever for his own happiness, perhaps. He thought of *himself* as a German in those days, and saw Jenifer as an incurably *English* woman who hadn't even been able to settle happily in Ireland – where after all they speak something that approximates to her own language. In the end he went back to Germany alone. I thought he was right to do so, but your uncle bitterly disagreed with me.' Her voice faded into silence; she found she could remember that conversation with Tristram so vividly and with so much grief that it might have taken place yesterday.

Morwetha watched her grandmother's face and reluctantly tugged her back to their present problem. 'Mummy sometimes forgets that time moves on,' she suggested with more tact than usual. 'I did my best to remind her that . . . that . . .'

'*She* is middle-aged and sorry for herself, and Kurt the broken survivor of unthinkable atrocities,' Lavinia finished for her bluntly. 'Jenifer will have faced neither of those harsh facts.' She saw the sudden anxiety as well as the tiredness in Morwetha's face and leaned forward suddenly to kiss her cheek. 'My dear, we can only wait and see. Kurt may hate Trebinnick, in which case we shall simply help him to get back to Switzerland. If it should happen to give him peace, we shall see nothing of him here – according to Tristram, he shuns people completely now. Fortunately your mother loathes Petroc's moorland hide-out, and won't make a misjudged habit of going there to try to lure Kurt out of solitude.'

It seemed to sum up all there was to say. They were left to seek their beds and wait for Tristram's arrival in the morning. But, at breakfast, it was impossible to pretend that they thought only of normal, every-day things – the preparations to be made for Easter, Lisette's visit, and the annual spring re-opening of Morwetha's shop at Polperro. Jenifer sighed a good deal, and thanked God so often for 'a fine morning at least' that Lavinia's patience finally snapped. She was pointing out that since Trebinnick had a roof, Kurt *wasn't* camping in the open air when the arrival of the mail provided a useful diversion. There was a rare letter from Luc, asking prettily if he just *might*, dearest Gran, come with Lisette to Prospect for Easter after all. The news distracted Jenifer, who enjoyed her nephew's company, and listened to his London gossip as avidly as an audience of old listened to the tales of the wandering story-teller.

Another letter from Pont Street was addressed to Morwetha. Hers, from Lisette, spared a line or two to hope that the travellers had arrived safely from Switzerland, and then dealt in detail with Cécile's recent cocktail party.

'Everyone's suddenly deciding to come to Fowey,' Morwetha observed, looking up from her letter. 'Lisette sounds rather irked by her brother's change of mind. She reckons it's because his self-esteem is a little wounded. He didn't make quite his usual impression on *her* new friend, Polly Penwarne – who is *also* down here with her father.'

Lavinia looked apprehensive. 'It only needs Cécile now . . .'

'No, Gran, it's all right. Aunt C. is on her way to Scotland to smarten up some baronial keep for an American millionaire. We, by the way, are to keep Uncle Tris here over Easter because she won't be able to get back in time.' She looked across the breakfast table at her mother. 'Do *we* know Lisette's new friend? . . . it sounds as if we ought to.'

It was her grandmother who answered. 'She's Loveday Penwarne's daughter, but you don't know her because she's always lived in London. Her only visit here, as far as I know, was just at the beginning of the war. She refused to be left behind when Loveday went back to London, and made it clear that Fowey fell a long way short of what she was used to!'

'How sensible of her,' Jenifer said inevitably. 'She must take after her father. Shouldn't we invite them here, Mama? I mean, if they go to Cécile's parties . . .'

Lavinia looked down her long, thin nose at the idea that her daughter-in-law's acquaintances were necessarily welcome, then relented a little. 'I admit to being curious to see Polly Penwarne again – Daniel, too, for that matter.' She picked up *The Times* again and they were meant to understand that the conversation for the time being was closed.

It was mid-morning before Tristram arrived from Tregenna, where he'd spent the night. Lavinia watched his face, certain that she would know at once whether he was filled with hope or despair. The sight of him now made her speak gently.

'It's too soon to judge, my dear. You can't expect miracles, even of Cornwall . . . just give a sick man time to be healed.'

'He's more likely to *die* up there,' said Jenifer, determined to strike a note of tragedy. 'You should have brought Kurt *here*, where we could have looked after him, not abandoned him in that dreadful place.'

'It didn't look dreadful last night, thanks to the efforts of both your children, and if I'd offered him Prospect he wouldn't have come,' Tristram explained tiredly. She opened her mouth to argue and his own fears spilled out into rare anger with her. 'For God's sake *try* to understand, Jen . . . He doesn't *want* comfort, companionship, human warmth. In some strange and terrible way he's got beyond needing those things; perhaps thinks he has no right to them, even, when so many others didn't survive at all.'

Morwetha's calm voice broke the silence. 'He'll need fresh supplies of food. How are we going to manage that?'

'Petroc's shepherd lives close by – he'll pick up anything Kurt needs when he goes to St Neot for his own supplies.'

'The shepherd will need paying,' Lavinia pointed out. 'We must do that, my dear, not Petroc.'

Tristram shook his head. 'I hope we shan't need to do it, either. Kurt would certainly hate it if we did.' He turned to look at his niece. 'Darling Mor, another lame-dog craftsman for you to take under your wing! Kurt's been supporting himself frugally for the past few years by doing woodcarving . . . small things that would just fit nicely on your shelves.'

She gave a little inward groan – still more amateur offerings that she hadn't room for and would never be able to sell. 'Well, of course I'll give them a try,' she agreed nevertheless. 'If they don't find favour with the customers we shall have to think of something else.'

Tristram smiled at last, comforted by her never-failing directness and generosity of heart. He tried not to make comparisons between her and his wife, but deep affection had prompted him to a rare protest when, during a visit to Prospect, Cécile had made the mistake of criticizing Morwetha's appearance.

'She's too busy to be thinking about her looks all day long; and in any case, with Peter dead, perhaps she doesn't care any longer,' he'd said sharply.

His wife had stared at him in genuine astonishment. 'My dear Tristram, *no* woman is too busy to neglect her hair and complexion – both of them with distinct possibilities in Morwetha's case. And a dead husband has nothing to do with it . . . there are still *other* men left alive to look at her.'

'All right, but she didn't have the benefit of a war spent in Washington. Clothes rationing was only abolished here a few months ago.'

'So I made her a present of a lot of things from my non-rationed wardrobe. What more am I supposed to do?'

'Nothing, of course. I'm sure you've been very generous,' he had agreed, and firmly put an end to the argument.

Lavinia suddenly remembered that they had news to report. 'Letters from Pont Street this morning. Poor Cécile is having to spend Easter working in Scotland, and she hopes you can stay for a while here. Luc is favouring us with a visit, and driving his sister down.'

'I was going to ask if I could stay anyway. I can't leave until I know whether or not Kurt is going to be all right.'

Jenifer hurried in with the last item of news before anyone else could steal it. 'Lisette has met Loveday's daughter. *She* and her father are in Fowey as well . . . really, with Kurt back here, too, it will seem almost like old times!' She smiled at them with a trace of her old bright gaiety, and bustled out of the room to break the news to their only daily 'help' in the kitchen – Mrs Bartlett's niece – that the house looked like being full for Easter.

'Kurt is a recluse, Morwetha a widow, and Loveday dead,' Tristram said harshly. 'For God's sake tell me, please, how times can seem remotely like they once were.'

Unable to oblige him, Lavinia said instead, 'It seems that we're expected to invite the Penwarnes here, but Lisette doesn't say where they're to be found – not with Hannah and William, surely?'

'No, but Mrs Penwarne is bound to know. I'll call in and ask *her*,' Morwetha promised.

She hadn't had time to visit Fore Street when Lavinia stumbled on a trespasser in the bottom level of the garden. A dark-haired girl, with a camera slung round her neck, stood there very still, staring out over the sparkling estuary. Then she turned to look up at the house, crouched like some old, grey animal amid a jungle of green, white, mauve, and spring gold. She had remembered it with strange and accurate vividness, just as she'd remembered every detail of her one brief visit there.

'Do I know you?' a quiet voice enquired behind her.

She spun round again, to find herself being watched by a tall, thin lady whose only concession to age was the silver-knobbed cane she leaned against. Age hadn't lessened her authority, and she was immediately recognizable.

'I'm Polly Jane Penwarne.' She was in the habit of giving the information in full, unconsciously agreeing with her father that each of the three names supplied something the others lacked. 'I came once before and was caught trespassing then, too. I'm very sorry to have disturbed you . . . I'll take myself off again.'

'There's no desperate need to rush away – my grandson isn't here this morning!' A gleam of amusement in her eyes brought an answering smile from Polly, reminding Lavinia poignantly of Loveday. 'Remembering your last visit, as we both obviously do, what lured you in here this time?'

'The gate was open,' Polly explained simply. 'It's hard . . . no, it's downright impossible *not* to peer in when you can glimpse something that promises to be absolutely beautiful. Once through the doorway, I kept being beckoned on. We live in the centre of London now, with only a backyard to grow things in. My mother would have hated that . . .' Her hand was lifted in a sudden, sweeping gesture that took in the garden and the immense view beyond. 'London's grand, but there isn't anything like this,' she conceded with aching regret.

'Admire the view, and the general effect of the garden by all means,' Lavinia suggested, 'but don't stare too closely. At the moment it's still a glorious mixture of *my* planning and Nature's abundance; a year from now Nature will have bolted with it altogether. I'm too ancient to keep a rein on her, and no-one else here has the time or inclination to crawl around on their knees grubbing up weeds.'

It was on the tip of Polly's tongue to say that *she* would crawl, but it seemed much too much like fishing for an invitation. For the same reason she stopped herself from mentioning Lisette Bossiney, but the lady in front of her seemed to guess what was in her mind.

'We heard of your visit from one of my granddaughters, and were instructed to find out where you and your father are staying. Lisette arrives at the weekend, and believes she can persuade you to come and visit us – neat and dry by the front door this time!'

A single dimple appeared in Polly's thin cheek . . . relict of a wound that had required stitching when she was a child. 'I should be glad to come, but I'd specially like to come *this* way, through the garden gate. My father dislikes hotels, but so as not to be a burden to Granny Penwarne we're renting a place called Salubrious House! I smile whenever I think of it, because it's such a perfect address for someone who's supposed to be resting for the good of his health!'

She saw a strange expression touch the face of the elderly lady in front of her, wondered if perhaps she had been kept standing there too long. 'My father says I chatter too much, Lady Bossiney. It looks quite a long climb up to the house . . . I could help you before I take myself off again.'

'I don't think it will be necessary, my dear!' She pointed her cane in the direction of the terrace, in time for Polly to see a dark head just disappearing from her line of vision. 'I think I misinformed you a moment ago . . . It seems that my grandson *is* here.'

A moment later a tall young man stood in front of them, and there was no need to be told who he was. How else would an arrogant and overbearing schoolboy have grown up, except into this personification of self-confident, self-controlled Cornish masculinity?

'Good morning, Miss Penwarne,' he said affably. 'Trespassing again? I see you got yourself another camera.'

19

On their first Sunday at Salubrious House, Daniel refused Polly's invitation to go with her to church, and strolled down to the Bodinnick ferry instead. The steep climb up from the landing-slip on the other side made him breathless, reminding him unpleasantly of Kirkmichael's warning. But it was level going along the Hall Walk, and he was comforted in spite of himself by the view of sunlit river and little grey town. Across the water, Fowey clustered round the battlements of Place House and the church tower, whose bells were launching flights of music through the still air. He stopped to rest in front of the monument erected in memory of Lavinia's friend, 'Q' – a Cornishman 'courteous in manner, charitable in judgement, chivalrous in action . . .' Even to a thoroughly modern expatriate, it was a citation not to be jeered at. When he turned away from the simple granite obelisk and looked downstream to the mouth of the river he could make out the grey bulk of Prospect, bowered in greenness. From this vantagepoint its superb position was made dramatically clear. Daniel inwardly saluted the long-dead Bossiney whose vision had led him to stake a claim there – a man after his own heart *that* one had been.

At last, he walked back the way he'd come – bell-song keeping him company on this side of the river, too, from Lanteglos Church across the creek at Pont Pill. He knew he could never have settled here, but on a morning like this of blue and green and gold it wasn't hard to see what kept an unambitious man from roaming. His cousin Charlie had spent the war years hazardly, at least, in North Atlantic convoys, but the girl he'd married had travelled no more than a hundred yards from the Old Ferry Inn to her next home.

He was outside when Daniel reached the cottage, inspecting the mass of pink and white bloom that smothered his camellias.

'Good to see you, Daniel – it's handsome weather you and Polly've brought with you.'

They smiled at each other, both pleasantly aware of their kinship and of their differences. Charlie worked hard and ran Daniel's boatyards at Polruan competently enough for them to have become very prosperous, but it was all the success he wanted. There was much more to life than running after money. His brother John was cast in the same mould as Daniel, always restless, always staring over the horizon. Charlie preferred the nearer view, but he was kind enough to appear impressed by all their industry.

'Polly's in church – she'll be over to see you soon, though.'

'Mary's away there too. I only go once a month, so's to give vicar a little something to strive for!' Charlie led the way indoors, and noticed Daniel's sigh of relief when he settled in a chair in the kitchen. 'Been overdoing things, Daniel?'

'Maybe. Polly will tell you if I don't that I'm supposed to be here for a rest. But there's nothing against thinking at the same time.'

'Petrol's coming off ration – I suppose that means the Penwarne garages will do very well again.'

'Certainly, but they don't need thinking about – John runs them better than I could. The electronics factories we started during the war don't need *me* now, either – I pay good men to keep us ahead of the technology.'

'So you're a mite bored, I reckon – looking for some new excitement. Maybe you've even found it by now.'

He saw Daniel's grin, and registered a fact that he hadn't been aware of before. Middle-age suited his cousin. The arrogance of youth had become the confident authority of a man accustomed to giving orders. His face was interesting now, and the strong features were set off well by a thatch of thick, greying hair.

'I'm thinking of getting into Cornwall's newest industry – there's no saving the old ones that I can see. For each mine that *might* be re-opened there are dozens that are now flooded for ever, and fishing's in the same hopeless state.'

'You're talking about china-clay then,' Charlie hazarded. 'That's had its ups and downs too; but it does pretty well now, and there's enough of the stuff up on Hensbarrow to last a good old while yet. Some people don't like it, of course – say it makes an untidy mess of the landscape.'

'Some people don't like whatever you try to do,' Daniel commented.

Charlie nodded, too intent on filling his pipe to notice that Daniel hadn't committed himself on the matter of china-clay. His cousin's next question took him by surprise.

'See anything of the family at Prospect nowadays?'

'Very little of Tristram, unfortunately, because his wife doesn't like Cornwall. The children mostly stay away too, which is probably a grief to her ladyship.'

'What about Jenifer O'Meara and her children – don't they still live there?'

'Mrs O'Meara does – where else would she go? Seems to me she'd like the war to be yet going on – happy as a lark she was by all accounts, when there were American officers up at Fowey Hall to be looked after, and an RAF air/sea rescue base at Caffa Mill; now it's all gone quiet again, and the poor soul's lost.'

'What about her children?' Daniel insisted.

'Well, Morwetha's there more often than not – real chip off her ladyship's block, that one is. Petroc's a farmer, with a big acreage to look after, but he manages to keep an eye on things for his grandmother as well. Quiet, watchful sort of chap – proper Cornishman, even if his father *was* Irish.'

A smile lit Daniel's face again. 'I expect that's why Polly took such a scunner to him when she was here before. She still remembers a disagreement they had. If my daughter's on your side, you're in clover; if she *isn't*, God help you!'

'It was before I joined the Merchant Navy that Loveday brought her down here,' Charlie said reminiscently. 'As it happens, I remember it as one of the few times when Tristram *was* here. He'd just come back from Berlin, looking very tired and sick. Cécile didn't stay, but he did, to recover a bit before he went off to Washington.'

Charlie busied himself putting the kettle on to boil and setting out crockery, unaware that amusement had faded from his cousin's face, leaving it cold and hard.

'It's a long time back – you've forgotten what happened,' Daniel said sharply.

'No, I haven't then.' Charlie turned round, the better to make his point, and saw at once a change that he couldn't account for any more than he could miss. Something in the conversation had disturbed Daniel, but even so it seemed necessary to insist that *he* hadn't been mistaken.

'I'm not likely to forget the only time in my life that I've been invited to dinner at Prospect. It only happened *then* because Loveday was here. Tristram and his wife had arrived that very same morning. Loveday and Polly left very soon after Cécile had gone, and that was a disappointment, specially to William – he'd been reckoning on having Polly, at least, for the rest of the war.'

Charlie was aware of talking too much, but there was nothing else to do when Daniel stared into space at some bitter reflection of his own and forgot that he wasn't alone. Then his expression altered again. A faint smile that had no amusement in it signalled another change of mood, and the strange little incident was over. He accepted the tea Charlie put in front of him and spoke as if nothing out of the ordinary had happened.

'Polly and I were honoured with an invitation recently in London. Tristram wasn't there, but his wife was "at home" in Pont Street. I had an interesting chat with *her*, and Polly got on well with her daughter. The boy's clever in his own way, apparently, but finds it necessary to wear fancy dress and make himself pleasant to middle-aged women.'

'Poor Tristram,' Charlie said simply.

Daniel grinned naturally again. 'Luc Bossiney prefers to stay in London, I gather, but Lisette is spending Easter here – so I think the Penwarnes may be about to cross the sacred portals of Prospect again!'

'They did before,' Charlie pointed out, determined that for once they should mention his sister. 'Don't forget Loveday lived there a longish while.'

'I don't forget *anything* about Loveday.'

The statement of fact fell starkly on the conversation, leaving awkwardness behind, until a small commotion outside gave Charlie the relief of knowing that help was at hand. His wife came into the room smiling warmly enough for Daniel not to guess the problem she was urgently considering – a small, rationed piece of lamb that had seemed barely adequate for two might now also have to feed an unexpected visitor. She was still the pretty, beguiling woman Charlie had married soon after the beginning of the war. Often enough since then he'd regretted wasted years, but it had seemed for long to him that Mary would marry no-one if she couldn't have John Penwarne. She'd taken John's younger brother in the end and been happy – Charlie knew that now for sure, but it had been a grief to both of them that they hadn't been blessed with children.

'You'll stay and eat with us, Daniel?' she asked in her soft mid-Cornish voice. 'There's plenty enough for three.'

'More than I dare do, today – we're expected in Fore Street when Polly gets out of church.' He smiled pleasantly at her. 'William may look frail enough to be blown away

by a puff of wind, but Hannah goes marching on as if only
the rest of us are growing old!'

He stood up with a little mock salute of farewell, and
promised to come again soon with Polly. When the door
had closed behind him Mary looked at her husband.

'Something's different about Daniel – he's never admitted to growing old before.'

'Didn't ask how business was, either, which is even
more unusual! Still, he did say he'd been sent down here
for a rest.' Charlie thought again of the strange, tense
moment when Daniel had been in the grip of something
unrecognized . . . anger or grief? Not knowing which it
was, there was no sense in mentioning it to Mary.

Polly came out of church while her father was still
across the river at Bodinnick. There was no need to
hurry, but in any case she was reluctant to leave the
lovely, tree-lined churchyard. Old almshouses huddled
round it in a friendly way, and wild daffodils nodded
and bowed in the wind between ancient gravestones recording names that were still familiar. Long-dead Baggas
and Trevenors, Rashleighs, Treffrys and Bossineys all
slept here peacefully amid their living descendants in the
town.

'Are you Polly Penwarne by any chance?' a pleasant
voice enquired behind her. She turned to find a woman
some years older than herself holding out her hand. 'I'm
Morwetha Kendrick, Lady Bossiney's granddaughter – I
hoped you might be here.'

'Granny would say that I ought to be at the Methodist
chapel, not here at all – she's strongly nonconform-
ist!' Polly smiled at the thought, suddenly reminding
Morwetha of Loveday. 'My mother looked after you
when you were small, so I'm told.'

'I hope you weren't told that I was a monstrous child
whom only she had the knack of handling! According
to my brother, I still like to get my own way, but at
least I've outgrown the habit of shouting for it.' She
glanced at the delicate profile of the girl beside her as

they walked along the path together. 'I expect you still miss Loveday,' she suggested gently.

Polly turned to look at her and nodded. 'Yes, but the odd thing is that I miss her more *here*, when we've always lived in London.'

'Perhaps that's why you haven't come very often.'

It wasn't even a question that needed answering; she could have said nothing at all. But she heard herself speak the truth. 'I only came once, and couldn't wait to flee back to London. I dare say it's why Fowey has haunted me ever since. This time perhaps I'm here for long enough to lay its ghost!'

'Long enough to get to like it, I hope,' Morwetha said with a faint smile. 'It's a place that grows on you.'

'I belong to London,' Polly insisted. 'I don't *want* to be grown on.'

The hint of desperation was startling, but Morwetha decided regretfully that she was intended to ignore it.

'My brother Petroc says you're rarely seen without a camera, although I've no idea how he should know. But being Cornish through and through himself, *he'd* expect you to give in to Cornwall's lure.'

'Then I shall be glad to disappoint him,' Polly said pleasantly. 'But he's right about the camera – photography is my job. I'm going to record some of Cornwall's sadly unalluring ruins while I'm here. If that would irritate him, I hope you'll tell him so!'

She smiled entrancingly again and indicated at the churchyard gate that she was now going in the opposite direction from the Esplanade. Morwetha went her own way towards Prospect, deep in thought. Polly was a Penwarne all right, and she'd inherited Loveday's smile; but apart from that she was much more Daniel's daughter.

Lavinia's dinner invitation was delivered the following day – formally phrased, and penned in her own flowing hand. Polly was aware, without knowing why, that her father's liking for Cécile in London didn't extend to the rest of the family at Prospect; she half-expected him to say, therefore, that he refused to be bored or patronized by three generations of Bossiney women while they sat through an interminable dinner. But Daniel smiled, and obligingly promised to give his very best imitation of the sort of gentleman they normally entertained.

'You'll find you can't be anything else with her ladyship,' Polly said thoughtfully. 'I suspect her of taming *much* uglier customers than you pretend to be.'

'As it happens, maid, I'm acquainted with her already,' her father pointed out. 'Jenifer O'Meara was, and probably still is for all I know, a sharp-tongued snob, and *her* daughter was widowed in the war. Not exactly sparkling company, but I shall put up with it for *you*, nevertheless, as a good parent should.'

For some reason she didn't understand he was not only amenable to going to Prospect, but actually looking forward to it. Beyond pointing out that he'd probably have to contend with a fourth Bossiney female in the person of Lisette, she contented herself with returning a note of acceptance as formal as the invitation had been.

During the intervening days she worked doggedly – observed and photographed, checked exposures, selected shutter speeds; but she was painfully aware of a struggle going on inside her that had nothing to do with the work in hand. William Penwarne's gentle flow of reminiscence threatened to trap her in the same web of fact and fantasy that her mother had known; but much worse even than that was the salty sharp reality of the little town itself, huddled alongside its lovely river. She found herself recognizing the steady rhythm of the tides, and the raucous lullaby of the gulls; knew that the immense solitude of sea and sky outside the harbour was always waiting to pounce on her. A dozen times a day she reminded herself that her father was looking better already. Soon they would be able to escape again and go back where they belonged.

On the evening of Lavinia's dinner party Daniel was ready and waiting when she came downstairs. Their invitation had considerably suggested that dress should be informal, but even the sharpest-tongued snob could have no fault to find with his dark lounge suit, white shirt and discreetly expensive tie.

'Elegance personified,' Polly said, grinning at him approvingly.

'You don't look too bad yourself – hooray for the Penwarnes!'

In this light-hearted mood they set off for Prospect, but for Polly, at least, gaiety didn't survive the discovery that there were more people present at Prospect than she had bargained for. Lisette's tedious twin brother was the first unexpected set-back, but there was worse to come. For one thing, Petroc O'Meara was handing round his grandmother's sherry. For another, and much, much worse, she couldn't fail to recognize the man who walked into the room a little later than the rest of them. His hair was silvered now, but in the lamplight it looked as she'd seen it once before, bright in the first rays of morning sun. She had hidden away in the darkest corner of her mind a picture of this man holding her mother in his arms as if he couldn't bear to let her go. But the picture had never faded – had always known, perhaps, that it would spring to life again like this one day.

'My son, Sir Tristram,' she dimly heard Lady Bossiney say. 'Tristram, I don't think you have met Mr Penwarne's daughter, Polly, before.'

'No . . . no . . . but I think I should have guessed who you were.' His eyes didn't leave her face, and they stared at each other, but now unaware of anyone else in the room. Watching them, and remembering what Charlie had said, Daniel knew that he'd finally found the missing piece of a puzzle that had always refused to complete itself. Petroc watched too, at a loss to account for the intensity of a moment that held his uncle and a white-faced girl wrapped in isolation.

'Sherry, Miss Penwarne? And for you, too, Uncle?' His tall body screened them for a moment, and the wine glasses they were obliged to accept broke their absorption in each other.

'*We've* met before,' Petroc reminded her brazenly. 'You were a trifle wet at the time.'

Her glance flew to Daniel's rigid face, then back to Petroc again and he thought her eyes begged him not to mention their subsequent encounter on the road to Par station.

She sipped the wine he'd given her and felt its warmth spread through her cold body. Tristram Bossiney moved away from her, and she could find voice enough to speak again, more or less calmly.

'You've forgotten a recent trespass as well, which makes this my third-time-lucky visit to Prospect. At least this evening I'm here by invitation, hopefully looking a little less bedraggled.' He thought she must know that she looked beautiful. Her dress of smoky-blue jersey hadn't been bought in austerity-ridden London. Her short dark hair reminded him of the curling petals of a chrysanthemum. Everything about her said that she was the indulged daughter of a wealthy man, and her eyes challenged him to remember that the Penwarnes weren't for being patronized now.

Lost in this second confrontation, Polly was unaware of Lisette having come to stand beside them.

'How *nice* to see you again.' The drawl was a passable imitation of her mother's social manner – cool and insincere – but her eyes were piteous in a way that Cécile would have despised. 'I should have warned you that it's thankless work fishing for compliments from my cousin; he's more used to noticing the finer points of ewes and dairy cows!'

Half-irritated, Polly also felt sorry for a girl whose airy rejection of marriage was a fraud that she practised on herself. Lisette was head over heels in love, and if and when Petroc O'Meara asked her to marry him, she would lay down brave independence without a second thought.

'You exaggerate as usual, little cousin,' Petroc said

blandly. 'I'm not so besotted with livestock that I can't be impressed with womanly charms. But you're up against stiff competition – my favourite Alderney is a beauty!'

'Which puts us *both* in our place,' Polly observed with a smile, but there was still only suspicion in Lisette's face of a girl who had been warned off *her* property. One way and another, it was turning out to be a thoroughly unpleasant evening, and Polly was ready to accept her father's estimate of the Bossineys. Like any other family whose forebears had barged their way to prosperity and power, they were still arrogant and self-satisfied, for no good reason that she could see. But the worst she knew of them now was the unhappiness they'd caused her own family.

She would have welcomed an excuse to leave this oppressively old-fashioned house and its oppressively self-centred inhabitants, but she could see her father now deep in conversation with Jenifer O'Meara. The unpleasant certainty was suddenly borne in her that he was using on *her* exactly the same combination of flattery and teasing that Petroc was now offering Lisette to coax her back to good humour again. She was swept by a sudden wave of distaste that threatened to suffocate her. Instead of clean, sweet air she seemed to be breathing in the fumes of an intrigue in which her father was unpleasantly involved. She took a deep breath and looked up to find Lavinia Bossiney watching her with a faint question in her eyes. It was necessary to take hold of herself and walk over to a lady who found it painful to rise from her chair and come towards her guests.

'My dear, *I* can say how lovely you look because I've reached the age when I can compliment another woman on her appearance and not be suspected of being insincere!' Lavinia's hand, once beautiful but now misshapen with arthritis, touched Polly's skirt lightly. 'Your dress is the colour of the wild scabious my stubborn old gardener used to uproot whenever I wasn't there to stop him. But Simeon's retired now and it's free to rampage happily all over the place.'

She was perfectly well aware that what she said scarcely impinged on the tense girl beside her, but Polly needed time to master whatever had almost overset her a moment ago. 'Morwetha tells me that you're a photographer,' Lavinia went on calmly, 'intent on capturing Cornwall on film!'

'It sounds ambitious put like that – even arrogant,' Polly muttered. Then the ghost of a smile chased anxiety from her face. Arrogance, at least, ought to commend itself at Prospect. 'I'm quite a good photographer,' she explained gently.

Lavinia saw her grandson hovering expectantly beside them and admitted him into the conversation. To Polly's surprise, Luc Bossiney improved on acquaintance; he was knowledgeable about her subject, and interested enough in it to forget that he was a rising star in London's firmament of talent.

'Dear Polly, surely *colour* film is the thing now,' he said earnestly, 'so much more exciting. Black and white will be dead as mutton soon, except for portraiture, like Karsh and Henri Bresson do.'

'Work like theirs no-one else *can* do . . . they are geniuses at it, and I'm only just beginning. But apart from the fact that I can develop black-and-white film myself, I still think it's preferable for certain kinds of outdoor shot – street scenes, buildings, cloud effects . . . that sort of thing. I'm not a portrait photographer.'

'Because you've inherited your mother's eye for landscape?' The question put in Tristram's quiet voice made her spin round to find him beside her again.

'My mother's gift was for painting,' she answered deliberately. 'I choose not to photograph people simply because I don't understand them well enough yet – they behave in ways that I find confusing and strange.'

He didn't look away from her, and his smile was tinged with such heartbreaking sadness that she felt suddenly ashamed of her intention to prick him if she could. Arrogance, at least, was not evident in this gentle, self-effacing man, and the truth was likely to be that his experience of the strangeness of life was a good deal more extensive than hers had so far been.

As if he'd been able to read her thought, he murmured, 'I'm afraid people may continue to confuse you for a long while yet . . . they still do me!' Then it was time to deny himself the painful happiness of talking to Loveday's daughter – dinner was about to be served, and he must lead the way with Lavinia across the hall into the dining room.

It seemed that the rest of the evening might go more easily. Seated between Lavinia's two grandsons, Polly chose to devote herself to Luc's maliciously amusing chatter about his mother's clients. Daniel was fully occupied in keeping his end up with her ladyship, and Jenifer on the other side of her son could scarcely inflame Lisette's jealousy. But it was Jenifer who catapulted them into serious trouble. Her voice, perhaps intended only for Petroc, reached everyone else as well in a sudden lull in the buzz of conversation.

'Darling, your uncle's been making the most *absurd* difficulties about the rest of us seeing Kurt. Imagine it, when we are all such very old friends.'

Petroc hesitated for a second too long and Tristram stepped in, frowning at his sister. 'The difficulties are anything but absurd, and I've explained them to you time and time again. Kurt doesn't *want* to mix with people yet . . . God knows, with reason. We have to respect *his* wishes.'

'*You* go, and so does Petroc, but Kurt was *my* friend . . . my very *dear* friend. How can I be expected *not* to be concerned about him?'

Polly watched her haggard face, flushed by sudden agitation into something like youthful beauty. Petroc glanced at Tristram's set expression and abandoned his position on the side-line.

'Mum dear, why not leave it for a little while yet?' he suggested gently. 'Kurt is still struggling to come to terms with life on Bodmin Moor in a beautiful but primitive

283

farmhouse! When we're certain that the experiment is going to work, then perhaps visitors can be welcomed.'

'When we're "certain", there will be no point in my going,' his mother said sharply, with her own maddening brand of logic. 'I have a right to find out for *myself* whether there is anything I can do for Kurt.'

Tristram stared at Jenifer's stormy face and tried not to shout at her. 'We none of us have any "rights" over someone else's freedom of choice – over Kurt's least of all. My dear girl, try to understand . . . The reason I don't take you up to Trebinnick is that he might easily not even open the door to you.'

'Whatever is to be the end of this discussion, it has gone on long enough here,' Lavinia put in firmly. 'My dears, remember that it can't be of the slightest interest to our guests.'

But it seemed she was wrong. Jenifer looked at Daniel across the table, and a smile of pure triumph lit her face. '*One* of our guests might be interested, Mama. Mr Penwarne has kindly promised to drive me up to see Kurt when he next goes to Lostwithiel. I can do without my brother's help, *or* my son's!'

Silence fell on the group around the table. Polly glanced from Tristram Bossiney's white face, to Petroc, now deliberately staring at the ceiling, and then to her father, smiling at some secret satisfaction of his own. Morwetha looked anguished, her London cousins mystified; and not even Lavinia's savoir-faire seemed adequate to deal with the emotions raging round the table.

'If Mr Penwarne has a grain of understanding of a complicated situation *he* will refrain from "helping" you too,' Tristram said finally with bitter distinctness.

Daniel lazily shook his head. 'You mustn't blame me for coming to the rescue of a lady in distress, my dear fellow . . . I thought it was what a *gentleman* was supposed to do!'

Polly watched her father and knew beyond the shadow of a doubt that this oblique duel with Tristram Bossiney was affording him the sweetest pleasure. She looked away, feeling faintly sick, and fell foul of Petroc O'Meara's contemptuous gaze. She was a Penwarne, it seemed to say, and the sooner she and her father took themselves back to the polluted haunts of London, the more breathable Cornish air would become again.

Her hands trembled on the table, and she buried them in her lap. Beside her, Luc sensed her distress and, having some of his father's innate kindness, tried to help by changing the subject of conversation. 'I'm here over the Easter weekend . . . May I come out with you, prospecting for photogenic ruins?'

About to say a blunt no, she saw Petroc's sardonic eye on them and smiled brilliantly instead.

'Why not? You're no more inclined to have your eye blinded by Cornish whimsy than I am!'

She got up from the table, and went towards Lavinia, holding out her hand.

'Thank you for an . . . an interesting evening, Lady Bossiney, but I believe it's time I and my father went home.'

Daniel, surprised but apparently not put out by this show of independence, shook hands with his hostess, bowed, and followed Polly out of the room. Morwetha interpreted her grandmother's glance correctly and got up to go with them to the front door.

'The rout of the Penwarnes?' Lisette suggested with a faint air of glee.

Lavinia stared at her coldly. 'Do you think so? My impression was that the victory went to Polly Jane Penwarne.'

20

The evening seemed to have exhausted Daniel's taste for conversation. On the walk back to Salubrious House he had nothing to say, not even the uncharitable commentary she was expecting on the family they had just left. It was something to be thankful for – her own strong inclination was never to have to see or think about the Bossineys again. Feeling weighted down with tiredness, she stumbled once or twice on the uneven pathway, but her father didn't notice, and she was aware that he was deep in some train of thought he didn't intend to share. She was thankful to reach the house, exchange brief good nights, and hurry off to bed; but it was Daniel who plunged them into battle at breakfast the next morning.

'I take it you're not serious about having Luc Bossiney mooning round you like a lovesick calf while you're supposed to be working?'

She smiled at the exaggeration, but let it pass. 'As serious as *you* are about taking Mrs O'Meara to call on someone who doesn't seem to want to see *her*.'

'Who says so? Lord God Almighty Tristram Bossiney! Of course I shall take her, if only to put a spoke in *his* wheel.'

Polly stared at him. '*Not* a gentleman riding to the rescue after all!'

She spoke lightly but the irony stung, and suddenly they were confronting each other like enemies. Daniel was aware that she hadn't grown up agreeing with him entirely – he hadn't wanted her to; but none of their differences of opinion had been serious. If that was about to change it was almost enough to make him scrap his plans, but an idea that had taken root in his mind was always hard to forgo, and this one had more than business attractions.

'On your high horse, maid? Well, if we're on the subject of behaviour, don't go stalking off from the dinner table in future the moment you get bored. The Bossineys are probably sniggering about us still . . . High tea in the kitchen is what they'll reckon we're used to.'

'It wasn't boredom,' Polly said sharply. 'I left because I couldn't bear to stay a moment longer. It was a beastly, hateful evening.'

'I'd have called it interesting, myself.' Daniel's brief grin appeared unexpectedly. 'I had the feeling in London that what I wanted to do was probably impossible; now I reckon I can pull it off after all, and there's much more satisfaction in it than I thought.'

Polly stared at his face – familiar as her own, known and loved since she could remember anything at all. She didn't understand why it should seem unfamiliar now.

'You might as well know – I've got it in mind to buy Prospect.'

Small sounds broke the silence – the chiming of the mantelpiece clock, reproved a moment later for being a trifle fast by the distant tones of the clock on St Fimbarrus' tower.

'To . . . to *buy* . . . as in take possession of, keep permanently?' she enquired faintly.

'Something like that,' Daniel agreed, still smiling.

'It happens to belong to another family.'

'It *has* belonged to them until now. They can't afford to keep it and it's time to let someone else have a turn.'

She wanted to believe he wasn't serious, but there was no gleam of teasing in his face; he actually meant what he was saying.

'We don't belong there,' she said desperately. 'What's the point of owning Prospect when we live in London?'

'I'm not buying it for us to live in – I've got a much better idea.' She took so long to frame the question that he couldn't wait for it to come. 'Fowey's on the holiday map

287

now . . . full of history and "quaint" charm for those who want such things, a lovely river to explore, and a good haven for the yachtsmen who arrive in ever-increasing numbers, I'm told. But visitors can't live on scenery and charm alone – they also need food; and a first-class restaurant is something Fowey *doesn't* have. That's what I'm going to turn Prospect into – the sort of luxurious place that people sick of austerity and Lord Woolton's fish-pie will come miles to enjoy. There's land there going to waste as well. With a bit of careful building-on, I might even make it into a small, exclusive hotel.'

It was hard to speak over the wave of nausea that suddenly threatened her. She wanted to shout her protest, but only a shocked thread of sound could be forced out of her dry mouth.

'You can't do that . . . can't even think of doing it. Prospect has been the home of generations of men and women who have helped to make the history of this town. It's *still* Lady Bossiney's home, and your "waste land" is the garden she has loved and laboured in for fifty years. It mustn't be just another challenge – another opportunity for you to make *more* money you don't need.'

A faint smile twitched the corners of Daniel's mouth. 'Who's talking about money? I'm thinking of this wretched county, as a good Cornishman should! Face the fact, Polly: the old industries are dead; the only thing that can save Cornwall from total stagnation and poverty is the holiday trade. I shall do my bit to help it along, that's all, by attracting here people with money to spend.'

'That *isn't* all,' she said with quiet emphasis. 'You're doing it because you hate the Bossiney family. You're revelling in the idea of ramming under their noses the fact that nowadays the race is to the strong, not the privileged . . . it will make you happy to have rich vulgarians gobbling down their food in Lavinia's drawing room, and swigging their gin on the terrace where Bossineys used to watch for their schooners to dip flags before making for the sea.'

Her scorn was terrible to Daniel, but she judged him because she didn't know what he knew. She had no *right* to judge him. Anger fermented inside him, rose and exploded in a roar that echoed round the room.

'Of *course* I hate them . . . I have cause to. Did I not live for twenty years with a woman who had to *pretend* to love me? Who closed her eyes when I touched her, so as not to see that it was me she belonged to, not Tristram Bossiney? She wasn't good enough to be made his wife – rough, crude Daniel Penwarne could marry her, work for her, prove himself the one to deserve her, but it didn't make a haporth of difference in the end. She went on loving Bossiney till the day she died.'

Polly saw the anguish in his face and knew that this moment, so long in coming, had been waiting for them all the time in Cornwall. She knew the truth of what he said, because her mother had once been driven to try to explain. Loveday hadn't revealed the name of the other man even then, only the despair of being unable to love her husband as he deserved. Polly wanted to weep for Daniel's pain, but now that her mother's true love had been identified she couldn't help but pity *him* as well.

'Something happened when you both came down here at the beginning of the war.' Daniel spoke quietly now, rage under control and only bitterness seeping through his voice. 'I didn't know what had driven her back to London, but I know now – and I think you do as well. It's why you refused to be left behind.'

'You imagine you know what happened,' Polly muttered through dry lips. 'Nothing did . . . they just . . . just said goodbye to one another and I stumbled on them doing it. I never mentioned it afterwards, but I was old enough to understand – they were renouncing happiness, not enjoying it.'

She stared at her father's face and knew that he didn't believe what a child had thought she'd seen. He gave a little shrug as if to say that the subject was now closed, and then tried to pretend that it had never been dragged out into the open at all.

'I think I'll go back to London soon . . . I'm sick of doing nothing. But you're to stay here, maid – I want to see those Cornish pictures materialize. You'll need to do a lot more than photograph Fowey, so Uncle John must find you a car to drive.'

She considered what he'd just said and finally nodded. 'I'll stay if you'll promise to be sensible, but I'll move in with Granny.' Then, in case it had sounded distant when her heart ached with love for him, she got up from the table and went to wind her arms round his neck. They stayed like that for a moment, both aware of an extreme danger passed. Nothing could be worse than losing trust in each other, but they had just come close to that over Tristram Bossiney. Prospect and the family it belonged to must be forbidden ground in future.

Daniel left for London two days later, and Polly moved into the little bedroom that had been her mother's in the cottage in Fore Street. She heard nothing from Luc Bossiney and felt certain, once Easter was over, that he must be safely back in London. Thinking about *him* reminded her that her father had left without making good *his* promise to Jenifer O'Meara. She would have to find someone else willing to take her to see her solitary friend. Polly was strongly of the opinion that Petroc would prevent more ruthlessly than Tristram Bossiney a visit of which they seemed not to approve. Morwetha Kendrick had described herself as a child who got her own way, but her brother had surely acquired the habit too. The memory of him at his grandmother's dinner party remained strangely vivid in Polly's mind, along with other impressions of that extraordinary evening at Prospect. She could still remember with pleasure Lavinia gently touching the stuff of her scabious-blue dress with stiff, swollen fingers; and with something that felt like pain Tristram Bossiney searching her face for some precious trace of Loveday.

Uncle John Penwarne came down from Lostwithiel, bringing a car for her to use, and her grandfather was given the immense pleasure of plotting from his armchair in the window of the parlour the places she must on no account miss seeing. Hannah watched the change in William and smiled on her granddaughter. With Loveday's death, he had almost drifted away from life himself, and although she had guarded him and refused to let him go completely, she hadn't been able to resurrect joy. Loveday's daughter had done that just by smiling at him in her mother's way.

Polly woke up early the morning after her arrival at the cottage, aware of a change but unable to account for it. The quarrel with her father, harrowing though it had been, had certainly exposed and finally laid to rest a worry that had troubled her for years. Still, it didn't explain why she felt strangely content to be where she was. She had no intention of staying longer than was strictly necessary, but it *was* a bit of a facer, nevertheless, for a dyed-in-the-wool Londoner to be feeling happy in Cornwall among the Penwarnes.

William observed her with satisfaction when she went downstairs. Hadn't he told Hannah that the little maid would do better among her own kin? Well, he could see that he'd been right; she was looking less wisht already.

The things she had to see, apparently, would fill months of wandering. First off, quite near at hand, the lunar landscape of the china-clay workings – white, spectral mountains of clay-waste mirrored in pools of dark-green water; and the remains of the great Caradon mine on the flanks of Bodmin Moor, where her great-grandfather had hacked tin out of the rock for years. Then she must go on across the windswept uplands to where the Atlantic hurled itself against the awesome slate cliffs of the northern coast. Next, down along to the last remaining huer's hut at Newquay, and the grassy arena of Wesley's holy preaching-place at Gwennap Pit, and the rock-strewn slopes of Carn Brea where Isaac's ancestors had toiled in foetid darkness half-a-mile underground . . .

'I shall be here for ever,' Polly pointed out, as her grandfather spoke the place names like a sacred litany.

'That's what I reckon, too,' he agreed with a contented smile.

She began methodically with the places closest to Fowey, and returned each evening to recount her wanderings over Hannah's pasty suppers while William waited to read to her from his second Bible – Tregella's *Cornish Tales*. Then one damp, misty morning she turned off the main Liskeard road to hunt for St Cleer, where Isaac had gone to live with his wife and sons after leaving Penwith. She found it easily enough, but having collected a nail in one of her tyres as well, crawled into St Neot with a slow puncture. While it was being dealt with she went into the church and sat entranced in front of the stained-glass windows depicting miraculous incidents in the saint's life – none more so, probably, than the survival of the glorious windows themselves during six hundred years of stormy Cornish history. She left the church reluctantly at last and walked back to the garage. A battered jeep was parked alongside her Austin, and her hope that she'd seen the last of the family at Prospect was proved to have been over-optimistic – Petroc O'Meara was standing beside the jeep, watching her walk towards him.

No such smile on his face now as he'd offered Lisette; his brows were pulled together in an unwelcoming frown, and disapproval seemed to stiffen every bone in his tall, straight body.

'Good morning . . . still snooping, I see!'

He had seen her in the past, she remembered, only at moments of weakness and disadvantage. This morning, being in no difficulty that required *his* help, she needn't make much effort to deal politely with him.

'I'm working, as it happens – recording the remains of Cornwall's fascinating past before they're allowed to fall into complete ruin.'

'Cornwall has a present and a future too; for those of us who live here, it seems more important to spend our time preserving *them*.'

She gave a little shrug as if to say his opinions didn't greatly interest her, and went to walk past him; but the tactic was a mistake. His hand fastened painfully on her arm, giving her no option but be pulled out of earshot of the curious boy taking a long time to fill the jeep with petrol. She was aware of strength, and of an anger which seemed disproportionate to the offence of stumbling on the same garage that he'd decided to patronize.

Petroc stared down at her flushed face beneath a cap of dark hair that curled slightly in the dampness of the air. Everyone agreed that she came nowhere near matching her mother's extraordinary beauty, although Lavinia had insisted on claiming for her other qualities, like humour, courage, and intelligence. There were more disturbing things to notice as well – the spare grace of her body, the tiny scar that became a dimple when she smiled, and the intense blueness of her eyes. Petroc acknowledged them to himself and almost regretted the need to distrust her because she was Daniel Penwarne's daughter. But he knew that distrust hadn't spoiled her for his cousin – Luc had gone back to London in a very entranced state of mind.

Petroc pointed to the camera slung round her neck. 'You're a professional now, I believe. What brought you up here? The chance of spotting our German friend at Trebinnick, so that you can take one of your damned photographs and caption it "Refuge for an Auschwitz survivor" for the gutter press?'

Polly took a deep breath and reminded herself that it would be unseemly to shout on the public highway.

'I don't know your German friend, nor do I know or care *where* Trebinnick is,' she said distinctly. 'If you'll be kind enough to let go of my arm, I shall retrieve my car and get on with the journey I was intending to make. According to my grandfather's itinerary, I should be well on the way to Dozmary Pool by now.' She sounded so cool and unconcerned that Petroc was tempted for a moment to believe that her only object was to hunt for Cornwall's more photogenic ruins. Even if he didn't approve of it, it was scarcely a programme he could object to, but she *was* Penwarne's daughter, and he had learned by bitter experience during the war no-one could match a woman when it came to *looking* honest and living an outright lie.

'There's no hurry, is there?' he asked smoothly. 'If your father succeeds in buying Prospect, you'll have all the time in the world to "record" Cornish remains.'

Her heart missed its normal beat, then hurried on to make up for it, but she'd found nothing to say before he spoke again. 'You look surprised, Miss Penwarne. Surely your father mentioned that he was going to write to my uncle – suggesting that the Bossineys should sell to him what they can no longer afford to maintain?'

Polly closed her eyes for a moment to shut out the anger in his face.

'My . . . my father spoke of it,' she muttered. 'I thought he meant to . . . to abandon the idea.' But when had he ever done such a thing, she realized. Certainly never when heart and soul were involved, as they were now in paying off a bitter score against the Bossineys.

'Your uncle has only to refuse the offer,' she went on unsteadily. 'Nothing forces him to do what he doesn't want to do.'

'Nothing but a strong-minded wife who can't wait to see the back of Cornwall, a son who doesn't want to inherit Prospect, and a chronic shortage of any money of his own!' Petroc's thin smile was like the flick of a blade across her skin. 'I'm sure your father has been careful to find out these things already.'

She remembered his long conversations with Cécile Bossiney. Yes, undoubtedly he had.

'It's your grandmother's *home*,' she shouted suddenly, forgetting the public highway. 'If you can't, between you, find some way of ensuring that she stays in it, perhaps you *don't* deserve it after all.'

She willed her feet to move away from him and hurried back to the safety of the garage hut and its attendant. The tyre had been repaired; she had only to pay the bill, and sweep out on to the road, with Petroc O'Meara still watching her. By God's especial grace she didn't stall the engine, and even found that she was heading in the opposite direction from a signpost she could now see, whose finger pointed clearly to the place she had been warned to avoid.

21

When Tristram reported that some of Kurt's carvings were ready for inspection, it was Morwetha who insisted that it was time to let her mother visit Trebinnick as well. He was accustomed to living with women who knew always that they were right and that he was wrong, but at least his niece took pity on his anxiety.

'I'm sure there's no need to worry, Uncle Tris. Either they'll find that they enjoy seeing each other, or the visit will be a failure and my mother won't ask to repeat it.'

When the suggestion was made to her, Jenifer calmly agreed to go, but from then onwards worked herself into a state of nervous excitement that her daughter found unexpected and touching. Only when she insisted on changing her dress for the third time before setting out did Morwetha try to lighten the atmosphere of tense anticipation.

'Darling, don't forget this isn't really a social call. A determined hermit like Professor Winkler will probably only notice if we go wearing nothing at all!'

Feverishly wiping off the too-bright lipstick she'd just applied, Jenifer scarcely heard. 'This colour makes me look like a hag,' she said in a trembling voice.

'You look lovely, just as you are,' her daughter said gently. 'Let's go, shall we?'

The journey was made in silence, Morwetha concentrating on the road, Jenifer constantly fidgeting with her bracelet and her rings. Then, as they climbed out of the valley of the little St Neot river, she suddenly began to talk.

'What a place to have brought Kurt to . . . it's depressing enough for a man who is completely *normal*, but . . .'

Her throat closed on the rest of what she'd been going to say. The man they were about to meet was anything *but* normal . . . she couldn't bear it after all . . . must ask if they could turn round immediately and go home.

Morwetha glanced at her white face and shaking hands.

'He's still Uncle Tris's friend, still the man who loved Cornwall,' she reminded her mother compassionately.

'But . . . but he went back to Germany without me – I never really knew why.' Her voice trailed away at the memory of a disappointment that had never quite lost its cutting edge.

'Well, don't expect too much. At least, not this first time,' Morwetha cautioned with gentleness.

It was as much as she had time for. Trebinnick was in front of them – a solid stone house tucked into a fold of the hillside for shelter. It wasn't anywhere near the highest point of the moor; Brown Willy was that, away to the north-west. But compared with Fowey, snug in its river valley, it seemed to be on the rim of the world. The wind always blew there, and there were days and days of sad, persistent rain. Jenifer shivered at the thought of them, and of the even worse times of winter storm when Petroc and his shepherd had to dig the sheep out of drifts of snow. Then she forgot everything else but the fact that someone had come to stand in the open doorway. Disbelief, then panic, made her clutch Morwetha's hand. This white-haired, bespectacled man couldn't be the Kurt who had waltzed with her at Place House, and kissed her because she taunted him with only knowing about books. She had to walk towards him, but it was left to him to find something to say.

'*Gnädige Frau, Fräulein . . . kommen Sie herein.*'

It was worse, far worse, than she had ever imagined. If he'd forgotten the English he could once speak as fluently as the rest of them, how in the world was this nightmare meeting to be managed at all?

'K . . . Kurt . . . you remember m . . . my daughter?' she stammered.

Morwetha smiled, and stepped bravely into the breach. 'I'm hoping you *don't*, Professor. Petroc still claims that I was a ghastly child and, allowing *something* for brotherly exaggeration, I dare say he was right!'

'That I do *not* recall.' Kurt stared at her gravely, then remembered to remove his spectacles. 'Always I forget to take these off when I stop working. Now I can see you better.' His glance travelled on to Jenifer – once upon a time a girl so beautiful and bright that it had broken his heart to return to Germany without her. Where was *she* in this agitated, middle-aged woman who seemed too frightened to look at the man he had become? He scarcely recognized her, but he recognized her fear and pitied her.

'So many years, *meine Liebe*, but so little change I find,' he said gently.

Morwetha thought it could scarcely be true, but whatever else the Nazis had done to him, they hadn't killed the kindness of his heart. It was the very quality she had perceived in him when she was still a small child.

'For you it is different,' he was saying to Jenifer. 'I'm afraid you even have difficulty in knowing me!'

'Well, yes . . . no, I mean, just a *little*,' she agreed desperately, then rushed on for fear of having been tactless. 'You should have let Tristram bring you to Prospect. This is such a lonely, uncomfortable place.'

He looked round the room he'd shown them into . . . remembered arriving dazed with travelling and dulled by despair. The peace and emptiness of the moor had fallen on him like balm; the sheep scattered on the hillside grazed but made no noise, and only a nightjar near at hand had been practising its evening song. Inside the house, bowls of primroses and wild daffodils had been left to welcome him. Trebinnick had seemed to him then, and still did, like the Kingdom of Heaven itself.

'I could have asked for *nothing* more than I found here,' he said quietly. 'Petroc is anxious because he cannot get the generator working immediately, but why do I need electricity when I have firelight, candlelight, and oil lamps?'

Jenifer almost forgot fear of him in the horror of his situation. 'It's *primitive* . . . absurd, when you could be comfortable with us.' His voice was reassuring, and so was his smile. This *was* Kurt, and if he would only come to Prospect, perhaps something from the past might be recaptured after all. Eagerness put a youthful glow in her face, but Morwetha knew that he would refuse and that her mother would feel rejected all over again.

'Dear friend, you are good enough to be anxious about me, but all I need is here – a home, a place to work in, absolute peace, and nothing but beauty on my doorstep.'

He didn't mention people, who might be needed to talk to, laugh with, or love. The omission was deliberate and couldn't be missed. Morwetha saw the light in her mother's face suddenly quenched, and felt angered by his inhuman self-sufficiency. It had been necessary for survival, but why couldn't he lay it aside now, among friends?

'Does Evan Nimmo bring you enough food?' she asked.

'More than I can eat! Tristram keeps me supplied with books and journals, and I have the wireless to listen to. My dear godson whom I remembered only as a baby even finds the time to help me search for the wood I need. I am complete.'

'Not quite,' she said coolly. 'I understand you need customers.'

He nodded, aware that her friendliness had been withdrawn. It was surprising enough to lure him into wondering why; not for a long time had he wanted to try to solve the puzzles set by other human beings; sanity had seemed to lie in simply avoiding them, and the habit was fixed now.

'Yes, I need customers,' he agreed. 'Will you come with me next door? The kitchen is my workshop.'

The room he led them to was unexpectedly pleasant – lit by a large window, and warmed by a Rayburn stove set into a fireplace so huge that it took up almost the whole of one wall. It wasn't now quite as Morwetha had left it ready for him, but it was still orderly and very clean. A store of wood was stacked neatly in one corner; beside the table, now pushed under the window, a rack had been made to hold rows of beautiful, wooden-handled chisels – the tools of his new craft. On the window-sill were ranged the pieces she had come to see – come without the slightest hope or enthusiasm, simply because this man would hate to have to live on charity.

She stood in front of them for a long time, speechless with surprise and sudden delight. Then she put out her hand because the little creatures in front of her demanded to be touched – a squirrel sat up on his haunches, examining a tiny, perfectly carved nut held between his paws, next to him a rabbit brushed his whiskers; a duck slept with his head tucked into a downy wing, uninterested in the wide-eyed owl next door . . . Each one insisted, like puppies in a pet-shop, 'look only at *me*, because I am the one that you must take away and love'.

Morwetha turned round at last to see Kurt's eyes fixed on her. 'Uncle Tris didn't warn me,' she said unsteadily.

'That you would be disappointed? *Liebe Fräulein*, there is no need to pretend; just say that . . . that you—'

'—that I find them lovely beyond words?' she interrupted him. 'All right, I *will*! I'll say as well that these will sell without difficulty if I can only bring myself to part with them! Finally, Professor, I shall say that my name is Morwetha!'

'And you remind me that you are *not Fräulein* at all,' he said miserably. 'Tristram *told* me, but my stupid memory is unreliable now. Forgive me, please.'

She nodded, and suddenly smiled. He was reminded of her grandmother – another woman who, like herself, became nearly beautiful only when she smiled. He didn't expect her to refer directly to the fact that, however briefly, she had had a husband. She wouldn't mention the man who had been machine-gunned to death by a Luftwaffe fighter pilot any more than he would speak to

300

her of his own suffering. In a way that was unexpected and strange, they understood one another without benefit of words. At last, the third person in the room reminded them that she was there.

'Kurt, the carvings are very charming, but you can't go *on* doing them, surely?'

'Different ones . . . better ones . . . these I hope I *can* go on doing.'

'But you are a famous doctor, trained to help people with sick minds. Isn't it a . . . a dreadful *waste* to do what you're doing now?'

He gave a little grimace at her choice of words, and Morwetha looked away from his face to stare at the ceiling.

'My dear, sick people deserve better than a physician who hasn't yet healed himself! Apart from that, what have I to go back to? My home and family were destroyed, my institute is in the hands of the Russians. That part of my life is over. If Petroc will allow me to, I shall stay here, learning to be a good woodcarver. Perhaps one day I shall even create something worthy of the man whose tools I use.'

'It's time we went,' Morwetha said quickly, before her mother could step further into error. 'May I take away everything that's here, and fix the prices? They'll sell like hot cakes, but I shall only let them go to people who look as if they understand that they are privileged. I'll ask Petroc to tell you when I'm ready for some more.' Kurt's expression made her add hurriedly, 'I'm inclined to be bossy, you know; you must always say if you don't agree with what I suggest.'

His austere face was suddenly softened by a look half-amused, half-rueful. 'Never shall I dare to interfere, when a lady is so firm and resolute! I work from drawings – you may take whatever is here.'

He watched her wrap each piece in the soft paper she had brought with her, and although her manner might be decided her hands were gentle. Their touch matched the instinct, he realized, that had prompted her to leave flowers in the house to welcome him. He remembered what else Tristram had said of her – the home for handicapped children would never be achieved at Prospect now. She would have done it very well, and it was still one more crime to add to the account of the men who had spawned Nazism in Germany.

With all the carvings safely in a box, she held out her hand to say goodbye. His own hand seemed reluctant to touch hers, felt cold when it finally did. She wanted to weep for such remoteness, as well as for the prison mark branded on his wrist. He walked outside with them to the car, but didn't say that he'd been glad to see them there, or would like it if they came again. He simply stood by the door, watching them drive away – a lonely, frail figure framed by the granite pillars that made a porch for the front door.

They drove in silence again, but after a glance at her mother's tear-stained face, Morwetha said gently, 'He's got out of the habit of including people among the things he needs. It's not to say he'll always feel like that.'

'He won't need *me* . . . I thought he might, that's all.' Jenifer wiped her tears away and frowned in the mirror of her powder compact.

'Darling, this was the first time you'd seen each other for twenty-five rather terrible years,' Morwetha pointed out patiently. 'Miracles *can* happen, but they don't have to happen immediately.'

'Mine have to,' her mother insisted, 'otherwise they don't happen at all. I'm glad to know, because now I shall accept an invitation from some of my war-time American friends to visit New England. Petroc will have to make the arrangements for me, but I suppose that isn't too much to ask.'

She was already half-way there in her imagination, the disappointment of a moment ago blurred by the prospect of a journey she'd scarcely thought about until now. It was only Morwetha's mind that was haunted by the image of a man too damaged by his fellow men to be able to mingle with them any more.

She reported briefly to her uncle that the visit wouldn't be repeated, but he noticed, as Kurt had done, the gentle reverence with which she unpacked the little carvings.

'They're almost too good for *me* to sell, but he seems dissatisfied with them. I suppose that's the difference between true artists and would-be experts like me.' Morwetha frowned at Tristram. 'You needn't be anxious about leaving your friend there. Even my poor little mum had to accept the fact that he's perfectly determined on being a hermit.'

'That's all right then, but you might help Petroc keep an eye on him for me – I must go back to London.'

'I'm afraid I shan't have time for that,' she said shortly and walked out of the room, leaving Tristram to stare in astonishment at behaviour so entirely unlike her.

It was true that he'd overstayed his time in Cornwall and was needed back in London – if not by his busy wife, at least by colleagues waiting for his judgement on the manuscripts he'd brought with him to read. With Kurt settled at Trebinnick, there were only two more things to be done before he was free to leave. An hour was spent composing a letter to Daniel Penwarne that politely but firmly declined his offer to buy Prospect. The fine courtesy of the phrases did *not*, Tristram hoped, conceal what couldn't quite be said – that if he ever agreed to sell, the last man on earth he'd sell to would be Daniel. No doubt it was altogether shameful to allow the bitterness of the past to colour the present, but for the very life of him he could not allow Daniel Penwarne to have had Loveday *and* Prospect as well.

His other task was less easy to accomplish, but he managed it by accident in the end. Having gone on an errand to Polruan for Lavinia, he walked on impulse up the hill to St Saviour's Point, on a blustery afternoon that mixed springtime showers with shafts of sunlight stabbing down dramatically between great banks of cloud. The headland wasn't empty, and it happened that the girl who stood there entranced by the spectacle in front of her was exactly the one human being he needed to see. She had a camera in her hand, but seemed content to watch the glistening fountains of spray that high tide flung against the rocks and inlets on the far side of the estuary.

She was unaware of him behind her until he spoke. 'I used to imagine that, having known this place all my life, I wanted to escape into the big exciting world outside. Now, I'd happily stay here always if I could.'

He was easily identified by the remembered pleasantness of his voice; she could have smiled and walked away, true to the conviction that she must have as little to do with the Bossineys as possible. But when she turned and looked at him it was impossible not to match his truthfulness.

'After one visit here ten years ago it seemed simple to pretend that I hated Cornwall. I was never going to come again – wouldn't have come now if my father hadn't been told to take a holiday.'

She turned away again to watch the sea, as if it had some irresistible attraction for her. Tristram stood watching *her*, and it was hard to remember that she was as much Daniel Penwarne's daughter as Loveday's. Not for her the hideous hats he remembered her mother wearing – she was bare-headed and her short, dark hair was damp and ruffled by the wind. A blue corduroy jacket, and blue-and-grey-checked skirt, looked practical but elegant; he thought Cécile would have said that she had style.

'I was here as well ten years ago,' he said abruptly. 'When we met at Prospect recently I felt certain that you recognized me. Was I right?'

Polly took so long to answer that he thought she was making up her mind to walk away and leave him there. Then, still staring at the view in front of her, she muttered, 'I saw you once with my mother. Long afterwards she explained a little, without telling me your name. I hated *you*, as well as Cornwall, because you were the reason why she was always sad inside . . . My father knew, as well, that when she was killed she wouldn't have minded dying very much.'

'Do you hate me still?'

She considered the quiet question gravely, and shook her head. 'No, because I think you've been as sad as she was.'

'We should have married – long, long ago. It was my fault that we didn't, and finally Loveday thought she would make things easier for me by marrying someone else. Measured against the sum total of human misery since then, it seemed only our little private tragedy, but perhaps it hasn't been so little after all if it has affected the lives of you and your father. I'm sorry for that, my dear girl.'

She turned to look at his face, thinking that he hadn't mentioned the lives of his own family; but there'd surely been a price to pay there as well. Luc and Lisette were both unsure of relying on the prompting of their heart, and Cécile Bossiney's brisk assault on public success might be compensation for a private failure.

'It's over now . . . the tragedy,' she said gently. 'You can't blame yourself for ever, any more than I need go on avoiding a place that's haunted me. I may even discover that I belong here, with the ghost of my mother, and with Grandfather William, and Isaac, and all the Penwarnes before *him*.'

'Does that mean you're going to stay?' Tristram asked.

'No, because my father would miss me too much in London, and in any case the people who buy my work are there. But first I want to put together a portrait of Cornwall before it changes too much. The only difficulty is *choice* – it's so endlessly photographable.'

'When you're ready, bring your "portrait" to *me*, please. I shall only publish it if it's good, but it would be the greatest joy I could think of to help Loveday's daughter.'

There was so much sweetness in his smile that Polly smiled whole-heartedly back, wanting to offer something that would ease the loneliness she sensed in him. Tristram was sorely tempted to leave their conversation there, but one more thing needed to be said if they were to understand each other enough to become friends.

'You said a moment ago that the past was over and done with. It *isn't*, quite. Your father would like to see the Penwarnes in the house that has always belonged to my family. I'm afraid I *can't* allow him to buy it in order to get even with the Bossineys, even if it would please you.'

'It wouldn't please me at all,' she said firmly, unable to decide which was the more shameful – to want to evict the Bossineys out of revenge, or out of an inbred commercial instinct for making money. Either way it reflected no credit on Daniel, but not even to this man could she allow herself to say so.

'My father is the best that anyone could have,' she murmured instead after a moment or two, 'and most of his ideas are brilliant; but very occasionally, as Uncle Charlie would say, he gets the wrong sow by the foot! Then you have to be firm with him until he loses interest and thinks of something else.'

'Is that what you do?' Tristram asked, fascinated by this matter-of-fact recipe for controlling a headstrong parent.

Polly nodded, smiled seraphically, and as a way of saying goodbye leaned forward on a sudden impulse to kiss Tristram's cheek; then she walked away from him across the headland towards Lantic Bay. She left behind her a moment's feeling of emptiness that he remembered from long ago whenever Loveday had parted from him. It was high time to turn his back on Cornwall, but this time he would go more happily. Kurt could be left in Petroc's safe hands, and his own empty heart now held the image of Loveday's daughter. It no longer mattered that the only thing Cécile would want to know when he got back to London was whether or not he'd accepted

Daniel Penwarne's offer for Prospect. She would be seriously displeased when he said no, but he was prepared for his clever, energetic, elegant wife not to understand about things Cornish. It grieved him far more that Luc and Lisette would probably agree with her.

22

Jonathan rashly put into words one day a thought that kept occurring to Lavinia. Their quiet, peaceful routine *seemed* to be undisturbed, but it was an illusion. Just as Prospect's seclusion insulated *them* from the invasion of noisy holidaymakers who were a reality to the rest of Fowey, so the Bossineys were like the inexperienced swimmers who came to grief off Cornish beaches every summer because they disregarded the invisible undertow that swept them out to sea.

'Inexperienced . . . at *our* age?' Lavinia enquired sharply. 'My dear Jonathan, face the truth. If we allow things to get out of hand, it's due to the selfishness or indolence that overtakes old people.'

He forgave her the severe reminder, but his smile was wistful. He was content nowadays to be a little selfish, and more than a little lazy; but if his dear Lavinia required action, he would have to bestir himself.

'Which mountains shall I command to reduce themselves to molehills for you?' he enquired gently. 'Shall I try to persuade Petroc that beneath his cousin's soft and winsome exterior lies all her mother's rock-hard determination to get her own way? Even if he believed me, I fear he might resent my interference. Shall I insist to the Almighty that I must be allowed to die when you do, so that you can stop worrying about me? Even so, I'm afraid you'll still go on agonizing about the future of Prospect.'

'I *know* its future,' she said bleakly. 'My daughter-in-law will make Tristram's life a misery unless he agrees to sell it the moment you and I are dead. I could bear it going to someone who would understand its value;

having it go to Daniel Penwarne, merely to satisfy some impudent ambition he has to get the better of us, is *more* than I can bear with grace.'

It was an attitude derived from the fulminating, outraged ghosts of St Clysts long-dead who jabbed their fingers at the upstart Penwarnes. It was arrogant and unacceptable in a democratic age; but it was so much part of Lavinia that Jonathan didn't mind. Still, he didn't dare smile – the matter was grave and he must tread carefully.

'My dear, it might not be Daniel who buys it,' he suggested. 'Did you and I not agree back along years ago that we would live to be *very* old parties? Daniel is an impatient man – he'll get bored with waiting for Prospect to drop into his lap. He's bound to have a dozen other irons in the fire, all keeping nicely hot.'

Lavinia shook her head. 'Lisette chatters too much, even in her correspondence, but some of what she lets drop is revealing. Cécile and Penwarne are as thick as thieves in London and I doubt if it's because they've discovered a liking for each other's company.'

'Why not? They're birds of a feather after all – clever, competitive, and ambitious.' Jonathan was tempted to add that it would also amuse Cécile to make a friend of a man Tristram particularly disliked, but remembered in time that his task was to reassure Lavinia, not make her anxieties worse. 'In any case, Daniel is a businessman; Prospect can have no real interest for him, and he doesn't even have a son to hand it on to – only a daughter who seems fairly unimpressed by the land of her forefathers.'

'That's true – he *has* a daughter,' Lavinia agreed thoughtfully. 'She's been travelling around a good deal but, according to Mary Penwarne in church last Sunday, she is due back in Fore Street now. I should like to see Polly Penwarne again, and I have the strong suspicion that she longs to get her fingers dirty working in my neglected garden! She's inherited from her mother a passionate need to grow things.'

Jonathan registered the pleasure in his friend's face and began to feel nervous.

'My dear, *dear* Lavinia, please *don't* feel tempted to play the role of *deus ex machina*. I believe it's found to be a very thankless one.'

Her expression changed suddenly. 'Not only that, but stupid and dangerous as well. I interfered once – in Tristram's life – with all the good intentions that the road to hell is paved with. I'm not tempted to make the same mistake again.' She saw the anxiety in Jonathan's face and offered him a faint smile. 'Not the smallest nudge at Fate, I promise you!'

But a week later the nudge came, though not from Lavinia. Cécile, who normally went out of her way to avoid visiting them, rang to suggest coming with both the twins while Tristram made a business trip to New York.

'She likes America and she hates Cornwall,' Lavinia observed crossly when Jonathan reported the telephone conversation. 'Why does she want to come now?'

'I could scarcely enquire since she needn't have bothered to ask at all, this being Tristram's house! Still, a reason *was* mentioned – she's been working very hard recently and needs a holiday. Luc is acting as chauffeur and general help, and Lisette doesn't want to be left behind in London in midsummer.'

'You mean she'd rather drape herself on the sand in Prospect cove, looking as naked and wanton as possible, in the hope that Petroc will stumble over her.'

Jonathan grinned at Lavinia's disapproval and couldn't help teasing her a little. 'My dear, he's a normal, healthy man – I'd be alarmed if he *didn't* enjoy looking at her, although I'm not sure I agree with Jenifer that he ought to get on with marrying her.'

Lavinia snorted with the disgust that her daughter's views often aroused in her. 'She's the drip of water on stone, constantly reminding him that he's monopolized Lisette ever since they were here as children. If Petroc should ever ask for *my* opinion – which he won't – I shall tell him that cousinly affection tinged with lust is not the best basis for marrying on.'

Jonathan's grin broadened. 'And he will tell you that it may not be the worst, either!'

For once Lavinia refused to be amused, because she knew the truth of something else Jonathan had once said. Underneath surface, cajoling playfulness, Lisette *was* very like her mother, but Petroc was a tougher kind of man than Tristram had been, and Lavinia saw only eventual misery coming of a marriage with his cousin. She was aware that he had returned from the war with some confidence in women lost. It had been tempting to ask what had gone wrong, but she had forbidden herself to do so. All she was certain of was that he would eventually want a wife. Lisette would do as well as any other since he couldn't have the woman he'd have chosen for himself.

Morwetha's shop at Polperro roused strong and differing reactions in her family. Lavinia and Tristram were genuinely interested in what she sold, Jenifer preferred to think of it as a gallery in which objets d'art were merely on display, and Petroc was bluntly opposed to anything that encouraged the visitors he didn't want in Cornwall. Knowing this, Morwetha had decided to call on Kurt herself when necessary, instead of asking her brother to act as go-between.

She had gone again a fortnight after her first visit with Jenifer, with the proceeds of her sales, and to report that her stocks would soon need replenishing. The pleasure of taking what she thought was good news had shone in her face; but the smiling warmth she unconsciously offered him had beaten in vain against a courtesy so remote and impersonal that only her promise to Tristram made her go again. Now, another visit was unavoidable, but she went determined to be as businesslike and brief as possible. Even so, she couldn't avoid noticing the tiredness in his face and the piece of bloodied rag tied inexpertly round the palm of his left hand.

'A piece of clumsiness,' he explained quickly, when he saw her looking at it. 'A chisel slipped . . .'

'Because you work too hard . . . do nothing *but* work, in fact.' The accusation sounded fiercer than she meant it to, because her heart was wrenched by a stained and messy strip of rag that seemed to sum up the ruin of their adult lives. She had wept when Peter died, but never since, because there had seemed nothing left to weep for. Now, tears pricked her eyelids again so that she had to march blindly out of the house towards the car. She returned a moment later, unaware that Kurt's careful formality had been shattered by the strange, sweet amusement of knowing that she was angry. He was remembering a small child in the nursery at Prospect stamping her foot with rage when he explained that he couldn't stay there for ever. She hadn't liked the country he was returning to then. He thought she had even less reason to like it now.

Morwetha banged her little first-aid box on the kitchen table and ordered him to hold out his hand. She could sense enjoyment in him now of something she didn't understand and it made her more unreasonably cross than ever.

'This is not quite right,' he murmured helpfully as she unwrapped the makeshift bandage. 'The nurse is always gentle . . . always kind and reassuring . . .'

'Not when her silly m . . . mutt of a p . . . patient works until he drives a sharp chisel into his hand.' She swallowed a sob, and blinked away the tears that persisted in clinging to her eyelashes. 'I warned you I was bossy . . . you only had to *say* you needed more time . . .' Her voice trembled and stopped altogether, leaving them silent and suddenly aware of each other in the quiet room. Kurt's free hand crept up as if to wipe away the tear that trickled down her cheek, then hid itself in the pocket of his coat again. She wasn't the small child in the nursery now to whom he had given comfort, but a woman with frank eyes, sweet-smelling skin, and the gentlest of hands touching his.

'I was teasing, *meine Liebe*,' he said unevenly. 'The nurse is kindness itself.'

'She'd probably have done better to take you to have that gash stitched,' Morwetha muttered. 'If you don't give it a chance to heal before you start working again, it will *have* to be stitched.'

She lifted her head to look at him and he nodded, but his eyes didn't leave her face. For a moment that seemed to have slipped out of time they were aware only of each other. Then she shook her head as if rejecting something she knew to be impossible, and made a brave attempt to ignore the moment that had held them paralysed.

'I'm sorry if I hurt you just now. If your ration will run to it, I think the best thing would be to make you a cup of tea.'

The suggestion was so absurd in its weighed gravity that it made him smile wholeheartedly for the first time in her new acquaintance with him. The smile became a chuckle, and then a roar of laughter that echoed round the room. She was caught up in its infectiousness, and had to join in, but mopped her wet cheeks at last, and tried to sound indignant. 'You're n . . . not supposed to rock with m . . . mirth at the offer of a cup of tea; it's sacred. Our unfailing standby in all life's trying moments.'

'I *know* . . . I remember!' Kurt fought against making his sin worse by collapsing again, and finally managed to sound sober. 'But I'm light-headed with the joy of discovering that life can still seem funny. I didn't expect it to, ever . . . I even convinced myself that it would be *wrong* to laugh again in the face of so much tragedy and horror. *Such* are the knots we tie ourselves into when life destroys the simple certainties we take for granted.'

'It's become simple again here, surely?' Morwetha asked. 'I don't mean in the way you *live*, which my mother considers unbearably primitive! But it's only other people who complicate things for us. You're spared that at Trebinnick, except for *me* nagging at you to produce more beautiful carvings than I ought to.'

313

'Yes,' Kurt agreed gravely, '*you* are my only complication.'

She wished she had the courage to ask what he meant; decided, against her brief knowledge of him, that he'd spoken without meaning anything at all, and reminded herself that there was the calming routine of making tea to be seen to. She would drink her share and go, and once away from this lonely, beautiful place her normal, calm, commonsense would be in charge again. She was only imagining that some boundary had been crossed, taking them into unfamiliar territory; the silence in the quiet room was *not* so dangerous that she must needs chatter like a frightened fool whistling in the dark, but it was still what she proceeded to do.

'Tristram's in New York, so Cécile and the twins are coming to Prospect. My mother is also away in America or she would see *any* visitor as an improvement on her usual humdrum life, but Gran discriminates – some arrivals are more welcome than others! She would welcome *you* if you ever felt like a visit, and so would Uncle Jonathan . . . but Petroc must have mentioned that a dozen times already.'

Kurt shook his head, looking amused again now. 'You should know better than anyone that your brother *never* says things more than once. I hope the girl he offers marriage to is listening carefully at the time!'

'She scarcely needs to, being already determined that she's going to be his wife.' It was possible to speak naturally again, and she could chatter enough about her family to see her safely out of the door. 'My cousin has known her future since she and Luc lived with us as children. I think Petroc knows it too, but a farmer's work is never done and he hasn't yet found the time to hustle Lisette in front of the vicar. Perhaps that's why Aunt C. is descending on us – she's a lady who dislikes loose ends.'

'Then perhaps I *should* come to Prospect and inspect my godson's "future",' Kurt said solemnly.

She stared at him for a moment, not sure that he meant it. Then her grandmother's luminous smile lit her face.

'You've begun to laugh again, and you've even decided that you can bear the complication of people after all . . . Professor dear, it's quite a day, *nicht wahr*?'

He thought it might also be a day on which he began to weep if she continued to smile at him with such heart-easing kindness. But she turned away suddenly from the expression on his face, clattered mugs in the sink, and then announced that she was late for her next port of call at a pottery ten miles away.

'I'll be back the day after tomorrow to change the dressing on your hand. Leave it alone until then, and please don't use it.'

The terse instruction might have misled him once, but not now; he was beginning to know Lavinia's grand-daughter. 'What will you do instead of work?' she asked, as he walked outside with her to her car.

'Walk, and sketch with my good hand – the models I need are here and they charge no fee! Evan Nimmo will probably call after supper. If it rains I teach him to play chess; if the evening is fine he shows me the haunts of wild animals and birds. Am I not blessed in my friends?'

His face was serious again, and she found no answer to the question except to nod. Courage seemed to be lacking altogether today, or she might have said that his lonely, self-sufficient life came near to breaking her heart. She drove away, conscious of him still watching her. He was dwarfed by the stone pillars of the porch, lost in the empty, lonely landscape that surrounded him.

The steep, winding route down to the valley needed care, but one certainty managed to bore its way through the concentration she kept on the road. If Kurt should come to Prospect, it would be to see old friends. She was too young to be considered one of those, but much too old to mistake a moment born simply of the isolation of that moorland place for something significant in their lives. He'd smiled at her in just the way he used to smile at Morwetha, the child. All she could do for him was

315

to sell his beautiful carvings. It wasn't for her to ease his loneliness, and bind up his wounds when he got hurt.

Petroc always kept his grandmother informed of the state of Bossiney property in the town, knowing that she accepted the responsibilities of ownership in place of Tristram.

'The rents scarcely justify the outlay, but repair work needs doing urgently,' he reported. 'Shall we go ahead, without waiting for Uncle Tris to get back?'

'Of course we must – Cornwall is no place to live in with a leaking roof.' Lavinia stared at her grandson's reticent face and wished she knew what else he thought about apart from missing tiles. 'Cécile and the twins are coming here while Tristram is in New York,' she said next, hoping for enlightenment.

'I know. Lisette has made matters clear! I'm expected to leave the farms to what she's pleased to call my "hired hands" so that for as long as she is here we can enjoy a holiday together.'

'It wouldn't do you any harm,' Lavinia said bluntly. 'You work too hard, and don't play at all as far as I can see.'

Petroc's amused grin was all the answer she got. 'I hope *you're* looking forward to the visit,' he said blandly instead.

'The children will cheer your mother up when she comes sadly home from her visit to America, and Cécile will bully her into not giving way to despair.' He made no answer to that either, and Lavinia shot a sudden question at him. 'I suppose you think I'm heartless where my daughter is concerned.'

He heard the note of sadness in her voice, and bent down suddenly to kiss her. 'No, love. A trifle bracing now and then, but never heartless. Perhaps something else will cheer Mum up as well. When Morwetha called in last night on her way back to Polperro she'd seen Kurt again.

Apparently he's recovered enough to think of paying you a visit.'

'Oh, my dear, I do *hope* so, and so will Jonathan. Jenifer said she scarcely recognized him, and there's nothing to be wondered at in that. But if the man *inside* hasn't changed, I shall know him instantly.'

Lavinia put aside past memories with regret and returned to the anxious present. 'Cécile is supposed to be coming for a holiday, but I doubt if that's her real purpose, since she gets no pleasure from being here. It's more likely that I'm to be reminded once more of my unreasonableness in clinging to a house that's a millstone round her husband's neck. The reminder will be delivered delicately, but it will be unmistakable all the same.'

'Dear Gran, why let her reminders, delicate or otherwise, bother you? She doesn't own Prospect, Tristram does. After him, Luc will; and we've got time to convince that mixed-up lad that he's got Cornish as well as Sabatier blood in his veins.'

'So we have,' she agreed without conviction, but smiled cheerfully because she knew Petroc wanted her to. For that very same reason she would have to look cheerful for him on her deathbed as well. Then she thought of something that lit her face with real amusement. 'In any case Jonathan and I have settled it between us – we're not going to shuffle off this mortal coil until Daniel has lost interest in Prospect!'

'That's the spirit, Gran – hurrah for the stubborn Bossineys, and down with the Penwarnes!' He kissed her goodbye, promised to think seriously about a holiday, and took the steps down from the terrace at his usual breakneck speed. Lavinia watched him go, and remembered too late to warn him that one of the upstart Penwarnes was even now working in the garden down below, at her invitation.

Not expecting any obstruction in his way, Petroc rounded a sharp bend at speed, collided with a body hunched over the job of staking up a rampant dahlia, and finished up with it in a tangle of arms and legs at the foot of the steps.

'Any damage?' he enquired, a trifle breathlessly.

Polly licked a grazed knee clean and glowered at him from her resting place in a flower bed.

'Not much, but no thanks to *you*. Couldn't you ring a bell, or something, if you must play at being an express train?'

'No, but I'll remember your talent for turning up where I least expect you to be in future. What are you doing here, anyway?'

Anticipating what would come next, she quickly interrupted him. 'Snooping as usual in what is going to be *my* garden one day? Yes, let's say *that's* what I'm doing, Mr O'Meara.'

He got up and put out his hands to lift her to her feet, then stood looking at her, faintly smiling. 'We could say it, but it wouldn't be true, would it? You come here to help my grandmother, because you know it hurts her to see the garden neglected. I'm always meaning to do something about it myself, but there never seems to be enough time.'

It was the longest speech she'd ever heard him make, and the most amiable. He was tall for a Cornishman, and she had to look up to discover for the first time what his face looked like when it wasn't angry or contemptuous. She was left with the ridiculous feeling that *now* he was being unfair – disarming her with a smile of treacherous and unexpected sweetness. There were scratches on her bare arms and legs, but she didn't feel them; for the moment, all she was conscious of was the touch of his hands, his dark eyes examining her face, and the blood that raced through her body, confusing her with messages she refused to understand.

At last he let her go and she was free to move away.

'I expect you've heard that my cousins are on their way here,' he said next. 'Perhaps you can interest Luc in some

318

navvying out here; my job, apparently, is to keep Lisette amused.'

It was obvious, now, the reason for his good humour. He had finally decided that monkish isolation had lost its charm. His cousin might occasionally be tiresome, but even the most single-minded breeder of prize cattle needed a woman in his life and heart and bed. Polly remembered Lisette's teasing smile and seductively curved body, felt her own racing heartbeat slow down, and struggled to grab at a topic that would return them to normality.

'Annie Trelear, next door to Granny in Fore Street, had rain dripping through her roof after last night's downpour. Is that how Bossiney tenants are supposed to live?'

Petroc's usual frown was suddenly back in place, and her pulse might never have known its agitation of a moment ago.

'Mrs Trelear has paid so little rent for the past fifty years that she might consider herself lucky to have a roof left at all. But, as it happens, the leak *is* being attended to.'

It sounded adequate if cool, but Polly required more – a sign of sympathy in his face for a woman whose lot had been cast in pastures less pleasant and privileged than his own.

'Generations of Trelears have been just as much a part of Fowey history as the Bossineys but, being fishermen, I suppose you think they're of no account?'

'They're of about as much account as the rest of us,' he said definitely, 'a mixture of good and bad, sometimes a credit to the town, at other times not. But I haven't the inclination to sentimentalize over them – I leave that to visitors from London with their intrusive cameras, looking for artificial local colour and encouraging phonies to dress up and play the part of Cornish "characters".'

Her assortment of grazes had begun to hurt now, and his unfairness stung as well. 'Intrusive or not, *my* camera records only what is *real*. I've spent weeks travelling round your precious county. There isn't much that's picturesque about it, and even less that's hopeful.'

'Don't tell *me* what our problems are. I live with them,' Petroc suddenly shouted. 'But what Cornwall *doesn't* need is outsiders like you and your father crashing in with their instant diagnoses of all our sores. Leave them to *us*, for God's sake.'

Calm again now that she had made him angry, Polly smiled faintly. 'With pleasure, but I'll play fair and warn you of something you won't like. Your uncle instructed me to take my Cornish pictures to *him* first. I shall do that when I go back to London!'

It was a huge comfort to have the last word; she could walk away from him up the steps they'd tumbled down together, smiling at the expression on his face.

Petroc had to watch her go, registering things about her that he would rather not have noticed. 'Down with the Penwarnes,' he'd said confidently to his grandmother. The truth was that he didn't feel confident at all, only tired and rather sad. It was scarcely the way to go into battle, and a battle – Gran was right – was surely what his aunt had in mind. He drove home trying to weigh up his chances of defeating a single-minded woman who had no scruples to inconvenience her and a certain amount of rational good sense on her side; but he had to chase from his mind the memory of Polly Penwarne's blue eyes accusing him of not sufficiently cherishing dear, fat, slovenly Annie Trelear.

23

Long before Luc had steered them into Fowey, Cécile was regretting the need to have made the journey; the usual mixture of boredom and frustration assailed her once the Tamar had been crossed and they were back in Cornwall. She had work to do there, and a spell of rare settled weather might make the slow, hot days more bearable, but who would there be to talk to? She could be sure already that not a man in that tight, complacent, little society would have heard of abstract art or the plays of Christopher Fry, and not a woman would care that Christian Dior had made it a crime to cling to the hideous uniform clothes of war-time.

Prospect itself was an added penance to look forward to – Victorian décor, bathrooms to match, and those huge, oppressive views from every window. For a woman who liked to feel in charge of things there was altogether too much visible sea and sky, too much sense of being perched on the very edge of the known, controllable world.

Two hours later she knew for certain that little had changed from her last visit. The discomforts were the same, and so were the tiresome members of her husband's family. For once Jenifer wasn't there to twitter around them in her usual state of well meaning muddle, but Lavinia's dry cheek still smelled of the lavender water she'd used for fifty years, and Tristram's uncle observed them with the relish of a lepidopterist studying rare butterflies. Cécile was accustomed to making an impression on men, but she always had the irritating feeling that the impression she made on Jonathan Bossiney was not the right one.

Bearing in mind Lavinia's strictures on the selfish indolence of old age, Jonathan exerted himself to be agreeable the following morning. He looked at Cécile's wide-skirted dress of cream tussore, belted with orange and brown-striped ribbon, and smiled with a pleasure that was genuine.

'My dear, how elegant you always manage to look! I know old men are tedious about times past, but women haven't seemed feminine to me since Edward the Seventh was on the throne. Bosoms and hips – that's what ladies' dresses ought to flatter.'

Cécile agreed smilingly and told Jonathan that he was looking very well.

'It's the peaceful life we lead down here,' he said artlessly. 'No wild metropolitan rush and bustle for us. What a good thing Lisette seems happy here, because nothing would persuade Petroc to live anywhere but in Cornwall.'

The satisfaction in his voice was maddening, and so was the inference that what Petroc wanted was the only thing that mattered.

'Nice to see Luc, too, enjoying himself,' Jonathan blundered on. 'He loved this place so much as a child that I always knew he'd come round to it again in the end.'

'My dear Uncle, his reasons for being here are simple – our potential clients leave the city in midsummer, and he was aware that Polly Penwarne is still in Fowey. That's the extent of Cornwall's attraction for him – temporary boredom in London, and a pair of very beautiful blue eyes beckoning him down here!'

She tried not to sound sharp, tried to sound confident, and knew as she spoke that this keen-eyed old man saw the fear hidden inside her. Possession of Tristram had never been achieved, so the children *must* be hers. Luc, especially, mustn't be seduced into thinking himself a Cornishman by sunlight on water, and lonely windblown headlands and mysterious river creeks. She had recognized the danger of letting him come now, but needed to remind him of the irrelevance of Prospect to their lives. He had to understand the absurdity of letting these old people stay in it, apparently for ever – since, like Jane Eyre, they seemed 'so tenacious of life'. Irritation suddenly provoked her into saying what was really in her mind.

'I often wonder why *you* didn't stay at Salubrious House, Uncle. It wasn't the impractical museum-piece that *this* is, and you must surely have grown attached to it over the years.'

He knew that she wanted him to confirm what she suspected – that the sale of his lovely Georgian home had contributed to the gift he'd made to Petroc. Without Prospect to move back into, he would have had to remain there and his great-nephew's purchase of the farms wouldn't have been possible.

'I was tired of living alone,' he said simply, 'and I couldn't look at the sea from Bull Lane.'

'And perhaps my mother-in-law wouldn't have agreed to join forces with you *there*!' Cécile pointed out with a thin smile. 'Jenifer would – she's sick to death of living here. I feel very sorry for her – but the lot of widowed daughters is as bad as that of unmarried ones; no-one cares what *they* want, poor things.'

It was neatly done, Jonathan acknowledged to himself. Without actually saying so, Cécile had managed to imply that Lavinia was a selfish monster feeding off a sacrificial daughter, and he a gullible fool content to help Petroc at the expense of Tristram's generosity. Anger flared like a lit match, giving him a moment's youthful vigour.

'Jenifer *chose* to come back here when she was widowed; she has *chosen* to remain ever since, not at all displeased to know that people like yourself feel sorry for her. But living in the Bossiney home still has a certain cachet! Petroc's farmhouse and Morwetha's flat above the shop at Polperro don't have quite the same appeal, although both have been offered to her.'

Cécile lowered her sword, aware that it had struck tougher steel in Jonathan than she expected. 'With Kurt

Winkler installed at Trebinnick, perhaps *that* will grow on her more!' she said with a charming smile. 'I am so pleased for dear Jenifer that Tristram took the trouble to find him and bring him back. Missed opportunities are not usually offered again, in my experience.'

'And never, in mine,' Jonathan agreed bluntly, 'but Tristram didn't rescue Kurt just so that Jenifer could indulge her romantic fantasies. I think even *she* has the sense to realize it now.'

Cécile acknowledged defeat with this tiresomely stubborn old man, and took herself away to a more important interview.

Petroc watched her arrive an hour later and realized that he might have expected a visit. Tristram's wife didn't believe in ducking what she saw to be her responsibilities. He felt a reluctant admiration for her as long as she didn't hurt the people he loved. She stopped the car and got out of it gracefully – something few women managed in his view – and smiled when he walked towards her. He knew she was only a year or two younger than his mother, but she could have belonged to a different generation. Hair and skin had been religiously cared for, and her dress sense never faltered. Even now he could see that in certain ways she'd been an enormous asset to his uncle.

'If you tell me that I'm *de trop*, my dear Petroc, I shall go again at once,' she said gaily. 'But I am too old to find lazing on a beach enjoyable, and even when young I *never* enjoyed getting wet in little boats! I leave that to Luc and Lisette.'

'I'm not sure how much Lisette enjoys it either. For a girl who spent most of her childhood here, she's very reluctant to trust herself to sailors!'

The opening was almost irresistible but Cécile managed not to take it. 'You didn't answer my question,' she pointed out instead. 'Shall I go away and leave you to get on with whatever farmers feel obliged to accomplish at this hour of the day?'

Petroc smiled and shook his head. 'This farmer only

feels obliged to drink a thirst-quenching glass of something. I can offer you beer, cider, or some white wine that almost certainly arrived here without benefit of customs duty. We still can't resist a little harmless contraband, the Cornish view being that the wine tastes all the better for it!'

Cécile chose the wine, allowed herself to be settled on a bench shaded by an ancient apple tree, and looked about her while Petroc disappeared inside the house. She had even less wish to be buried alive here than at Prospect, but on a fine day of summer it looked attractive enough. More to the point, it looked prosperous and well cared for.

'How much of this land is yours?' she asked idly when he returned with wine for her and beer for himself.

'By Cornish standards the acreage is quite big – as far as the river to the west, and about the same distance all round. The farm buildings are almost exactly in the middle, which makes it a very convenient arrangement.'

She nodded and sipped her wine; the convenience or otherwise of his arrangements was of no interest to her, but the subject led easily to the conversation she had come for.

'I now see why the cards are stacked against me so heavily! I want Lisette to see the exciting promise of what others offer her in London, and all *she* can think of is living in these admittedly idyllic surroundings.'

Petroc leaned back, brown hands clasped round one knee – the picture of a man at his ease; but she knew that his eyes were watchful.

'The living on a Cornish farm is sometimes a good deal less than idyllic,' he suggested. 'I have tried to explain to her that there's more to it than stroking foals and watching the antics of new-born lambs.'

'My dear Petroc, I'm sure you have, but without the slightest success that I can see. My daughter is *convinced* that she was born to be a farmer's wife!' In the silence that followed, Cécile glanced at Petroc's expressionless face, and gave a rueful little smile that said they were companions in misfortune. 'Awkward, is it not, *mon ami*, when you are convinced of nothing of the kind! But unfortunately she has her father's loyalty, and an *idée fixe* about you – childhood friend, dashing war-time hero – that is hard to dislodge. I expect you've been too kind since then to hold her at arm's length, but perhaps it would be still *kinder* now to be frank with her.'

It was beautifully done, Petroc acknowledged, even as rage consumed him for the corner she had boxed him into. She gave a little shrug that regretted her daughter's heartache, and then put it aside. 'I suppose you know that Tristram chose to refuse Daniel Penwarne's generous offer for Prospect.'

'I wasn't aware that he was looking for a buyer,' Petroc answered as calmly as possible, 'but I did hear about the refusal.'

'How can he *not* want to get rid of a hideous and expensive white elephant in Fowey when our life is entirely in London? Tristram hasn't lived here for thirty years – he is completely *dépaysé* as far as Cornwall is concerned, and Luc has no interest in it at all.'

For the first time Cécile sounded sharp, and the knowledge made Petroc feel slightly better. 'Other members of the family *do* still live at Prospect,' he pointed out gently. 'It's their home. It's always been the home of the Bossineys.'

'Which means precisely nothing at all to present-day Fowey or to future Bossineys. Luc is the only one of you who can carry on the name, and he will want to play the part of an outmoded, impoverished, country gentleman even less than his father does.'

It was a telling argument hard to counter except by offering the unvarnished truth – that, but for her, Tristram himself might have come back contentedly to Cornwall.

'Is Daniel Penwarne minded to become a property-owning countryman?' he asked instead.

'How should I know *what* he has in mind?'

Petroc smiled, seeing his opportunity. 'I thought he

might just have mentioned it to you . . . He certainly knows about *our* difficulties, because in fact his offer was scarcely generous at all. With inside knowledge, he reckoned he had his opponent on the ropes!'

A slight flush crept up Cécile's beautifully made-up cheeks, but she didn't lose her head. 'He's a businessman, driving the best bargain he can, no doubt. Who is to blame him for that?'

She sat twisting the wine glass in her fingers, then threw down her challenge.

'I expect you realize that the battle isn't over. I shall urge Tristram to change his mind before Daniel loses interest.'

'And I shall expect him to give Penwarne the same answer as before. One of us, dear Aunt, is bound to be wrong!'

Cécile acknowledged to herself that in any other circumstances she would have enjoyed fighting Petroc O'Meara. She smiled suddenly and he saw again what had snared his uncle into marrying her.

'*Mon cher*, I'm not suggesting that we turn your grandmother and Uncle Jonathan out into the street! Of course we should buy a suitable house for them – build one if necessary.' She glanced round, and delivered her *coup de grâce* as a gentle afterthought. 'Why not here? Surely you could spare a little of all *this* space?' Bought with Jonathan's money, she skilfully implied, without actually mentioning a fact so crude.

'It's good agricultural land, and Cornwall doesn't have enough of it to waste on unnecessary buildings.'

She allowed a flash of anger to appear at last. 'In other words, your grandmother, Jonathan, Cornwall even, not to mention your *own* interest are all to be catered for at *our* expense. I do not find this amusing.'

'Perhaps not, but you've overlooked something *we've* all been taught to believe – it's accounted more blessed to give than to receive! Or perhaps that *wasn't* taught in Belgium?'

327

She ignored the smiling suggestion and announced coldly instead that it was time to go. The last remaining shot in her locker was only fired as they walked towards her car. 'What a relief to know that you've never had any *real* intention of marrying my daughter, Petroc. I should quite hate to have you as a son-in-law.'

He smiled, bowed, and held open the door for her. Cécile drove away, measuring the results of her interview. She now knew for certain that it was Petroc who was bolstering Tristram's courage and unusual obstinacy; and she had manoeuvred him into a position where he must immediately do something about Lisette that would give her the strongest possible dislike of Cornwall. On the whole, Cécile decided that her trip to Tregenna had been very worthwhile. She smiled suddenly – it had also made a self-controlled man angry, and that was an added bonus!

After anxious consultation with Jonathan, Lavinia decided that Kurt's return visit to Prospect should take place while other people were there to absorb some of its first emotional shock. Apart from meeting him as an old friend, Cécile was the undoubted mistress of any social occasion, and the presence of the twins and Polly Penwarne would mean that the conversation had to concern the present. There would be time to come to terms with the past when Kurt had grown used to them again.

Jonathan agreed with this point of view, and also suggested that with Cécile or her daughter there to supervise the preparation of the chickens, eggs and butter provided from Petroc's farm, the catering arrangements would be far better than usual.

'Selfish, indolent, *and* greedy?' he asked wistfully, harking back to a conversation he hadn't forgotten.

Lavinia smiled and shook her head. 'Not at all . . . after ten years of rationing it's a crime not to make the most of good food and enjoy it when we get the chance. Let us eat, drink, and be merry, my dear, for tomorrow we . . . Well, who knows about tomorrow?' She took care to sound as if it didn't worry her. Having put them all to rights, on matters of dress, politics, philosophy, and the best way of cooking freshly killed chickens, her daughter-in-law would return to London and leave them in peace for another year. Tristram would keep Prospect for them in her lifetime, and after him Petroc would fight its battles still. The scars of war were fading, even for people like Kurt, and gaiety was creeping back, despite the austerities of Mr Attlee's government and the fears that hung over the world. Lavinia refused to allow herself to whimper about the past or fear for the future. Both were the most futile occupations an old woman could sink to. She sat down at her desk instead to write her little notes of invitation, while Jonathan went to inspect the few dusty bottles that remained in the wine cellar.

The other members of the family considered the evening ahead with differing feelings. Lisette hoped to impress Petroc by taking charge of the kitchen, Morwetha felt ashamed of the longing she recognized in herself not to have to share Kurt Winkler with the rest of her relatives, and Luc, with nothing else to do, irritated Polly by following her about the garden where she was working. When she lost patience one morning and told him to help or go away, he suddenly made a grab at her, pulled her down to the ground, and began to kiss her with a great deal more skill and fire than she would have expected him to possess. His habitual dandyish languor was a pose, after all, and she was shaken and dishevelled when he was finally forced to let her go for lack of breath.

'At least I've got you to notice that I'm here – it's a step in the right direction!' Luc said unsteadily.

'Oh, I notice you all right; I can't help it when you're always in the way. But I'll let you know when I want to be mauled in future.' It wasn't an entirely fair description of his technique, but she was too flustered to be fair.

'It's your own fault – in that rig-out, in any rig-out if it comes to that, you're an open invitation to any normal male. Darling Polly, you'll have to hie you to a nunnery if you don't want to be kissed. *Why* don't you, by the way? Or is it just me you spurn so brutally?'

His voice reminded her of Tristram Bossiney's, and now that he'd been jolted out of his London affectations she could recognize a charm of manner also inherited from his father. But instead of answering his question she asked one of her own.

'Why *not* do some work here if you're bored with lounging about on the beach all day? You can see for yourself that there's plenty to do.'

Luc dragged his eyes from her mouth and concentrated on the distant view instead. A yacht was tacking round St Saviour's Point into the safety of the estuary, mainsail and jib spread to catch the breeze. Nearer at hand he could see that slack water was past and the tide was flowing again gently into Prospect Cove – *their* special place, that had always been, where they'd gone in childhood to paddle and swim and shrimp and pretend that they were valiant lifeboatmen rescuing sailors stranded on the little rocky island that jutted out of the water twenty yards away. Since it was their beach, they'd laid claim to the rock as well. Those days, enchanted in memory, were over now, but it was the cove that he would regret most when Prospect no longer belonged to the Bossineys.

'I know nothing about gardening, but even if I did, there'd be no point in working out here,' he said abruptly. 'A few weeds more or less don't matter now.'

She went suddenly pale beneath her summer tan. If he knew about her father's offer, why didn't he also know that it had been refused? Or was he *better* informed than she was? With another stab of fear she remembered something Petroc O'Meara had said – Luc wasn't interested in inheriting Prospect.

'Weeds *always* matter,' she insisted desperately, 'especially to someone who has worked for fifty years to make a garden beautiful. In any case, surely it isn't pointless to make your grandmother happy?'

Her eyes, fixed on him steadily, were the same deep

blue as the sunlit sea, and her brown face under its cap of short, dark hair was hauntingly different from the faces of the girls he knew in London. He wanted to tell her his fear, wanted to explain, so that she wouldn't despise him; but it was too dangerous to admit that if he gave in over the garden he might want to give in over much more important things as well.

He made another sudden confession instead. 'Oh, God, how I *hate* having to take sides, don't you?'

She gave the question careful thought before answering. 'Yes, although it's not quite so bad if you're sure which side to be on. When things you thought you were sure of start turning upside down, *then* it all begins to get difficult.'

She was referring to a difficulty of her own – he was sure about that; but before he could make the mistake of asking what it was she glanced at her watch, and then scrambled to her feet.

'Thanks to you I've wasted almost half an hour, and I meant to finish this bed before I went home. As it is, I shall have to sprint all the way to Fore Street to change for her ladyship's party.'

'And I shall come and escort you back again.'

She smiled, liking a courtesy of which William Penwarne would certainly approve.

'All right – if I'm not quite ready you can listen to some of my grandfather's stories. He knows even more about Cornwall than my mother did.'

'No . . . Mr Penwarne must talk of *anything* but that,' Luc said strangely. 'I can't bear to hear about Cornwall.'

Polly stared at him, understanding the sudden desperation in his voice. But just as there was no need to ask what he meant, there was no comfort she could offer either; he must choose for himself the side he was to be on.

'In that case I'll make sure of being ready,' she promised, then smiled more warmly on him than she'd done so far, before disappearing in the direction of the potting-shed with her trug of tools.

24

Petroc changed reluctantly out of working clothes, being of the opinion that his grandmother had for once been doubly mistaken – it would have been far better to invite Kurt to Prospect when Cécile and the twins had gone back to London, and it was far worse to have included Polly Penwarne in her invitations. He could see no sense at all in opening their gates to the daughter of the enemy, to let her observe the Bossineys at odds with each other. But these were surface anxieties; beneath them lay his own problem of what to do about Lisette.

He went downstairs still feeling depressed, and found that Kurt was ready first, looking surprisingly composed for his re-entry into society.

'Look, my friend, no more shaking!' Kurt held out steady hands to prove it. 'I am being made whole again up on the moor. That is what Evan calls it, you know – just "the moor", as if there were only one.'

'There *is* only one that counts to a Cornishman,' Petroc agreed. He looked at his godfather's quiet face and smiled faintly. 'You can manage this evening well enough, but I doubt if you'll be sorry to get back to the peace of Trebinnick tomorrow.'

'No, I shan't be sorry, because I feel safe and happy there. But I remember always that it isn't mine – you must tell me, Petroc, when you need the house yourself.'

'I *don't* need it, and since it was bought with Jonathan's money you could say that it isn't mine, either. It belongs to the family, and we *all* beg you to stay!'

Kurt smiled, but fell to examining his left hand. He was thankful that the wound was healing now and no longer needed the attentions of a nurse, because Morwetha's visits had become painful. When she came briskly to bring him money for the carvings she sold, he could manage to be as brisk and impersonal as she was herself; it had been hard to be that when her hands, at such tender variance with her manner, had been touching his.

He and Petroc arrived at Prospect just as Luc escorted Polly back through the garden. They walked hand in hand, and Petroc registered the entranced expression on his cousin's face, understanding its danger – if anything else had been needed to put Luc completely in the Penwarne camp, it was needed no longer. This slender, graceful girl would convince him easily enough that greedy men like her father should be allowed to buy for their own ends whatever bits of Cornwall suited them; it didn't matter what became of a place that had no meaning in his own life. But there were memories that refused to match the image in front of him. Instead of this elegant nymph in a sleeveless white silk dress that flattered her brown arms and throat, he saw a different girl – one who sat on the ground, licking dirt off a graze, or shouted at him on the highway that it was up to him to keep Prospect safe. Such pictures in his mind made him want to believe that he was wrong about her, but she *was* Penwarne's daughter. She would compile her sharp, one-sided, little portrait, exposing Cornwall's scars and jeering at its superstitions, and then go back to her sophisticated haunts in London. Tristram wouldn't buy what she offered, of course, but someone would.

Knowing nothing of these things, Kurt smiled with pleasure when the introductions were made. 'I am more fortunate than these *young* men,' he said simply. 'I can remember your mother when she lived at Prospect.'

'And you sang German lullabies so beautifully to Morwetha that she refused to go to sleep. My mother used to say that you were a mixed blessing to a conscientious nursemaid!'

He bowed and held out his arm to conduct her into the house.

For a determined recluse he was doing very well, Petroc reflected, then grinned because Luc's face looked resentful and nonplussed.

'It's called continental finesse,' he explained kindly. 'Even *you* won't get a look-in!'

But things improved for Luc indoors, where Kurt was caught up in recollections of times past. The atmosphere of Prospect hadn't changed at all – the salt-tinged air still drifted in through every window, mingling with the scent of flowers and beeswax polish. His friend, Lavinia Bossiney, smiled at him as she had always done, and the only difference now was that her cheeks were wet with tears.

'Oh, my dear Kurt . . . welcome back,' she murmured unsteadily.

He kissed her hand, and her wet face, and then looked at the rest of them – Jonathan, Cécile, and a smiling girl with a faint resemblance to Tristram and a much stronger likeness to the young man he had met outside. Memory held him speechless, but Cécile found something to say in the language they had always used together, and the moment of paralysis was past. He could move and smile now, clasp hands and talk, without fear of breaking down. He was among dear friends, even if the oldest of them – Tristram – was still in New York, and the most recent of them – Morwetha – was absent for some reason of her own.

Lisette spared a friendly smile for the middle-aged stranger in their midst with the haunted face, and then promptly forgot him because Petroc was talking to Great-Uncle Jonathan. She went over to the two men and tucked her hand in Petroc's arm.

'I'm inclined to feel very fed up with you,' she said severely. 'You were supposed to come out to play, not stay hidden among your wretched livestock.'

He smiled but gently disengaged himself. 'Don't come too near, then, in case I still smell of the cowshed!'

Her little trill of laughter was engaging, and she stayed

close enough to share with him the pleasure of her own expensive perfume. 'Silly, you smell lovely . . . you always do.'

'Not when I've been dipping sheep, or herding cattle for market on a hot day.'

Beside them, Jonathan listened unashamedly, aware that the conversation was not as trivial as it seemed. Petroc reflected that it was scarcely the moment he would have chosen for a dialogue that might shape the whole of his life in future; but in a way it helped to have old Jonathan there, alert and interested, but unemotional.

Lisette was frowning now, and her large hazel eyes fixed on Petroc's face insisted that for once he must take her seriously. 'You like to pretend that I'm a stupid, fluffy-headed idiot. Darling Petroc, I am *not*! I understand perfectly well that a farmer's life sometimes has to be very real and earnest.'

'You're not stupid at all,' he said with rare gentleness. 'You're very pretty and very sweet, but I doubt if you *do* understand that a farmer can never leave the job. Whatever else he feels inclined to do, his livestock must be cared for and messily delivered of their offspring; his cows must be milked, his land ploughed, sown, harvested, and ploughed again. His wife gets the excitement of an occasional trip to market if she's lucky; otherwise, she puts up with mud and manure outside her home, and a good deal of lonely monotony inside it.' He spoke so gravely that Lisette couldn't miss the intention behind a picture as deadly as he could paint it; she was to understand now, if she hadn't before, the realities of being a farmer's wife.

She heard what he said, but looked at his close-lipped mouth, and thought of his brown hands touching her. Petroc saw her smile and knew that she was still lost in the enjoyable game they had been playing for years. He should never have played it at all, but when he returned from the war, tired and heartsick, she was back at Prospect as well – a revelation in her pretty American clothes of what carefree youth ought to be. Cécile hadn't accused him of vanity in allowing her hero worship to go on, but he thought she might well have done.

Lisette saw in his face a mixture of affection and rueful sweetness that seemed more important than what he suggested next. 'I think I've made you remember that you're really a city girl at heart. If we exchanged childhood vows, sweetheart, now is the moment to forget them!'

He waited with a curious sense of detachment for what she would do or say next. If she offered him the smallest chance that Cécile had lied, he would take it; if not, it would be impossible to smile and walk away. Lisette turned to talk to Jonathan, but her smile wobbled suddenly on the edge of tears.

'He's very stupid, isn't he? Not to understand? Shall I do the asking, Uncle J.?'

Petroc's hands on her shoulders forced her to look at him. In her face he saw such a brave attempt to cover hope and longing with a smile that it was almost no effort at all to lean down and kiss her trembling mouth. '*I* shall do the asking, but not here and now. I insist on a little privacy when I propose to a lady!'

She caught her breath, uncertain whether or not to believe in happiness until she saw him smile. Then her face flushed with delight and she almost stammered that it was time to remember she was in charge of the kitchen. When she'd floated away, leaving silence behind, Jonathan stared at his companion.

'Shall we join the others?' he suggested after a moment or two. He had the strong impression that his great-nephew had forgotten where he was until Petroc smiled, and said 'Why not?' politely.

Morwetha arrived only as they were sitting down to dinner. She looked weary and plain, and was still dressed in the crumpled cotton skirt and blouse she'd been working in all day. A muttered apology wouldn't normally have been enough to turn away her grandmother's displeasure, but after a glance at her face Lavinia merely remarked that she was glad to have the dinner table complete.

'Unusual forbearance on Gran's part,' Morwetha murmured to her brother sitting next to her. 'Any idea why?'

'Benevolence inspired by having Kurt back in the fold, I expect. He's bearing up under all this jollity rather well, don't you think?'

She registered in Petroc's voice a note she didn't understand, but most of her attention was on Kurt across the table, smiling at something Cécile had just said. He seemed at ease sitting there, but she guessed that he would rather have been in his peaceful, lonely kitchen at Trebinnick.

The food was delicious, and the wine unearthed by Jonathan still very drinkable; even so, Lavinia was of the opinion that true conviviality was missing from her dinner party. Lisette, looking even prettier than usual, was very gay, and Luc clearly asked nothing more than to monopolize Polly's attention. Jonathan savoured each small pleasure of the evening with the care of a man who understood that he could no longer afford to waste any experience of enjoyment, but the others struggled to give the appearance of contentment. It was a relief to hear her daughter-in-law announce that she must take herself back to London.

'So soon?' Luc asked quickly. 'You were meant to be taking a little holiday . . . I thought we *all* were.'

'I'm going to stay, Maman,' Lisette put in. She smiled revealingly at Petroc, then with a little flicker of triumph at her mother, who had finally been proved wrong about him.

Cécile interpreted the message received from her daughter, queried it with a glance at Petroc, and saw him give a faint nod. She made no comment on it, but after a moment held up her hands in a little gesture of resignation before turning to Luc.

'Stay if *you* want to, *chéri*, but one of us must return. Clients soon grow impatient, and if we are not immediately at their beck and call, they find another decorator.'

He hesitated, aware that he ought to agree, and that

he didn't in the least want to. The silence was beginning to grow awkward when Polly stepped into the breach with a charming smile at Luc.

'I'm afraid it's time for me to leave Cornwall as well. I've a huge heap of films waiting to be processed, and I prefer to do them myself.'

His face changed, but he was tactful enough to talk only to his mother. 'Of course you can't go back alone; if you're going to start work again, so must I.'

Cécile looked at Polly. 'Why not drive back with us? I'm sure your father would prefer you not to be travelling alone.'

On the brink of making a polite excuse she found herself meeting Petroc O'Meara's measuring gaze and suddenly changed her mind. 'My father thinks I'm old enough to fend for myself, Lady Bossiney, but cameras are weighty things to add to one's luggage – I should be very glad of a lift.' She couldn't help glancing again in Petroc's direction, but he was intently considering now the pattern engraved on the wine glass in front of him. How she travelled home was no concern of his. How could it be, his expression clearly said, when she had chosen the side of the enemy?

Petroc drove Kurt back to Tregenna for the night, relieved to find him untalkative. But finally his guest roused himself. 'It was a pleasure to see your grandmother and Dr Jonathan again . . . Indeed, I found the evening most enjoyable altogether.'

'It's more than I can claim myself,' Petroc said after a moment. He was tempted for a moment to add that it had provided him with a future wife, but perhaps Kurt would be shocked by an attitude so strangely English and dispassionate.

'Because you are worried, perhaps . . . don't entirely trust your uncle's wife? Tell me that it's not my affair if you like, my friend; I shall not be offended.'

Petroc's shoulder lifted in a little shrug. 'The blunt truth is that I don't trust Cécile at all, and the thing that bothers

338

me most is her friendship with Daniel Penwarne. Granny is safe, of course, but in the long run unless we can work a conversion in young Luc, Prospect will go under the hammer – to someone else if Penwarne is too old to care about it by then.' His hand came off the steering wheel in a revealing gesture. 'It's only a small family drama – completely trivial, God knows, measured against your own experience of tragedy. But the same thing is happening all over Cornwall. One by one old families are having to let go of what they've preserved for generations, and each time something is lost that can never be replaced.'

'That is *not* trivial,' Kurt corrected him quietly. He debated with himself and then risked his question. 'Have you considered first trying to convert Loveday's daughter? Interest *her* in Cornwall and I have the feeling that *she* might then persuade Luc to keep his inheritance.'

Petroc took a long time to answer. 'I first met Polly Penwarne ten years ago and she informed me very clearly that she *hated* Cornwall. As far as I know, her opinion hasn't changed, but even if it had it wouldn't be allowed to affect her loyalty to her father.'

Kurt regretfully put Polly aside as the answer to Petroc's problem, but a grief of his own clamoured for the relief of being mentioned.

'Morwetha wished not to be present this evening.' He stated it as a fact needing no argument.

'She was tired . . . works too hard,' Petroc said, unable to pretend that her quietness hadn't been noticeable.

'Then she must *not* trouble to come to Trebinnick in future. I can borrow Evan's bicycle and bring my work down to you. Tell her this for me, please.'

'I can tell her but it won't make the slightest difference – she'll come anyway.'

'Yes, but she comes coldly, and this I do not wish. I am cold and formal in return, but all the time I know that she is not to blame. How should she *not* hate me when my countrymen killed her husband and left her lonely?'

The note of anguish reached Petroc, insisting that he must struggle out of his own preoccupations.

'You're wrong . . . completely wrong. Morwetha is the last woman on earth to bear such a senseless grudge. Peter Kendrick was doing his best to kill some poor German sod when he was shot down himself. That's what bloody war is, but we can't go on being haunted by it, and I'm quite sure Morwetha *isn't*.'

'Then tell me why she behaves in this way when normally her heart is so warm.'

Petroc realized that it was the reasonable question he should have been expecting. It was also the one he couldn't answer without giving his sister away.

'You'll have to ask her yourself,' he said wretchedly, and the rest of the journey passed in silence again.

On the long drive to London, Polly found herself wishing that she had made the journey by train. The back seat of the car made her feel faintly sick, and she couldn't respond to Cécile's comments on the narrow, self-satisfied attitudes of people she referred to as 'provincials'. It wasn't expressly stated that her husband's family at Fowey came into this category, but she allowed herself an amused sneer at their friends among the Cornish gentry.

A stop for luncheon helped the problem of car-sickness, but not Polly's feeling that she was proving a disappointing travelling companion. It was better, but only marginally so, to appear stupidly dull than to be at loggerheads with her hostess. Luc smiled at her, sensing none of her difficulty, and it was he who raised the subject of Lisette.

'I can't think why she wanted to stay – she'll be bored stiff as soon as Petroc disappears back to his rural slum.'

Cécile stared coolly across the lunch table at her son. 'You're quite wrong, my dear. I took the trouble to visit Tregenna and it's anything but a slum. Even if it were, it would make no difference to Lisette; she's determined to live there.'

Luc looked unimpressed. 'That's an adolescent dream she hasn't quite grown out of. Petroc doesn't share it, I'm sure.'

'You're wrong about that as well,' his mother said with a certainty there was no arguing with. 'The next thing we shall hear is that she is finally engaged to your cousin.'

The interminable journey was over at last. Polly could direct Luc to stop at the house in Wilton Mews and escape from a family that weighed on her too heavily. But when her luggage had been deposited on the doorstep, Luc ignored the hand she held out to him.

'I'm not saying goodbye,' he said quickly. 'Darling girl, I want to see as much of you as possible in future.'

'Shall we get our London bearings back first, and then see how we feel?' she suggested.

Luc smiled but shook his head. 'I *know* how I feel already, sweetheart . . . it's a blow if *you* don't!'

She remembered her first impression of him and realized again how wrong it had been. He wasn't arrogant and self-satisfied at all, but truly Tristram's son – sensitive and diffident beneath a veneer of sophistication. She hoped he was strong enough to withstand being in the middle of his mother's and his cousin's tug-of-war. The thought made her smile so kindly that it encouraged him to kiss her mouth before he walked back to the car and drove away.

'You seem to have got on very matey terms with *him*,' said Daniel's voice behind her. She swung round to find him standing in the open doorway, and suddenly ran into his arms.

'Glad you're back,' he muttered into her hair. 'I've missed you . . . thought you might have decided to become a Cornish maid after all.'

Polly leaned back against his encircling arms in order to inspect him more thoroughly.

'You look all right. Is Dr Kirkmichael pleased with you?'

'Enchanted! You didn't answer *my* question.'

Her eyes held his steadily, and he was stabbed by a sudden shaft of pain because they were Loveday's eyes, deeply blue and beautiful. Then she grinned cheerfully.

'Well, ducks, I decided to stay the same old me – Lunnon-born, Lunnon-bred, and prahd of it, me ole cock-sparrer!'

He pulled her into a brief, rib-cracking hug, and then normal relations were resumed. 'I hope you've done some work, as well as idled away weeks down there.'

'Yes, *good* work I think, but I shan't know for certain until it's all processed.'

'Then what? Do we start looking for a suitable publisher?'

'Well, the photographs we select will need captioning first, but I've got an idea I'd like to do more than that – unless you tell me that "vaulting ambition" is about to overreach itself!'

'Now, am I likely to tell you anything of the kind?' Daniel asked truthfully. 'If we're *not* ambitious we might as well be dead. What is the great idea?'

'To make the portrait complete – link the pictures with text that's just as illuminating but in a different way. Look, here's an example for you. I've got some lovely shots of Restormel Castle that will show what it *looks* like – a marvellously photogenic ruin – but I want an extract from some vivid contemporary account as well that brings the picture to life. People must be able to imagine they hear the shouts, and the jingle of harness, and the horses' hooves clattering on the cobbles – all the excitement and bustle of a medieval cavalcade arriving.' She pulled herself up at the expression on her father's face. 'You *do* think I'm mad!'

'Mad or not, you're going to need some help.'

'It's fixed already. I reckon Grandfather William knows more about Cornwall than anyone else alive, and he's *promised* not to die for a long time yet, so that we can select the material together! You never saw a man so happy, and Granny's only complaint is that she can't keep up with all the books he wants her to track down for him!'

Daniel tried to sound disgruntled, although the eagerness shining in her face made it difficult. 'So you *have* gone over to the Cornish after all.'

'*No*, I've told you,' she said with sudden fierceness. 'But it's important to do this before all the things that make Cornwall a special place get lost. In any case, I want it to be a . . . a sort of memorial to my mother – it's why Grandfather wants to help so much as well.'

She was careful not to watch her father's face, and it seemed a long time before he answered coolly.

'All arranged, I see. Well, I suppose *my* job is to talk some publisher into accepting the idea.'

She nodded, suddenly knowing that she wasn't going to mention Tristram Bossiney's offer of help, or to allow herself to grow fond of his son. There was a deep-rooted conviction in her bones that it would be better now for the Bossineys and the Penwarnes to part company.

The summer slowly died, but she scarcely noticed its passing, except for the smouldering bonfires of dead leaves hazing the air when she wandered through the park; she was engrossed in the enterprise she now shared with her grandfather. Her photographs *were* good, and she half-lived in the world they and William's texts created for her. It was curiously dividing – to be among the noise and bustle of London, and to lie awake at night listening for sounds that didn't belong there. She sometimes fell asleep with tear-stains on her cheeks, only half-aware of what she wept for.

Cécile had been right – Lisette's engagement to Petroc O'Meara was announced, and they were to marry in the late autumn when a farmer could spare a little time away from his land. It seemed to Polly that Luc was saddened by his twin's engagement, but she didn't ask whether it was because he disapproved of her chosen husband, or because her choice meant a life to be spent in Cornwall in future. There wasn't any doubt at all that Cécile disliked her son-in-law to be, but Polly could imagine Petroc's dark eyebrow raised to enquire what difference this need make to *them*. She knew with strange certainty what his attitude would be. A woman would have no need of the tents of father, mother, brother who had the 'red pavilions' of *his* heart.

She was surprised and touched to discover that none of her own discouragements made any difference to Luc. If anything, they made him the more determined that she must finally agree to fall in love with him. She wasn't sure of his mother's approval of their growing love affair, but knew that it gave Tristram happiness to see them together. Luc was a charming companion, and Bossiney arrogance only sparked a quarrel between them when she refused to go with him to a country house weekend party.

'Any other girl I asked would be *glad* to go . . . she'd fall over herself to accept,' he said furiously. 'Why can't you?'

'Perhaps because I'm *not* any other girl,' Polly shouted. But the unhappiness in his face made her drag him up the stairs to her little attic studio. She put photographs in front of him and he stared at them in silence for a long time. Then a sudden torrent of words seemed to be torn out of him.

'They're marvellous . . . of course they are, because you're brilliant. But, Polly love, *this* Cornwall is dead and gone. For God's sake wake up, and live in the present – preferably with *me*! We're only young once, and we can't waste precious time looking over our shoulders at the past.'

She feverishly selected other sheets from the rack and pointed to them.

'Luc, this is Cornwall *now* . . . and this . . . and this.' He was offered in turn the white, spectral beauty of a clay-waste mountain mirrored in its own dark-green pool; next, the weathered face of a fisherman aboard his Mevagissey 'tosher', patiently mending the torn intricacies of his net; and then a moorland shepherd's dog, crouched with ears aprick, waiting for his next instruction.

'*This* Cornwall still exists, and *can* do for as long as it isn't trodden underfoot in the stampede of outsiders who only see it as a holiday paradise. That old man on his boat should be allowed to go on being an honest-to-God fisherman, not have to dress up like a Venetian gondolier to offer a "trip round the bay"!'

She broke off, but it was too late – Luc was staring strangely at her, and she knew why.

'I suppose you realize you sounded just like my cousin Petroc,' he murmured.

She opened her mouth to deny it, but no sound came; instead, the tears that were suddenly pricking her eyelids overflowed and trickled down her cheeks. Luc enfolded her in his arms with a gentleness that might have belonged to his father, and they stood there for a long while – aware of torn loyalties shared and the comfort that came of trying to deal with them together.

25

Morwetha scarcely listened to Kurt's message when her brother relayed it. 'Don't be silly,' she said shortly. 'Even a strong man, which he *isn't*, would take hours to cycle down here and back to Trebinnick.'

'I told him I'd be wasting my breath,' Petroc observed, 'but you might as well hear the rest of it. God knows what he considers *himself* now, but he's convinced that *you* still see him as a German and hate him for it.'

She considered for a moment a point of view so simple that it hadn't occurred to her. 'So I am to blame him because Peter is dead, and he must loathe me for what the RAF did to places like Dresden. Is that it?'

'I tried to explain what nonsense it is,' Petroc said wearily, 'but he's about as willing to listen to me as you are. I think I shall talk to myself in future.'

A gleam of humour brightened her face, but quickly faded, leaving it sad. She hadn't expected to be surprised by joy again – it had been known briefly in loving Peter Kendrick, and had died when he died. But when there was no joy, there was no pain; she'd reckoned to be safe from *that* in future. She loved her family, Petroc especially; but she wasn't sick with longing when she was away from them. It was absurd now – beyond all reason – that in order not to feel achingly incomplete she should want the company of a frail stranger nearly twice her age.

She attended doggedly to all her other needy artists, ran her shop, cajoled her customers into buying, and continued to visit Trebinnick – reminding herself each time she heard Kurt's grave, impersonal *'guten morgen, Frau Kendrick'* that, if he thought of a different life at all, it was of a time when he had been young and Jenifer O'Meara had been beautiful. It was a painful surprise, even so, to discover one morning that he intended leaving them. She saw evidence on his table in the kitchen that he'd been busier than usual, but the reason didn't occur to her.

'Kurt, these are beautiful – every one of them; but there's less need now to work so hard. The summer visitors dwindle every week. In a fortnight I shall close the shop, and we shall have the whole winter ahead to replenish stocks for next spring.'

In the sudden silence that fell on the room she knew what he was going to say.

'I shall not be here next spring – I am going back to Switzerland.'

The pain she'd supposed she was safe from tore at her heart, making speech difficult. 'I thought . . . hoped . . . that you were happy here . . . loved this bit of moorland,' she mumbled at last.

He gave a little shrug, keeping his hands hidden and his face turned away from her. 'It has been a time of . . . of great benefit to me, and you and your family have been very kind,' he said stiffly. 'But I have been here too long already. I shall leave as soon as I have made a good stock of carvings for you.'

Not knowing what she did, Morwetha wrapped squirrels, and rabbits, and beautiful birds caught in mid-flight, and a fox that Kurt must have seen running free on the moor. She thought of the miserable room in Zurich that her uncle had described, and struggled not to shout at him that it was impossible.

'Does Uncle Tris know?' she managed to ask.

'Not yet – I shall write to him soon and tell him myself, of course.'

'We shall miss you, and so will my customers next year. They come from far and wide now to buy a Winkler carving.'

He bowed, but stood clearly waiting for her to leave, and there was nothing else to do but go. She drove until she could no longer see him framed in the doorway and it was safe to stop and bury her face against the steering wheel of the car. Then, when she'd wiped away her tears, she switched on the engine again, and drove down the winding road to St Neot and her next port of call

Kurt's letter arrived in Pont Street in time to settle an uncertainty in Tristram's mind. He would spend his fiftieth birthday in Cornwall after all, arguing with his friend, instead of tagging behind Cécile and the twins in the hectic social round of a visit to Paris. She was irritated when he said so, but then he had expected that she would be.

'*Why* must you go to Cornwall to see Kurt, and what good will it do?'

'Probably none if he's made up his mind to leave, but I can't let him go without being sure he's not acting under some quixotic impulse.'

Tristram stared at the expression on Cécile's beautifully made-up face. Quixotic impulses were not things she readily understood, but, as always when he looked at her, he acknowledged that she did him more credit than he deserved. None of his colleagues could boast a wife so elegant and so successful. It was true that behind its smooth public façade their marriage was a less than perfect thing, but Tristram accepted the blame for this himself; his punishment, self-imposed, was to be unfailingly considerate to his wife.

'My dear, with so many friends in Paris that you know, you won't need me . . . In fact, I should only hamper your style!'

It was true, she reflected. Tristram was a disappointment to her in middle age, lacking any taste for the fashionable, sophisticated society she shone in so easily. He now disliked formal entertaining and loathed dressing-up, so what was the point of dragging him to a brilliant charity ball at the Hotel Lambert, where he would refuse point-blank to wear a domino and fancy dress? She gave a long-suffering sigh and conceded that while she and the twins were away he might as well use the time to make a duty visit to Prospect without her.

He made all the necessary travelling arrangements for his family and solved the currency allowance problem by finding French acquaintances willing to advance funds in Paris against expenses settled for them in London. Cécile kissed him amiably when he waved them off at Victoria Station, and Lisette even murmured that it would have been nicer if he'd been going with them. Still, he could prevent Petroc being lonely while she had this last little fling before settling down to become a good farmer's wife.

Two days later he drove himself down to Cornwall, feeling thankful that Cécile was already on French soil. She was always a poor sailor, and with gales beginning to sweep in from the Atlantic, even the short Channel crossing would have been a trial. When he reached Prospect the wind was still strengthening from the south-west – true Cornish weather. He stood at the bay windows of the drawing room, relishing what was going on outside. A flock of gulls, swept by the wind, tumbled through the air, and high-water in the cove was a churning, dark-green mass that thudded against the sea-wall, sending showers of spray into the lower levels of his mother's garden.

'Rough, and getting rougher,' he said over his shoulder.

'Novemberish,' she agreed. 'I suppose you forget about the seasons and the weather in London.' From where she sat his face looked reticent as usual, but more fine-drawn. She wished again that she could pretend she'd had no hand in influencing his life, but it wouldn't have been true. 'You're here to see Kurt, of course?' she asked abruptly.

'To see you *and* Kurt,' he corrected her with a faint smile. 'It seemed a good opportunity. Post-war gloom is definitely over in Paris, apparently, but fancy-dress balls aren't quite my dish of tea!'

Lavinia nodded, unable to say that she preferred it when he came alone. 'Morwetha bumped into Charlie Penwarne on Polruan ferry yesterday. Polly is down here too – her grandfather is helping her to put Cornish material together for a book. After being a confirmed invalid for the past ten years William has taken on a new lease of life, and Hannah isn't sure whether to be pleased or irritated!'

'I know about the book – in fact I still hope Polly is going to let me see it eventually.'

'It's stupid to want the people one loves to love each other,' Lavinia said thoughtfully, 'but I can't help wishing that Petroc didn't seem so convinced that she's an exact replica of her father.'

'Never mind, perhaps marriage will make him more tolerant. If it's any comfort to you, Luc *doesn't* share his cousin's prejudice; quite the reverse, in fact. He's head over heels in love with Polly.'

'Does that please you? Or not?'

Tristram smiled wholeheartedly this time. 'She's Loveday's daughter, as well as Penwarne's. Of course it pleases me – more than I can say.'

'And if she and Luc married it would seem to complete something left unfinished from the past?'

It was a more probing question than Lavinia normally allowed herself, but she wanted for once to break the shell of gentle, courteous detachment in which her son habitually hid himself. His only answer was to nod, but it was enough, and she judged it time now to talk of what had brought him to Cornwall.

'Morwetha thinks that our dear woodcarver is tired of living at Trebinnick, but you should also hear Petroc's view before you go up there. He promised to call in tomorrow before attending a town council meeting.'

Tristram nodded again, as the telephone rang out in the hall.

'Jonathan ringing from Place to check that I'd got here,' he explained, coming back into the room. 'The Treffrys want to persuade him to stay the night in view of the weather. It's a good excuse for another rubber or two of bridge, but he'd certainly have a job to struggle home in this, and the barometer is plummeting.' He listened to the rising shriek of the wind outside, and the fusillades of rain now being flung like grapeshot against the windows. 'I'm rather glad I *am* here.'

Lavinia smiled serenely. 'Jonathan would have got back somehow if you hadn't been, although he ought to be able to remember by now that the sound of the wind doesn't frighten me. It's part of living at Prospect.'

It was, nevertheless, one of the wildest nights she could remember, with gusting winds that, like the waves pounding all along the coast, gathered themselves every so often for the final onslaught that was to sweep everything away. But when dawn came Prospect still clung to its rock above the sea-wall; only a trail of havoc in the garden spoke of the night's bombardment of wind and rain. She surveyed it from her bedroom windows, saddened by the knowledge that she could no longer go out and do battle with the damage. The rain had stopped and the wind was slowly slackening, but the sea still churned violently in the rivermouth and flung curtains of spray over St Saviour's Point.

Tristram spent the morning staking up battered shrubs, under Lavinia's direction, and Jonathan returned with news gathered at the Yacht Club of ships in difficulties, and flooding along all the south-facing estuaries.

Lunch over, Tristram opted for a clifftop walk that promised to be exhilarating. He took with him a picture of the tranquil scene in the library – his mother smiling at him and then returning to her reading, Jonathan nodding over the crossword puzzle he was trying to solve. It pleased him deeply that his family were within Prospect's stone walls, safe no matter what tempest blew outside. Cécile would never be able to understand that satisfaction, but somehow before he died he must ensure that Luc did.

He climbed up out of the rain-sodden garden on to the path leading to St Catherine's Point. There out on the open headland the remaining force of the wind met him head on. The sky was shredded with tatters of rain-cloud being driven in from the sea, and the grey-green waves below him pounded against the rocks that still kept them from invading the land. It was a sight grand and primeval enough to be exciting, but Tristram was aware as well of the Cornishman's twinge of superstitious fear – only a stranger from across the Tamar could fail to understand that elemental Nature was ultimately in charge. He took a deep breath and fought his way on towards Gribben.

In Fore Street, Hannah grumbled a little – being of the view that one more storm, though worse than most, was nothing remarkable.

'It *is* to someone who wants some winter shots in her collection,' Polly said, smiling at her grandmother. 'This wild and wonderful weather is just what I need.'

'Then make for Lankelly Cliff, maid,' advised her Uncle Charlie. He had for once used motor-power to get across the swollen river to check up on his parents, and now sat eating a huge slice of Hannah's potato cake to strengthen him for the journey back to Bodinnick. William looked anxious, but Charlie smiled at his father.

'No need to fret about her, Dad. She's a good little lass, with too much sense not to keep to the path.'

Polly promised to be both good and sensible, deposited a loving kiss on them all round, and set off to catch the best of the early-afternoon light. Stopping to photograph, she made slow time on the ups and downs of the cliff path. At this rate the light would be fading before she got as far as Lankelly Cliff, but she went on all the same, too entranced to turn back towards her grandmother's hot little parlour. She was alone in a wild, cruel, beautiful corner of the world, but she felt none of the loneliness that occasionally attacked her in the middle of a throng of people in London. It was time to accept at last that all the Penwarnes and Eliots stretching back through generations past had seen to it that she must recognize *this* as her home.

On the exposed curve round the top of Southground Cliffs she could see Lankelly jutting out ahead of her, but there was something unexpected to see as well. The figure of a man showed up against the skyline, walking slowly as if, like her, he got pleasure from the struggle. She raised her camera to capture the composition of lone figure, windswept clifftop and immense sky, and in that moment the figure in her viewfinder disappeared. She stared at the sudden emptiness in front of her, and heard at the same time a long, dreadful roar of sound that wasn't the noise of the wind or the sea far below. Fear paralysed her for a moment, and then she began to run.

Between the turfed headland she was on and the outward swell of Lankelly, the cliff-face curved inwards, rearing up from a tiny, inaccessible cove; beyond it, a tangle of rocks ran out to Southground Point. But the sheltering backdrop to the cove had been pounded once too often. Instead of the path that should have led safely round the top of it there was now a gaping void. Only twenty yards further on did the torn edges of rock and muddy grass manage to knit themselves into firm ground again.

With the sound of her own sobbing breath in her ears, Polly lay down where the soaking turf still seemed intact on her side of the hole. Below her was the chaos of torn earth and rock that had been the cliff-face until a few minutes ago. Her eyes searched downwards, and found on the boulder-strewn floor of the cove the still, spread-eagled figure of the man she had seen. He lay just out of reach of the incoming tide, but there was half an hour still to highwater. If he was unconscious or unable to move, he would drown before she could reach Fowey and bring back help.

Instinct alone operating, she tied her camera to a stunted thorn tree that leaned away from the wind, and then crawled out on to the tumble of mud and rock. At least it *sloped* down, thank God, instead of falling vertically. An eternity later that measured five minutes by her watch – mercifully still working – she slid to a stop among the rock rubble at the water's edge. A sharp stab of pain reminded her of an ankle wrenched on the way down, and her legs and hands were bleeding. She was very frightened, but she was at the bottom and she could now see who it was that lay there. He wasn't unconscious, and he recognized her when she limped over to kneel beside him. She found a handkerchief in her pocket and wiped his face free of rock-dust and mud, and the trickle of blood that oozed from a graze on his temple.

'I can't think what to do next,' she said hoarsely. 'Tell me, if you can, where are you hurt?'

The pale face looking up at her tried to smile. 'I've no idea,' he said in a thread of voice she scarcely heard, 'I can't seem to move, but there isn't any pain at all.'

She began feverishly to clear a path along the rock-strewn sand, unaware that her hands were already raw in places. Then, sitting behind him with his head in her lap, and her arms linked under his, she struggled to edge her way backwards, dragging him with her an inch at a time. She had to keep stopping to ease the terrible pressure on her back, but at last they were safely away from the water's edge. Then, trembling from that huge effort, she crawled about on hands and knees, building into a protective ring around him any bits of rock that she could manage to move. He might still get wet, but he wouldn't drown if she left him now supposing that she could possibly manage with God's help to crawl *up* what she had slid and bumped her way down.

Drifting out of unconsciousness, Tristram's eyes focused on her and saw that she was staring up at the broken cliff-face.

'You mustn't think of going ... please ... I want you to stay with me,' he whispered. 'Someone will come ...'

Would they? If she prayed with all her heart and soul to Mary, Mother of Jesus, and all the saints of heaven, *would* Grandfather have sent Uncle Charlie to make sure she got home safely? Could the coastguard on St Saviour's Point already have seen and reported the cliff fall?

She looked down at Tristram Bossiney's grey face, and clouded eyes, and knew that whether anyone came or not, she couldn't leave him; if he were to die all alone, it would be more than she could bear.

'Talk to me,' he murmured, ' just talk to me as . . . as Loveday used to . . .'

She wrapped her coat over him, and sat holding his cold hand. The stories that Isaac Penwarne had told her mother, she told again, while her voice grew thick with unshed tears and the November afternoon slowly waned around them. High tide came, showering her with cold spray, but the water did no more than seep through the base of her improvised little wall. They were safe from the peril of the sea, at least.

She stopped talking at last, thinking that Tristram had drifted into unconsciousness again. In another hour it would be dusk, and after that the night would fall swiftly. Wrapped in a cloak of sadness, she remembered suddenly her first visit to Cornwall and the overpowering grief she'd felt, staring at the sea from Prospect Cove. That same prescient feeling had returned outside the picture gallery in London. It was familiar to her now and she understood that this moment had already been ordained; perhaps it was why she also felt strangely unafraid. She knew what her grandfather would have said '*Thy* Will be done'. It made everything seem very simple.

Then, beside her, Tristram spoke with sudden distinctness, as if he'd been gathering enough strength for this one effort that he had to make. 'Polly . . . Petroc will make Lisette understand about Prospect and Cornwall, but Luc *doesn't* understand yet . . . he will if you help him . . . he will, *then*, I think.'

'I think so too,' she agreed gently.

'Something else,' Tristram murmured. 'Don't turn your back on happiness; searching for it again is as useless as writing your name in the snow of a spring day, a West Country poet once said. But Luc will make *you* happy, my dear.'

His eyes pleaded with her to agree, and she leaned over to kiss his cheek.

'Yes, I think he will,' she promised. 'Now, don't talk any more. I'm going to sing to you. My mother told me the names of the German songs she heard at Prospect, and after she died I made sure of learning them.'

'Kurt's songs,' he whispered. His hand slowly grew colder in hers but she clung to the idea that the sound of her voice could still reach and reassure him.

She was in the middle of *'Du bist die Ruhe'* for the third time when she stopped suddenly to listen. The storm had moved on, leaving stillness behind, and above the alternate thud and retreating wash of the waves, surely she could now hear the echo of human voices? Her neck was stiff but she twisted her entire body in time to glimpse figures silhouetted on the next headland, before a dip in the path hid them again. Blackness swept over her and she ducked her head into the sodden wool of her jersey that smelled of sea-water.

Then, through waves of dizziness she heard another sound, and lifted her head to find that the grey, unfriendly ocean was no longer empty. A motor-boat was beating steadily through the rough water under Southground Cliffs. Five minutes later it anchored thirty yards off and an inflatable dinghy began to bob its way into the cove, with three men manoeuvring it.

The first of them to splash ashore was a stranger, but behind him came someone she recognized. His face was frowning and intent, but her relief in that moment of seeing him was enough to halt the beating of her heart. Nothing unbearable would happen now that he was there, and it seemed impossible to remember that she could ever have thought she hated him. He glanced at her, and then his entire attention was on the silver-gilt-haired figure lying on the sand.

'Dear God . . . it's Uncle Tris', she heard him say, before he knelt down, touched Tristram's face, and then searched for the pulse in his uncle's wrist.

'Do you know where he's hurt?'

'He couldn't say . . . only that he wasn't in any pain,' she croaked, almost unintelligibly.

She watched Petroc and his companion lift Tristram on to a blanket, then on to the stretcher they'd brought with them – and so gently and competently did they work that she knew this wasn't the first time they'd done such things together.

'I'll be back for you,' said Petroc as they lifted the stretcher. She closed her eyes so as not to watch their struggle to get it into the waiting dinghy, but then he was beside her again, examining her muddy, blood-caked hands and legs. She had begun to shake, as if in the grip of some consuming fever – was scarcely aware of him pulling off her soaking sweater and skirt and wrapping her in a blanket that smelled of salt air and pipe-tobacco. Then she was lifted into his arms, and he sat on the sand, holding her.

'We've a few minutes to wait,' he explained quietly. 'It's a ticklish operation, getting a stretcher aboard, but your Uncle Charlie is in charge and there's nothing he can't manage.'

She nodded, aware of having reached the dangerous stage of exhaustion where every sense she possessed seemed painfully alive. The hairy comfort of the blanket against her bare skin, the shape of Petroc's brown hands cradling her, the unsuspected gentleness of his voice – just so, she thought, would he speak to a badly frightened child. These things would stay in her memory however old she lived to be.

'I met Charlie in the town; there'd been an urgent message from the coastguard, so we sent men along the cliff to fence it off, and came this way ourselves. I suppose you were walking with my uncle.'

She shook her head where it rested against him. 'He was ahead of m . . . me, and suddenly disappeared when I heard the n . . . noise of the cliff collapsing.' Her voice was ragged but she took a deep breath, and tried again. 'When I got to where the path was torn away, I could see him lying down here. I'd have run back for help then, but he was too near the water not to . . . to drown. After that he didn't want me to leave . . .' Her voice failed altogether, and Petroc stared up at the broken cliff-face she had had to get down. God alone knew how she'd done it without killing herself, but at least Tristram had managed to stop her trying to climb up it again. He thought of his uncle lying sheltered behind her careful little ring of stones, and buried his face against her wet hair, suddenly afraid of weeping. Then the dinghy scraped over the shingle again, and Charlie was smiling down at her.

'Your turn now, maid.'

The stretcher filled the cabin space, but Petroc sat holding her in the cockpit for the rough journey back to the haven. He saw her lips moving, and leaned down to listen to the hoarse notes of the lament she was singing – '*Kennst du das Land . . .*' – 'Knowest thou the land where the lemon tree grows?'

Ambulances were waiting at Town Quay, and there she was lifted out of Petroc's arms. She wanted to implore the kind-faced people around her to let her stay with him, but the words were only in her mind, making no sound. Then, as if perhaps *he* had heard them, Petroc stooped to kiss her grimy face before she was put into an ambulance and driven away from him.

26

Tristram died in Truro Hospital a week later. The injury to his spine would have left him paralysed, and Lavinia tried to believe that he would have preferred not to survive the pneumonia that killed him. Cécile and her children got back from Paris in time to say goodbye to him, but Jenifer was too late in returning from America to do more than attend her brother's funeral.

The Church of St Fimbarrus was crowded for the service, but still there were people who couldn't be squeezed in – old friends who reckoned that twadn't right of the widowed lady to keep so many of the pews for the smart ones from London. None of 'they' had known Tristram from childhood, and watched him and Charlie Penwarne take on the might of Looe and Polperro at Town Regatta. Only Fowey people had been aware of his kindness since to anyone in trouble, and of the courtesy that treated mad old Willy Bagga the same as if he'd really *been* the Duke of Cornwall he sometimes imagined himself to be. They left Cécile Bossiney to her 'foreign' friends and offered their shy words of sympathy to the lady who stood with 'Doctor' at the church gate to thank them for coming – a frail, dignified figure in her old-fashioned black coat and velvet beret; but, though old, she didn't need reminding of anybody's name, and they went home feeling proud of her, without knowing quite why. Jonathan thought he knew why. She behaved as they still expected Bossineys to behave. In a world that changed day by day Lavinia refused to change at all.

Polly walked home with her grandmother and Uncle Charlie, having refused Cécile's invitation to join her other

359

guests at the Fowey Hotel after the service. She had also
shaken her head at Luc's plea for her to sit with them in
the front pews, preferring to be among her own family.
Petroc's deep voice had reached her at the back of the
church, etching on her memory the lines he read.

> '. . . my soul, like a quiet palmer, travelleth
> toward the land of heaven, over the silver
> mountains, where spring the nectar fountains
> . . . My soul will be a-dry before, but, after,
> it will thirst no more.'

She thought he'd chosen well, to give his uncle the
company of Walter Raleigh's pilgrim, but there was no
chance to say so. A tearful Lisette absorbed all her fiancé's
care, while Luc stayed beside his mother. Both women
looked beautiful, Polly thought – black suited them and,
in an unexpected way, so did the grief that made most
other women look plain. She didn't doubt that both of
them grieved for what they had lost, but it was Lavinia's
tragic face she couldn't bear to watch.

In Fore Street, she refused Hannah's offer of food,
and gently commanded her grandparents not to worry
if she went off alone. *This* day couldn't be dangerous; it
was December-grey, but very still and mild. She walked
instinctively in the direction of Prospect, because that was
where she needed to be. There would be no danger of
meeting anyone – the family and their guests would all
be at the Fowey Hotel. She let herself into the garden and
climbed up to what had been her resting-seat whenever
she worked there. The storm had been discriminating,
she noticed sadly; only the precious things were lying
broken.

From where she sat she could easily make out Grandfather Tom's cottage above the ferry-slip at Polruan. She
imagined him there now, keeping his eye on the river
as usual while Jane put his lunchtime pasty in the

oven. Upstream, but just hidden by the curve of the riverbank, Aunt Mary would be performing the same service for *her* husband. From the boat-scattered river, Polly looked towards the great stretch of sea and sky outside, distinguishable only because one element was a slightly darker grey than the other.

'Make Luc understand about Prospect and Cornwall,' Tristram had asked, and she had promised that she would. She'd thought much since then about a promise that might change the whole course of her life. She didn't blame Tristram for laying this responsibility upon her – Loveday would have said that it had been meant all along.

'My dear . . . I thought you were in that scrimmage at the hotel,' said a quiet voice behind her.

She turned to see Lavinia leaning on her cane – still composed, but looking very tired after the strain of the morning.

'Why is everyone there, instead of here?' Polly asked, making room for her friend on the bench.

'Too many people, I was told. I have no idea who many of them are, but having come so far they need of course to be looked after. My daughter-in-law does that very well.' Her ladyship's beautiful, precise voice gave no hint of her conviction that Cécile had deliberately chosen not to bring her guests to Prospect – to underline the fact that its relevance to their lives was over now.

Polly stared across the river, seeing instead of the familiar view other images fixed in her mind's eye . . . her own little spray of white chrysanthemums, 'from Loveday and Polly', not quite lost among the flowers waiting to be heaped on Tristram's grave, Petroc with his arm protectively about Lisette's shoulders as they followed the coffin to the graveside, and Luc's white face, suddenly aged by what had happened.

'It was a beautiful service this morning,' Lavinia said quietly beside her.

'I thought so, too,' Polly agreed. Then she turned to

361

look at her companion. 'Luc managed it all beautifully – lovingly attentive to his mother, but thoughtful to everyone else as well.'

Lavinia nodded, vowing to herself that this time she would *not* interfere. 'I think perhaps he's growing more and more like his father,' was all she allowed herself to say.

Polly stared at her hands; they were beginning to heal, and hurt very little. She wouldn't ever forget Southground Cove, but soon now the memory of being taken out of Petroc's arms would hurt as little as her hands did. She would remember, but she couldn't bear to talk about him.

'If I were to marry Luc, would you mind a . . . a Penwarne in the family?' she asked suddenly.

Lavinia took time to answer. 'Only if you married him for the wrong reasons,' she said carefully.

Polly nodded, thinking that for once her friend hadn't been of much help to her. One person saw as blue a colour that someone else swore was green. She thought it might be much the same with right and wrong reasons; but it was *her* problem, and she put it aside with a faint sigh.

'There's still a lot of storm damage to repair,' she said, pointing to a myrtle tree whose bare, rust-coloured branches now drooped disconsolately to one side. 'I'll be able to help before I go back to London.'

'There may be no need to do anything at all.' Lavinia said in a voice that was suddenly harsh with pain. Her hands trembled but the shocked expression on Polly's face made her struggle for self-control again. 'My dear, it doesn't matter very much. If *we're* not here to put the garden to rights, someone else will do it, I'm sure.'

Someone like Daniel, Polly wondered, ready to tear up the garden to make room for a car-park? 'It would matter to *you*,' she muttered through the taste of sickness in her throat. 'Where else would you and Dr Jonathan go?'

Lavinia had almost recovered herself. 'Cécile is being tactful at the moment but there have been hints in the past of a delightful bungalow on some of the land Petroc could do without – so much more comfortable and convenient than this old house! In a way, of course, my daughter-in-law is right – she very often is.'

'Except that you don't *want* a delightful, convenient bungalow.'

'The problem in a nutshell!' Lavinia agreed.

Polly still sounded fierce. 'It's not for *her* to say . . . Prospect belongs to Luc, now.' She spoke vehemently, but couldn't drown the echo of Tristram's voice saying that his son didn't yet understand.

Lavinia's hand reached out to touch Polly's scarred one. 'Dear girl, I think *he* may decide in the end that his mother is right. If he does, you mustn't blame him. His life is in London; why should he struggle to keep what he can't afford and doesn't enjoy, simply for our benefit?' She glanced at the little fob-watch pinned to her jacket, and got stiffly to her feet. 'I must go back to the house again – some of our old friends may come looking for me to say goodbye.'

She looked too frail for any further effort, but Polly knew that whatever effort was still needed would be made.

'Petroc will see that nothing changes,' she said desperately.

Lavinia nodded, unwilling to point out that in the matter of Prospect he had no chance of seeing to anything at all. She allowed Polly to help her up the steps to the terrace, and had just kissed her goodbye when he appeared round the corner of the house, with Lisette clinging to his arm.

'Darling Gran, we've come to make sure you're all right. Petroc was beginning to agitate a bit about you—' She stopped suddenly, catching sight of Polly behind the tall figure of her grandmother. 'Oh, we didn't know you had company *here*.'

Loving concern was splintered by something else, reminding Lavinia of what she already knew – her granddaughter resented Polly. It wasn't generous, but it wasn't a surprise; Lavinia had lived long enough to know that grief didn't ennoble many people, at least not for longer than a day or two. Polly had played a spectacular part at Southground Cove, and Lisette couldn't help wishing that she hadn't.

'I was just leaving,' Polly said quickly, anxious to go, even without the knowledge that Lisette didn't want her there. Nothing remained that could safely be said, least of all to Petroc, whose eyes had skimmed her face and looked away again. He hadn't called at Fore Street after she was released from hospital. There had been no need, of course; as soon as Luc had flown back from Paris *he* had come every day. Petroc didn't speak to her now because he was remembering a conversation with Cécile, who had sadly explained how much Tristram had looked forward to having Polly as a daughter-in-law. She had been careful not to mention Daniel Penwarne, but Lisette had been less tactful.

'So the Penwarnes will get Prospect after all, in one way if not another.' She had smiled defiantly at the disapproval in her mother's face and gone on to make matters worse. 'My father would have hated *that*, Maman; you know it as well as I do.'

The memory of that conversation was still so bitter that it held Petroc rooted where he stood, even though his heart wept for a sad, pale girl whom mourning colour didn't suit. She looked sallow and plain, and he wanted above all things to enfold her in his arms . . . wanted *not* to remember the truth of what Lisette had said.

Lavinia watched Polly's hand lift in a little hopeless gesture that he didn't see, and fall back to her side again. Then she walked away from them down the steps and out of the garden.

The room at the Fowey Hotel was crowded, and Morwetha found herself trapped in a corner with an old friend – 'Q's daughter, Fay Quiller-Couch. She could see her mother talking earnestly to Kurt, but it was scarcely surprising that he should look as if he needed to escape; Tristram had been to him more like a brother than a friend. When he walked out of the room a moment later, Morwetha sadly concluded that he'd had as much of Cécile's reception as he could endure.

The ordeal was finally over for them all at last. The visitors from London took their leave, and old Cornish friends called at Prospect only long enough to say good-bye to Lavinia. A sad, uneasy emptiness lay over the house, grief and uncertainty waiting to fill the post-funeral vacuum. Jenifer felt that silence was unbearable, and chattered to Morwetha about her conversation with Kurt.

'You said *what*?' The terse question was unexpected and fierce, and Jenifer repeated aggrievedly what she'd said.

'Darling, I've just told you. I thought Kurt ought to know that Tristram only came down to see *him* – it was bound to make him think he ought to stay here after all.'

It was also bound to make him think that they blamed him for his friend's death, but Morwetha forbade herself to say so. It would deeply offend her mother, and do no good at all; but it was one more grief to bear, to know why he'd left looking so haunted.

At Tregenna, Petroc and Kurt both made a pretence of eating supper, but stayed sitting at the kitchen table afterwards, unable to talk, unable to think of anything else to do.

'Shall we comfort ourselves with a glass of contraband brandy?' Petroc suggested at last.

Kurt waited for him to return to the table with decanter and glasses, took a sip of the spirit, and felt its warmth against the back of his throat. He'd been shivering inside ever since his conversation with Jenifer – it seemed hours ago.

'What is going to happen? Or is it too soon to know?'

Petroc stared at his own long fingers laced about the glass in front of him.

'Not too soon, because it seems to be pretty well arranged already. My cousin will marry Polly Penwarne, and then sell Prospect to her father. What could be neater all round? Everyone gets what they want – except Gran and Uncle Jonathan, of course; but we must remember that *they* have had their day.' His voice didn't shake, but anguish was kept only just under control.

Kurt's hand touched his in a brief gesture of comfort. 'Can I convince you that your grandmother *won't* mind, dearly as she loves Prospect? It is sad, yes, if the Bossineys own it no longer; but that scarcely matters to her now. As long as *someone* cherishes Prospect . . .'

'Do you see Daniel Penwarne as the "cherisher" of something that belonged to the Bossineys?' Petroc interrupted bitterly. 'Because I'm damned if I do – he's much more likely to pull it down.'

'Polly won't allow him to do that,' Kurt said with gentle certainty. He watched Petroc's face, thinned to gauntness by too much work and strain; his marriage to Lisette had been postponed, of course, and Kurt supposed that the tension his godson couldn't entirely conceal wasn't only to do with the future of Prospect. He badly needed the comfort and companionship of a wife.

Petroc poured out more brandy, then asked a sudden question of his own. 'What about you? Are you still determined to go back to Switzerland?'

Kurt took a reckless gulp, and swallowed it without even noticing that he did so. 'This morning, driving with you to Tristram's funeral, I thought it right to stay for a while, in case I could help your grandmother. Now I know that I was wrong. I do not help *any* of you by being here, and I must leave as soon as possible.' He emptied his glass and stood up, trying to smile. 'It's time while I'm still sober to "go over timberen hill". That is Evan Nimmo's beautiful way of saying I must climb the stairs! Goodnight, my dear friend.'

In the morning the carrier who brought Petroc farm supplies offered to drop Kurt off at Trebinnick on his way north, and they both found themselves relieved that no more talking was necessary.

The house waited in its fold of moorland when he climbed the track from the main road. The first sudden sharpness of winter was in the upland air, and he could see a kestrel hanging motionless while it searched the hill below. He would have been happy to stay in this harshly beautiful, lonely place for the rest of his days, but the choice wasn't his now. Then he saw that he wasn't alone – a car was parked outside the house, and it was a shock to find Morwetha sitting on the stone step of the porch.

'What are you doing here? I have nothing ready.' This time even the formal pretence of welcome was absent, and she shivered, not only because she'd grown very cold, waiting for him to come. Her face looked drained and sad, but there was no comfort he had the right to offer; instead, he could only try to make her smile.

'A cup of tea . . . *that* is what you are needing, *nicht wahr*?'

She didn't smile, but she followed him into the house, wondering whether she would ever find the courage to explain why she had come. He clearly reckoned it a purely social call because he led her into the sitting room he rarely used. The laid fire was quickly lit and she was told to get warm. She crouched on the rug, still shivering from something more than the cold air outside. The crackle of the logs beginning to burn on the hearth, and the rattle of crockery next door, were homely sounds, insisting that normal life existed still. Happiness might be very hard to find, but it hadn't vanished entirely for those brave enough to seek it out.

Kurt came back into the room, put a steaming mug into her hands, and busied himself with the fire, carefully stacking peat at the back, as Evan had taught him. When it was done he moved away from her to the safety of a chair.

'Yesterday was a bad day for you all,' he said quietly. 'But it is over now.' Over but not entirely done with yet; he supposed that was why she'd come – to escape Prospect's troubled atmosphere.

Morwetha stretched her hands to the blaze, and firelight shone golden on her skin. 'My mother told me what she'd "explained" to you at the hotel,' she said abruptly. 'Her brand of logic is entirely her own, but I ask you to believe that she hadn't the slightest intention of hurting you.'

'Is *that* why you came – in case I had been hurt?'

'I saw your face when you walked out of the room yesterday. Please . . . you *must* ignore what she said. Uncle Tris was obliged to live in London but he remained a true Cornishman, and superstition goes hand in hand with fatalism down here. He would have known, as everyone does, that there's a proper time for "goin' round land". When it comes it doesn't matter *where* you are.'

The firelit room was growing warm, and hidden in the empty moorland outside it seemed more intimate than she could bear. Her other purpose in coming seemed impossible now, but somehow she must find the courage to say what she had come for, or regret it for the rest of her life.

'Perhaps I should have remembered that you know my mother too well to misunderstand anything she says. She'll return to America soon – has, I think, made up her mind to marry an old war-time friend there, since happiness *here* is not forthcoming.'

'Are you by any chance suggesting that it might have been forthcoming with me?' Kurt enquired gravely out of the silence that had fallen.

'You thought so once – so did she.' The flat, quiet statement didn't accuse, but it goaded Kurt to rare vehemence.

'I *wanted* to think it, because I was young and desired her beauty. But I knew I couldn't make her happy – knew it even before we were engulfed in the horror that was surely coming. Now, nothing is left of the young man she thought she knew, and in her heart she knows as well as I do that the man I have become fills her with a kind of terrified shame!' He heard what he'd just said, horrified that it might have sounded like a cry for sympathy. 'It doesn't matter, of course,' he added hurriedly. 'I've grown selfish, content with my own company, and confident – since there is no-one here to argue with me! – that I'm always right! It is a very happy way to live.'

'Then let me tell you, *Herr Doktor Professor*, that you are not always right,' Morwetha suddenly shouted. Drained and sad-looking no longer, she was flushed with firelight and rage. 'You're as wrong as you can be about a lot of things. I don't hate you because you're a German and Peter was killed by a German; you *mustn't* hate *me* for all the terrible destruction we did; and there's nothing happy about living alone, with no-one to love, pretending that you enjoy talking to yourself . . . I know . . . I've *tried* it.'

Angry tears sparkled on her lashes and she smeared them away with the impatient gesture he remembered a small child making. The memory was precious, but it reminded him that he was almost old enough to be her father.

'Very well, *meine Liebe* – the truth is that I live alone *not* from choice – although I must insist that my choice would *not* now be Jenifer O'Meara. I am aged by more than the twenty years that separate you and me, I own nothing except my tools and a few books, and even the roof that shelters me belongs to your brother . . . Morwetha, I have nothing to offer a woman.'

She heard his voice tremble despite the effort he made to hold it steady. The worst was still to come, but she felt calm now, knowing some things for certain that she hadn't known before.

'It's a good thing you took up carving,' she said quietly, 'you're better at understanding wood than you can ever

369

have been at understanding women. What you could offer *me* is all that I've missed since Peter was killed – tenderness when I feel poorly, companionship when I'm lonely, courage when I'm afraid, and love all the time. I'd have the right to ask *these* things because they're what I would offer *you* if you weren't so happy to live alone.'

'This is madness that must stop. You don't *know* what you are saying.'

The whisper barely reached her, but she could see his face. It said clearly that he would reject what was being offered him because it was only being offered out of pity.

'I know perfectly well, but *you* don't understand,' she said fiercely. 'Go back to Switzerland, and your self-sufficient, little life, and pretend for the rest of your days that carving wood is all you need for happiness. You've become a coward, Kurt.'

His smile was so strange that she thought he'd only been listening to her anger, not hearing what she said. 'You used to get cross like that when you were very small – a sudden storm that raged through the nursery until you smiled through your tears and peace was restored. Will you smile now, please?'

'Yes, because I can't leave shouting at you, when I may never see you again.' She did smile, but tears were beginning to trickle down her face as well. 'I came here meaning to seduce you into making love to me! It would be *something* if I'd belonged to you just once, and if I was very lucky you might even leave me with a child beginning its creation inside me. What a hope! Not nearly enough continental allure, my bloody seductive cousin would say. And she'd be right, because all I've done is rail at you!'

She began to laugh because suddenly it seemed insanely funny, but Kurt moved at last, throwing himself down beside her to grab her shoulders in a grip of desperation.

'Stop laughing . . . stop jeering at yourself. Great God in Heaven, don't you know that you're everything a man could desire?' The shout sobered her, and they were left in the sudden silence of the room, confronting one another.

'*Meine Liebchen . . . Mein Herz . . . Ich liebe dich,*' he said softly.

She began to smile, because joy at last was in sight, and all miracles were possible. 'Let me stay then, and be loved, please,' she whispered.

They remained where they were in the firelit warmth of the quiet room, tenderness growing easily into passion, desire flooding inevitably as the flowing tide. When they were at peace again, fulfilled and complete, Morwetha turned her face from its resting-place against him to smile contritely. 'Dear love, I didn't mean to be so rude; I'm sure you were a brilliant psychiatrist, but *they're* probably ten a penny, while woodcarvers of genius are very rare. Will you stay and work here now, or are you absolutely set on forsaking Cornwall?'

'How can I go, not knowing whether we have made the child or not? If not, we have to try again, *nicht wahr?*' He kissed her laughing mouth, and held her close. 'Such happiness, my heart . . . I didn't know that it was possible.'

'We won't broadcast it yet, though,' she murmured. 'Not until yesterday's awfulness isn't quite such a present memory.'

Kurt nodded, drawing his hand down her cheek in a gesture of loving tenderness. 'Not the others yet, but Petroc must be told that I am going to marry his sister. I owe him so much that he must be at least given the truth immediately.'

Morwetha's luminous smile was beautiful. 'Marry? Oh, my love, I only came to seduce you, not to trap you into marriage!' Then her face grew sober again. 'Petroc will be glad, but not only for *our* happiness. There's going to be a battle over Prospect, and most of the weaponry is on the side of Aunt C.'

'The same was true of Goliath but remember, please, who won!'

She nodded, remembering, too, the expression on her brother's face when he'd returned to the hotel yesterday. More than anxiety over Prospect had carved those deep lines in it, but he wasn't a man to disclose what private sorrow ailed him, or to thank anyone who tried to prise it out of him.

'I'm in that idiotic state of bliss that requires the rest of the world to be happy so that I needn't feel guilty,' she confessed.

Kurt tried not to smile, knowing that she was serious. 'Well, *Liebchen*, I who thought it was wrong to laugh a little while ago now don't feel guilty at all!' He watched her get ready to leave, and exchanged for her promise that she would drive with the utmost care, a promise of his own – that at last he would carve for her something that was worthy of his dead friends, Hans and Tristram.

27

Cécile was being unusually patient with her daughter; a girl who had loved and just lost her father must be forgiven for being difficult. But in any case it didn't greatly matter if *she* had begun to see Prospect through Petroc's eyes. It was Luc who must understand it clearly for what it was – a hideous, money-consuming white elephant, and *not* the last precious bastion of Bossiney pride. She might have expected that, by dying in Cornwall, Tristram would have strengthened his son's distaste for the place, but in some strange and irritating way this hadn't been the case. It had required much patient tact to convince him that a brilliant future awaited him in London, and that nothing but stultifying boredom could come of life in Cornwall. She had expected help in this from Polly Penwarne, and had only now begun to realize that Daniel's daughter wasn't by any means her ally after all.

A few days had to be allowed to elapse before the subject of Prospect could decently be discussed with her children, but the moment came when Lavinia and Jonathan were out, making a call at Place House.

'Maman, does it absolutely *have* to be sold?' Luc asked desperately.

Cécile fought against a longing to shout at him, and gave a regretful sigh instead. 'My darling, yes . . . I fear it does. For one thing, there are death duties to pay; for another, your father's income in London died with him. Without what you and I earn, we should be rather poor.'

'But we own half Fowey,' Lisette put in impatiently. 'Something must come from that to keep Prospect going.'

'We own a *little* of Fowey, by no means a half, and it's occupied by tenants who have lived in Bossiney property for generations. Their rents are never raised because, although Cornwall was once rich, it hasn't been so for fifty years. If there was ever anything left of our income here that Prospect itself, or rising damp in one cottage and dry rot in another, didn't instantly absorb, your father would hear of someone's misfortune and *give* the money away.' She saw the expression on Lisette's face and tried not to sound sharp. 'My dear, I know that people loved him for his kindness, but *we* are the poorer as a result.'

'That's what the Cornish motto – "one and all" – means,' Lisette said obstinately. 'I'd forgotten it until Petroc reminded me.'

'He's obsessed with things Cornish,' her mother snapped. 'I can't imagine why, when his father was an Irishman.'

'He says it makes him doubly Celtic. I think it makes him doubly interesting!'

It was, if anything, doubly infuriating, but Cécile was still clear-headed enough not to alienate her daughter. It would be playing straight into Petroc's hands to have Lisette side against her completely and perhaps influence Luc as well.

'He can be anything you like, darling,' she said with a faint smile. 'But *please* don't let him persuade you that your brother should spend the rest of his life trying to keep this ugly barn of a house upright; it simply isn't fair. However, if you've set your mind against poor Mr Penwarne, then we shall have to try to find another buyer.'

It was the right note to end the discussion on; Luc would agree to sell, and she was almost sure that in the end he would allow a deal to be struck with Polly's father.

The Penwarne home in Fore Street didn't run to the luxury of a telephone, and Polly was obliged to walk to the post office each morning to ring her father with the same message: the work she was doing with William was nearly finished and she would be back in London for Christmas; she was fully recovered from her bruises and cuts on the cliff; she was quite all right, and there was no need for him to worry or to come and see her for himself. Some of this was true, but there were moments when she was thankful that it wasn't a face-to-face conversation, because Daniel had too keen an eye for a fib. Her grandfather, too, had a glance made sharp by love, and she thought he was aware of the grief and uncertainty she struggled to hide as they sifted through his material together.

One day they stared sadly at her photograph of Maen Porth, where incomers' chalets and bungalows – tiled as a final insult to their surroundings, instead of being slate-roofed – smirched a once-beautiful clifftop.

'It might happen here – did happen, I s'pose you could say,' William murmured, 'when all those houses were built up on the height at Lawhyre; still, we've been lucky, maid. Even St Catherine's headland was threatened, but a good man – Mr Stenton Covington – bought it and gave it to the National Trust.'

'What shall we print alongside the Maen Porth photograph?' Polly asked, leading him gently back to the task in hand.

'Well, how about something Petroc O'Meara brought me? He was here one day about a repair and saw me looking at the photograph. Next day he comes back with *this*, written by an old friend of his grandmother's – name of Sir Arthur Quiller-Couch: "To any right Cornishman, Cornwall is a mother with a character, definite and dear. Having that character, she has a character to lose . . . the coastline used to be *ours*, the priceless if barren inheritance of a little clan . . ."'

Polly agreed that the words were apt enough, but she thought she could hear Petroc O'Meara shouting them at her, and pointing out at the same time that her father was the sort of Cornishman that 'Q' would have abhorred. She didn't want to be reminded of Petroc, and it was a relief when Hannah came to insist that it was time for William's little rest; while he took it there was an errand for her granddaughter over to Boddinick.

'A breath of air for you, my dearie, won't do any harm,' she said, looking at Polly's pale face, 'and you can take this parcel of wool across to Mary for me at the same time.' She had perfected the art of killing at least two birds with one stone, and would have thought it wasteful not to get some extra benefit from her granddaughter's need for fresh air. Polly smiled, and promised not to linger talking for hours across the river, because Hannah was going to make hot potato cake for tea.

In fact there was no need to linger at all, because Mary Penwarne was not at home, and Polly could only leave the parcel inside the porch, propped against the door. But she walked on *up* the hill, instead of down to the ferry-slip. With the words William had shown her still in her mind, she wanted to go along Hall Walk with 'Q's memorial as her objective before she turned back again.

It was a damp, soft, sad sort of afternoon, in keeping with the feeling hanging over her that something important was almost finished and done with. She would take her thick folder of material to the publisher Daniel had found, and then it would cease to belong to her; Cornwall would cease to belong to her too, because the life that was waiting for her with Luc would have to be lived in London. As she walked along the springy turf it was finally clear in her mind what she must do. Tristram Bossiney had made and exacted promises that afternoon in Southground Cove. She must let his son provide all the happiness she required; she must see to it that Prospect was kept safe, and that Luc remained in his heart a true Cornishman. The legacy handed down from Bossineys and Penwarnes must still be theirs, and the legends of Kirrier, Pyder, Powder, and Trigg that

Isaac had taught William and Loveday, she would teach her and Luc's children some day.

She had the Hall Walk entirely to herself. Summer visitors left before the swallows did at the beginning of October, and no local resident would think of walking from Bodinnick to Polruan; a short pull downstream was quicker by far than this meandering land passage. But when she got to 'Q's memorial, where the path turned sharply eastward to the little bridge across Pont Pill, the wooden seat looking down on the estuary was occupied. A friendly greeting died on her lips as she identified the man who sat there; he had nothing more urgent to do apparently than watch a vessel laden with china-clay being tugged downriver before starting its return voyage to Oslo. She made herself sit down on the far end of the seat only because it would have looked strange not to do so.

'For a farmer you seem to spend a lot of time away from your farm – isn't there a cow or a crop you should be attending to?' she asked politely.

'My herd is in excellent health, thank you, and my fields are flourishing. At the risk of tempting Fate, who amuses herself by breaking farmers' hearts, I shall say that everything is as it should be at Tregenna. And since my working-day began at five this morning I think I'm entitled to sit here and watch the world go by.'

'You're a long way from the Lerryn Valley. Why not watch the world from there?'

The smile that Lavinia knew to be dangerous but Polly had scarcely seen turned up the corners of his long mouth. 'I'm beginning to get the strong impression that Miss Penwarne thinks I shouldn't be here.'

'She has no opinion on the subject at all,' Polly stated untruthfully. Her first sideways glance had shown him leaning back, half-turned towards her, very much at his ease. He might have been a different man from the one who had ignored her on the terrace at Prospect after Tristram's funeral, and different again still from the one whose arms had sheltered her in Southground Cove. She would never know or understand him, but it didn't matter now; that was the only important thing to remember.

'I come to Fowey quite often because I seem to have inherited my grandfather's involvement in local affairs,' Petroc was explaining. 'No-one remembers that my name isn't Bossiney – I'm considered part of Prospect . . . part of this place altogether.'

She didn't comment on what he'd just said, but chose to stare at the view instead. Petroc looked at her profile etched against a soft, grey sky; it was slightly tilted away from him and showed the delicate line of cheekbone, jaw, and slender throat. There was a sheen of moisture on her dark hair that always reminded him of the petal-head of a flower. She was as boyishly thin as a medieval page, as brave and merry at heart and unknowingly provocative as Shakespeare's Rosalind. She was all these things, but more – she was Daniel's daughter, and she was going to belong to Luc Bossiney.

Suddenly her hand sketched a gesture at the view in front of them. ' "The priceless if barren inheritance of a little clan," ' she quoted. 'That's how *you* see Cornwall, isn't it?'

Petroc forced himself to concentrate on what she'd just said. ' "Q" was talking about our coastline, and I agree with him about that; but inland Cornwall has been rich in the past – could still produce wealth enough to keep our people fed and self-respecting if they were prepared to forgo easy options . . . if they weren't content to be waiters and potboys for four months of the year, and nothing at all for the other eight.'

She heard in his voice the deep, sad conviction of what was closest to his heart. It was hard – it was nearly impossible – not to pocket pride and say that she agreed utterly with what he said. But loyalty to Daniel remained, and insisted on being heard.

'It's so lovely that less fortunate people are bound to want to come here,' she pointed out. 'Why should they *not* have the chance to see a seal poking its grey nose out of a green wave, or a hillside golden with primroses and gorse?'

'They must come, of course, but on *our* terms,' Petroc said definitely, 'that means investment first in any local industries that can be revived *before* government money is lavished on the things we can do without – like extra roads that bring in more holidaymakers, who in turn need more cheap, ugly accommodation run up for them, and more tawdry amusement arcades to make them forget our Cornish weather when they get here.'

Polly clung to her role of devil's advocate, because after all *he* had a case as well. 'Have you asked any young Cornish people whether *they* mind roads they can drive on, or ugly housing they can at least afford, or somewhere to go and enjoy themselves when it's pouring with rain on their day off? Old-time wrestling matches and Wesleyan revivalist meetings went out of fashion at least fifty years ago.'

'Perhaps, but it doesn't mean that all they're good for now is a cheap sneer.'

'It wasn't intended as a sneer,' she insisted quietly.

He answered after a little pause. 'I know . . . I didn't really imagine that it was. We understood each other better in Southground Cove, Polly.'

Her eyes flew to his, then looked away from the yearning sadness in his face.

'How is Lisette now?' she managed to ask.

'Very unsettled still – missing her father greatly, I think. She wants to stay at Prospect, but I can't help feeling that she'd recover more quickly in London. Our marriage has been postponed till the new year.'

Polly gathered nothing from his expressionless voice, but perhaps that in itself spoke of natural frustration, and accounted for some of the unhappiness she sensed in him. It left nothing more to talk about since the subject of Prospect itself couldn't safely be mentioned. But this entire conversation wasn't safe – they were isolated from the rest of the world, and between them there seemed to

379

be growing, as naturally as a flower grew, the knowledge that the rest of the world didn't matter at all.

Petroc stared at his hands that were locked together to resist temptation. 'What about you and Luc? I gather you're going to marry soon.'

'Not soon, and he hasn't even asked me yet – but there's no hurry; in the end I think we *shall* marry.' The words were said, and the real world was all around them again. She turned bravely to look at Petroc. 'We shall be sort of cousins then. No more squabbling! Shall we "clap hands and a bargain"?' Her hand was held out, and her smile was beautiful, but Petroc stood up, knowing that he must ignore what she offered.

'No, I don't think we'll do that, Polly Penwarne.'

A moment later he walked away from her, down the track that led to the footbridge and the creek. His rejection was as sharp as a slap across her cheek, but she was more painfully aware of his sadness. Worst of all, there had been no chance to say that he no longer need worry about Prospect, because *she* was going to make sure that it was kept safe for Lavinia. She turned in the direction of the ferry back to Fowey. Even if she hurried she was bound to be late for Hannah's potato cake. It was a reason for the tears that trickled slowly down her face, but not a very good one.

Petroc retrieved his car from where he'd left it by the bridge and drove home to Tregenna. It seemed a long time ago that he'd set out on his favourite walk to 'Q's memorial, to wrestle with a decision of his own that must be taken soon or not at all. But at least the decision *had* been taken, at some level of his mind where conscious calculation ceased to operate; it was a huge relief – something to blot out the memory of Polly's expression when he had thrown her little olive branch back in her face.

At Tregenna, Kurt's bicycle was propped against a pile of straw in the yard, while he let Henry Dingle polish harness and talk at the same time. Henry was retired now, but Petroc still hadn't convinced him that he might enjoy not working if he would only give it a try.

'I'm a nuisance coming without warning,' Kurt said with a glance at his godson's face.

'Only if you've still come to say goodbye. Shall we leave Henry to his polishing and go inside? *Have* you come to say that you're leaving?' he asked when they were alone.

Kurt shook his head, smiling a little, and there was a different air about him. Petroc registered it as something inexplicably like joy, and it seemed a puzzling but redeeming end to a day that had coloured itself as grey as Cornish drizzle.

'Morwetha wanted to come with me but I couldn't allow that,' Kurt said hesitantly. 'It is only for *me* to break news that you may find very bad.'

'If you've changed your mind about going, and want to stay on at Trebinnick, that isn't bad news at all.'

'I want to stay to marry your sister,' Kurt said, taking his fence in a rush. 'I have tried to explain to her how very remarkable and strange it is that *she* should be prepared to marry me, how very . . . very objectionable *you* are bound to find this idea, but . . .'

'But she doesn't listen?' Petroc interrupted, with a smile beginning to drive sadness from his face. 'For once she's quite right not to, because I don't find it objectionable at all. In fact I find it such gloriously good news that for two pins I'd dance and sing!' He held out his hand, and Kurt took it in both his own trembling ones.

'I'd nearly convinced myself on the way here that you would think I had abused trust and friendship most shockingly.'

'You've convinced yourself for far too long that happiness is something only other people are entitled to! If you *must* insist on that fat-headed idea, then just remember that Morwetha is due for a little happiness as well.'

Kurt nodded gravely. 'That I shall remember every day of my life.' His face shone for a moment with relief and happiness, then grew serious again. 'I should feel like dancing myself if this were not also so sad a time.' He hesitated, on the verge of permitting himself a probing question, but his own joy was too recent for him to forget that pain was not helped by the well meant prodding of friends. 'Sad times pass,' was all he allowed himself to say instead, 'this I can now promise you.'

Petroc smiled with rare warmth and affection. 'And who am I to contradict a *Herr Doktor Professor* who is about to become my brother-in-law?'

28

Polly went back to London quieter than usual, but Daniel thought it was bound to be so. Beyond the briefest description of the accident in Southground Cove she left the subject of Tristram Bossiney so pointedly alone that he was warned not to refer to it. Nor did she enquire whether he still had any interest in Prospect. He had the strong impression that, with her photographs and her grandfather's texts delivered to William Collins, she preferred to think no more about Cornwall.

They spent Christmas quietly together – a walk in the park after church, listening to the king's broadcast message to the Commonwealth, and dining with Cécile and Luc in Pont Street. Afterwards, Daniel waited; with a patience that would have astonished his employees, to be told that she'd agreed to marry Luc, and that Cécile had persuaded him to sell Prospect to the Penwarnes. The Cornish blood in Daniel's veins had thinned with time, but even he couldn't help feeling that these events would complete a circle begun long ago – would even, in a way, make sense of them, so that Loveday's troubled ghost could rest in peace at last, and Tristram Bossiney's would have no cause to complain. It was time that these things happened, even if, to Daniel's way of thinking, they were happening very slowly.

Polly might have said to him what she'd said to Petroc O'Meara – there wasn't any hurry, and they all had to recover from the loss of Tristram. Then for a week or two at the end of January she saw nothing of Luc at all, because the settlement of his father's affairs required a visit to Cornwall. When he reappeared in London she was immediately aware of a change – it was as if some temporary hiatus was over and his life was in motion again. He shared a meal with her in Wilton Mews made more peaceful by Daniel's absence in the Midlands to inspect a new factory, and began by answering her enquiries about Lisette.

'She's still at Prospect, but looking rather bored, if you ask me. No wonder, of course – there's nothing to do down there in winter, except take long walks in the rain and play backgammon with Uncle Jonathan. Still, even that's better than sitting by herself at Tregenna, waiting for Petroc to stop working. I suggested getting on with marrying him so that she'd have something to do, but she didn't seem grateful for the advice – said she was sick of hearing it from everybody else! Petroc's too gentle with her; it seems to me she needs a firm hand.'

'I believe that's what all brothers think about their sisters,' Polly said absently, remembering with painful vividness a man to whom patience didn't come naturally, although gentleness sometimes did.

'Darling love, we've got more to talk about than Lisette,' Luc said with sudden urgency. 'Listen carefully now, because this concerns *us*. It's so exciting that I hardly know where to begin, and it's all Maman's idea, of course.'

'Of course,' she agreed without a smile, but he would have heard no irony even if it had been intended.

'We're doing well in London – *very* well, as a matter of fact; Bossiney et Fils are on the crest of the wave.'

'Is there something wrong with that?'

'No – there's only the problem of staying there! But Maman's answer is simple – we expand – in Paris! Different textiles, different furnishing ideas, different clientèle, and all the kudos of having a continental atelier as well as the London showrooms.'

She saw the shining eagerness in his face and smiled at him with warm affection.

'Dear Luc, it sounds marvellously exciting, and if your

384

mother is going to be in Paris in future, it means that you'll be in sole charge here at last.'

'*No*, it doesn't mean that at all. I was certain it would be that way round, but my blessed, darling mother insists that *I* must have the fun of getting the new Bossiney's started.'

His smile was brilliant, but she knew him well enough to realize that his excitement, although real, was laced with fear. She realized also that Cécile's great idea would have the effect – perhaps deliberate – of finally detaching him from Cornwall. Her own promise to Tristram seemed to have been useless after all.

'Sweetheart, don't look so sad,' Luc begged. 'Like the child Granny still thinks I am, I've saved the best bit till last.' His face was finely featured in the way Julian Bossiney's had been, but saved from mere handsomeness by the charm that had belonged to Tristram. Now, it was full of smiling tenderness and pleading. 'I can't go without you – you've got to come to Paris and help me.'

His hands grabbed her shoulders and pulled her close. She could feel him trembling, and knew that he meant what he said – he wanted her, perhaps, but he would *need* her very much as well.

'We'll get married before we go. Say yes, *please*, my sweet. Polly, you've *got* to come.'

'I'll come,' she agreed slowly, but the rest of what she'd been going to say was lost against Luc's mouth. When he finally let her go, she was flushed and smiling, but this time she laid a finger across his lips to prevent him speaking.

'You didn't let me finish. Shall we just be engaged for the time being? We shall still be sure of each other, but starting a new venture in a foreign city is quite enough to cope with all at once. Getting married is a serious business – we should need too much time to concentrate on *that*.' She saw the hesitation in his face, and added gently, 'I'm sure that Maman would agree.'

Luc considered this afterthought for a moment and finally nodded his head. 'Perhaps you're right, sweetheart.

Marriage a little later on, but what blissful fun it's going to be.' Then, suddenly brightness died out of his face. 'Oh, God – I suppose it's heartless not to be still plunged in gloom . . .'

Polly put up a consoling hand to touch his cheek. 'I don't think so – I promise you that your father would *want* to see you happy. But, Luc dear, I want you to promise *me* something, too. Don't sell Prospect to *anyone* while your grandmother is still alive, and *never* sell it to my father just to use. When we can no longer afford to keep it, it must go to someone who will live in it and cherish it as a part of Cornish history.'

She didn't know what she expected, but certainly not Luc's shout of amusement before he hugged her again.

'You haven't promised,' she reminded him breathlessly.

'Sweetheart, I *can't* – Prospect was sold a week ago! That's why I went down there.'

The shock of it drove the colour from her face. Behind anxiety for Lavinia lay the knowledge that Cécile had won, and that *all* her promises to Tristram had been useless.

'What about your grandmother?' she asked with dry lips. 'It doesn't concern you what becomes of her and Uncle Jonathan?'

'The new owner is allowing them to stay.' Luc saw the fierce anger in her face, but smiled at her again before he explained. 'Darling, it's not fair to tease you, but I can't help it when you get worked up about Cornwall and Prospect. Can you really see Petroc evicting Granny?'

She took so long to answer that he wondered if she'd understood what he'd said. 'You mean that . . . that *Petroc* has bought Prospect? How could he possibly do that?'

Luc gave a little shrug that didn't entirely conceal embarrassment. 'Darling, it wasn't exactly my business to ask him – but I *think* he's probably had to mortgage his farms.'

He saw the expression on her face, and suddenly the grip of his hands on her tightened painfully. 'Don't look like that – it *had* to be sold, and Petroc has always wanted to own it. This way everybody's happy.' Then a shadow crossed his face as he remembered something. '*Not* everybody – your father loses the house, and my mother wanted me to accept *his* offer; it was much more than Petroc could afford to pay, and the extra money would have been useful to us in getting our Paris venture started. Maman was furious with me for not agreeing.'

'Why didn't you then?' Polly asked coolly.

'Because I knew Lisette was right – my father would have hated Daniel to get it.' He needed her to say that he had done right – had done well, after all, in opposing Cécile for once.

She nodded, accepting the truth of it. What did it matter to her if Petroc O'Meara had beggared himself to keep safe something he believed was important? It didn't matter at all because she had committed herself to going to live in Paris with Luc, and if it hadn't been Paris it would have been London. It wasn't for her – the joy of tending Lavinia's garden, of listening for the cry of gulls, and the wind blowing round the old grey house. It was time to put such dreams away.

'Tell me when we have to be ready to leave,' she said quietly.

A month later, when spring was knocking at the door in Cornwall but not in London at the end of a bleak February, she went down to Fowey to say goodbye to her grandparents. William looked sad, even when she explained that the publishers had liked their Cornish material so much that she'd been commissioned to take photographs of Paris.

'A female view of a feminine city,' she explained cheerfully. 'It sounds rather a silly idea to me, but I can't help feeling a little bit flattered that they've asked me. And it will be something to do when Luc doesn't need my help in the shop.'

Her grandfather seemed unimpressed by the idea of a

place so unimaginably different from the world he knew, and even Hannah looked unhappy. She had been born in Victoria's century, Polly remembered; how could she approve of her unmarried granddaughter going off, even with gentle, upright Luc Bossiney, to a city that was well known for its bohemian depravity and godlessness. There wasn't a single Methodist chapel in Paris, she felt sure, to restrain the behaviour of its citizens.

Polly did her best to reassure them both, but it was a relief to visit Prospect.

She was welcomed with such pleasure that it seemed sad to have come only to say goodbye, wrong to be going so far away. Lavinia saw the shadow in her eyes and understood that, for Polly at least, it was grief as well as excitement to be setting off for a strange country.

'I envy you and Luc Paris in the spring,' she said gently. 'It was much less magical in a wet November, shared with a husband who thought it a waste of time to be there at all! Rome seemed even worse to Julian, and it was great relief when his father's ill-health gave us an excuse to cut short our wedding journey. Cleopatra combined with Helen of Troy *might* have roused my husband to passion, but I never managed it!' A reminiscent smile lit her face, insisting that Polly need not be sorry for her, because as time went by life had a way of turning such very small tragedies into something comical. 'I'm so glad you're going with Luc,' she added after a moment or two. 'With you he won't entirely forget, however much Cécile would like him to, that he is his father's son.'

Polly nodded, hoping with all her heart that what Lavinia said was true.

'Luc told me about selling Prospect,' she said abruptly. 'Does it make any difference to you?'

As if it was a question she found hard to answer, Lavinia took a long time to reply. 'It makes *this* much difference, my dear. I used to think that nothing was more important than keeping this house and its history intact; now I see that it isn't nearly worth the sacrifice that has had to be made for it.'

'Petroc seems to think differently.'

A smile, half-wry, half-tender, touched her ladyship's mouth. 'He is careful to insist that he hasn't beggared himself for me or Jonathan – only for Cornwall!' She lifted her thin shoulders in a gesture that said her own anxiety must be put aside. 'There's other happy news apart from your own. Having given up the struggle to pretend that she is not floating on air, Morwetha confesses that she has persuaded Kurt Winkler to marry her. Kurt pretends that she has taken pity on *him*, and smiles like a man who sees the kingdom of heaven in front of him. Tristram would have been . . . comforted by their happiness.'

Polly's nod acknowledged more than the truth of what Lavinia had said – they both knew that he had been in *need* of comfort. 'But for him Professor Winkler wouldn't be here – it's something, isn't it?'

Her grave question was answered by a nod this time from Lavinia. It *was* something, at least, to set against the loss of a man who couldn't be replaced. They sat in silence for a moment or two, content to be together, needing no conversation to understand one another. Then, as Polly was about to say that it was time for her to leave, the door behind her opened and Lisette walked into the room. Her face looked thin and pale, and she seemed a ghost of the girl who had sparkled at Lavinia's long-ago dinner party. She murmured a brief hello that gave no impression of pleasure at the sight of her grandmother's visitor.

'Luc asked me to give you his special love and good-byes,' Polly said quickly.

'Tactful of you,' Lisette murmured with a cool smile. 'I expect the truth is that he's far too busy to remember his twin sister. He's got Paris to look forward to, and so have you. Lucky Polly Penwarne!'

The tone of her voice pulled Lavinia's brows together in a little frown of displeasure, but Polly allowed no time for it to be put into words.

'Yes, I agree with you, but I've still to go over to Polruan, where Grandfather Tom is bound to tell me that the Seine is nothing to the Fowey River when it comes to "liquid 'istory"!' She hugged Lavinia goodbye and was warmly kissed in return, but this evidence of their deep affection for one another seemed also to irritate Lisette when she went with her across the hall to the front door. Polly thought Petroc had been right – she would have done better away from a place that didn't constantly remind her of her loss.

'I suppose your father was rather irked at not getting Prospect after all,' Lisette observed. 'With you and Luc engaged, he must have thought it was a foregone conclusion.'

There were limits, Polly discovered, to sympathy for a bereaved girl. She took firm hold on a flash of anger, but her voice was crisp.

'In matters of business he never takes anything for granted. If he is disappointed, he sees no point in saying so.' She glanced at Lisette's unhappy face and spoke more gently. 'You're bound to have plans of your own by now – surely the thought of marriage must be fairly exciting.'

'Fairly,' Lisette conceded without enthusiasm. Then a little colour tinged her cheeks because Polly was staring at her. 'Sorry . . . I'm in what Luc calls my spoilt brat mood – it seems that I always *am* nowadays. Petroc's so marvellous that he puts up with me, gentle as a lamb. I almost wish he'd turn fierce and masterful, and drag me to the altar, but he's made up his mind that I'm to be handled like a fretful child. The result is that I go on behaving like one – certain one minute that we must get married immediately, convinced the next that it won't hurt to wait a little longer.'

Polly's irritation was mixed with pity for a girl whose parentage itself probably confused her, pulling her in different directions that she didn't fully understand.

'Why not trust Petroc enough to get on with it,' she suggested gently. 'I think it's what your father would have wanted you to do.' It was tempting to add that her fiancé deserved some consideration too, but she reminded herself that they were not on sisterly enough terms yet to permit such plain speaking.

'I expect I shall soon,' Lisette agreed. 'All the same, he *should* have consulted me before he took on this wretched house. It isn't as if we're ever going to live in it.'

Polly heard the note of genuine resentment in her voice, but instead took refuge in a glance at her watch. 'I *must* go, but we'll be sure to come back for your wedding.'

'Everybody's having them,' Lisette said glumly, as if this was another slight she couldn't overlook, 'you, Morwetha, and even *Aunt Jen's* decided to go back to America and settle down with some elderly war-time admirer!'

'The more the merrier,' Polly suggested, trying not to grin.

It brought no answering smile, only a parting shot that Lisette had just thought of. 'I don't know that I *do* envy you Paris, after all. Luc speaks the language like a native, but you'll have a lot of catching-up to do, and the French don't make things easy for an outsider.'

'Never mind; I'll catch up in the end. My father would tell you that cussedness is my only saving virtue!' She smiled cheerfully and walked away, wondering whether Lisette or Grandfather Tom would prove to be the greater Job's comforter.

A fortnight later she set out with Luc on their great Parisian adventure. It had been hard to say goodbye to her father, but it was time to face the future, not steal glances over her shoulder at a past that had never been quite real. She smiled confidently at Luc as they stood by the rail of the Channel steamer.

'No regrets, sweetheart?'

She shook her head, thankful that she could answer him without hesitation. 'None . . . I'm *glad* to be a traveller with "promises to keep, and miles to go, before I sleep"!'

He didn't understand her but it didn't matter; her lovely mouth was smiling when he bent to kiss it, and

all the excitement of their life together lay ahead. The
ship slowly cleared Dover harbour and swung round to
meet the open sea. He was safe now. They were going
to Paris, and he needn't even remember Cornwall at
all.

29

In September Paris was coming into its own again. The
tourists had mostly left, and the people who belonged
there were back in their shops and offices and cafés.
Daniel preferred it that way, seeing no point in coming
to a place that was full of bemused-looking foreigners.
It had been hard to wait this long before coming to
check up on Polly, but it had been only fair. By now he
thought they ought to be ready to receive visitors, and –
fair or not – his plan was simply to arrive, without fuss
or warning.

Installed in the Lutétia in the Boulevard Raspail, he
telephoned what his daughter called the shop, although
Luc did not, and heard her voice, subtly changed by the
different vowel sounds of the French language. Stupid of
him not to have expected that – she lived in France for God's
sake; but if Polly Jane Penwarne had gone for good and
only a Frenchified stranger remained, it would have been
a mistake to come at all. Familiarity returned when she
recognized him, but he refused her offer to come and
fetch him from the hotel. He would find the Rue Jacob
himself.

The neighbourhood he walked through had been
Cécile's choice, and Polly's first letters had been en-
thusiastic – the *quartier* was perfect, combining past
elegance with modern Left Bank chic; the premises
themselves were ideal – spacious ground-floor rooms
for Luc to use, and living quarters above that could
soon be made habitable again once they got to work
on them. In short, Polly had written blithely, everything
in the *jardin* was lovely. It still was as far as he knew;

only instinct had been suggesting for weeks past that her regular letters continued to sound cheerful because she wouldn't let them sound anything else. But the instinct had been strong enough to bring him here; without it he wouldn't be walking along a Paris street trying to make sense of the cock-eyed French numbering system.

Here it was . . . Bossiney et Fils, in discreetly elegant lettering, above a window occupied by one sumptuously modern chair, and a gilt bird-cage from which hung swathes of rainbow-coloured material. It was eye-catching, Daniel supposed dubiously. Then he forgot the window-dressing because Polly had seen him and was at the door. He caught her in a fierce hug, and then held her at arm's length to inspect her.

She was . . . no, *not* the same . . . seemed taller for one thing, but that was because she was even more slender now, with the bone structure of her face clearly visible. Her dark hair, cut shorter than before, should have seemed boyish, but its effect was the reverse, subtly accentuating femininity. A striped grey-and-white cotton shirt, and a wide grey skirt cinched in with a belt of scarlet raffia looked simple enough, but this was his Polly with a high French gloss, no question. She had learned things from living in Paris, and Daniel didn't know whether to be pleased or not.

'You're as thin as rake,' he said roughly. 'I thought the food was what people came here for.'

'Well, they seem to manage better here with what's available than we do at home, but I expect I've been too busy to "get the benefit" as Granny Eliot would say!' She struggled with a strong inclination to burst into tears, and smiled instead. 'It's *lovely* to see you . . . just lovely! Now, come upstairs – we shall be able to hear if the bell goes down here.'

Daniel followed her up a narrow staircase and through double glass doors into the salon that stretched across the width of the house. Its two balconied windows were simply draped in white muslin that muted, but didn't obstruct, the light that streamed into the room. It was *all* light and space and emptiness – white walls, polished wood floor reflecting low tables made of glass, and chairs that seemed to Daniel to be made entirely of bamboo. The only colour in the room came from yellow silk lampshades shaped for no good reason he could see like Chinese pagodas; they echoed the brightness of a sheaf of sunflowers in a tall white jar. It was studied and strange, and not a bit like home.

'God Almighty – is this where you live?' he asked.

'Well, it's where Luc lives – I'm still with dear old Madame Martin at the other end of the street, of course. This is the new style; Luc says English chintz and polished mahogany are as passé as Louis Quinze.'

Daniel snorted, aware that he must be considered more than a little passé himself – he thought of his home, to the extent that he thought of it at all, as a refuge full of comfortable, cluttered, familiar things. *This* would be like living in the middle of an iridescent bubble. 'It's not my cup of tea,' he said truthfully, 'but I dare say the French like it. Now, shall we start on our catching up, or wait for Luc?'

Polly shook her head. 'You've arrived on a day when he isn't here at all; that's why I'm minding the shop. Normally his assistant would be here, but she's with him out at Saint Cloud. An old friend of the Sabatiers has given him the biggest commission he's had so far, to redesign a villa for her. He won't be back until very late, so *we* can dine together at a little bistro round the corner and talk English to our hearts' content!'

'You make it sound like a rare treat. What else would we talk?'

'Well, Luc only talks French to me.' She saw her father frown, and was quick to explain. 'He's quite right; it's the only way if I'm ever to learn. Lisette and he grew up equally at home in both languages, but I'm still struggling to turn schoolgirl French into something that people here are prepared to recognize.'

'Bloody-minded lot, but then they always were. You'd think their language was something special, the fuss they make about it.'

She grinned for the sheer pleasure of listening to a man who'd never held with weakening his argument by admitting that there might be another point of view. She'd missed him more deeply than she'd realized.

'Smile if you like, maid, but I've had to fight with them in one war, and deal with them in another. We were supposed to be on the same side, but there were times when I doubted it.'

'All the same, you encouraged us to come here,' she reminded him.

'Was I wrong? Do you wish I hadn't?'

It was a tactic she should have remembered from the past – the quiet probe slipped in when least expected. His expression was familiar too; just so would a terrier wait outside a rabbit-hole, ready to pounce on anything foolhardy enough to emerge from cover.

'No, I don't think you were wrong,' she answered after a moment. 'Luc is beginning to do well now, and his talent is appreciated among people who think it's important to live with style. He's happy here – seems to belong to Paris.'

'What about you. Do *you* belong?'

This time she had anticipated the question and was ready for it. 'Not quite to the same extent yet, but I expect I soon shall.'

Her smile was confident, and he believed her because she hadn't made the mistake of claiming too much. His frowning expression relaxed suddenly. 'What about a cup of tea, then? I'm sick of ersatz coffee already.'

Dinner in the bistro she recommended deserved more attention than they could spare from talking. Even the patron's *gigot d'agneau farçi* earned only an approving nod from Daniel as he listened to Polly's account of their first weeks in the Rue Jacob. Her face grew bright with the memory of them – hard work shared and plans laid as they'd scrubbed and scraped and painted. The joy of the adventure had been strong then, and she had been sure of being needed.

'Who's Luc's assistant?' Daniel asked eventually.

'The daughter of a family friend – Monique de la Vallée. Her English is much better than my French, and she's useful to Luc in a lot of ways, because she's got a College of Art diploma, as well as a clutch of well-connected and rich relations. Cécile is very pleased with her.'

Daniel's keen ear caught the slight emphasis on that, but he allowed it to pass. 'I assume she doesn't work for nothing, so she's an expense on a fledgling business. I know you've got your own work, but couldn't *you* do whatever she does?'

Polly linked long fingers round her wine glass and stared into the red heart of the wine. 'Probably not, and in any case Luc is afraid I don't make quite the most favourable impression!' She glanced at her father's face and gave a wry smile. 'He's right about that too, I expect. His fees are moderate but, even so, his clientèle has to be wealthy, and they aren't people I seem able to like very much. Luc says it's because I accuse them in my mind of being those of the French who did well out of the war.' She gave a little shrug unconsciously learned from the race she lived among. 'It's hard to explain, but we were probably different people *before* 1940, and then we lived through a different kind of war. London, battered and burning, at least was always ours, not swaggered over by occupying Germans. Even now the French want to meet present adversities with a flourish, whereas I think *our* aim is just to meet them with humour if we can.'

Daniel glared at his *tarte aux pruneaux* in a way that broke the patron's heart. 'Which camp does Luc favour?'

'He spent the war years in Washington – yet another experience from ours – and also he's half Belgian; it wouldn't be fair to expect him to think as I do. But in any case, he's *obliged* to be tactful here and he can't help feeling that I'm not tactful enough.'

She ordered coffee for them both and a *fine* for Daniel, and then touched his hand consolingly. 'Don't worry about the expense of Monique. The sale of Prospect financed Luc's start here, and he's bound to do well. He works very hard, and his talent is appreciated.'

'I only worry about you. Isn't it time you got married? Long engagements are an unnatural strain.'

She didn't deny it, but said instead, 'We'll marry as soon as the Saint Cloud house is finished, but I'm afraid the ceremony will have to be here. I'd wanted us to go back to Fowey for our wedding but it's too soon to disappear when he's just beginning to get known.' In case it had sounded too wistful, she smiled with the sudden sweet gaiety he remembered. 'Cornwall seems far away, though, and I'm so nearly used to living here that I've even given up coveting Grandfather Tom's cottage by the ferry at Polruan . . . that shows you!'

'Well, it *reminds* me of something,' he said instead. 'Your publisher in London is saving postage. I've got the proofs of your *Cornish Portrait* in my hotel room – he wants them back within a month; publication early next year, to catch the summer season.'

A tinge of pleased colour warmed her face. 'Does my dear William know that it's actually coming into print?'

'I asked Charlie to tell him. He's very frail, but the thought of it might be enough to get him through another winter. They all send their love, of course, and miss you very much. Your letters are hoarded like miser's gold, and the postman regularly enrages your grandmother by telling everyone in Fore Street when another envelope with a French stamp arrives. Hannah doesn't mind them knowing, but she wants to give out the news herself!'

It was a laughing note to end the evening on. Daniel walked back with her to Madame Martin's house in the Rue Jacob, and suggested that if she wasn't needed in the shop the next morning she could give him a guided tour of Paris. 'After that we'll have a little celebration in the evening.'

'Can we invite Lisette as well?' Polly asked. 'I expect you know she's here, now, staying with Luc.'

'I heard from your grandparents that the engagement was off. Don't know that I blame her – damnably awkward chap Petroc O'Meara, but I'm not sure we couldn't do with a few more like him. I suppose she didn't fancy marrying a man who'd been fool enough to make himself poor over a matter of principle.'

Polly had no comment to make on a man who was proud as well as 'awkward'; more than most, he would loathe pity, and the knowledge that he was being generally discussed. For that good reason alone she hadn't encouraged Lisette to talk about her failed love affair. 'Lisette is working as an assistant at a rather famous cookery school called Maxim's Academy – it's run by a grand friend of Cécile's, the Comtesse de Toulouse-Lautrec.'

'It *would* be,' Daiel said unfairly.

Polly kissed him goodnight, but then stood staring up at him for a moment. He hoped the moonlight was to blame for throwing light and shadows on her face that made it look sad.

'Have I mentioned that I'm *very* glad you came?' she asked suddenly.

'Not in so many words, but then *I* haven't said that I didn't really come for the guided tour!'

They smiled at each other with huge, unstated affection before she unlocked the door and went inside, and Daniel began to navigate himself back to the Boulevard Raspail.

She went early to see Luc the next morning, stopping to buy fresh croissants on the way. With their shared breakfast on the kitchen table, she offered her news as well. 'Luc, I've got a lovely surprise for you. My father arrived out of the blue yesterday . . . just for a little visit. He's flying back to London tomorrow.'

Luc made a real effort to detach his mind from the problem of how best to convince Estelle Mérigny that she didn't really want a bedroom that resembled a sheikh's desert pavilion. 'Splendid, Polly . . . give him my love.'

'You can give it yourself this evening.' She saw the expression on his face and her smile faded. 'Don't – *please* don't – say that you're unable to take *one* evening off from dancing attendance on that wretched woman.' It was a mistake; she knew it even before she saw the offended look on his face.

'She is a charming and valued client,' he said stiffly, 'not a wretched woman. If your father had seen fit to let us know he was coming, I could have explained that this is an inconvenient time. Polly, he's a businessman – he'll understand, better than you do apparently, that appointments aren't made just to be broken.'

'He might *not* understand that you can't spare even a couple of hours to have dinner with *him*. It's downright unkind.'

'He should have given us warning,' Luc said furiously. 'I suppose he wanted to find out if we were sleeping together.'

'Nothing of the sort,' she shouted. 'And even if we were, he'd think it was *our* affair, not his.' She saw her angry face in the mirror and was shocked by it into quietness. 'He's here for affection's sake. Can't you understand that?'

Luc smoothed back his long fair hair. It made him look very English in this city of dark-headed men, but in other ways he seemed to become gradually less familiar, day by day. 'I'm sorry if I misjudged him, Polly, but dinner with your father is less important than neglecting the most valuable commission we've had so far.'

'Very well, then; there's no more to be said. Father and I will have our little family celebration alone.' She poured herself more coffee and drank it, but the croissant on her plate had to be abandoned because she no longer felt like eating.

Luc stood up and she waited for him to hurry out of the room, but he stayed where he was, staring at her downbent head. Then he spoke again, in a different tone of voice.

'I hope the family celebration can include Lisette.' When she looked at him in astonishment his face was kind. 'Sorry, sweetheart – I'll square Estelle, somehow. Just tell the *bon papa* to be ready at eight o'clock! There's no need for you to stay here; Monique is back downstairs today.'

He was gone before she could reply, and she was left still sitting at the table, aware that some point of danger had been approached and narrowly missed.

The day that followed was unexpectedly enjoyable. The mellow warmth of September lay over a city whose beauty she knew she had unconsciously resisted. Now, sharing it with her father, there seemed no need to resist it at all. The faint shadow at the back of her mind wasn't dark enough to spoil her pleasure, and she had to convince Daniel that it wasn't there at all. They sampled all the simple tourist pleasures that could be crammed into the day before it was time to meet Luc and his sister at the Deux Magots.

They were already there, waving from a corner; but they were not alone. The elegant woman beside Lisette, *entre deux ages* as the French tactfully say, was Estelle Mérigny, and the dapper young man opposite them she introduced as her nephew, Jean-Pierre. For the space of a moment or two Polly assumed that the meeting was accidental, the sort of coincidence that sometimes occurred to upset the best-laid plans. But Luc's nervously smiling face denied the possibility, and Estelle Mérigny confirmed with a raking glance at Daniel that she had been unable to resist meeting the father of Luc's 'so enchanting English fiancée'.

Both aunt and nephew were capable of speaking excellent English for Daniel's benefit and it seemed to Polly, struggling to conceal murderous dislike, to give them an advantage they kindly pretended to ignore. Lisette, changed almost out of recognition by two months in Paris, flirted impartially with Daniel and Jean-Pierre, as if she had no recollection of a very different man she was once supposed to have adored, and Luc struggled to be equally solicitous to both his fiancée and his self-invited guest. As a family celebration it failed miserably, Polly decided, and she was equally ready to write it off as a pleasure of any kind until, crisply slaying a compliment from Jean-Pierre, she caught her father's eye upon her. It moved in a sly, deliberate wink, and she knew with immense relief that he was enjoying himself.

She had always loved him very much, but never more so than now. Whatever language they had to speak, it was clear that *he* was in charge. After that it seemed possible to taste what she was eating, and even to listen with a show of interest to Estelle's waspishly amusing anecdotes about people they didn't know.

All was going well until Lisette pounced on the name of a Belgian acquaintance living in Paris, whom Estelle mentioned as a likely client for Luc. A little flown with wine, and irritated by Jean-Pierre's tendency to stare at Polly, she ignored her brother's frown of warning.

'You'll have to conceal the fact that you've got an English fiancée,' she told him brightly.

He did his best to head off the disaster he saw coming. 'I suppose you'll say next that if French people don't employ *me* it's because they still resent the Battle of Waterloo!'

'What Madame de Senlis still resents is the English retreat from Dunkirk,' Lisette said stubbornly. 'Her son was left behind there and captured by the Germans.'

'Then let her resent the right people,' Polly said swiftly before Daniel could intervene, 'her own *king* for one, who surrendered while our troops were still fighting on Belgian soil to try to save *his* country.' Feeling pleased with her own self control, she managed by a hair's-breadth not to say his 'rotten' country. Aware that both Luc and her father were silently willing her to hold her tongue and not go on to deal with the French surrender that had left Paris unscathed, she took a sip of wine and smiled sweetly at them. But the evening seemed interminable until relief came, with Daniel bowing over Madame Mérigny's hand with an aplomb that astonished his daughter. Even more surprisingly, he said as they walked away from the restaurant together that he'd enjoyed the evening.

'Well, it was more than I did,' Polly commented briefly, aware that Luc, walking ahead with Lisette, was out of earshot.

'I realize that.' He gave her hand, tucked inside his arm, a sharp little pat. 'Be fair, maid. You said yourself that Luc's bound not to see things quite your way; but if there's a side to be on, you have to be on his. You know that as well as I do.'

'I do know,' she agreed after a while, 'and I do try.'

They walked on in silence until Daniel said, 'I've got a very early start for Le Bourget airport tomorrow, so I don't want *you* rushing round to the hotel in your nightgown to say more goodbyes. I hate 'em anyway. Both of you just try to come home for Christmas – tickets on me. Luc won't be working then, and you might even find time to get married.'

She hugged him gratefully at the entrance to the hotel, and managed to smile instead of weeping at having to see him go. Afterwards, walking back to the Rue Jacob, his words echoed in her mind. She was committed to Luc; she *must* be on his side, and somehow be glad that it was so.

'There's no need to say it,' Luc suddenly muttered. 'You objected to Estelle and her nephew being there tonight, and made it fairly plain. But haven't you learned by now that the only thing to do with the bloody war is forget it? We can't go on for ever remembering who did what.'

Polly had a fleeting memory of Morwetha and the man she'd married, whose child she was soon going to bear. It wasn't likely that either of *them* had found it easy to forget the war. But she wouldn't say so, because in one way Luc was right. Instead of reminding him that it was Lisette who had dragged the subject up, she smiled half-apologetically. 'I'm sorry . . . and I can see that Madame Mérigny's curiosity about your English connections would have been hard to refuse. Still, she was disappointed if she expected my father to have two heads!'

He didn't smile, and she realized as she had sometimes done before that he was mystified by the sense of humour she'd inherited from Daniel. She cast around for something safer to say and remembered her father's parting offer.

'I know it's ages away, but can we spend Christmas in England? Father wants to give us the air tickets, Luc – it sounds lovely, don't you think?'

There was a silence that warned her of what was to come. Then he found the courage to answer.

'Maman is already looking forward to spending Christmas with us *here*, and Estelle is planning a huge party to show off the villa, which has to be ready by then. Darling, it would be madness not to be there, and very unkind – because the party is really to help *us*.'

She stared at his face – half eagerly ingratiating, half ready to insist that she would be cruelly unhelpful if she refused to understand. It was very hard not to rage that his mother and his clients couldn't entirely control their lives, but after a struggle with herself she managed to remember the choice of sides she had made. 'All right, Christmas in Paris it is,' she agreed gently.

He smiled at her with sudden, brilliant gratitude, because he loved her, and because he understood that the surrender had cost her something. Cécile insisted that she would *never* change enough to please his French friends, but Jean-Pierre hadn't found any fault with her tonight; in fact, he'd scarcely stopped looking at her. She remained stubbornly English, it was true; but she was beautiful and brave and generous, and there were times, like now, when he teetered on the edge of insisting that they should marry first and consider Bossiney's afterwards. He kissed her goodnight lingeringly, but Polly closed the door, grateful that he knew Madame Martin listened in her room for only one set of footsteps on the stairs.

'*C'est toi, Mam'selle?*' – the usual enquiry came as she crept past her landlady's door.

'*Oui, Madame . . . bonne nuit.*' The response was as usual, too, but *something* was different now and, tired as she was, it was necessary to work out what it was. Twice today she had come close to looking at Luc as someone detached from herself, whose mind and heart didn't function in ways she could understand. She prayed that her father was right – engagements were an unnatural strain. As soon as Luc's work at Saint Cloud was finished they must allow nothing else – not even Maman, with her eternal insistence on what was best for Bossiney's – to stand in the way of their getting married.

Her little attic room was flooded with the light of a nearly full moon, and she sat by the window, watching it sail across the sky. As inevitably as it tugged the ocean tide towards land, its silver track led her thoughts straight back to Cornwall. The same light that filled her room washed over that land beyond the land, and touched the sleeping face there of a man she might never see again.

She was transfixed for a moment by the clarity with which memory pictured him; then she drew the curtain across the window and blotted out the moon.

30

After Daniel's departure, Polly blamed the sudden tang of autumn in the air for the sadness that hung about her – there was always something desolate in the dying of the year. She pretended to herself that it had nothing to do with the reminders contained in every page she had to check of the proofs Daniel had brought her. Luc was aware of the work that occupied her at the kitchen table above his studio, but he went in and out apparently too busy to pay any more attention to it than Lisette did. She, at least, was honest enough to *say* that Cornwall didn't concern her any more; it was a boring, backward place compared with Paris.

'You didn't always think so,' Polly reminded her with rare sharpness, 'you were going to spend the rest of your life there.'

'I was going to be a farmer's wife, God help me!'

'Petroc O'Meara's wife – would that have been such a hardship?' Her steady blue glance required an answer that wasn't flippant and wasn't untruthful, and for once Lisette provided it.

'It *would* have been a hardship as a matter of fact, but not just for the reason you're thinking. I know he signed everything away without consulting me, but Maman was right all along – it was because he cared more for that ugly old house than he did for me. I *lavished* love on him, and it didn't seem unreasonable to expect a grand passion in return. What I got instead was the sort of fondness that kind people feel obliged to offer children!'

'I'm sorry,' Polly said, gently this time. 'I didn't understand before.'

Lisette stared at her across the table, aware that she had no idea whether her brother's fiancée was happy or not. 'Polly, if you and Luc really love each other, don't let my mother get in the way,' she said with sudden urgency. 'Maman means well, and wants what *she* thinks is best for Luc. But she *could* be wrong about you.'

Polly thanked her for a warning that was unexpected but well meant, even if it made too clear Cécile's resistance to having her as a daughter-in-law. It explained the painful hesitation she sensed in Luc – inclination always at war with the advice he was being offered. But it was difficult to know what to do about a woman who found frequent reasons for visiting them. She was adept at stressing whenever she came that she and Luc and Monique comprised the Bossiney *équipe*. Like a trio of dedicated musicians, they had no need of a fourth player unfamiliar with the scores they pored over.

'Maman reckons it's safe to harp on Monique's virtues,' Lisette confided in a final burst of indiscretion. '*She* isn't a threat, but *you* are.'

Polly smiled and shook her head, refusing to allow depression to settle round her heart. Cécile's deliberate exclusions lasted only while she was in Paris; they could be endured, like the social round that must never be ignored in case it led to some professional opportunity. Polly had learned to smile a lot at these meaningless events, looked as elegant as Luc required, and hid behind surface cheerfulness the fear that she was among people who would always remain strangers to her and she to them.

Her only real pleasure lay in the work she did for William Collins, even though Luc was clearly doubtful about the photographs she put in front of him.

'They're interesting, darling, of *course* they are,' he murmured one day, 'but need your subjects be quite so ordinary? Why pick on *these*, when Paris is so beautiful?'

He pointed to a couple that had given her particular pleasure – in one of them an old man rummaged with mittened fingers among the second-hand books on a river-side stall; in the other an aproned concierge talked to the caged bird she'd brought out under the *porte-cochère* for a little taste of freedom. Luc was right; they weren't in the least elegant – one of his favourite words – but they were part of her own vision of Paris.

'I prefer small, humble people myself,' she explained gently. It was a temptation to add that attitudes like his had helped bring about the French Revolution, but she knew that he would only smile, believing it to be one of her jokes he could never understand.

As winter settled on the city, she was often left to mind the shop alone, while Luc and Monique worked for long hours together on the villa at Saint Cloud. It was to make his reputation and, although it would be a close-run thing, every final touch would be in place by the time the guests arrived for Estelle Mérigny's glitter-ing pre-Christmas party. Polly tried to share Luc's tense anticipation, behaved as if she didn't notice the growing hostility in Monique's eyes, and waited for a moment when she could warn Luc of a problem he must face as soon as possible. One evening he led up to it himself by mentioning Estelle's villa. What he said explained, she thought, the air of suppressed excitement about him.

'It's *almost* finished, thank God, and it's a dream, even if I say it as shouldn't!'

'Why not?' she asked, smiling at him. 'You've a right to feel proud of your work.'

'It's Monique's work as well. The ideas were mine, but they couldn't have worked without her – she always managed to find someone who knew someone else who could provide what we needed. She's a marvel, *tout court*, as Maman would say!'

The opening was there, and Polly knew that she must take it. 'She's also in love with you.' The words fell more coolly on the warmth of his enthusiasm than she intended, and she hastened to explain. 'I don't mean that it's the only reason she works for you so devotedly but, dear Luc, it really would be kinder to let her go and be a marvel to someone else.'

She realized with a little shock of surprise that he wasn't put out; one hand brushed his mouth in a faint gesture of pleasure that would have reminded his grandmother of Julian Bossiney. Then he shrugged the suggestion aside. 'You sound like my sister, darling – making a little drama out of nothing at all.'

'It's not a drama; it's the truth,' Polly said quietly. 'Monique can't bear to be in the same room with me now, and it's cruel to leave her slaving away downstairs, imagining *us* enjoying a passionate love affair up here.'

She spoke thinking only of a girl she felt deeply sorry for, intending no irony about themselves. But a flush of colour stained his fair skin with anger, as if she had reproached him for a personal failure.

'We've scarcely had time to *talk* to each other for months – she might have noticed *that*.'

'Women in love aren't very rational, poor things. Luc, let her go, please. Find someone else if you won't let me learn how to help you.'

He smiled unkindly for once, to expose the futility of the suggestion. 'Monique stays, *chérie*. Thanks to her, I've just landed the prize that every designer here would give his chance in heaven for – a friend of the de la Vallée family wants his eighteenth-century *château* in the Touraine entirely refurbished. Without her I shouldn't have got the job, and without her I shan't be able to pull it off.'

Polly stared at her hands, gripped together on the table in front of her. So much for the idea that he'd been excited because they would have time to get married at last. The faint, sad echo of Tristram's voice promising happiness returned to mock her. Then Luc's voice, so like his father's, broke across her memories with a rush of stammered words.

'Polly sweet, don't look sad. I must keep Monique

because I need her help, but it's *you* I love – always have, always shall.'

It was true; she had no doubt of it. But she must accept as well that whatever virtues the male Bossineys had, the capacity for a grand passion wasn't one of them – Lavinia, Loveday, Cécile, and even Lisette, had had to reach the same conclusion.

Luc's hands reached out to cover hers in a desperate grip. 'We'll marry as soon as Estelle's party and Christmas are out of the way – start the new year together, sweetheart. Say that's what we'll do, please.'

She nodded, and saw his face break into a blinding smile. Yes, it was perfectly clear that *that* was what they must do.

It was what they would have done, but for one thing. William Penwarne didn't survive the winter after all. As Hannah made her usual frugal preparations for the Christmas festival she knew that her companion of more than fifty years was slipping away from her. For once he knew better than she – it was time to be going round land at last. His only sadness, whispered to her one day, was that he'd promised to wait long enough to see the little maid again. When Hannah reported this message to Charlie, he rang Daniel in London, and Daniel's immediate telephone call to Paris found Polly holding the fort in the shop, as usual. By the time Luc returned from Saint Cloud that evening she was ready to leave for London the following morning.

His reaction to her news was slow in coming, but sufficient of a shock to drive the blood from her face.

'You meant to go all along. What a fool I was to think otherwise. I suppose the air ticket arrived from your father this morning.'

She scarcely remembered telling him of Daniel's offer; the enormous horror of discovering that Luc thought she was lying blotted out everything else.

'My father telephoned this afternoon; I *bought* the ticket as soon as I could close the shop, because I *promised* to see William again before he died. Say you believe that, Luc.'

Her eyes burned like jewels in the whiteness of her face, with a mixture of anger and despair that he couldn't fail to recognize, even in the midst of his own terrible confusion.

'I'm sorry,' he said hoarsely. 'I believe you. But admit that you *wanted* to spend Christmas at home – admit that this *isn't* home for you, because you can't stop yearning for that bloody, hopeless corner of England. You'll go rushing back every time a fading, elderly relative gives you the excuse to do so, instead of learning to live here.'

She was halted on the very brink of shouting that William was much more than just a fading, elderly relative, because what Luc had said was true. In her heart she remained an exile – might always be so, however long she had to live in Paris.

As if he sensed that a slight advantage had been won, Luc's voice changed. It was full of tender persuasion, and his arms reached out to pull her close to him.

'Polly love – I know I've neglected you shamefully for months, but I promise I won't in future. Forget all this nonsense about rushing back to Cornwall now. We *can't* cut Estelle's party – it's much too important. But we'll get married straight after Christmas while Maman's still here, and *then* make a dash over to see William together.'

He smiled, sure that what he'd said was generous, sure that she would understand, as she always did. His face was familiar and beautiful, his mouth against her own more possessively demanding than usual. But she didn't yield, and his hands became hurtful, insisting on a response that would meet the unaccustomed fire in his own blood.

'Sweetheart, let's go to bed together – this minute.

We've waited much too long. My fault, I know, but we can make up for it now.'

The feverish murmur against her mouth might once have persuaded her; she had longed for sheer desire to swamp the murmur of Cécile's voice telling him that the girl he'd chosen would never understand the importance of his work. But now it was too late – she struggled to free herself, sick with the knowledge of how little they had to share after all.

'I have to miss Estelle's party, and Christmas here,' she said distinctly. 'I *must* . . . I deserve to have William die if I don't go at once to see him.'

Luc's arms fell away from her, and hung limply at his sides. 'I'll ask you once more – stay and behave as I need you to in front of my mother and all our friends, or admit that nothing matters but what you were supposed to have left behind in Cornwall.'

Polly lifted her hands in a little gesture of appeal that he ignored. 'I hoped we needn't leave it entirely behind . . . hoped we could remember it enough to teach our children where we came from.' She stared at his face, but it had become the rigid mask of a stranger, and to speak of her promise to Tristram would cause more pain than she could inflict on him.

'My mistake was in staying too long, I think,' she said gravely. 'You'll manage better without me from now on. I'm glad you've got the *château* job to look forward to.' She leaned forward to kiss his cheek in a little gesture of farewell, and he wanted more than anything in life not to let her go. But longing wasn't quite strong enough to batter down hurt pride and the conviction that she wouldn't change enough to make life easy for them. He watched her walk out of the room, and his heart died a little.

She managed to ring her father before she left the following day and he was waiting at the air terminal in London – a solid, powerful man identified for her simply by the way his feet claimed the space they stood on. No-one in the crowd jostled Daniel, but he looked surprised when she pointed this out to him.

'You make me sound dangerous, maid. I'm as gentle as a lamb if left alone.'

'That's what they all realize,' she agreed with a smile.

His sharp glance registered the thinness of her face, but he supposed that anxiety about her grandfather accounted for the impression that her bright spirit had been dimmed.

'I wanted William to stay long enough to see our book come out,' she said as they drove home. 'Do you think there's any chance of that?'

'Not much, love, though the sight of you will perk him up a bit. By the way, I've to be off to Glasgow first thing, but Charlie will be waiting for you at Lostwithiel.'

Daniel asked how things were going in Paris, and she replied in a voice that didn't tremble that everything was going very well. But when they were home in Wilton Mews, and supper was over, he mentioned Luc again. 'Pity he couldn't come with you.'

Polly accepted a cigarette for once, and inhaled its smoke gratefully. 'Perhaps a worse pity is that I shan't be going back.'

'Thought so,' Daniel muttered after a while. 'There seemed to be a lot of luggage for a flying visit. Are you sure, maid, or is this some silly quarrel just because you've come rushing back to see William?'

'That brought things to a head, because Luc felt very strongly that I ought to be doing something else. But I've known for months that I'd made some bad mistakes – I thought I could live happily over there . . . thought Luc would always need me . . . thought we could remain ourselves even though we lived the lives of Parisians – all wrong, apparently!' She tried to smile but anger stirred in Daniel because she'd had to accept a defeat she found heartbreaking.

'It wasn't Luc's fault,' she went on, as if her father

413

had just insisted that it was. 'He prides himself on becoming a cosmopolitan; however hard I tried, I seemed to remain stubbornly English!'

'It's what you are, for God's sake. What's wrong with that?'

'According to Luc, it's the kind of narrowness that makes wars inevitable. But apart from that, there were other problems.'

He knew he would have to guess what they were – she would come to terms with them in her own way, and wouldn't thank him for the indignation and hurt and love he couldn't in any case put into words.

The room they sat in was at the back of the house, and the roar of traffic came only faintly. The curtains had been left undrawn, and she got up from the table to look out at the silver crescent of a new moon that hung above a neighbouring chimney-pot. For the heart of a great city it seemed very peaceful.

'Shall you stay here always?' she asked, with her eyes still on the sky.

'Can I bear not to finish up on the other side of the Tamar, you mean, like a proper Cornishman? Yes, easily, although that's not to say I wouldn't like to give my native folk a helpful shove here and there. But London's my place now. I still walk out into our backyard at night for the pleasure of seeing a sky lit by moonlight instead of searchlights, knowing that some poor sod *isn't* going to have his little house blown to pieces before the all clear goes at dawn.'

Polly turned to look at him, hearing in his voice the echo of more feeling than he usually allowed to appear. She had loved her mother very much, but Daniel had been her sheet-anchor for as long as she could remember. Middle-age had abated his fierce energy a little, but brought hard-earned tolerance and wisdom. She thought that if Tristram Bossiney had still been alive, they might even have learned by now not to hate each other.

414

'What about you, maid?' he asked eventually, 'where do you belong?'

'Here, I expect. Cornwall is only where I go in dream-time.' She feared she might have sounded forlorn, and tried to look cheerful instead. 'Do you mind having me back? I don't intend to sponge . . . I can be self-supporting.'

'By the look of you, you need a damned good rest,' he said roughly, 'and as it happens, I don't mind having you back at all. But you'll have to get a new ration book from the Food Office when you come back from Cornwall. The bloody war only ended seven years ago, and we can't expect miracles!'

She grinned naturally now, aware amid her sadness that one of the many things she had missed in Paris was the dry humour belonging to her own people. If the French had their own brand of irony she hadn't been able to master it.

'I must also call on Mr Collins some time,' she told Daniel. 'He might like my Paris photographs enough to send me somewhere else, but that must wait till William doesn't need me any longer.'

It seemed strange that night to be back in a bedroom unadorned with Madame Martin's treasured scenes of the martyrdom of all her favourite saints. But even without St Lawrence spreadeagled on his gridiron above her bed, Polly still found it hard to sleep for the images that chased each other through her tired brain. Most vivid of all was the torment in Luc's face when she'd kissed him goodbye. Cécile had won only if he learned to be content with the choice of sides he had made.

The following morning she and Daniel went their separate ways – he to Euston and the north, she to Paddington for the train to Penzance. The months in Paris seemed already to belong to a life that she had only dreamed. Reality was this journey through London's dreary outer suburbs, with their war-wounds still showing. She supposed they might seem ugliness itself to a stranger's eye;

they didn't to her, and they were leading her back to Cornwall.

She left the express at Lostwithiel, looking for the burly figure of her uncle. But it wasn't Charlie who finally detached himself from propping up a convenient wall and came to meet her.

31

Petroc's first impression was that an exotic flower had strayed into a field of English daisies; his next, that it was the wrong word for her, suggesting a gaudiness that was the opposite of her cool and simple style. But something about her caused the women around her to stare – perhaps her cropped dark hair, so different from their own sausage curls and frizzy bobs. It didn't seem to be a London fashion either, because even the other passengers off the train looked more like *them* than her.

'You're giving the good ladies of Lostwithiel something to think about,' Petroc murmured by way of greeting. 'By tomorrow they'll all have their collars turned up, and a choirboy's haircut.'

After a moment's startlement, like having tried to step on a stair that wasn't there, Polly found that she could smile at him; but she overcame the French habit almost ingrained in her now of holding out her hand. He'd refused it once before, up on Hall Walk; she wouldn't offer him the chance again.

'My father told me to look out for Uncle Charlie,' she said. 'Are *you* taking the Fowey train as well?'

'No, and nor are you. I told Charlie I'd collect you.'

She stared at him, uncertain whether to laugh, or weep. Nothing had changed – she was still little Polly Penwarne, being hauled home on the back of a schoolboy's bicycle. Only this wasn't a schoolboy, but an experienced man whose eyes assessed her for Paris changes. On the margin of her mind was the memory of a moonlit vision that had never quite faded. Its flesh and blood reality staring at her now wore faded corduroys and a tweed jacket that had seen better days. Above the rollneck sweater, his dark hair was windblown and his face looked tired. He had made himself poor to keep Prospect from going to her father, and he had lost Lisette to a man whose only obvious merit was a rich and childless aunt.

The recollection prevented her from insisting childishly that she would prefer to take the train, and she followed him to where his shabby, old car was parked in the station-yard. She was handed into it in silence, and in silence they drove out on the St Blazey road, then turned off towards Fowey. In the end she was obliged to find something to say herself, because the car seemed to isolate them in a pool of intimacy she found hard to deal with. There was altogether too much of him to be ignored.

'Your grandmother is a very good writer of letters,' she said at last. 'We've been kept up to date with all the news – including, of course, the arrival of Morwetha's baby.'

'Lavinia probably *didn't* mention that she's had a bad dose of influenza; recovery is on the way, though.'

It seemed to deal with the subject of the family in Fowey, and if he wanted to hear about the Bossineys in Paris he would ask. No enquiry came, and she decided to abandon the thankless task of making conversation. Reality seemed to be playing tricks with her; during the train journey from London the long months in Paris had taken on the hazy quality of a dream; now the illusion was reversed. In a moment she would wake and find herself back in the Rue Jacob, buying sprays of beautiful, scentless, white lilac for Luc's elegant room.

The slowing-down of the car jolted her out of memories. They were stopping outside an old stone farmhouse whose name – Lantyan – was chiselled on a piece of slate above the front door. She wanted to say that she could have got to Fowey more quickly by train if he had calls to make along the way. It was too long already since Daniel's telephone call had brought her away from Paris, and the journey to William was beginning to seem endless and unbearably slow. Petroc ignored the sudden anxiety in her face, and said briefly that he'd be gone only a minute or two.

When he came back he threw a napkin-wrapped package in her lap. 'There was no food on the train – I enquired. Eat it. My friend Anna makes a good pasty.'

It was still warm from the oven and smelled delicious. She hadn't been aware of hunger until now; she started on it resentful of his autocratic ways, but finished it touched by unexpected kindness.

'I'm glad you haven't forgotten the correct way to eat a pasty,' he said suddenly.

She smiled faintly, glad that she hadn't forgotten. 'It was the best I've ever tasted; thank Anna for me, please.' She folded up the napkin neatly. 'I expect you know I was getting all het-up – blaming you for delaying me when I just wanted to get to William.'

He didn't answer except to steer the car on to the grass verge at the side of the road. This time she didn't feel like protesting because his face looked grave.

'We must stop again, now that you're feeling stronger. My dear, I'm afraid there isn't any need to hurry. Charlie wasn't at the station because he's in Fore Street with your grandmother and John. William died in his sleep just about when your train was steaming out of Paddington. There wasn't a chance to stop you coming, but I expect you'd have come anyway.' The gentleness in his voice reminded her of another occasion when she had felt that anything could be borne because he was there.

She got out of the car and stood looking over a gate a little further along the road. It had been bitterly cold in Paris, but here the air felt mild, and the field in front of her was covered in a shimmer of green. Somewhere close at hand a robin thought the winter was past, and began his small, sweet song. Blinded by tears, she only felt Petroc beside her, and then his hand covering hers where it gripped the top of the gate.

'I visited William quite often,' he said quietly. 'Apart from wishing that he could see you again, I think he died

a contented man. It's more than most people can claim
. . . but then he wasn't like most other people.'

She wiped away her tears with her free hand, thinking
that for the moment she asked nothing more than this –
Petroc's hand holding hers, and his gentle voice insisting
that there *was* serenity and contentment to be found,
because her grandfather had found it.

'What is it like, living in Paris?' he asked suddenly.

She answered merely the question he had asked, unable
for the moment to correct his assumption that she would
be going back.

'It's interesting . . . exciting, I suppose, and Paris is
beautiful in a way that London isn't. I've had a lovely
time trying to photograph it, and Luc is thoroughly happy
and at home there.'

'You don't mention your own happiness, but I suppose
I'm bound to take that for granted.'

She wasn't looking at him, and he could examine her
thin face wondering if only grief for William made it look
sad.

'I have to admit to a little homesickness. I've walked
sometimes to the Seine, to follow it in my mind's eye
to where the estuary meets the sea – just to imagine
that I could smell salt water again and hear the seagulls
squabbling over something they'd found on the shore.'

'Does Luc go with you to the river?' Petroc asked
abruptly.

'He doesn't need to – he belongs in Paris. It's something
to remember when . . . when it seems that I've failed to
make him understand that he also belongs *here*. Perhaps it
doesn't matter now, but there was a time when I thought
it did.'

She glanced at her watch in a gesture too obvious to
be ignored, and Petroc walked with her back along the
road. He had wanted to ask what she meant, but even if
there'd been time he thought she wouldn't have told him.
Ten minutes later they were threading their way down
Fowey's steep lanes towards Fore Street, and Hannah's

door was open before she was even out of the car. She ran into her grandmother's arms, and heard behind her the sound of Petroc driving away. She hadn't thanked him for bringing her home, but he wasn't a man who waited while people remembered the things they had to say.

The following day she walked along the Esplanade to Prospect. Its garden had the sad look of winter, but she thought it only needed the spring to make it burst into wild, free beauty again. A pleasant-faced woman opened the door and agreed that her ladyship would be all the better for a visitor – being a mite lonely at the moment with the Doctor away. Lavinia was sitting by the fire in the library, with a heavy volume in her hands.

'My dear . . . what a lovely surprise – well, not quite that; I knew you were here, of course, but I thought you might be too occupied with duties to visit me.'

Her smile and her voice were still the same, and so was a room that smelled of woodsmoke, Jonathan's pipe tobacco, and, at this season of the year, the white stephanotis that she persuaded to burst into bloom. Polly kissed her cheek, and then brought a low stool to put beside her friend's chair. 'My uncles have everything beautifully arranged, and Granny is full of courage as usual, so I could easily be spared. I am told that *you* have been unwell.'

Lavinia waved the dose of influenza aside, and laid down her book as well with a sigh of relief. 'Jonathan *will* insist that I should prefer Charles Dickens to Jane Austen if only I would persevere, but I *can't* be doing with all those milksop heroines.'

Polly smiled at a statement that caused her no surprise. 'Tell me about Morwetha and your great-grandson. Are they all right?'

'Flourishing, I'm thankful to say, even though he chose to arrive in the middle of the only snowstorm the moor has so far had this winter. There was no hope of getting Morwetha down from Trebinnick, so Petroc got our large but fearless midwife up there. She swears he hauled her bodily through the drifts on the hill, and I dare say that it's true.'

There was no surprise about *this*, either; Polly knew it was exactly what he would do. 'It must have been an anxious time,' she said gently, 'but worth every worry in the end.'

'Anxious for Kurt, especially,' Lavinia agreed, 'but now his son seems like a miraculous gift from God. *Proof* that evil doesn't destroy good in the end.'

Because he, and Morwetha as well, hadn't permitted it to. Polly remembered what another German psychologist like Kurt had once written: 'Courage is the health of the soul.' It was something to cling to, something to make a little sense of the terrors that more than ever now seemed to beset the human race.

She got up to throw another log on the dying fire, and remembered what her father had once said about their poverty. Luc's start in Paris had been financed by the sale of Prospect, but beyond supposing that any spare income from Bossiney property in Fowey still went to Lavinia, he seemed to have very little knowledge of how his relatives lived; it had always been Petroc's job to look after them.

'Are *you* all right here?' she asked suddenly.

'Perfectly, although we live more frugally than my husband would have approved of! The truth is, of course, that *then* we had more than was good for us.' But Lavinia's smile quickly faded, leaving her eyes old and sad.

'*Something's* wrong, though,' Polly suggested, and her hand tucked inside her ladyship's mutely asked to be told what it was.

'The wrong thing is that we are still here at all . . . useless, antiquated limpets clinging to the past as ship-wrecked seamen cling to a piece of floating timber.' She saw Polly's anxious expression, and tried to sound less anguished. 'I used to think it mattered that the Bossineys should be here for ever, part of the on-going history of this small place. I still agree with Petroc that Prospect itself mustn't be destroyed, but I know now that we ourselves don't matter at all.'

'Once upon a time my father *would* have destroyed it,' Polly said bluntly. 'Not its four walls, perhaps, but its lovely, peaceful continuity. Now, in a funny sort of way I feel sure that he *does* understand – knows as well as I do that something precious is contained here, and has to be preserved.'

'Petroc didn't trust Luc to preserve it, but the result of doing it himself is that he doesn't even own the land he toils to look after, and he can do nothing about making Trebinnick less primitive for Kurt and Morwetha. They prefer to be there, because privacy is important, but life on the moor in winter is harsh.' Her voice trembled slightly, then stopped altogether, leaving a silence that Polly filled.

'Does Petroc know that you worry about these things?'

'We don't speak of them, but I think he realizes how I feel – it's why he calls in for just long enough to make sure we're still alive, and rushes away again.' In case she had sounded fretful as well as forlorn, Lavinia smiled resolutely at her visitor, and spoke of something more cheerful. 'Your father arrived here unexpectedly one day – soon after he'd been to see you in Paris. The decoration of Luc's sitting room had made a deep impression on his mind, and I'm not altogether surprised from the way he described it!'

Polly's grin appeared briefly. 'You were hearing about it from a man who favours Turkey carpets and tables with fat legs like biscuit barrels! His taste isn't to be trusted, but Luc's is.' Then she was suddenly grave. 'We're not going to get married after all. It must make us seem very muddled and juvenile, but it would be worse not to admit to a mistake while we still can.' She glanced at Lavinia's face and mistook the reason for an expression that had grown sombre. 'I'm afraid that both Luc and Lisette *seem* to love living in Paris, but it doesn't mean for sure that you'll lose them completely.'

423

'Whether I lose them or not is up to them,' Lavinia said slowly. 'That's something else that I now see more clearly than I did. If, between us, Tristram and I seemed to make *you* responsible and to put the burden of the past on your shoulders, it was criminally *wrong* of us. I suppose there's no need to ask if my daughter-in-law is still in charge?'

'She is at the moment,' Polly agreed cautiously, 'but I'm not sure for how long. Luc's French assistant is quite formidable, too, and has the unfair advantage of being in love with him!' Humour shone in her face for a moment, then faded as she stared at the glowing heart of the fire, lost in thoughts of her own.

'What about you, my dear?' Lavinia's quiet voice prompted her. 'You haven't said what *you're* going to do.'

Polly thought she started to frame a cheerful, glib reply, but found without the slightest warning at all that she was beginning to weep instead. All the desolate, cold misery growing inside her in Paris for months had chosen *this* moment to melt into the tears that now poured down her cheeks, hot, humiliating, and unstoppable. She turned her face into Lavinia's lap and kept it hidden there until the storm was over.

At last she lifted her head and accepted the lavender-scented handkerchief she was being offered. Mopped dry, and more or less mistress of herself again, she tried to smile.

'To think I was supposed to be cheering *you* up! I expect all that pother was about getting back too late for William, don't you?'

Her friend gravely agreed that it was likely to be so, but while she debated whether to repeat her question Polly answered it.

'I think I have to find something *useful* to do. Photography is what I *enjoy* more than anything else, but I can't make it my life's work.' She absent-mindedly stuffed the borrowed handkerchief in her pocket, but Lavinia waited, knowing she had something more to say. 'My tears weren't only for William; they were washing away failure – it was a new experience for Daniel Penwarne's clever daughter. Chastening and very painful!' She tried to speak lightly, but Lavinia sensed, as Daniel had done, the damage that had been done to her in Paris.

'The blame for failure has to be shared, in my experience,' her ladyship commented calmly. 'Luc has weaknesses that I'm aware of, and others, no doubt, that I know nothing about. There is no need to flagellate *yourself* unduly!' She saw Polly's tragic expression fade a little under this bracing treatment, and decided that it was time to talk of other things.

'If you don't have to hurry back to London, why not go and see Morwetha? She doesn't get many visitors up at Trebinnick to show Peter Hans Winkler off to. Kurt chose his son's names, by the way – to bind up old wounds, he said.'

Polly nodded, thinking that Morwetha had got the husband she deserved. If courage was the health of the soul, generosity was surely the gift of a heart so loving that all trespasses could be forgiven.

'Yes, I'd like to go and see them,' she said slowly. 'Perhaps Morwetha will need some help with the shop this summer.' She got up to go, promising to come again after the funeral, and Lavinia was left alone. Solitude didn't worry her, and in any case she had more to think about than she could share with anyone but the one friend who wasn't there.

He walked in on her unexpectedly an hour later, while she was still sitting in the room's firelit dusk.

'Feeling a trifle hipped, my dear? It's always the way when you're getting over influenza, but I've got just the thing for you.'

She smiled at him as he switched on lamps, but spoke severely. 'You were supposed to come home tomorrow, not today.'

'I know, but two days of Edward's conversation were as much as I could bear. The poor fellow is *still* maundering on about our schooldays seventy years ago. But when I said you'd been poorly, he insisted on giving me six bottles of the most priceless, pre-war sherry you've ever tasted. According to his medic, he mustn't drink it any more. I explained that he should *never* take his doctor's advice in such matters, but fortunately it did no good, and my conscience is clear!'

Jonathan reverently poured the golden liquid and handed Lavinia a glass. She sipped it to please him, but then began on her task.

'Polly came to see me this afternoon. She *isn't* going to marry Luc, and for the moment has slightly lost her way – having been mauled, I think, by people more ruthless than herself.'

'Cécile, no doubt, for one,' he said calmly.

Lavinia nodded, but refused to be side-tracked by a discussion of her daughter-in-law. 'Jonathan, we may not be able to convince Petroc that it's wrong for us to go on living here, just the two of us in this great house, but if we *could*, would you very much mind leaving, my dear? It's your home as much as mine.'

Jonathan came to sit beside her and take her hand. 'I don't mind anything at all as long as I'm allowed to stay with you.'

It was the simple statement of a simple man, and it made her smile a little tremulously, but she did her best to sound brisk as usual.

'Jenifer is happily settled at last in Vermont, so we've only ourselves to consider. Perhaps Petroc could find us a Bossiney cottage somewhere. I should *like* that now, with dear Ada Bartlett looking in to keep us neat and tidy.'

'Somewhere overlooking the water, maybe. I can easily do without Prospect, but it would seem very strange not to be able to watch the river. That would take care of us, but what about this house.'

'I'm not sure yet,' Lavinia said slowly. 'I've got an idea in my mind, but it needs thinking about.'

She was still thinking about it on the day of William Penwarne's funeral, which Jonathan wouldn't allow her to attend. He joined Petroc in the Methodist chapel, to represent the Bossineys, and afterwards explained that Daniel had been one of his uncle's pall-bearers.

'I suppose he was going straight back to London afterwards,' she suggested casually.

'Probably, although I think I heard him mention the Fowey Hotel. Perhaps he's got it in mind to buy *that* now!'

Lavinia smiled faintly. 'I think I shall put on my best coat tomorrow and go and find out!'

32

If Daniel was surprised to receive a morning call from Lady Lavinia Bossiney he didn't allow astonishment to show. She was conducted to a seat in the deserted lounge, and a nod of his head at someone hovering in the background produced coffee for them both on a silver tray. After a glance at her arthritic hands he lifted the heavy jug himself, and was rewarded by the smile with which she thanked him.

'My aunt was touched by your flowers yesterday,' he said politely.

Lavinia waved the courtesy aside. 'It's a sad time, I'm afraid, made more so by the news of Polly's broken engagement. We had so hoped that she and Luc would be happy.'

This time the dismissive gesture was Daniel's, while he wondered what they could find to talk about next. But his guest took a sip of coffee and then came to the point with a speed that he recognized as masterly – the deliberate feint, followed by a thrust that her opponent wasn't ready for.

'Mr Penwarne, do you by any chance still wish to own Prospect?' She observed the expression on his face but went on calmly. 'That is not all I have to ask, of course, but if your answer is to be an outright "no", it would be pointless to continue.'

'Let us say that my no is not outright, at least,' Daniel commented warily. 'Does that make it worth continuing?'

She nodded, but he had the impression that, under the disciplined manners of a lifetime, lay much more anxiety than she wished him to see. 'My son refused your original offer, and then my grandson took over Luc's inheritance in order to . . . to . . .' Bluntness failed for a moment, but Daniel supplied it for her.

'In order to block another offer from me. What makes you think he would ever change his mind?'

'Only the fact that *you* might have changed enough to see Prospect differently now – as something that needn't be destroyed, but must be put to better use than housing two useless, superannuated creatures like Jonathan and myself.'

'What sort of use?'

His tone was not encouraging, but Lavinia took comfort from the fact that he had bothered to ask the question at all. 'Before Morwetha's first husband was killed she'd arranged with my son that Prospect should become a home for the sort of unfortunate children that no-one else seemed to want. She couldn't do it alone and the scheme was abandoned; but Tristram died not knowing that she would remarry – a man who had actually been trained in the care of such children. Between them, she and Kurt could make use of a house that is now three parts empty, and for such a purpose I think Petroc *might* be prepared to sell.'

'He could just give it to them, of course,' Daniel pointed out bluntly, and then felt ashamed of himself. The sight of her swollen fingers clutching a shabby old handbag hurt, and he wanted to shout that her husband, son and grandsons should have taken better care of her. But *that* was unfair. Petroc O'Meara, at least, had beggared himself to keep her safely at Prospect.

'It's a question of cash, I suppose,' he said more gently. 'Adapting the house for children and running it would take more money than you have.'

'We don't have *any* to speak of,' she answered with a simplicity that disconcerted him. 'Petroc provides us with enough to live on, but I don't know how.' He couldn't guess what it cost her to say so – perhaps no effort at all, because false pride had long since been discarded from the luggage this patrician lady carried through life.

He replaced his cup on its saucer, and the finality of the sound in the quiet room seemed to mark the end of the interview. She waited for his outright no to come at last, but it wasn't in the end what he said.

'I shall need to think about it, and talk to my opinionated daughter, who always reckons she knows what I should do. For the moment will that content you?'

A smile he hadn't seen before lit Lavinia's face to beauty. 'It will content me very well.'

Then she took the arm Daniel offered her, and allowed herself to be piloted back to her own front door.

Nine months later, on a fine Saturday morning in early September, Polly was working in the garden at Prospect as usual. She stopped to hold an interesting conversation with her companion, who was strong enough now to haul himself upright and laugh at her over the rim of his playpen. Sunlight sparkled on the river below them, and out at sea the water colours deepened from hyacinth-blue to indigo. She was accustomed to the view, but now couldn't take its changing beauty for granted.

'It's not a bad day for revisiting old haunts,' said a voice behind her.

She spun round to confront a chic young woman, half-smiling but holding friendliness in reserve – Lisette Bossiney, now Madame Mérigny since two months ago.

'Goodness, what a nice surprise! But why didn't we know you were coming?' Polly asked.

'Because I wanted to walk in and take you all by surprise. I arrived last night and stayed at the Fowey Hotel.'

It was said without emphasis, leaving unspoken the fact that much had changed since she was last in Cornwall. Polly decided to leave it unspoken a little longer. 'Matrimony suits you,' she said instead. 'You're looking very well, and elegant enough to put me to shame. Is Jean-Pierre here too?'

'No, I left him settling into his new job in London. Just as I was counting myself a real Parisienne, his bank decided to transfer him to London. We're with Maman in Pont Street until we can find a flat of our own.'

'Have you come to see whether you can inflict lovely, backward Cornwall on a French husband in future?'

'No. To see whether I should ever want to come again myself.' If she had decided which it was to be, she didn't say, and Polly plunged into the topic they seemed to be avoiding.

'Have you seen your grandmother and Uncle Jonathan?'

'I called at Cob Cottage first. They said I'd probably find you here.' Something faintly hostile had crept into her voice and she stared unappreciatively at the ordered loveliness all around her.

'Saturday is my day off from Morwetha's shop,' Polly explained. 'I can work in Lavinia's garden with a clear conscience.'

'My grandmother's garden? Not quite *that* any more.'

'She created it; I still think of it as hers.' They had reached the heart of the matter now, and she chose her next words carefully. 'I expect you feel unhappy about her, but the truth is that she and Jonathan are entirely content now, and thankful to know that Prospect is going to be put to good use again.'

Lisette's shoulder lifted in a faint shrug, but Polly soldiered on. 'Come inside and see how busy we've been. The ground floor is still as you remember it, but some of the bedrooms have been partitioned into small ones. Kurt says it's important for children to have a little private place of their own.'

'Is woodcarving to be forgotten in future? I thought he was so good at it.'

'He is, and he'll go on doing it; but living here he can help Morwetha with the children as well. The first of them are due to arrive soon.'

'Rather grim for you,' Lisette observed, 'to be sharing Prospect with a bunch of deprived children.'

'I don't think so, but in any case I don't live here. During the week I use the flat above the gallery in Polperro; at weekends I stay with my grandmother in Fore Street.'

Lisette stared at her oddly for a long moment, but then pointed at the child, who refused to smile in the presence of a stranger. 'Morwetha's, I suppose?'

'Yes, but a little bit mine as well. He's my godson! She and Kurt will be back soon – they're only up at Trebinnick, clearing things out for a new tenant.' After a glance at Lisette's unreadable expression, she added something else that needed to be said. 'Luc must miss having you in Paris. I hope he's happy, and still doing very well.'

'My brother's only *un*happy if he isn't being rushed off his feet by several demanding clients at once. Monique manages everything perfectly, and one of these days he'll find that she's arranged a wedding ceremony for them at the *mairie* among the morning's appointments! You and Luc wouldn't have done nearly so well together, but I expect you realized that before you left Paris.'

Polly nodded, then asked a pointed question of her own. 'You didn't say – *is* Jean-Pierre to be brought to Cornwall in future?'

Lisette answered slowly, as if surprised at herself. 'My mother won't like it, but yes, he is. She associates this place with failure, because the hold *she* should have had over my father, Cornwall had instead. That's why it was so important to detach Luc. I didn't understand it for years, but I do now.'

Polly realized that past history still hadn't quite finished haunting them – perhaps it never would; but for the first time in their interview she smiled her lovely, friendly smile. 'I'm glad we haven't lost *you* completely, and so will your grandmother be. If you can stay another night, there are plenty of beds – come and take your pick.'

She lifted up the baby, kissed the tip of his nose to make him laugh again, and led the way towards the house. His fat little arms were tight round her neck, and he confided in her ear some secret she seemed to understand. Watching them, Lisette was obscurely aware of resentment. It should have been Polly envying *her* a sophisticated life in Paris or London, but she couldn't see a trace of regret in the serene, tanned face beside her.

'I told Gran we ought to have a little party this evening,' she said, trying to regain the upper hand. 'For once I'll even separate Petroc from his entrancing livestock and make him come too.'

'You can try,' Polly agreed calmly, 'but he never comes if he thinks I'm likely to be here.'

Lisette stopped to stare at her again. 'He sold the house to your father – he didn't have to if he hated the idea so much.'

'It suited everyone else so well that he thought he *did* have to. Then my father made matters worse by handing Prospect over to me, having the strange idea that Petroc would prefer that. For once my darling pa got things wrong, because it merely looked as if at last *I* had got what I'd always wanted!' Lisette remained where she was, still staring, and Polly smiled to show that Petroc's hostility didn't matter. 'Your cousin and I have to meet occasionally at meetings of the Prospect Trust, but we manage to be beautifully polite to one another!' She could say it cheerfully, but not bear the effort of smiling any longer. She hid her face by hugging her godson, unaware that Lisette had seen the desolation in her eyes.

The evening party was enjoyed by everyone except Petroc, who had explained regretfully that a farmers' meeting couldn't be postponed. After a night at Prospect with Kurt and Morwetha, Lisette left the following morning with the intention of driving straight back to London, but the car seemed to turn itself in the direction of a queue of vehicles waiting for the Bodinnick ferry. Once across the river there was no more doubt about it – she was going to Tregenna, although she had no idea what she would say when she got there.

Before the summer was quite over Prospect had come alive again, and its cove was a children's heaven once more. Morwetha shared their pleasure with the memory in her heart of Peter Kendrick, and Kurt smiled on the world because his wife was entirely happy. Lavinia could watch the cove from the bedroom window of her new home, and knew every time she did so that the rearrangement of their lives had been right and good. They owed it, of course, to Daniel Penwarne, and perhaps even more to the memory of Loveday. He had never said it in so many words, but Lavinia's conviction was strong that Prospect now was a memorial to his dead wife. A ferocious charge of anger and pain long hidden inside a hard man had been transmuted at last into *this* healing act of love.

She put the idea to Petroc one day but was discouraged by his lack of interest. In fact, she was altogether discouraged by him nowadays – reluctant to probe, but aware during his visits to them of the restless unhappiness he made such efforts to hide. On a morning when their conversation seemed even more laboured than usual she finally begged him not to bother to come at all.

'Not welcome, Gran?' he asked with a rueful smile.

'Not required to waste what little free time you have on coming to see us.' She put out her hand in a rare demonstration of affection. 'My dear, perhaps it didn't *sound* like a well-meant suggestion, but that is what it was.'

He lifted her hand to his lips and then returned it to her lap again. 'It sounded more like a well-merited scat round the ears! Sorry if I've been a bit surly of late, Gran. It must be the thought of the winter ahead – I'm getting too old to enjoy digging sheep out of snowdrifts!'

The only thing she asked of life now was that she might be allowed to see him happy. But all she could do for him, apparently, was pretend that she didn't see his sadness.

'You're not quite thirty yet – can you manage another winter or two?'

He grinned and nodded, but felt relieved when she went on to talk of someone else. 'I received a letter from Lisette this morning. She wants to introduce her husband to Cornwall – suggests that Morwetha might let her use the flat at Polperro as soon as Polly closes the shop.'

'Typical of my little cousin! She'd like to stay there herself so she assumes Polly will move out to make room for her.'

Lavinia didn't comment on this. 'She was disappointed that you refused to dine with us when she was here.'

'I know . . . She came and told me so in no uncertain terms, having got very *grande dame* on the strength of a French husband!' Petroc's brief smile faded, leaving his expression sombre. 'She fired one or two other home truths at me as well – the most telling of them being that, even now, I couldn't pocket hurt pride and accept with grace the idea of Polly owning Prospect. There was enough substance in that to hurt, unfortunately.'

He looked up and found Lavinia's compassionate gaze fixed on him. It made him admit what he'd intended never to say. 'I've been wrong about Polly and Prospect all along . . . known it in my heart for years, really, without needing to be told that she even tried to get Luc to promise never to sell it to her father! Luc mentioned *that* to Lisette one day when she was being snide about the Penwarnes, but she didn't believe it until she came here and found the new owner not even living in what she owned.' His voice was steady but he could do nothing about the misery in his eyes.

Lavinia saw it, and painfully abandoned her vow never to interfere again. 'Lisette was right about the Polperro flat, as it happens. It *will* be free, because Polly is leaving very soon – the gallery closes today. I'm very glad; she looks badly in need of a change to me.'

'She's going to London for the winter – is that what you mean?'

'No, something much more exciting. Her publisher is sending her to Paris to see her collaborator there, but then she has been commissioned to make a photographic portrait of Rome. I'm afraid we shall lose her until next spring. Might even lose her altogether, of course; she's becoming sought after already. By the time the Paris book comes out, she'll be a rather famous photographer.'

Petroc stared at his hands as if they belonged to someone else, shoved them in the pockets of his jacket, and then stood up. He remembered to kiss his grandmother goodbye, but entirely forgot that he hadn't left an important message for Jonathan.

Lavinia sat still after he'd gone, certain that his next stop would be the gallery at Polperro. She had no idea what his reception would be, and had to face the knowledge that in the past interference had been ruinous. If she found the courage to tell Jonathan she could guess what his opinion would be – that old ladies who meant well should be locked up out of harm's way.

33

Polperro on a fine day looked like paradise, but there was nothing appealing about stone cottages running with water, and a grey sea that looked a shade more coldly depressing than a grey sky. Persistent Cornish rain had been falling for hours, sending into Morwetha's gallery at the tag-end of the holiday season a trickle of disgruntled visitors. Polly tried to welcome them, knowing even as she smiled that they would like little or nothing she offered them. They bought when they felt well disposed and generous, but that wasn't how they'd felt today. The season had been long and she was tired. It would be a huge relief to close the door for the last time, but there was still a stout, peevish lady at the counter with her husband, equally unwilling to choose something or go away. The jingle of the doorbell announcing yet another customer was unwelcome, but for the moment Polly's attention was on the woman who rifled through a tray of delicately wrought ear-rings and complained that she could get the same things at home.

'Perhaps not *quite* the same,' Polly suggested patiently. 'These are made locally, you see, of Cornish silver, and the silversmith uses authentic Celtic designs.'

The lady from Birmingham was unimpressed. 'You don't say! Well, they don't look much to me, and I've got ear-rings by the dozen already.' She pushed the tray aside, waiting to be offered something else she could reject, then spotted for herself on the shelf behind the counter a row of Kurt's magically carved birds.

'What about *them*?' she suggested disparagingly to her

husband. 'Fancy a seagull, Bert? It might look all right on the mantelpiece in the lounge.'

Polly spoke firmly before he had time to reply. 'They're wild geese, not seagulls, and I'm afraid they aren't for sale. Now, if there's nothing else I can show you . . .'

The stout lady could, at least, take a hint. 'Nothing, I'm sure. Come on, Bert, we're leaving.' He followed her to the door, with an apologetic smile at a girl he reckoned had been more courteous than his wife deserved.

Polly hung the 'closed' sign on the door, heaved a sigh of relief, and then remembered that there'd been that other warning tinkle of the doorbell. Her last remaining customer was still there. Then he turned from inspecting a display at the far end of the room and she saw who the latecomer was.

'Do you make a habit of turning away buyers for Kurt's things?' Petroc asked.

She could manage very well when she was prepared for meeting him; it was much harder when he suddenly appeared. 'Not a habit,' she said briefly, 'but they have to look as if they deserve them. Morwetha feels the same way.' She could think of no reason that would bring him to Polperro except the one that now occurred to her. 'There's nothing wrong, I hope?' He shook his head and she thought of something else. 'Have you come to see what sort of a mess I make of things here? It doesn't usually go as badly as it did just now.'

She sounded and looked tired, and he wanted to kiss away the little frown between her dark brows. But no man was ever receiving less encouragement to linger. He knew as surely as he knew anything that she waited for the moment when he would go away.

'Morwetha says you do very well, and I thought you were angelically patient with that harridan because your heart bled for poor old Bert.'

'There aren't many of "they" left here now. It's time for all good visitors to go home,' she said pointedly.

'Time for you to relax,' Petroc agreed, missing the point entirely. 'Shall I take you out for a restoring drink, or will you offer me a cup of coffee upstairs?'

He'd come to be pleasant, she had to suppose, and would only leave when he was ready to, not before. 'I can do better than coffee,' she conceded reluctantly. 'Jonathan insists on sharing the contents of a well-stocked cellar that an old friend of his is passing on.'

'I know – he murmurs a toast "to Edward, God bless him", every time he blows the dust of ages off a bottle.'

She led the way upstairs, and Petroc followed her to rooms that were familiar because they still contained Morwetha's furnishings. But some rearrangement of them spoke of a dweller there now who was not his sister. More books overflowed the shelves, and a guitar was propped against the wall in one corner, beside a stack of sheet-music. White dahlias in a dark-blue bowl looked rare and beautiful, reminding him that *this* girl had learned such effects from his cousin in Paris.

Polly poured the wine, wondering what had suddenly made him look grim. His face was fine drawn, too old and disciplined for the age she knew him to be. Perhaps it was a grief to him to know that Lisette would soon be there with the man she'd married instead of him.

'Do you play that thing?' Petroc asked, pointing at the guitar.

'I'm learning to . . . I must, because it was the valued possession of a young Spaniard who came into the gallery one day. He hadn't any money to buy, but he kept looking at Kurt's carving of a donkey, and touching it gently. When he said, "It's the one that carried Christ into Jerusalem", I remembered Chesterton's donkey – "there was a shout about his ears, and palms about his feet!" The young man tried to refuse when I made him a present of it, but he couldn't. The next day he came back to give me the guitar, and I knew I mustn't refuse *that*, either. His father had been horribly killed by the republicans in the civil war, and because of that he'd wanted Germany to

439

win the *last* war . . . So I told him about the man who carved the donkey – I don't, as a rule.'

She stopped speaking, aware that the incident had meant too much to her to share with anyone else, even Morwetha. Petroc thought of what it revealed about Polly Penwarne. She was learning to play what the young Spaniard had given her, as Kurt had learned to use the tools of his dead friend. She'd taught herself, too, the songs that Loveday had heard sung in the nursery at Prospect; he remembered – would never forget – hearing her croon them to herself the afternoon they brought Tristram back to Fowey. Life insisted on weaving these unlooked-for patterns, so that people who had never even met had precious parts to play in each other's lives.

'Lisette called on me before she went back to London,' he said next. 'She seemed to think that Luc would soon be marrying some French asssistant he's got out there. Does the idea upset you?'

Polly looked blankly at him for a moment, so long ago did it seem, and so unreal now, that she should ever have been going to marry him herself. 'No, it doesn't upset me,' she said eventually. 'I wanted the wrong things for him . . . tried to keep him faithful to Cornwall; but that wasn't how he could be happy. Monique and Cécile between them will see that he is.'

It seemed to Petroc that the statement gave away more than she intended, but she made it so calmly that he had to accept it to be true; at least the strain Lavinia believed she'd observed in her wasn't the grief of losing Luc.

Polly was aware of his eyes inspecting her, and found it an ordeal that she could scarcely bear. He absorbed altogether more space and air in the room than her own body could spare, and each silence that fell between them became a little more electric.

'Lisette was disappointed not to see you at Prospect the evening she was there,' she said at random.

'Not *very* disappointed . . . you'd already warned her, apparently, that I'd refuse to appear.'

440

His eyes, holding her own, said that this point of danger had been reached because he'd intended it . . . it was the very thing he'd come there for.

Polly took a deep breath and plunged, wildly, into waters that might sweep them out of reach of land. 'She arrived hating me for having the right to be at Prospect; she found it hard to accept, just as *you* do, that your grandmother is happy at Cob Cottage . . . that it gives her joy, *not* pain, to see Prospect filled with children who've never known what it is to have a proper home.'

'Lisette accepts it now, and so do I,' Petroc said quietly. 'She accused me of arrogance, and I'm sure she was right. But you have to understand that it wasn't *only* not wanting the Penwarnes to have what the Bossineys could no longer keep. I was brought up in the belief that Prospect's owners were required to be part of the continuing life of Fowey, doing what they'd done for generations . . . holding things together, looking out for the people who weren't very good at looking out for themselves. I know the Welfare State is supposed to have taken over those responsibilities, but it's not how the Cornish have always done things.'

She wanted to weep for the humility in his voice, wanted to say that she understood to her heart's core how the Cornish preferred to do things. But he'd come to make peace with her, not to listen while she made a tearful, abject fool of herself.

'You were right not to trust my father's intentions once upon a time,' she said with difficulty. 'But what he does now is not done to get the better of your family; *he's* learned to understand important things as well.'

'My grandmother told me Tristram's story after he died – your mother's story too, of course. I loved him enough to heap the blame for their unhappiness on Cécile and Daniel. It was quite unfair, and there's been time since then to see that *they* had their share of unhappiness too.'

Polly nodded, forgetting her immediate difficulties in a vivid memory of the past. 'Do you remember overtaking a sullen evacuee on the road to Par station? I'd just stumbled on my mother saying goodbye to Tristram up on St Catherine's headland. For years after that I thought I hated Cornwall, but when I finally got to know him I realized that he was a man to love, not hate.'

'His epitaph, in fact,' Petroc agreed gently. What he'd come for had been accomplished now. His apology had been offered to a girl he'd been less than fair to in the past; but still he seemed in no hurry to leave. His long body seemed reluctant to move, because it found rest there. As far as she knew, no woman ever waited for him at Tregenna; he'd lived alone for long enough to come to terms with solitude. Or perhaps Lisette had been right, and only things and causes fired his heart. Without her noticing it, the day-long drizzle had relented, and the evening sunshine that now filled the room made a nimbus of light around his dark head. It was all she would have to remember when he went away.

'Gran says that you've got an exciting winter planned,' he said after a while.

'It's not what *I've* planned exactly, but yes, it is exciting. My dear William would have been proud to know that our Cornish portrait has done well enough to earn me other commissions. The Paris photographs are already being got ready for publication; after that I'm to tackle Rome for Mr Collins.' She got up to refill Petroc's glass because it was easier than sitting still, but suddenly his long fingers encircled her other wrist, holding her a prisoner.

'My grandfather always claimed there wasn't much to Rome except overblown architecture, scowling Swiss guards, and smiling Irish nuns – see one and you'd seen them all, he said!'

The atmosphere in the room had changed, but she was more aware of the burning of her skin where his fingers touched it. She had to contend with the turmoil in her own body, not notice that a normally self-controlled man sounded suddenly, strangely, off balance as well.

'Your grandfather was a very peculiar man, by all

accounts,' she managed to say breathlessly. 'Imagine not enjoying a wedding journey with Lavinia. He must have been a *very* cold fish indeed.' She did see, now, a gleam in Petroc's eyes, but it didn't halt the nervous flow of words that tumbled out of her mouth. 'I used to blame *myself* that virtue was intact after months with Luc in Paris, but when Lisette said . . .' It was clear to her at last that what Lisette had said would be better left unspoken, and she took a huge gulp of sherry instead. When she'd finished coughing, Petroc was waiting to finish the sentence for her.

'Lisette complained that *my* hot-blooded lust was lacking as well! Of course it was. Cynicism and vanity having led me into Cécile's trap, I had to wait for Lisette to realize that she could do better for herself than marry a poor, struggling farmer. And so, my dear heart, could *you* – much better!'

He had let go of her wrist. She was free to move away if her legs would carry her. But they didn't seem up to the task, and she could only stand where she was, trying to make sense of the words he'd just spoken. Perhaps she'd imagined them – dreamed them in the long, lonely night-time hours of the past summer.

But he was on his feet in front of her now, and his expression said that what she'd heard was *not* imagined. 'Polly, my career has to remain firmly grounded in Cornish mud, but yours is about to become airborne. I have no right to ask, beg, shout that you *mustn't* prefer the delights of Rome to marrying me – even though you're the light of my life, and my only hope of happiness. I'm not so arrogant that I don't realize, now that it's probably too late, what I'd be asking you to give up, or what a mess I've made of loving you.'

He saw the sudden flush of colour that made her thin face beautiful, and knew how easy it would be to snatch her in his arms and leave the rest to chemistry. But they couldn't afford any more mistakes now.

'Listen to me before you say anything, please,' he

443

insisted gently. 'I don't want to marry you to redeem an old unhappiness – Tristram and Loveday's story is over; I'm not trying to get some grip on Prospect again, because I think it should still belong to my family; above all, I'm not hoping to enjoy the result of marrying the daughter of a rich man. If Daniel still has money to spare I'd try to persuade him to invest it in some worthwhile Cornish industry. What he won't be allowed to do is give it to us. I should work for you with joy and with all the strength I have, because I love you more than words can say, but life would have to be what *we* can make of it together.' He tried to smile, acknowledging that what he insisted upon must seem unreasonable. '*Now* it's your turn to say something.'

She tried to look prim, but it was hard when happiness was unfolding inside her like the petals of a flower opening to the sun. Already she could scarcely remember how life had seemed only an hour ago, because now it shone around her with a thousand dazzling points of light. 'I'm leaving for Paris the day after tomorrow . . . It's all arranged, and I have to meet my collaborator there. After that . . .' It was no good, she couldn't look grave a moment longer. 'After that, poor Mr Collins must find himself another photographer. Oh, Petroc!'

She was caught in his arms, and then his mouth came down on hers in a kiss that sent the rest of the world around them swinging unheeded into space. They were home at last, no longer separate, lost minds and bodies. He released her just enough to look at her flushed face.

'Any doubts still, Miss Penwarne, that passion might be lacking?' he asked unsteadily.

The single dimple danced in her cheek, but she answered with gravity. 'None, but the truth is that it probably wasn't lacking in Luc, either. The fault was mine, but I didn't understand that until I saw you waiting for me at Lostwithiel station. I realized then that I'd been trying for months to talk myself into loving the wrong man.'

'And I failed to recognize in that dogged little evacuee

the one indispensable woman in my life! My love, we shall have to do better in future.' He caught his breath at the smile she offered him, then clamped his hands on her shoulders in a grip that hurt.

'Polly, are you sure? Tregenna isn't much to offer you, even though it belongs to me again, at least – just a small bit of Cornwall, lovely beyond the telling at times, but often enough bleakly sodden and uninviting. And whenever we think that things are going rather well, old Ma Nature will be sure to send a drought or a flood to cut us down to size.'

She reached up to kiss away the anxiety in his face still marvelling that this privilege was now hers. 'I've repeated to people a dozen times the lie that I couldn't wait to leave for Rome. But each time I said it I died a little at the thought of going so far away from you. I *know* what Cornwall is, and it's where we belong to be.'

His features were familiar – she'd pictured them often enough in her mind's eye; but she'd never seen them as they were now, transfigured by joy. 'In that case I shall wait for you to come back from Paris with all the grace and patience I can muster. But we must tell Lavinia before you go. She guessed I was coming here, but didn't look as if she rated my chances very highly!'

Polly smiled at the thought of her friend. 'I prefer to believe that she's infallible, and even now warning Jonathan to blow the dust off his wedding suit!' Then she grew serious again. 'I'm glad to be going, apart from having work to do. I parted from Luc in the wrong way, with both of us feeling that we'd been a failure. I see now that we were bound to fail, but if *he* can understand that too he'll be able to remember Cornwall kindly in future – might even want to visit Lavinia occasionally.'

'As Lisette is going to do,' Petroc agreed slowly. 'Yes, that would have pleased Tristram.' His arms tightened about Polly for a moment before he let her go. 'I'd give anything to stay here now, but I've got animals that need seeing to. Will you come and inspect your new home

445

before you leave . . . tell me what it needs to make you happy?'

She nodded, wondering what in heaven or earth might give more happiness that she hadn't got already. Then she said gravely, 'I think we've *all* got the right hang of things at last, don't you?'

Her choice of words would have made him smile except that they required answering seriously. 'I think we have, my blessed love. Even Prospect is still true to itself – past history living hand in hand with present usefulness. With luck and a lot of hard work from people like us, perhaps we shall be able to say the same of old "Q"'s "priceless inheritance" – Cornwall?'

Polly held a hand to one ear as if listening for something. 'Did you hear a little sound? I think William would have said it was the great King turning in his sleep!'

THE END

A ROSE FOR EVERY MONTH
by Sally Stewart

James Rushton dominated both his thriving wine business and large family with all the style of an old autocrat. It was part of his plans that Jane, his only daughter – already thirty-one and likely to become a spinster if she wasn't careful – should marry her cousin William, not a love-match exactly, but highly convenient for the family.

But Jane, slight, plain, quiet, wanted more than William's obedient acquiescence, for she had loved her careless handsome cousin for a long time. On the point of settling for the little she *could* have, she discovered a shameless betrayal. Humiliated, not really wanted at home, she took the most daring decision of her life – to go and live and work in Italy.

It was to be the beginning of a long, passionate, and overwhelming involvement with the Buonaventura family, aristocratic, and torn apart by the strife of Mussolini's new Italy. To Jane, Ottavio Buonaventura and his family were a fascinating challenge. And the impoverished aristocrats at Castagnolo were to discover that the quiet English-woman was to revolutionise their lives.

0 552 13938 6

A SELECTED LIST OF FINE NOVELS AVAILABLE FROM CORGI BOOKS

THE PRICES SHOWN BELOW WERE CORRECT AT THE TIME OF GOING TO PRESS. HOWEVER TRANSWORLD PUBLISHERS RESERVE THE RIGHT TO SHOW NEW RETAIL PRICES ON COVERS WHICH MAY DIFFER FROM THOSE PREVIOUSLY ADVERTISED IN THE TEXT OR ELSEWHERE.

❏	13933 5	THE LEAVING OF LIVERPOOL	Lyn Andrews £3.99
❏	13718 9	LIVERPOOL LOU	Lyn Andrews £4.99
❏	13829 0	THE SMOKE SCREEN	Louise Brindley £3.99
❏	13255 1	GARDEN OF LIES	Eileen Goudge £4.99
❏	13686 7	THE SHOEMAKER'S DAUGHTER	Iris Gower £4.99
❏	13688 3	THE OYSTER CATCHERS	Iris Gower £4.99
❏	13384 1	A WHISPER TO THE LIVING	Ruth Hamilton £4.99
❏	13977 7	SPINNING JENNY	Ruth Hamilton £4.99
❏	13872 X	LEGACY OF LOVE	Caroline Harvey £4.99
❏	13917 3	A SECOND LEGACY	Caroline Harvey £4.99
❏	13976 9	RACHEL'S DAUGHTER	Janet Haslam £4.99
❏	14104 6	LOVE OVER GOLD	Susannah James £3.99
❏	13758 8	PHANTOM	Susan Kay £4.99
❏	13708 1	OUT TO LUNCH	Tania Kindersley £3.99
❏	13706 5	THE GOLDEN TULIP	Rosalind Laker £4.99
❏	13880 0	THE VENETIAN MASK	Rosalind Laker £4.99
❏	13910 6	BLUEBIRDS	Margaret Mayhew £4.99
❏	12641 1	THE SUMMER OF THE BARSHINKEYS	Diane Pearson £4.99
❏	13904 1	VOICES OF SUMMER	Diane Pearson £4.99
❏	13969 6	AN EMBARRASSMENT OF RICHES	Margaret Pemberton £4.99
❏	13093 1	WHITE CHRISTMAS IN SAIGON	Margaret Pemberton £4.99
❏	13921 1	ALICE DAVENPORT	Audrey Reimann £4.99
❏	12803 1	RUTH APPLEBY	Elvi Rhodes £4.99
❏	13636 0	CARA'S LAND	Elvi Rhodes £4.99
❏	13346 9	SUMMER VISITORS	Susan Sallis £4.99
❏	13545 3	BY SUN AND CANDLELIGHT	Susan Sallis £4.99
❏	14106 2	THE TRAP	Mary Jane Staples £4.99
❏	13838 6	A ROSE FOR EVERY MONTH	Sally Stewart £3.99
❏	13834 7	THE DARKNESS OF CORN	Caroline Stickland £3.99
❏	14118 6	THE HUNGRY TIDE	Valerie Wood £4.99

All Corgi/Bantam Books are available at your bookshop or newsagent, or can be ordered from the following address:

Corgi/Bantam Books
Cash Sales Department
P.O. Box 11, Falmouth, Cornwall TR10 9EN

UK and B.F.P.O. customers please send a cheque or postal order (no currency) and allow £1.00 for postage and packing for the first book plus 50p for the second book and 30p for each additional book to a maximum charge of £3.00 (7 books plus).

Overseas customers, including Eire, please allow £2.00 for postage and packing for the first book plus £1.00 for the second book and 50p for each subsequent title ordered.

NAME (Block letters) ....

ADDRESS..

....